The
MISSION

The
MISSION

A Clairmont Series Novel ~ BOOK 2

L.J. WILSON

AB Edge

ISBN 978-1-943020-04-1

www.ljwilson.com

PROLOGUE

Present Day
Nickel Springs, New York

ALL EYES WERE ON A WORN, LEATHER DUFFEL BAG. ALEC HAD HAULED IT, with urgency, through the kitchen door where it hit the floor with a thud. Honor startled. Aaron swallowed hard. Troy sucked in a breath like he saw a ghost. Ruby, sitting at the kitchen table, looked curiously between the Clairmont siblings.

Years before, when Alec left for Navy SEAL training, Sebastian Clairmont had given him the leather bag. *"It saw me through a vicious scrape or two, son. I hope it does the same for you."* Inside the Clairmont house were family photos and family recipes, the little jewelry that belonged to Evie—a wedding ring, of course, not among her possessions. But with its supple scarred hide and nicked brass buckles, the duffel bag differed from other mementoes. Its mere existence told a story, and Alec had sometimes wondered about the secrets it could tell. A thick leather strap was attached to either end of the bag, and every Clairmont kid could picture it hanging from Sebastian's wide shoulder—sometimes coming, sometimes going. Today the duffel bag held Alec's things, and it definitely said he was going.

After receiving Jess's cryptic texts and remote crash site photos, the Clairmonts had been unable to reestablish contact. Alec had moved forward with a plan and his family, the *Tribe of Five*, agreed to it. There was a plane wreck that might hold answers to their parents' mysterious disappearance years before. Then there was Jess Donnelly—journalist, buddy, and roommate—the woman Alec was determined to find. All of it required he get his ass to Colombia ASAP. His flight left in a few hours. Standing in the Clairmont kitchen, Alec took out his phone.

"No word?" Aaron said.

"Nothing. I thought maybe there'd be a text. This isn't like Jess. Worse, it's such an isolated region of South America. I don't like it. Almost anything could have happened. I did put a call in to her ex, Julian Silva."

"The way Jess talked about him..." Honor drew a breath and shrugged at Alec. "I'm not sure how much help he'll be."

"I guess we'll find out. Julian agreed to meet me at the airport in Bogota, and he did say he'd seen Jess before she left on her assignment." Alec bent over the duffel, tightening the straps until leather squealed. "I mean, it makes total sense, right? What woman travels three-thousand miles and doesn't pay a visit to her fucking almost ex-husband?" He stood upright. A room full of blank stares met Alec's. "Anyway," he said, letting go of the bag. "Right now, he's our only plausible connection to Jess."

"And if Julian Silva hasn't been totally forthcoming," Aaron said, "my guess is he'll get a frogman-type lesson in the art of communication."

"Count on it," Alec said.

The brief exchange about Alec's SEAL past was the closest thing to a conversation they'd had on the subject in some time. It always happened that way. The moment Alec wrestled that part of his life silent, there it was again—like a weed. His brother's recent go-round with crime and punishment, evil and justice—namely Stefan Gerard—had been enough to stir memories Alec would rather forget. He refocused, glancing at his watch, calculating ground zero coordinates for the Sneak and Peek—aka, recon mission. He had spare time, which wasn't his strong suit. "You packed?" he said to Troy.

"Yep. Ready to ship out." Alec heard military lingo that made it sound as if his brother was reading his mind. "But maybe with all this happening I shouldn't be heading off to a movie set."

"Go," Honor insisted. "Jake is expecting you. You'll know anything the minute we do."

"Yeah, but I was thinking," Troy said. "Since I'm already packed, maybe I should go with Alec—be his wingman or something."

"I appreciate that," Alec said. "But I've got it covered. Stick with the plan, Troy. Go soak up Jake's movie star life. At least it'll be air-conditioned." He tried to sound upbeat and loose. The potential hazards of dragging Evie and Sebastian's youngest son into the unknowns of Colombia was more responsibility than he needed.

Sitting at the kitchen table, Ruby had been flipping through a photo album. While the pictures were new to her, any Clairmont could describe the next page before she turned it. "Heaven forbid I inflate a Clairmont ego, but you are a ridiculously handsome bunch," she said, tipping back her head to smile up at Aaron.

"It felt... *necessary* to take the album out," Honor said. "Maybe I just needed to see their faces."

"I get it," Alec said. With Honor and Ruby seated, Alec, Aaron, and Troy huddled tight to get a closer look at the album. In the next room, the dining room—a space they rarely used—was a sideboard. It was cluttered with family photos. First pictures of Evie and Sebastian from the late 1970's—when they'd first met. Those photos were followed by pictures of Alec; the kind you'd take of a first-born—like he'd been the first of a species. Pictures of Aaron came next, the brother who looked even more like Sebastian with the same striking green eyes. Photos racked up fast after Alec and Aaron, showing off the Clairmont twins, Jake and Honor.

They looked largely unalike—but maybe that was more of a boy-girl thing. The sideboard held just enough room for photos of Troy, the last of the *Tribe of Five*. The progression of photos ended with a final Christmas snapshot. It was taken not long before Evie and Sebastian's fateful flight to South America. It showed a messy mob of barely adult children, piled like dogs under the tree, a mountain of torn wrapping paper surrounding them. After their parents disappeared, the *Tribe of Five* decided there would be no more photos added to the dining room sideboard. They kept it exactly as it was—a small piece of the Clairmont house where time stood still.

Others photos were scattered about the rooms of the Dutch colonial—Troy's high school graduation, Alec on leave in Dubai, deployed to Iraq, Honor with Rowan, her fiancé, before he was killed. He guessed there'd be a wedding photo to come, Ruby and Aaron's. Alec shook his head at what seemed like a wild concept. For some families there might be the amazement of a first-generation college graduate. In Alec's family, amazement would describe the first Clairmont to marry—his parents included. Good for Aaron, if that's what he wanted—and it seemed he did. His brother had hardly taken his eyes off Ruby, who looked at the photos, gleaning bits and pieces of Clairmont family history.

Honor turned the page. Her fair hand wasn't reminiscent of their mother's, which was sturdier, less delicate. Honor's fine bone structure always stood out. In the photos, her blonde head was shades lighter than Evie's and even Jake's. Alec sometimes wondered if the loss felt different to Honor. She was the only girl, the only daughter who'd lost a mother. She'd been the person capable of ruffling Sebastian Clairmont at his core. Alec could remember the way Sebastian looked at his daughter—as if stunned by her existence, unlike his four sons, who were subtle variations of one man.

Alec stepped back, blindsided by a loud memory. It was clear in his mind how his father had also looked at him. He recalled the prideful gaze as he'd graduated from SEAL training, the medal ceremonies that had followed. But there was also the way Sebastian would catch himself, sometimes losing his temper at a younger Alec. He'd loved his children—categorically—but Sebastian could also be abrupt. Over the years, his work had taken him away for months at a time. Once, on Alec's first leave home, he remembered doing shots with his father. Sebastian didn't drink often, but on those rare occasions he did it up right. It had to be the booze talking, Alec had thought, as Sebastian wove in and out of conversations about the past—a time before Alec was even born. "Your mother and I—it wasn't an easy thing. In fact, every day, I still wake up amazed she's mine."

Alec was quiet. He'd been half drunk, half listening to a story that didn't sound like one he'd heard before. "Evie, she never saw where I came from. It was bad enough what she did know. Truth be told," his father had said, "I should have never made it off those docks—a man soured on life, an older version of the punk prick who didn't give a fuck about anyone." He'd snickered. "I was supposed to turn out to be my old man."

Alec's woozy gaze had traveled to his father, who'd stood an inch taller than his eldest son. He'd never met his grandfather. He didn't know anything about him. Sebastian never talked about life before Evie. Maybe that's why the description had made such an impression—*soured, punk prick* didn't fit. Sebastian Clairmont was rock solid—albeit a little unsteady in that moment.

His father had poured them each one more shot, downing his. "Remember that, Alec. We all work with what we're given. I wasn't given anything but a will to survive. A skull too thick to know to quit. If you knew where I started, who I was... Well, the last thing you'd want me to be is your father." Alec had stepped back from the bar. The mirror image, the steely interior—he couldn't fathom another man in that role. No Clairmont could. "Years before today... what you see now..." His father's words slurred and his lumbering frame had leaned hard into the bar. "This wasn't me. Not even close." He swiped a broad hand across his mouth. "God and Evie, they know I wasn't always Sebastian Clairmont."

CHAPTER ONE

1976
Philadelphia, Pennsylvania

Sebastian Christos rolled over and looked at the body breathing next to him. Easy girls from the neighborhood behaved this way. She wasn't from the neighborhood. He knew because he'd fucked all those girls—twice. Daylight pointed out bottled blonde hair and a tangle of sheets. Her skin, he now saw, had a ruddy Irish look. She stirred. Sebastian tipped his head at her fluttering eyelids—one set of lashes looked fur-lined, the other skimpy and paper-bag brown. He supposed it was her natural color. He lifted the sheet draped across her midriff. Yeah. Natural color. Along with her willingness to sleep with him, she'd been predictable—nothing special. Raking a hand over his stubble-covered face, Sebastian thumped a fist unceremoniously into the mattress.

Nothing special.

That was his life.

He was ready to get out of bed, but she stopped him, her hand coming across his body, stroking his broad chest. She cleared her throat—a croaky combination of tequila shots, come, and cigarettes. Sebastian wondered which might kill her first. He arched his brow and examined the scene—bare toe to pillow top. Considering how quickly she'd slept with him, this girl would fuck the wrong guy long before the booze and cigarettes got to her. She groped downward, reaching. His dick did the opposite of his brain by responding. On the nightstand were condoms, a bottle of tequila, and two empty shot glasses. "What the hell..." he muttered, grabbing the bottle and taking a gulp like mouthwash. He tossed a condom wrapper onto her stomach. She tore it open and went to work sheathing him. He'd been damn clear about that.

A moment later, Sebastian, whose frame largely shadowed hers, rolled the woman onto her back. She moaned softly as her legs parted on cue. She closed her eyes again, and he felt flamingo pink fingernails rake down his back. That woke him up—maybe more so than the mechanical thrusts into her. Her noises were more prostitute than passionate lover, although she wasn't either thing. She wasn't anybody. Her long legs wrapped around his body, and her breathing amped to complementary gasps. Could be she really was enjoying it.

"God, Sebastian... I've never done it so many times, not like this."

He doubted that.

"Maybe... uh, maybe after..." she said on airy whispers, "we could get some breakfast. Or I can make you something." She giggled. "I'm guessing we can use your kitchen to cook."

The remark threw him—or maybe it was just her breath. But she shut up, her pouty mouth connecting with his unshaven neck. Images of last night jutted through Sebastian's mind—fucking her against the refrigerator. *Coffee.* A canister of coffee had shimmied from the counter onto the floor, the rousing scents of java and sex filling the air. One jacked him up enough to get through the days, the other delivered distraction. She was talking again, although Sebastian wasn't listening. Now that she'd proven to have remembered his name, Sebastian was trying to remember hers. It seemed like the decent thing to do. She moved her hands lithely down his back and onto his ass as she hitched her legs up, urging him on. Other odors hit him hard. Her hair reeked of cigarettes and the sheets smelled of a different girl's perfume. One from the neighborhood who he'd fucked two nights ago.

That girl had slipped from his bed before dawn, saying something about leaving a kid at home. Super good-bye to that, he'd thought. Kids belonging to anyone were an absolute point of avoidance. Random thoughts replaced those as he thrust harder into her, striving toward precious seconds of nirvana. The ones that indicated he was alive. A thundering orgasm shot through him, a powerful sensation.

Maybe too powerful.

The whole bed rattled. An object rocketed past them like a Russian missile. It slammed hard into the wall above their heads. The girl screamed. Shock, instead of ecstasy, penetrated Sebastian's ears.

A thickly accented voice boomed from the doorway. "You 'bout done in here?"

The girl tried to wrench away, but Sebastian's body had her pinned to the mattress. She clawed for the sheet, legs still wrapped around his ass. Her wide-awake hazel eyes blinked starkly into his. He looked away, annoyed when specifics registered. Sebastian reached around and hauled the sheet over them.

"Yeah. We're done. Give us a minute," Sebastian said.

"I'll give you thirty fucking seconds and not a speck more. Do your banging on your own time, Bash—you hear me? I'll not pay you to put your cock in chickies after sunup. You and your dick were supposed be on that dock at dawn."

Sebastian rose in a pushup-like movement, twisting his neck toward the warning. In the doorway, he caught a glimpse of the old man and, he suspected, his future. Sebastian looked to his right and saw the telephone lying where his head had been. It made sense—

hurling it at him was classic Andor retaliation. The phone had sat on the hall table. It was the closest, hardest object within Andor's reach. A sprinkle of freshly dented plaster flaked downward. Sebastian glanced at the girl, whose ruddy complexion had turned redder. "I said I'll be right there."

"See that you are." The door slammed but opened again. Sebastian sighed, stiffly holding his body over the girl. "And clean up that fucking mess of coffee on the kitchen floor."

He peered down at the girl. "No coffee. Explains his off mood."

"Off mood?" she said as Sebastian rolled away. The girl darted to a stance more erect than his dick had been. "Who... who the hell was that?"

"The man who calls the shots," Sebastian said, getting out of bed. Wadding the spent condom into a tissue, he threw it into the trashcan—a dead center shot from six feet out. He pulled on his underwear and glanced at his watch. A shower was out of the question. The girl gathered a telltale trail of clothes that led from the doorway to the bed. "Hey, do you, um... have a way home?" They'd come back to the house in his car. He hadn't thought about how she'd arrived at the pool hall where he'd picked her up. "I could take you, but... Well, you heard."

"I, uh..." She reached for her purse, which had spilled onto a chair. It seemed to hold all the cosmetics that held her together. With the bed in between them, she skimmed her gaze down his body, a more distant full daylight view. She seemed to forget things like fear and embarrassment. "Wow. It's a mind-blowing combination."

"What's that?"

"Muscles and scars. Last night I thought your eyes were the best part—guess I was wrong."

"Guess we better keep on truckin'." Sebastian shuffled into jeans and yanked on a thick crewneck sweater. He couldn't do anything about the eyes, an unusual milky green. They attracted attention—

all kinds. The sweater smelled of salt air and sweat. He often wore it to the docks. The wind was cutting and the sweater was bulky over his jeans, which was helpful.

As soon as he opened the nightstand drawer, the girl reverted to surprise. She gasped as Sebastian withdrew a Beretta and tucked it in the back of his jeans. He shifted his shoulders. "Docks can be a bad scene." For the first time since last night's game of nine-ball they made real eye contact.

"I'll call a cab." She looked at the phone, the cord ripped from its wall jack. "Maybe you have another one?" She busied herself by stowing away the contents of her purse. "I... I, um, don't even know what part of Philly we're in."

He hesitated, considering the possible fates she might have met with his part of town. "You should. And you're probably lucky it was just me." They traded a look. It was meant to remind her that he was twice her size and that he had just tucked a gun into his pants—a different guy, a different circumstance, and her night might have ended in a bad shit different way. Sebastian shook it off—nameless women weren't his problem. "Near Whitman," he said. "Not too far from the docks. There's another phone in the kitchen." Sebastian reached into the nightstand again, retrieving some cash. As he passed it across the bed, his glance caught on a black caterpillar. Eyelashes. He plucked the delicate feathery thing from the bedsheets. "Here." He held out a twenty-dollar bill, gently placing the lost lashes on top.

She touched her eye, which did look off-balance—one eye dressed like she'd been on her way to Cinderella's ball, the other offering a glimpse of where she came from. The middle class suburbs of Philly, he guessed.

"Are you offering me money for...?"

Sebastian snorted a laugh. He wanted to warn her again—*Well damn—fill name in blank—you did go to bed with me after a couple of drinks and sentences. What should I think?* "It's for a cab," he said instead.

"Oh." Sheepishly, she accepted the cash and prop. "Thanks. You, um... you work for him, that man?"

"Andor? Yeah, I work for him."

"Does he always talk to you like that?" she said, finally pulling on her clothes.

She'd worn no bra. No name, nothing memorable, no personal history, but her ample tits had registered. "Nah, sometimes he can be a seriously mean bastard. In that case, he woulda hit me with the phone."

Her expression captioned her reaction—things didn't go down that way in her middle-class neighborhood. The girl talked as she tugged on a bell-bottom jumpsuit, like perhaps keeping him busy might keep him from shooting her. Sebastian bit down on a smirk as the girl realized the error of her ways—wrong town, wrong man, wrong everything. "So... so why do you? Work for him. I mean, why let him talk to you that way? Where I live, there's decent work, nicer people. You seem like an okay guy—nicer than some."

And there you go. She'd officially moved through all the phases: find him, fuck him, fear him... *save him*. Like that was possible.

"Couldn't you change jobs, get a different boss?"

Sebastian thumbed over his shoulder. "Well, I suppose I could—get a different job... move, get a different boss. But that wouldn't do a damn thing about changing the fact that he's my father."

———

The girl—whose name Sebastian never did recall—didn't cross his mind again that day. Not until Vinny Danato's wife showed up at the dock's edge, Sebastian's shipmate racing down to meet her. They stood on the cement pier as a kid clung to each of Vinny's hands. His wife held a baby... toddler... mouth to feed. Having loaded and unloaded freight all morning, Sebastian's arms ached and he was ready for a break. On the deck, he leaned against crates of cargo. They were bound for the Port of Piraeus that night. He lit a cig, inhaling deeply, and zoned in on the family below. He didn't know the wife's name. Damn, did he ever bother to learn any woman's name? He stared, trying to remember Vinny saying it. Jesus, he talked about her enough. Sebastian narrowed his eyes at the scene. Christ, it was like Little Italy had crashed their South Philly dock, the entire Danato clan hanging out. *Wops...* Andor was particular about who he hired. He had a problem with most nationalities. Italians were bad, though not as worrisome as thick Micks. Micks went to confession, which meant they talked. "First it's the priest, *gios*," Andor would caution. "Then it's the cop that comes to Sunday supper."

Despite his Italian heritage, Vinny had proven himself by making two undercover narcs who'd worked the docks last summer. This act of loyalty had earned Andor's trust. Still, if his father had his way, he'd only hire Greeks. But that was tough in a corner of Philadelphia that spun like a miniature globe—Wops, Micks, Pols, Spics, Gooks, Blacks and so on.

Sometimes Sebastian wondered what they said about the Greeks.

Vinny's conversation with his wife grew more animated. Sebastian couldn't hear, but the Italians talked with their hands, and Vinny's gestures were increasingly fervent. Sebastian read it as angry. He leaned into the rail and braced for a strike to the face of Vinny's wife. Years ago, he'd seen his father do it, strike his mother in public. She'd been dead a long time now—an eleven-year old Sebastian finding her that way on the kitchen floor. If Vinny's wife died, he supposed his crewmate's reaction would be different than his father's. *"Life is full of hard things, gios... Just take this as proof and move on..."* The same voice Sebastian heard in his head boomed from the forward deck.

"Is everything so loaded, Bash, you've got time to stand about?"

He turned from the railing, Andor approaching. Sebastian stood six-foot three while his father was six-foot four. It summed up his life—always an inch short. "I'm workin' on it. I'm waitin' for one more crate to board. The one from Atlantic City. Paulos is bringing it."

"Your uncle is delivering the most important one. Make certain no one touches it but you. It goes in the safe, in the belly. Then you lock it." He poked at his son's chest. "Nobody but you locks it. Last man out, you understand, *gios*?"

"Yeah, I got it. So it's not cash?"

Andor's eyes, which were a shade deeper than his son's—*gios*—narrowed. "I thought you don't like to know. I thought my money-making ways are of no interest to you. Naturally, eating interests you—this is true since you were born."

Sebastian heard the harsh Greek accent, words that had filled his head for twenty-four years—guttural consonants and exaggerated vowel sounds. He didn't have the accent, though his appearance was similar enough—oil-colored hair (Andor's peppered with gray), imperial noses, the eyes surrounded by thick dark lashes. Shit that seemed to leave women in a puddle. But the mirror-like reflection only left Sebastian leery. How much of Andor Christos was bound to him? Most days he didn't want to know. Sebastian squinted as if this might alter the fingerprint image. "I'll watch for Uncle Paulos. You can count on me, Pater."

It was only an inch. Even so, Andor had a way of staring down his son. A smile pushed into the hollow of broad cheeks—like airplane wings. He moved closer. Sebastian tensed. The close proximity rarely resulted in anything good. "Our new product line. Heroin was the drug of yesterday—the sixties, still a decent business," he said, waving his hand in a so-so gesture. "Today these young men and women have jobs. They're earning money, wishing for a classier high. It's a new dawn, Bash."

"Cocaine," Sebastian said. The girl from last night had asked if he had any. At the time, he didn't think so.

"The finest grade money can buy. The shipment includes both product and profit for our Godfathers of the Night on the other side of the ocean. I believe they'll be impressed. They'll want to invest. I could move up."

Sebastian nodded, waiting for more. There was always more.

"If things go well, we'll be adding a new route to our schedule."

"New route?" Sebastian said. For as long as he could recall, a bi-monthly trip to Greece and back had been their bread and butter run.

"Yes. Our brother godfathers here, they wish us to expand to a southern course—down through the Panama Canal into South America."

"What the fuck are we going to do in South America?" Sebastian didn't like the sound of that—the routes they sailed were dangerous enough.

"Like I said, we're expanding. Our product and our transport. I'll tell you more when it's a fact. I'm not getting younger, Bash. You will have to decide. Are you willing to take my place? If you want, you could rise above me. If you don't," he said, his drifting gaze moving around the seedy dockyard, "you'll be a ship's hand until you die. Tell me... what is your biggest ambition, *gios*? To collect whores like pennies?" He spit on the wooden deck. "Worthless, both things."

Sebastian supposed the girl from last night was a glaring example. That and he did lack true ambition—the kind that took you to college or to trade school. But neither were options Andor had encouraged. It didn't matter, he thought, glancing at Vinny. He wouldn't know what to do with that sort of everyday life. "The Godfathers of the Night, Pater," he said, looking at his father. "It... I'm not sure it's where I belong."

"Where you belong? It's who you are, Bash." The way he spoke, it was like saying the sky was blue. "You can't deny it. What?" he said, peering over the rail. "You think you belong with that, down there? At Sunday mass with Danato and his kind?" Sebastian and his father watched. Vinny patted his wife's stomach while holding their son in his arms. Sebastian had mistaken joy for anger. He took a long drag on his cigarette, skeptical of both lives.

"The Wops, they reproduce quicker than the Micks. One son is all a man needs." A sideways glance cut to Sebastian. "One mouth to feed—as long as he doesn't disappoint. One woman..." He slapped at Sebastian's arm and laughed. "Now that's a different tale. Right, Bash?"

Andor puffed out his cheeks, lighting a cigar as he strode toward the bridge of the Diamatis. As the dock manager and mid-ranking member of the Godfathers of the Night, it was Andor's business to oversee the Greek ship's imports and exports, legal and otherwise. It was Sebastian's job to make certain his father didn't fail at the latter. On occasion, depending on the cargo, he'd made the crossing too. Sebastian neither loved Greece nor did he hate it. It was more like relatives—you couldn't choose your heritage. He'd been to other European ports, not feeling an attachment to any of those either. But looking to the west, he also couldn't picture sailing to South America.

As Andor disappeared from view, Sebastian felt a tap on his pea coat. He turned, having to look down. "Bim. I wasn't sure if you'd show—well, not on deck." Sebastian shook the slight hand of a man who was the color of coffee.

Bim worked for the vendor who supplied fruits and vegetables to the ship's galley. Years before, when the two first met, Sebastian had laughed at Bim's everyday ambitions. He said he'd come to America to get a college degree. Then, some time ago, Sebastian quit laughing. Not only had Bim finished college, he was now in medical school. But, as incredible as the feat was, a poor medical school student wasn't in a position to help his family. The one he'd left behind in the Sudan. That's when he'd approached Sebastian. Cautiously, Bim had asked if the stories were true. Did the dock manager's son—his friend—run ocean-wide errands for cash?

It wasn't untrue.

"I was fearful the balance of my funds would not arrive in time," Bim said. "Mercifully, they did. Here—it's all here." Anxiously, he shoved an envelope at Sebastian.

With the stub of the cigarette pinched in his lips, Sebastian thumbed through the contents. One-thousand dollars, just as they'd agreed. "Good. But you've got to take care of your end. Have your sister at the dock in Piraeus on the twenty-first. Tell her escort to ask for Vinny. He'll take her to a safe spot on the ship. It won't be the Ritz, but if she doesn't mind crappin' in a bucket for ten days, she'll be in America on the other side—no questions, no immigration."

"I understand." Bim continued to nod as if taking copious mental notes. "I've used most of the cash to secure safe transport out of the Sudan and into Egypt. My parents, you have to understand— they have no choice. They were to marry Nafy to the son of a neighboring family. In turn, his family would pay my parents' debt to the warlords. There is nothing these men do not control."

Sebastian nodded back. "So marrying her off to the son, that wouldn't be any better than the warlord option?" He couldn't absorb it beyond the plot to a movie.

"My friend, you've no idea. This happens every day to women in my village—unspeakable atrocities. Girls no more than twelve and thirteen turned into sex slaves... or resold again. Death, I think, is a better fate."

"Twelve and..." Sebastian shook his head. "How old is your sister?"

"Much older. Sixteen. Even so, the man my parents will marry her off to... These warlords are his cohorts. Nafy, she is smart, so sweet. In this arrangement, the best she could hope for is producing many sons then a swift fatal illness."

"You're kidding, right?" Sebastian waited for Bim to smile, to tell him it was some twisted joke. "That's, um... some heavy shit. And so you're gonna do all that for her?"

Bim's tiny face grew more curious. "Nafy is my sister. How can I not help her?"

"Yeah, well... that's something I wouldn't know anything about." Sebastian flicked his cigarette butt overboard and returned to fingering the cash. Warlords and sisters, they weren't his problem. "Bim... how'd, um... How'd you get this—and the rest, the money to get her out of the Sudan? Poor med students and part-time produce vendors don't have that kind of bread."

"Bread?" he said, his newfound roots had taken, but not the slang.

"Dough..." Sebastian sighed when that didn't register either. "Money. How'd you manage so much cash?"

"Ah!" he said, holding up an index finger. "After being accepted to medical school, I was sent the dowry of my to-be wife, Devi. Her family is wealthy." He pushed the envelope closer to Sebastian. "There was just enough to pay you after funding Nafy's escape from my homeland."

"Damn," he said, thinking about Bim's willingness to invest his last dime. It made Sebastian think of the crate he was about to load and the cash value attached to it—how the money was earned and how it might be spent. "This girl... the one with the dowry. She's the chick you plan on marrying and you haven't seen her in four years?"

"Nearly five. And, yes, absolutely. We are lucky. It was love at first sight."

Sebastian's brain balked at the concept.

"Nafy—she is not as fortunate. She had no suitors. The men of my village do not care for women wiser than them. Daughters not as clever as Nafy, they are often given to warlords or if they're lucky, to decent village men. Repayment of debt and bearing children are their only worth."

Sebastian inched back. "Jesus... Sucks for the daughters."

"Sucks?" Bim said, wrinkling his dark brow. "Perhaps. But sons do not provide what these men want."

Sebastian raked his hand through his hair, considering the universal concept—guys thinking with their dicks. He recalled stories he'd heard while getting drunk in the bars near the Port of Piraeus and the Port of Rize in Turkey—a particularly unsavory stop. Young girls traded like livestock, treated worse than chickens in a cage. At the time, he didn't think the stories were real. "But as long as you get your sister out..." He clung tight to the envelope, shaking it at Bim. "That's all that matters, right?"

"For Nafy, yes."

"I mean, you can't save the fucking world."

"I suppose not. I mean... correct. Our plan for Nafy is perfect. My family won't be implicated in her disappearance. The village, the warlords, they will believe she was stolen or eaten. Both can happen."

Sebastian nodded vaguely at the grisly fate. "And this Dev..."

"Devi," Bim said, a bright smile consuming his face.

"I'm curious... You're set on marrying her?" Sebastian waved a hand at the harbor and distant land and dropped it brusquely. "With all the women on this side of the map? I mean, eventually you'll be a rich doctor."

"This side of the map or that one—there is only one Devi."

Sebastian had a better feel for being eaten by a lion. One girl mattering that much? Impossible. "Whatever, man..." Slipping the envelope toward his coat pocket, he hesitated. "The money. Won't you have to explain what happened to it?"

"Safe passage for Nafy. That is our agreement," he said, pushing the envelope at Sebastian. "You're right. One day I will be a doctor with a good income, and Devi's dowry will be repaid. This is not for you to worry about."

Bim was right and he tucked the envelope away. "Well, I'm a man of my word, Bim. Your sister will be here on the first."

"Excellent! It's going to work out, my friend. This life... this country. My days as a produce vendor are numbered. I could never say that in my country."

"I think it's a lot to say here."

Sebastian watched as Bim retreated, the small man and his huge ambition disappearing into the stairwell of the Diamatis. Whatever drove Bim, Sebastian suspected he didn't own an ounce of it. *Ounce...* It brought him back to reality and Sebastian went about his business, directing cargo and waiting for his uncle's delivery. But as he plotted the future of crates bound for distant shores, Sebastian couldn't shake Bim's life. He stared east feeling... *something*. Or maybe it was more about feeling anything. The things Bim had talked about, his family, this Devi. Sebastian shook his head, his gaze set on the horizon. Could be that on his next run, he'd get off the freighter and set down roots in the land of his ancestors. But seeing Paulos's car turn into the dockyard, the idea short circuited. Nothing would change, even on the other side of the world. A different life required a reason, and that Sebastian couldn't see.

He leaned over the rail where Vinny remained at his wife's side. "Hey, Vin, you ever gettin' back to work?"

Vinny turned, waving at Sebastian, indicating he'd be right there. The wife offered a smaller, shyer wave, her hand barely rising past her breastbone. Awkwardly, Sebastian's large hand returned the gesture. Vinny kissed his children and he kissed his wife. The menial crewman then bent and kissed his wife's stomach.

Sebastian stepped back from the rail. The scene below was wrought with things he couldn't comprehend—like Sanskrit or doing the drugs he shuttled. But as he came away from the rail a name bubbled in his brain. "Antonia." Sebastian remembered the endearing way Vinny said his wife's name... *Antonia*.

CHAPTER TWO

Fifteen Months Later, July 1977
Good Hope, Pennsylvania

IT BAFFLED EVIE NEAL HOW HELL COULD BE ANY HOTTER THAN THE Fathers of the Right meeting hall. But the fact seemed evident to Duncan Kane, who slammed a hymnal onto the pulpit, warning of brimstone and doom. It had its affect. If you dosed off mid-sermon, the jolt, jarring as the Devil's pitchfork, snapped you wide awake. Evie sat up straighter, though she'd listened dutifully. She had to trust that eventually she'd know what to do with the words. Not everything was meant to be revealed at nineteen.

Temptation caused her attention to dart right, a distraction from pending brimstone and the sweat trickling down her back. She did think Ezra Kane handsome with his starlight-colored hair and lagoon blue eyes. She'd decided on lagoon blue years ago, after seeing real lagoons in *World Missions* literature kept in the meeting hall vestibule. Evie was awed by the tropical settings, the heathen and beautiful places where religion needed to be introduced. Sin and exotic destinations—why did they always go together?

From her peripheral glance, framed in the greenish tints of the hall's single, stained-glass window, Ezra looked particularly handsome. This was good since Evie was going to marry Ezra that fall. The Fathers of the Right, distant relatives of mainstream Quakerism, decided as much years before. It wasn't a decree—as that would be archaic—but an understanding that the eldest daughter of Gideon Neal would marry the son of Reverend Kane. Next to Hannah Wheaton, Ezra was her closest friend. And as the sect's women often reminded Evie, "How lucky you are… What more could a girl ask for?"

Aside from Evie's luck, the marriage would also help to uphold the longevity of their sect. Two more families had left the Fathers of Right that year, lured into lives beyond their rural haven of Good Hope. Evie couldn't imagine such a thing, though sometimes she did dream of venturing beyond their sanctuary. She didn't mean to, but in her sleep the dreams would find her, and who could help that? Awake, Evie was certain no place could feel more like home than Good Hope. And it wasn't as if they lived like the Amish— they had electricity and conservative but modern clothing, even a community station wagon. But those who had abandoned their ways seemed to have wanted something else.

Sitting in the pew, her thoughts went the way of dreams, seeing Ezra's eyes rise from their prayerful direction. A lightning fast wink sailed across the aisle. Quick as a hiccup, she smiled back. Evie did love Ezra's rare mischievous behavior. It released little pieces of him that otherwise Reverend Kane might smother like a demonic serpent. Wary of demonic serpents and a nudge from her father, Evie forced her eyes onto the pulpit. But a cough from across the aisle drew her glance back. Ezra mouthed the word, *"Revelations."*

Evie understood that it had nothing to do with scripture.

After the sermon, Evie kept her distance from Ezra. She chatted with an assortment of girls and women, including Ezra's sisters and mother, Adah. Evie stared at the woman who looked like she'd been etched from ivory, her devoted daughters at her side. But admiration ebbed as envy washed over Evie—a horrible thing to feel. Ezra and his sisters had a mother. Evie did not. She admonished the selfish thought. It wasn't Ezra's fault, nor his mother or sisters. Keeping her glance low, Evie looked toward a group of men. She held her focus on Reverend Kane, and blame settled in the pit of her stomach until Hannah plucked her from the blasphemous state. She handed Evie red-berry punch and a different conversation.

"The Reverend was on a tear this morning, and with it so hot in the hall, I thought for certain the Widow Vale would pass out at the piano." Both Evie and Hannah looked toward a woman past her prime—at least thirty-five. Even so, she was attractive with delicate bones and a natural curl to her earthy-toned hair. She had a gift for music, leading the sect's choir. It was how the Widow Vale provided her worth to Good Hope with no husband to do it for her, no children to add to their future. "If Nolan Creek had been nearby to catch her, it might have been worth fainting," Hannah whispered.

"And what good would that do?" Evie asked, sipping the punch.

"Everyone knows it's as good a match as the Widow Vale and Brother Creek will ever find. Why it hasn't happened by now..." Hannah shook her head. "My mother said she's baked Brother Creek a pie for every fruit that's come into season."

Evie glanced at Nolan Creek who stood apart from the other men. "I don't think Brother Creek favors... *pie*."

"What a silly thing to say. And why is that? Everyone loves pie."

Evie's mouth gaped as she held the punch glass midair. Her understanding wasn't clear enough to articulate. But Evie had once overheard Brother Creek in deep prayer, alone in the meeting hall. Or at least he thought he'd been alone. With solemn, pained words, he begged God to smite him blind if he continued to lust for other men. Evie thought she'd heard wrong. Such a thing had to be impossible. But watching Brother Creek skirt away, yet again, from the approaching Widow Vale, she supposed she might have heard right. "Oh, I don't know," she said, shrugging at Hannah. "Maybe when a man gets to be his age—what is Brother Creek, thirty-two? With no wife, I suspect he's set in his ways."

Hannah accepted the answer and took Evie's hand in hers, drawing the two into a tight corner. "Tell me something else. Is it true that Ezra's going to be gone for an entire week?"

"That's what he said. He's going with his father to meet with the other sects—common Quakers. They'll decide if they want to fund a full mission for the Fathers of the Right."

"And this doesn't bother you? To marry Ezra knowing he'll be gone from Good Hope so much of the time? I don't know what I'd do if Tobias were gone more than a day."

Evie knotted her brow, her stomach muscles following. Hannah was that way about Tobias Blyth. She suspected if Tobias were to ask, "Will you—" Hannah would reply, "Yes!" before he could finish saying "pass me the salt." Evie tugged at the braid draping her shoulder. "Ezra will be back," she said firmly. "Do you really think it's the Reverend's plan for us to marry, only to send my new husband away? Besides, when I'm Ezra's wife—"

"When you're Ezra's wife, you'll be Reverend Kane's daughter. I should think, without Ezra, living in the Kane house will not be like living in your own," she said, pointing to Gideon Neal.

That much was true, her father being a subdued, obedient sect member. Evie shook her head. "We're to live in the cottage behind the Kane house. It will be Ezra's and mine. It's not as if I'll be living with them while Ezra's gone."

"Perhaps not," Hannah said, sipping her punch. "But I still wonder whose house you'll obey—the Reverend's or your husband's?"

Evie didn't reply, uninterested in debating any man's rules—another notion Hannah wouldn't understand. But nibbling on a corn cake, the question hung in her head. Evie pushed back her shoulders and looked toward her intended husband. With Ezra's sweet nature it wouldn't be that way. She was sure of it.

Adah Kane appeared beside the two girls, having floated in like the Holy Spirit. "I know this surely isn't gossip. But it might look that way to watchful eyes."

Evie looked toward the men, her father's glance concerned. The Reverend's hard stare was more on point, and Evie looked away. "Not gossiping, just talking about your corn cakes, Mrs. Kane. They're so delicious I was thinking about having another."

"I thank you for the compliment, Evie." A blush colored the woman's pale cheeks. "But I say with certainty that two would be indulgent." She paused. "And put a knife to your throat if you are given to appetite."

Evie's mouth hung as Hannah, a better student of verses, offered the proper reply. "Proverbs, 23-2."

Adah Kane smiled and shooed the girls toward the other women. The verse was a reminder about moderation. Plain language, social order, temperance, and simplicity, these were ideals that connected their sect to the common core of Quakerism. The things that didn't separated the Fathers of the Right from not only Quakers but the outside world.

Evie listened to a wider circle of women vigorously discuss the oversized quilt they were working on. It was to be sold at the North Good Hope fair, an annual undertaking that brought nearly a thousand dollars to the sect. There wasn't a Quaker, Amish, or Mennonite who could compete with Fathers of the Right quilting. Evie paid attention, though she knew her contribution would be close to nil. She hated sewing of any kind and would spend most of the project trying to keep her bloody, needle-pricked fingers on the red squares of fabric.

Adah led most of the quilt talk, Evie sinking into the soft lilt of her voice. It was reminiscent of her mother's. Elizabeth Neal died in the coldest part of last January. It was thought to be a stroke, but no one knew for certain. Medical intervention was strictly forbidden. Evie had been bold, outspoken, suggesting a hospital in Philadelphia or even Lancaster. It might have made life "God's will," as opposed to death. As Evie kept vigil with her languishing mother, the Reverend, her father, and prayer, she'd openly raised her demand about medical treatment. It had led to nothing but a stinging backhand from Reverend Kane.

Renouncing medical aid was a core principle and part of what drove the group from mainstream Quakerism. The Reverend's father—Ezra's grandfather—founded the Fathers of the Right. He'd forsaken medicinal interference and proved it by way of his three wives. Each died, in turn as Malcolm Kane proclaimed it to be God's will, not man's choice. For his part, he'd stayed true to his foundation, leading by example in his own passing.

Only since her mother's illness and death had Evie thought to question the unyielding belief. If God allowed everyone else in the twentieth century to survive—with regularity—things like fevers and child birth, why would He want a member of the Fathers of the Right to die? Her father's reaction had been equally troubling, Gideon Neal so accepting of his wife's fate. And that night, from the wooden floor where the Reverend's slap had landed her, Evie blinked up at her father. She faltered, losing respect for a man who had not intervened in Evie's life or her mother's death.

———•◦••◦•———

Revelations' nose was deep into a bucket of oats, Ezra scratching his ears when Evie slipped through the crack of the barn door. She watched the two gentle souls, feeling as if she were interrupting. Finally, she cleared her throat. Ezra didn't look but stared toward the dark of Revelations' stall. "I spy a sweet for the prettiest girl in Good Hope."

"Then I'll fetch Rachel Pruitt. She'd do double time to the barn if I told her Ezra Kane and a sweet waited for her."

He turned, smiling. "She'd be disappointed."

"Why's that?" Evie asked, poking into the thick of a bale of hay and peeking into the tack room on a casual search. "She's made it clear that turning your attention from me wouldn't take more than a snap of her fingers."

"I promise you, it'd take a lot more than that," he said, leaving the horse and heading toward the loft ladder.

"Not in her mind." Giving up on the tack room, Evie moved toward a storage area. She peered between discarded household items and under old quilts saved for the horses. "Rachel said you and I made as much sense as snow in June."

"Did she?" Ezra mused. "Well, did I mouth '*Revelations*' to her during service this morning?" He took a step up the loft ladder and Evie leaned, guessing where the sweet was hidden. "I don't suppose I did." He scrambled up the rest of the way.

Before following, Evie looked into one of several mirrors—some cracked, some not—in the storage area. These objects, along with other household items like a hair dryer, portable television, and electric can opener—some broken, some not—had been left by those who'd abandoned the Fathers of the Right. Most modern conveniences were frowned upon, and mirrors reflected vanity. On the other hand, convenience was hard to resist, especially with five children. Evie knew that Hannah's mother had taken a microwave and hidden it in her pantry. Televisions, however, were another argument entirely.

Glancing in a mirror, Evie knew that Rachel Pruitt was the hands-down beauty. She supposed that's what you got for looking. The girl was a hot-house flower, blooming brighter in hundred-degree heat. Evie traced her fingers over her cracked reflection. "Charm is deceitful, beauty is vain, but a woman who fears the Lord is to be praised." That verse she knew.

Despite the heat, she only wanted to look nice for the boy she was going to marry. What was so wrong about that? *"Nothing..."* Evie decided, shuddering at her candor. Ezra's father would be outraged by her free-thinking while Ezra's mother might try to distract her with a cross-stich. As it was, Evie had made a solid excuse about leaving the meeting hall, needing to run home and tend to loaves of rising bread. She wasn't much of a seamstress, but Evie had a way with food. In the years to come, Ezra might find himself in rags, but he'd be well fed. While precious time ticked and Ezra waited, Evie wasn't ready to let go of hopeful vanity. "Wilted... plain," she said, brushing beads of sweat from her forehead, hoping for something different. She tugged a rope-like, blonde plait, thinking of town girls she'd seen in Our Daily Bread.

Two years ago, Reverend Kane deemed it God's will that they add an ice cream parlor to the sect-owned bake shop, doubling profits in summer months. The women's pies and cakes already attracted buyers from miles away, tourists who invaded the area to eat, gawk, and wonder how such simple lives were lived. Along with curious crowds and revenue, the ice cream parlor drew town girls—North Good Hope girls who went to public high school and dances and read glossy-covered magazines. While working the counter, Evie was often distracted by them to the point of mixing the sherbet scoop with maple walnut.

Giggling groups poured through the door, defying heat with their skimpy clothing and permanently waved hair. They wore jewelry and fingernail polish and bold unapologetic attitudes. Evie once matched their nerve, asking where they purchased their jewelry. Women of the sect wore none—not even a wedding ring. A red-headed girl with unnaturally glossy pink lips looked Evie up and down. Then she'd laughed. "The mall, stupid. Haven't you ever been to the mall?"

Evie's face still burned, recalling the ridicule from within the safety of Good Hope, almost damning the barn mirror. She licked her pale lips and pinched her cheeks with unadorned fingers. She tried to capture wisps of humid hair. It wasn't wavy like Ezra's or lush like Rachel's, which was darker than Revelations' coat. Brown, ordinary eyes and an upturned nose, not a freckle on her face or anything that might strike a soul as interesting. She turned the mirror away, shutting out her simple image and the girls from North Good Hope.

"Evie!" She looked up, seeing Ezra hang over the side of the loft. "Are you coming? Won't be another twenty minutes and they'll send out a search party."

Strict courting was a rule—nothing beyond public hand-holding before the wedding night. Certainly private moments were forbidden. But like the Wheaton's microwave and vanity, it was a rule Evie and Ezra had already broken.

Evie and her knee-length, blue skirt shuffled up the ladder, her heel catching her hem on the last rung. It sent her tumbling face-first into the hay. She thought Rachel Pruitt to be not only beautiful but less clumsy. While Ezra laughed, he was quickly at her side, asking if she was all right. She pushed up on her hands. In her ankle-high sightline a purple and pink sugar-dusted flower twirled. It was as shiny and tempting as the girls from North Good Hope. "Where did you get that?" she said, examining the unusual sweet. She did love Ezra's thoughtfulness.

"My father had one of his meetings in North Good Hope—that lot of ruffians from down toward Philadelphia. He never likes me to be around, he even sends the other Brothers on errands while he meets with them. Father says they're so far from salvation he'd be afraid we'll catch something. I must admit, his bravery is remarkable. Not even Brother Creek goes."

"That is surprising. I thought Brother Creek attended all sect matters."

"I'm sure my father has his reasons. Perhaps he's trying to find a wife for him through his Philadelphia connections."

"If Brother Creek wanted a..." Evie quieted. "From what you've said, they don't seem the type your father would welcome here, even if it were to save Brother Creek from his own cooking."

"True enough. And if Brother Creek would only give the Widow Vale a chance..."

Evie nodded and remained silent. It wasn't her place to suggest ideas to Ezra. "Tell me where you came across such a beautiful thing?" she said, twirling the treat. Ezra grinned, which Evie did love.

"You'll be pleased to know I took the time in North Good Hope as my own."

Evie smiled back.

"The meeting went on longer than usual. They are a tough-looking bunch—thick accents. As for the flower, a group of Mennonite women were selling them. I managed this one all the way back without crushing it. You know Duncan would rather see me share soup with the devil than purchase something from Mennonites." Shameful as it was, Evie loved it when Ezra showed sparks of defiance—interacting with Mennonites and calling his father by his first name.

She sat up and sniffed the flower, sugar dust filling her nose. Evie was pleased, not only about the flower but Ezra's daring use of time. Last year he would have waited in the station wagon even if it were a hundred degrees. "Is it for eating or for looking at," she said, examining the delicate work of art.

"I'm not sure. I didn't get a chance to ask. My father finished his business and I had to go." His fair face perplexed. "For as often as he meets with those men, I'm not sure he makes much progress."

"Why do you say that? They keep coming back."

"Because I catch their talk as they get into their own cars—fancy looking vehicles that don't look right even in North Good Hope. That and I've never heard the Lord's name taken in vain with such regularity. But if my father says he's making progress, he must be."

Evie considered Ezra's observation and obedience. Surely, after they were married, that would ease. Ezra inched over and plucked a straw of hay from her hair. "Ah, it must add to the appeal," she said, thinking of her wilted appearance.

"Evie, you're here. It's all the appeal I'm after."

A shiver raced through her sticky skin. Evie did love the way Ezra looked at her. The first time Ezra had touched her, odd sensations bubbled. Evie was sure she was on the verge of knowing what Hannah so often spoke about. The way Tobias Blyth's mere presence made her heart pound. Today was their fifth private meeting—first kissing by the pond, then behind Our Daily Bread. After that came the barn. The barn had led to the loft and the loft to things only married people shared. But Ezra had good reasoning for this. In only a few months they would be those married people, so God was likely to have given the go ahead. Evie had given it too, persuaded by Ezra's daring position on the matter.

Now, in a different position, she felt Ezra's mouth meet with hers. Evie liked the way his full lips covered hers, his tongue darting playfully. He smelled of summer sweat and hay, tasted of the corn cakes his mother brought to Sunday service. *Sunday.* It did make Evie think twice. "Ezra, I don't know. Today is Sunday. Maybe we shouldn't do it today."

"I've never heard that rule," he said, already working the buttons on her white cotton blouse. Evie glanced down, seeing the Peter Pan collar slip open then off her body. But she tensed as his fingers hooked the strap of her slip, his body guiding them into a thatch of hay.

"Even so…"

"Even so, I'll be gone all week making missionary arrangements. And my father—"

"About that," Evie said, pushing up on her elbows. He didn't stop kissing her, just adjusted to the angle. Gentle touches of his lips covered her face and neck, his hand nudging the slip down. "Ezra, does your father say how long you'll be away after we marry?"

"Not specifically." He rose back to eye-level. "I suppose it depends on our funds and my progress." Ezra groped at her skirt, fishing, without success, for the zipper.

Evie wasn't as convinced. "But shouldn't I know... whether my husband will be gone a few weeks... or months. Maybe if it's longer, I could come with you."

Fumbling with what was a generous amount of fabric, Ezra stopped. "Come with me?"

"Yes. Would it be that incredible for a wife to accompany her husband on a missionary trip? I've read it in the *World Missions* literature—often men and women, husbands and wives, they go on missions together... a team."

"A team?" Ezra said, resting back on his heels. "I hadn't thought of such a thing. Why don't we talk about it when we have more time," he said, leaning toward the open loft door. "Evie, it won't be long until somebody realizes we're the only two missing."

Her hands pressed to his slender chest. "But we will, talk more about it?"

"After..." he said, "we can talk about whatever you like." Evie nodded as Ezra's whole body urged hers into the hay, his hand wrestling again with the skirt. "Just easier to push it up, I suppose." He gathered the fabric that kept most of Evie hidden from view.

As Ezra's hand skimmed her thigh, Evie told herself to breathe. The first time she'd been terribly nervous. She believed Ezra had done his best, making certain it wasn't awful. And she appreciated his effort, especially after overhearing so many of the women insist sex was a necessary act, like plucking game. Evie waited, anticipating Hannah's version, the one that included a luxurious rush of dreamy emotions.

All she felt was Ezra's clammy hand burrow beneath the slip, bumping over her stomach.

"Ezra," she said, losing focus, though she followed protocol, lifting her bottom so he could shimmy off white cotton underwear. "Promise me you'll talk to your father this week. I'd like to know that I'm to be more Ezra Kane's wife than Reverend Kane's daughter."

"Evie," he said, his tone a tad harsher. "I prefer not to think of him at all while we're..." Ezra glanced at her naked lower half.

"But..."

Ezra's finger pressed firmly to her lips. "I said not right now."

She complied, reaching around to unhook the bra as if undressing in her bedroom. Last time she'd left that to him, it had taken all his concentration and minutes they didn't have today. Now she'd give him what he wanted in hopes of getting an answer.

For a moment it seemed to work. "Yes, I'll speak to him," Ezra said. "I prom—" But his promise ended abruptly as the brassiere followed the lure of gravity. A tremulous wave of air pulled into Ezra as his gaze traveled down her. It made Evie overly aware that this wasn't her bedroom. The cutting Sunday light, surely that was the reason Evie's hands flew protectively over her breasts.

Ezra continued to stare as if he might say something. Although what, exactly, didn't seem to be crossing his mind.

"Sorry," she said, dropping her arms. This was hardly the action of a dutiful wife.

"Don't... don't be sorry," he said. "Modesty is a right thing. But, you're just..." Another swallow bobbed through his throat. Evie felt her face go hotter than it had inside the church. On her slim frame, Evie was aware that she was fuller up top than every girl she knew. And the way Ezra was looking, it didn't make her feel proud of the fact. She glanced left, seeing her underwear cast aside, having landed on a pitchfork. Ezra's focus remained solely on her. He was quiet, poised over her then tall on his knees. His stare didn't move from her naked torso as he hurriedly unzipped his pants. Evie's eyes widened as the male part of him sprang forward—its shape surprising her again. She thought it funny looking and somewhat menacing at the same time—painful, or so she'd discovered. She also knew, having babysat the Yeager boys—a family who'd joined the sect more recently—that boys born elsewhere were built differently from Ezra and her younger brothers. Evie sighed, realizing none of what was on her mind seemed evocative of the sentiments Hannah prattled on about.

With the fat gather of the skirt wrenched around her waist, Evie waited for Ezra to move forward. It all seemed a bit better when Ezra was close. Her nervous heart slowed as his cheek touched hers. She did love the familiarity of Ezra. Evie closed her eyes and tried to think of that, burying her awkwardness into his shoulder.

His words mirrored her thoughts. "It'll be better this time, Evie." But as his hand slid to her breast, she stiffened. "It'd probably help if you moved your legs a little."

Evie tried to make herself comfortable with the moment and changing boundaries of their relationship. Tag, leap frog, decorating sugar cookies, blind man's bluff, skipping stones on the pond—these were the things she enjoyed with Ezra. Why wasn't this falling into suit? But there was no more time to think as his breathing grew heavier, his body pushing into hers. None of it seemed to fit. Evie's eyes squeezed tight and she bit down on her lip. The worst part was over. Her eyes opened, purposefully focusing on the sweet color of Ezra's hair and what a good person he was. She did like that about him.

Out of nowhere, Evie's heart jumped in the way she'd been anticipating—then she realized the thought attached to it had little to do with passion. "Ezra, what about... Well, you said it couldn't happen the first time... But what if, you know..."

He inched away, his face studying hers. "August... September... October. I shouldn't think you'd be showing by the time we get married. No one will say anything—they never do. Do you really think Abigail Strand's son arrived at ten pounds six months after her wedding day?"

"Well, I..." Evie mentally checked his math. She adored children. She would love Ezra's child, certainly. She calmed, picturing a brood of blonde children—girls surely—all with his lagoon-colored eyes and cheerful disposition. With that pretty thought in mind, Evie bit down harder on her lip—so much so that she tasted a droplet of blood. But it kept her from crying out as his maleness pushed harder into her.

"God, I love you, Evie Neal..." There was a pause, similar to last time, followed by a thunderous shudder from Ezra.

Twice now Evie wondered what that fuss was all about, Ezra's body collapsing on top of her. Between the heat, him, and the hay, she fought a smothering sensation. Moments later a more familiar Ezra returned to her. He kissed her nose and reached right, the sugar flower in his hand. "It's going to be a wonderful life, Evie Neal. You'll see."

CHAPTER THREE

September 1977
Philadelphia, Pennsylvania

It was the first morning Sebastian had dared to let light into the bedroom. He dragged his near naked ass out of bed and to the window shade. Andor had warned him to stay away from the windows, but he needed to see something that said the world was still moving. Three snowy TV channels weren't cutting it. He held gingerly to his side and hobbled to the dresser mirror, a nasty bruise on his hip slowing his pace. *Christ... what a mess...* For the first time in his life, green irises weren't his most startling feature. One eye remained swollen shut, the other so bloodshot it looked more like a cherry than an eye. The skin around it was an angry mix of purples and yellows. He wanted to shave. He looked like a beaten bear. Maybe he could. He'd just have to navigate around the stitched-up cut on his cheek.

He shrugged one shoulder—the arm of the other perched in a sling. Searing pain surged through like a hot poker. The shoulder had been dislocated weeks ago, and he'd hoped the arm could come out of the sling today. He'd see what *the doc* had to say. He turned away from his beaten image. He'd always anticipated dying young—maybe it was why he could never envision a future worth living. This beating had come damn close to proving the theory.

During the past year, he'd taken on more responsibility. Andor's health had begun to fail, and it demanded Sebastian either step into a role with the Godfathers of the Night or run from it. He was a lot of things—none of them particularly good, but he wasn't a coward. He'd do what his father—and the Godfathers—expected.

More and more frequently, Sebastian had accompanied the freighter's cargo to Greece's Port of Piraeus. Andor was right about the cocaine. The Athens faction wanted to do business—big business. But on the last shipment, he'd been caught with bogus goods. The Godfathers had done a spot check in a warehouse off the dock. The product Sebastian had delivered was worth an eighth of what the Godfathers of the Night were paying. They'd suspected Andor's son of a double cross, selling the coke elsewhere—maybe the ports in Turkey or Italy—for a higher profit. The accusations, demands, and Sebastian's denials had led to a monstrous beating. As each question came, a tire chain alternated with brass-knuckled fists. *"How could this have happened?" "How is it possible when only you oversee our coke?"*

Eventually, Godfather underlings had carried his beaten body to the dock. In a hazy half-conscious state, he'd been certain his life would end there—the men holding Sebastian's own gun to his head and dumping his body into the sea of his ancestors.

To his surprise, he'd woken up a day later on the homebound freighter. Vinny stood over his broken body. Through slits of eyes he'd traded wary stares with his shipmate. "If..." he'd said. Vinny leaned in closer, as if memorizing a dying man's words. "If I die, you make sure to dump me on the old man's doorstep."

Vinny had smiled cagily. They'd both known medical help was an ocean away. Their sad humor vanished as Vinny delivered an even more cryptic message in return. "The men who brought you, they said if it wasn't your swindle, you'd better come up with the name that goes with the bad goods."

Sebastian had heard the ultimatum. He was more on the inside of the organization than he ever wanted to be. Clearly, the Godfathers would decide how long he'd be a breathing, card-carrying member.

"I thought we were importing coffee," Vinny had said.

Sebastian hadn't replied but mercifully passed out again. In the meantime, while overseeing his usual tasks and caring for Sebastian, Vinny also saw to the nearly one hundred stowaways Sebastian had ferried to the belly of the ship.

After docking, Andor and a few of his cohorts had taken Sebastian from Pier 53 to his bedroom. "You lived this long. You don't need a hospital," his father had said. Anticipating as much, Sebastian asked Vinny to seek out his own medical resources and to call Bim.

Standing in the middle of his bedroom now—because moving was a bitch—Sebastian watched the door pop open. Andor never knocked. With him was Bim. A fourth-year medical student wasn't a hospital, but it'd been good care. After Bim had assured Andor he'd ask no questions, he'd been allowed to treat Sebastian. His friend had tended to Sebastian's cuts and bruises, some infected, and taped the ribs that Bim had so desperately wanted to X-ray. On a third, scream-filled attempt, he'd popped Sebastian's shoulder back into place.

"Why are you out of bed?" Bim said, rushing to Sebastian's side.

"Got to take a piss once in a while." But Sebastian allowed Bim to help him back to the rumple of sheets.

"Hasn't stopped him from eating," Andor said from the doorway. "How much more time until he's on his feet for good?"

Sebastian had lost track of dates, but he assumed the freighter was ready to leave port again. Andor would expect him to be on it.

Gently pressing on Sebastian's taped ribs, Bim barely glanced at Andor. "It will be at least a month until he can safely return to work."

"That's not what I asked," Andor grumbled, a cigar in hand.

Sebastian pushed his puffy eyes wide as the slight man rose from his bedside and crossed the room. "I am here to see your son. It is bad enough that I have to treat him here—a setting no better than my ravaged village in the Sudan. The room is dark, the bed covers filthy. I will not have you fill the air with vile smoke."

Andor left, closing the door behind him.

Bim returned to Sebastian's side and there was a slight tremor to his hands as he reached into his medical bag. "We will cut down the tape today. If you can stand the pain, my assumption is the fractures were small. I guess this will be welcome news for your father."

Sebastian eased back onto the pillow. "I guess you're gonna make a hell of a doctor."

"Yes, well, my preference is psychiatry. I'm interested in the body but fascinated by the brain." The medical work went on in silence, Bim going through a series of checkpoints that improved with each visit. He advised that the arm remain in a sling for another week.

"If, um... if I haven't said so, thank you. I'm not sure what you're saving here, but thank you."

Bim gathered his supplies and stood—his small face grim. "You joke, my friend. It's me that owes you a great debt."

"Your sister... your family, they're doing good?"

Teeth the color of snow shone against Bim's dark skin. Sebastian couldn't recall having a man of another nationality in the neighborhood, let alone the house. "My sister... yes. And my parents. And the brother of my father and his wife, their daughters... And all the others. I don't know how you managed—"

Sebastian didn't answer, holding onto his side. "So I take it the village is safe?"

"The village has been relocated to the United States, the loss of life none. We are all so grateful, Sebastian, I can never repay..."

"Don't sweat it. The ship was sailing in that direction either way."

"Yes, but on no other vessel would the fare be free and safe, transport out of the Sudan possible for so many. But the other part... the part that is not free. I know the money and arrangements it took to get Nafy from the Sudan to the port. I cannot fathom the price for extracting an entire village. Where did this money come from? I must repay—"

Sebastian held up a hand. "It was a bad situation. I had a way out. That's all you need to know."

Bim stared skeptically.

"Sometimes," Sebastian said, elaborating slightly, "there's satisfaction in turning ill-gotten gains into good."

"*Ill-gotten...?*" Bim said.

"Dirty money into... Never mind. Anyway... you're the one who stowed the extra consumables. I just led them to the belly of a ship and gave them a bucket."

"You gave them a life. You got them out of the Sudan. The means for that had to come from somewhere."

Sebastian looked away.

"If your present condition is the result of that, then I owe twice the debt."

"I said don't worry about it." Sebastian had summoned a tone that said to stop asking questions.

Bim went back to his work. "I hope you understand what you did... what you prevented. What your life is worth." Bim glanced around the shabby surroundings. "I only wish you'd give yourself the same chance you gave my family."

Sebastian coughed and reached to the nightstand. The glass was empty.

"Let me fill that for you."

"Andor will do it," he said, hanging onto the glass. They traded doubtful stares. "I can do it. I was on my way to the john when you came in, remember?"

Bim nodded and added a few medical instructions. Short walks outside would be good for Sebastian. It would keep pneumonia out of his lungs. The first time Bim had seen his patient, he'd gasped loudly asking Andor what he knew about his son's injuries. When there was no reply, he'd gripped Sebastian's hand—one of a few uninjured parts. His caregiver had whispered, "My God, my friend, how did this happen?"

Sebastian had seen no benefit in making the burden Bim's.

As Bim—an immigrant from a destitute, brutal country—left he seemed to take civilization with him.

Andor was back in the doorway. "Verdict?" he said.

"He thinks the ribs were cracked, not broken."

"If they are as thick as your skull, this would be likely." Instead of a cigar, he sipped clear liquid—Tsipouro, a homeland drink that always made the voyage. At the pier, Andor had collected a new batch along with his son. "And how long until you are on your feet—this is what I need to know from... *your friend.*"

Sebastian figured his bedridden state was holding up supply and demand. Andor couldn't make the trips, and he trusted no one but Sebastian with the movement of product. He tried to boost himself up, but pain thwarted the effort. "I can't haul crates, but I can be back to overseeing cargo in a few days. Bim wants me to start walking outside. If I can do that—"

Andor pounded into the room. Sebastian withdrew into the sour sheets. But it was the open shade that had his father's attention. He pulled it down. "I told you not to raise it."

"The light's not bothering me like it was. I feel like a mole in here, Pater."

"Better a live mole than a dead son."

"What does that mean?"

"Sebastian..." He glanced up. His father rarely called him anything but Bash. Then he did something even more curious and sat on the edge of his son's bed. "It's not your return to the dock that concerns me. It's your life. You need to leave here. It's been weeks since you came back. I've been in constant contact with your Uncle Paulos. We don't have a name. We don't know how or where the supply went bad. I do know it was grade-A product when I picked it up in Philadelphia. My source would not tamper with it. Paulos and I tested it." Andor banged the heel of his hand to his head, truly confounded. "I don't know if another crew member learned the safe's combination or if it's a scam by our own Godfathers in Greece... It could be either."

"It wasn't the crew," Sebastian insisted. He glanced sheepishly at Andor, thinking his father's second stab at an explanation sounded plausible. "But a double cross on the other end... maybe that was it. Maybe they only said it was a bogus shipment."

"Why would they do that? Besides, without proof... and without returning the $100,000 they spent on product they say was no more than baby powder...Well, the Godfathers will take the inch of life you have left."

As the words sunk in, Sebastian went numb, wanting to become part of the bed—something inanimate. Something that couldn't feel.

"You are young, Bash. I kept you for as long I could at the low end of the business—a simple courier shouldn't end up with a price on his head. But the Godfathers of the Night, it takes them years to gain trust. They do not have that trust in you."

"And beating me... dumping me off at the dock wasn't the end?"

"No. It was a warning. A warning they will make good on."

Sebastian pushed past the lump in his throat. "What, exactly, are you saying, Pater?"

"I'm saying you can't walk on the sidewalk in our neighborhood. You can't ever go back to the dock or sail to Greece. I'm saying if you don't leave here soon, they're going to kill you."

Damning the pain, he pulled himself up and met his father's eye. The inch of height seemed to have evened. "And where am I supposed to go, Pater? Do I just disappear into the streets of New York or LA? Would I be safe there?"

"I doubt it very much. The Godfathers of the Night, they're strong in New York. They have firm connections on the West Coast. You'd still be a dead man."

A shudder rippled past Sebastian's cracked ribs. "What then? Do I spend my life running?" He shook his head. "Seedy, low-life way of earning a living—drugs, mafia, dirty money. I hate that I was born into it." And for the first time, Sebastian wanted out of that life. Damn, he wanted his own.

"*Gios*..." Andor said. "You are right."

Sebastian stared, fairly certain he'd never heard those words come out of his father's mouth.

"I am a ruffian with unsavory ties. But when I came to America, it was with a debt. I did what was needed to repay it. I never moved past it. I was busy feeding you and your mother. I should have been wiser—"

Sebastian listened harder.

"I should have taught you something more than a questionable trade and taking pride in fucking women. But..."

Sebastian watched as a contemplative breath pulled in and out of his father.

"If you think I wish to watch my *gios* die..." A quiver settled over Andor's square chin. He didn't finish the sentence, which only told Sebastian how grave the situation was. "Right now, the Godfathers are searching for you in Atlantic City. Paulos led them on this trail. Your uncle has done a great deal to keep you safe, and not without risk. But it won't last. That's why I need to know your ability to move about, to travel."

"That's comforting," Sebastian said. "Where do you suggest I go?"

"I have a business acquaintance. He owes me a substantial favor—"

"No," Sebastian said, making the strongest motion he could with his free arm. "No more Godfathers... No more contraband."

"This is different. You'll be safe there for as long as is necessary. This man... his people, they won't cross me. Just do as they say and don't make trouble. But you need to leave—tonight if possible."

"Where are you shipping me off to, Pater?"

"Not far. The Godfathers of the Night, their net is large. Sometimes the best hiding place is in plain sight... odd but plain sight. If you think you can manage, you can leave for Good Hope right away."

CHAPTER FOUR

Sebastian felt like contraband being shuttled from a large sedan to the back seat of a station wagon. The sedan had smelled of cigarettes and cheap ouzo, the station wagon a sweeter scent—like a bakery. But smells were nothing compared to the striking difference in language. As Andor's colleagues drove, the car had filled with familiar Greek accents and the crude talk that went with the place Sebastian called home. It all changed without ceremony as Sebastian and his duffel bag were handed off to the two men in the station wagon.

The sun crept up and he was plunged into more light than he'd seen in weeks. The men in front spoke in whispers and plain language. No cursing. When he croaked a question, the man in the passenger seat—clean-shaven, older than him—looked at Sebastian like he was livestock, like the idea that he'd speak was crazy. Without answering, the passenger faced forward. Waves of nausea kept Sebastian from asking anything else. Along the way, he thought he saw a wooden cross dangling from the rearview mirror. It was as out of place as the men and their sanitized conversation.

For miles he drifted in and out of sleep until the highway shifted to the bump of an unpaved road. Opening his eyes, he saw chips of blue sky and endless evergreens. Rural... isolated. He wondered if Andor had double-crossed his son, offering him to the Godfathers to save his own hide. Was it possible? Hit men could easily lead a weak prisoner to a remote patch of earth. His body left for coyotes and turkey buzzards. Finally, the station wagon rumbled to a halt. The men got out, one saying to the other, "We may need another hand, Brother. He'll be dead weight."

On that hint, Sebastian forced himself alert. He managed to sit up and blinked at swirling dust. He needed a plan. Outside the car was a scattering of buildings. It reminded him of an Old West town his mother had taken him to when he was five or six. Trying to gain his bearings, Sebastian took a fast inventory. No, this was more modern. Telephone wires and simple small structures—a church, houses, and a barn, maybe two. It all seemed... *connected.* But the buildings petered out and beyond them were fields and thick woods. Sebastian wasn't sure about his rural survival skills, but that was where he needed to go—into the woods. The car door opened.

"Need a hand, Brother?" A man leaned in, the one who'd sat in the passenger seat.

With his arm in a sling and his ribs still tender, Sebastian realized it was the only way of hoisting himself out of the car. He swung his long legs around, struggling with bright light. The man gripped Sebastian's hand and his heart hammered as he stood.

"Nolan Creek," he said. Sebastian got a good look at his face. It was as expressionless as any executioner.

He didn't draw any more conclusions but heaved a hard left hook that connected with Nolan Creek's jaw. It was enough to knock him to the dirt. Slowed by a hobbling run, Sebastian headed toward the trees. Since his mother had died, it'd been up to Sebastian to keep himself alive. Why should today be different? But the shouts of men weren't far behind. He was amazed he didn't hear gunfire. Seconds later footsteps eclipsed his. A man toppled him. Sebastian sensed that his captor's stature was no bigger than Bim. But Sebastian's weakened state couldn't compete. It was all he could do to contain the searing pain.

"Where are you going, Brother? I doubt you'd last the night in these woods." The man was straddled on top of him. Sebastian had twisted as he'd fallen and he stared up into a face. "Are you crazed in the mind in addition to your injuries? I wasn't told of anything like that."

Sebastian blinked hard into blue sky and blue eyes of the same color. "Who... who are you? Where am I?"

"Ah, I see my Fathers of the Right Brothers held their tongues as instructed."

"Fathers of the..."

"Fathers of the Right," he said again. It took a moment for Sebastian to separate the words from *Godfathers of the Night*. Or maybe they were an extremist offshoot—anything was possible. But as he heaved pain-filled breaths, gazing at his captor, Sebastian did not see the eyes of a killer. In fact, he wasn't sure it was a man—or at least a full grown one. Grinning, the blue-eyed boy extended a hand. He remained straddled over Sebastian as if having been acclaimed the victor in a wrestling match. "Ezra Kane," he said. "I'm pleased to meet you."

—•••—

For days Sebastian saw only men—strange men dressed in similar dull clothing, shirt collars buttoned to the throat, and not a whisker of facial hair. He'd been led from the main arc of buildings and down a long path, hauled into a ramshackle cabin. Compared to the outside, the inside was sterling clean, smelling of strong soap. From his bedridden position, Sebastian could see one large room and a bathroom. Furnishings were sparse. The carvings of a dove and an oddly layered star stood out, sitting like trophies on a mantel. The stone fireplace was set to the middle of the space, its flame visible from either the bed or living area. It was the cabin's only source of heat, and it allowed Sebastian to be watched without the men coming too close. When it became marginally clear that they weren't going to kill him—feeding him delicious soups and crusty bread that arrived warm—Sebastian let his guard ease.

The men, on the other hand, remained wary. The one who'd sat in the passenger seat of the station wagon and said his name was Nolan Creek did most of the caregiving, or maybe it was guarding. Other than his name, the *brother* hadn't offered much else. He did notice the man's intense, almost ogling stare when Sebastian limped from the bed to the john. Less frequently, the young man, Ezra, came to the cabin. He wasn't forthcoming with information either, but on his third visit he did ask Sebastian if he was feeling better.

"Some," he said. The man-boy had smiled and sat down to read. The day before Sebastian had discarded the sling. It was curious. For as much as *the brothers* saw to his food and shelter, no one paid attention to his injuries. He was still sore to the touch, but for the first time since being carted off the freighter, Sebastian felt like he might recover.

This morning when Ezra asked again how he was feeling, he finally replied with more than a nod.

"Good to hear," Ezra said. "Shall I fill the tub?"

"Tub?"

"I don't mean to be rude, but it's been mentioned that you can be smelled from the door."

Sebastian glanced down at the yellowed T-shirt he'd worn since arriving and took a quick sniff of his armpit. The leather duffel bag sat nearby, untouched. He'd almost forgotten it. Sebastian inched back from his odor and ran his hand through greasy waves of hair. Yeah, he could see where showering was a reasonable idea. Ezra moved to the bathroom and Sebastian heard water running. *A bath...?* Come to think of it, when he'd been in the john he did notice the giant cast iron tub had no shower. Without much difficulty, he swung his legs around to the side of the bed and peered toward the bathroom. Ezra's backside was to him, and he was on his knees filling the tub. He continued in a man-servant way, folding a towel and placing it on the back of the toilet. The activities went on, Ezra retrieving a mirror from inside the cabinet, propping it on the sink. Shaving items followed. *Who are these bizarre people, and how the hell do they know Andor Christos?*

Sebastian made his way to the bathroom door. "I'm wondering, *Brother*," Sebastian said, using the word all the men seemed to respond to, "are you a colony of monks?"

Ezra stood. He was so very different from Sebastian in height and build, with a complexion that rivaled snow. The man-boy almost seemed to sparkle, reminding Sebastian of a storybook character, the kind who might kiss a sleeping princess.

"Monks?" Ezra laughed. "Is that what you think of us?"

It was a notable speck of humor. "Just a guess," Sebastian said. The few times two men had kept vigil, Sebastian listened from his bed. There was no inflection in their formal speech with conversations nearly as dull. It'd been better than a sleeping pill. The only burst of information had been about a late-season calf being born. Sebastian had rolled his eyes and rolled over. Aside from this, the men spent time reading aloud, all of it having to do with religion and the righteousness of modest, uniform behavior. Sebastian was aware that from every angle, he did not belong in this place.

Ezra turned, swishing his hand through the water. "Won't scald you, but it'll clean you. The Widow Vale adds lavender to the lye soap. Sorry to say it won't catch her a husband either, but it smells better than you or the lye."

"The Widow Vale?"

"Yes. Well, how else would you refer to an unmarried woman of such an age?"

And under his breath Sebastian mumbled, "In this place? Damn lucky, I'd think... Uh, just sounded odd, that's all."

Ezra stood, hands on his waist. "She fancies herself as the future

Mrs. Creek. But I don't see that happening. Brother Creek has passed on the suggestion again and again. Though I'm not sure why."

The way Brother Creek had gazed as Sebastian walked past in his underwear to the bathroom and back—well, he had an idea. Once, in the Port of Piraeus, a drunken sailor had offered Sebastian a blowjob—or the other way around if he preferred. He'd declined, moving to the other side of the bar. It seemed the concept of homosexuality was completely lost on young Ezra, who stood before him, mild mannered, an almost effeminate body. *On the other hand...* "Uh, you weren't planning on watching, were you?"

Ezra widened already large eyes. "Watch another man bathe? I should hardly think..." His fair face reddened. "Why? Do they do such things where you're from?"

"Where I'm from?" Sebastian said, thumbing his chest. "Uh, no, not usually. Not me, anyway."

"Good to know," Ezra said, making a circle, wide as possible, around Sebastian as he exited the space.

Sebastian moved into the bathroom and gingerly removed his T-shirt. Ezra remained near the doorway. Maybe it was the talk of *men only*, but Sebastian felt overly conscious of their dissimilar frames—his lumbering and dark, Ezra's meek and understated. It forced his next thought out of his mouth. "So the Widow Vale, is she like the only woman on your planet?"

"On our..." The sarcasm slowly connected. "Of course there are other women. Who do you think made the soups and bread and other meals? But it wouldn't be proper to send one inside. Not with you being a strange man in a bed—even if you are a broken one."

"I see. I guess."

"I understand your questions. I suppose I'd have the same myself, but my father—Reverend Kane—he feels it best we keep our distance until he's had a chance to speak with you. He'll tell you all you need to know."

"Reverend Kane?"

"Yes," he said, bending to swish the water. "Duncan Kane. He's our sect leader."

"Your... And when might that happen?"

"Soon, I would think." Ezra started to shut the door but hesitated. "We're good people," he said as if suddenly aware of their peculiarities. "As for women, we have our share. In fact, I'll be marrying one of the finest soon."

"Marrying? How old are you—twenty?"

"Twenty-one last week. If I'd made it to twenty-two it might be thought Nolan Creek and I have a lot in common."

Sebastian's jaw hung for a second. "A confirmed bachelor, right?"

"What else would there be? Anyway, I'm one of the lucky ones— not only am I marrying the girl, but I love her dearly."

"Would you marry her otherwise?" Sebastian asked, reminded of Bim and Vinny's reasons for marriage.

"Hmm, it is an anointed union. But fortunately, I needn't consider that, and neither does she. Besides, a man should have a wife, and a wife a man."

Sebastian couldn't get his mind around the thought, language that sounded more like 1777. And for a moment, he wondered if he'd fallen through a time warp.

Ezra pulled the door shut. But he didn't leave the cabin, Sebastian could hear him stoke the fire and then begin reading aloud. He looked around the scant space and full tub. With Ezra reading religious materials, he guessed the bath would feel more like a baptism. Sebastian stripped off his underwear and climbed into the tub. The bruises had faded to pale yellows. He could see his ribs, guessing he'd lost a solid twenty pounds. Sebastian dunked his head in the just warm enough water.

It felt good and he soaped himself from one end to the other, the lavender masking the pungent scent of lye. He closed his eyes and tipped his neck into the curve of the tub. Squeezing out a washcloth, he flopped it over his whiskery face. The bath water was the most soothing thing to have touched him in ages. His hand slid downward as his mind moved to the last woman he'd taken to bed. He had trouble picturing her face—her name was a total loss. The sex had been decent enough. It was almost a forgotten body part, certainly neglected, as his hand wrapped around a half-hard dick. Sebastian wanted to escape, if only for a few minutes.

He had himself hard in seconds and was slightly relieved to know that things were still in working order. He'd taken several knees to the groin as the Godfathers of the Night beat him. Slipping toward a familiar place, he worked an erection that now demanded satisfaction. His mind gave up on the last time he'd really touched a woman. They were all too inconsequential. There were certainly no evocative memories attached to anyone. Instead he pictured girly magazines— full breasts and pretty pussies—the common reading material that accompanied the crew on overseas voyages. He couldn't recall the last real, hot set of tits he'd seen—clothed or otherwise—maybe in one of the bars near Piraeus. Grinding against his hand, Sebastian found himself at a precipice—a moment away from a no-strings explosion of pent up frustration, stress, and boredom. His soapy hand was committed to the task, Sebastian holding his breath. He only wanted to hang on a second longer when a knock interrupted.

"Brother Sebastian."

Like a spike through a tire, the sound of Ezra's voice deflated his hard-on. "Christ..." he muttered.

"Pardon?"

"What?"

"If you're all right in there I'm going to get more firewood."

"Yeah. Fine. Whatever." Sebastian supposed that for now he and *the brothers* knew he wouldn't bolt. That or it was another indication of Ezra Kane's naiveté. Hearing the cabin door close, Sebastian sunk down, unfulfilled, into the now cool water.

CHAPTER FIVE

Evie was on the path to the cabin. She'd trudged more than halfway, struggling along with an oversized, over-filled picnic basket.

"Now here's a treat," Ezra said, coming toward her. "I didn't think you'd be to the cabin so early."

"I told your mother I'd help her can green beans this afternoon, so I had to make an early lunch delivery."

He took the weighty basket from her. "I thought you were working on the Christmas quilt today."

"Why do you think I offered to can the green beans?" Evie turned up the palm of her free hand, showing Ezra pin-pricked fingertips.

He laughed and nodded. "Good point. I suspect I should learn to sew if I'm ever to have anything mended."

"Or we could buy new clothing at the mall," Evie said. The spark in Ezra's eyes met with hers and he was silent. They'd argued the week before when Evie stopped outside a bridal shop on the main street of North Good Hope. She'd boldly remarked to Ezra how much she admired the fancy store-bought wedding gowns, even suggesting they go inside.

"Evie—"

"I'm sorry." She didn't want to quarrel with Ezra. "I don't know why I said that, or why I got so angry about the wedding dress last week. Sometimes I believe your father's right—maybe the outside world is more temptation than I could manage."

"There's a first, Evie Neal, openly agreeing with Reverend Kane."

"And yet," she said, "ideas about other places continue to turn up in my dreams."

He quickly tucked loose strands of hair, defiant and determined to escape, behind her ear. "Think of it this way, if you were to take such trips—mission trips, of course—there wouldn't be much temptation in South American shopping. There aren't any Rodeo Drives in that part of the world."

"Rodeo…?"

"It's a famous, fancy shopping place in California." He nodded hard. "I know a few things, Evie Neal." Ezra looked her up and down. "It's what makes us such a good match—you being so full of questions. I might have the answers." She didn't respond. "What? Go on. Say it—whatever's on your mind."

She shrugged, focused on the dirt surrounding their shoes. "Sometimes I think I'd like to answer my own questions."

"Within Good Hope, you'll have plenty of chance to do that. Anyway… there's no one in the cabin right now, so you'll have to bring your basket back later. I'd take it myself," he said, handing it back to her, "but I'm on my way to get a wheelbarrow of firewood."

From where they stood on the path, Evie glanced at the distance she'd already walked. "What if I leave it near the door? You can take it in yourself."

He nodded. "There you go. A better answer than mine. That'll be fine."

But Evie furrowed her brow. It was her answer, yet it required his permission.

"*The mission* is bathing—praying, from what I heard," Ezra said. "I thought he'd benefit from time alone with his sorry soul and some cleansing water."

Evie tipped up her chin, peering toward the cabin. "Ezra, what… what's he like?"

"The Reverend's *mission?*"

She nodded, her wandering mind having wondered about a man that sect members only referred to as *the mission.*

He shifted his slim shoulders. "More healed than when he arrived, so I suspect God wants him that way. I don't know beyond that. My father says we're not to question him, and I haven't."

"Of course you haven't," she said softly.

"What?"

"Nothing." She fiddled with the lid on the basket. "I just don't understand your lack of curiosity—that's all. I don't know how any of you can sit with him day after day and not want to know—"

"Evie," he said, cutting her off. "I believe my father has a point about you."

"What point is that?" she said, making firm eye contact.

"I'd have an easier time breaking a wild mustang than breaking Evie Neal."

"Is that what he says?" Evie glanced away, unsure if she liked being compared to a horse.

"Evie... look at me."

She refused to obey.

"I'm sorry. I shouldn't have said that—and I certainly don't agree. Thank you for bringing the food." She didn't reply or look at him, and Ezra changed the subject by tipping open the basket's lid. "Hmm, no matter who *the mission* is, if you keep feeding him like this we'll have to roll him out of here." He lifted a tea towel. "Did you bake him an angel food cake? I'm not sure I like that idea."

Ezra loved her angel food cake. "I made the cake for you."

He looked toward the main thoroughfare of their community. Brushing his fingertips across her cheek, Ezra cupped her chin. The small but intimate gesture was enough to tell Evie that the street behind them was deserted. It also forced her gaze onto his. "Maybe the canning will go quicker than expected. You can tell my mother you've gone to help with the Christmas quilt."

"But I hate to quilt."

"I know," he said, letting go of her chin. "That's why you'll meet me in the barn."

She did love Ezra's adventurous moments. Yet Evie didn't jump at the chance. "I, um... I can't. I have a lot to do today."

He opened his mouth, hesitating, as if choosing his words. "All right, Evie. As you like." But Ezra's broad grin vanished and a faint glimmer of his father laced through his placid face. "It's not as if you're my wife yet."

Evie set the food on the wooden step of the cabin. Nolan Creek had lived there until the Reverend insisted he build a proper house closer to other sect members. Outsiders rarely visited their community, and the cabin had been empty until *the mission* arrived. Without explanation, Reverend Kane had directed the women to prepare the threadbare wooden structure. Evie and Hannah had scrubbed the interior while the men supplied sparse furnishings. When they were done, Evie thought the cabin rather quaint with its stone fireplace and cozy single room, a feather bed tucked into the far left corner. She'd made up the bed herself and hung new curtains on the windows. But someone had left the curtain open today, and she leaned left, peeking inside. Evie suspected the bed sheets hadn't been changed since *the mission* had arrived.

She did know something about him, a little more than she'd let on to Ezra. The day before *the mission* came to Good Hope, Evie was in the meeting hall vestibule. She was minding her business, working on a game for the children to help memorize their lengthy doctrine rules. From inside the Reverend's office, she'd heard him give several brothers instructions. *"We'll not allow his wicked life to*

invade ours. You're to keep this mission sequestered, fed, and sheltered.
God will see to his injuries... or not. If it's the latter, you're not to interfere."
His words had infuriated Evie, a burning reminder of her mother's
death and the Reverend's unyielding commitment to Fathers of the
Right doctrine.

Evie peered inside the window again. "Good for *the mission...*" she
thought. No thanks to the Reverend, if *the mission* was bathing, he
must be improving. And if that was the case, he should have clean
bedding. One would do as much for a litter of puppies. Evie looked
through the open curtain on the right. It offered a view of the living
area and bathroom door, which was shut.

She turned toward the distant cluster of buildings that
comprised Good Hope—the direction Ezra had gone. She'd tell
him there were clean sheets in the cabin closet. He should change
them. Of course, she couldn't picture Ezra changing bed linens.
Besides, he was getting firewood. Surely *the mission* would want to
lie back down before Ezra returned. Evie looked between the cabin
door and the path that led back to the main sect. If women weren't
allowed in and men refused to change bed linens, how would their
cloistered *mission* ever get clean sheets? She looked inside again.
The bathroom door remained closed. Evie reached, barely turning
the rusted metal knob of the cabin door as it opened.

CHAPTER SIX

Once inside, Evie absorbed the result of leaving the brothers to housekeeping. The neat as a pin cabin she and Hannah had prepared was littered with dishes and reading materials, chips of wood from Brother Creek's carvings. Spent ashes from the fire dotted the floor. It was cold, which Evie suspected wasn't good for whatever ailment *the mission* was battling. Evie stoked the fire. In moments she had it burning bright. She peeked through the open firebox—on the opposite side of the hearth were the bed and a woeful tangle of sheets. She'd change them and go before anyone discovered her disobedient choice. In a small closet she located the spare sheets.

In seconds, Evie was engrossed in her task. She stripped the dank sheets, the smell unfamiliar—something like when the brothers came in from the fields in July. Yet it was different. Earthy, foreign—curious. After tucking the last corner and plumping the pillows, she stood back and admired her effort. At least he'd be comfortable. She almost giggled—perhaps *the mission* would think the bed fairy had come by while he'd bathed.

While making the bed, Evie's gaze repeatedly caught on the odd item in the room—a tall leather bag. It seemed forgotten in the corner. The wondering part of Evie got the best of her, and she found herself crouched beside it. She ran her fingertips over the

bag's heavy straps and hard buckles. Evie couldn't see *the mission*.
She knew she couldn't speak to him. So maybe she only wanted to
know what he smelled of, other than stale sheets. Impulsively, she
unbuckled the straps. It looked as if the contents had been packed
in haste, she thought, plucking out a white cotton T-shirt.

She raised the soft fabric to her nose, breathing in something
less pungent than the sheets—a vigorous mix of manly qualities.
Closing her eyes, she sniffed it again. The scent drew Evie in, the
way fireflies fascinated the eyes. Her brain was instantly engaged,
the evocative aromas more intriguing than anything in the air of
Good Hope. She couldn't describe it, vaguely aware of a tingling
sensation the scent of *the mission's* undershirt induced. Captivated by
a simple undergarment, Evie hadn't noticed any sound—not until it
penetrated through her. It was a voice much stronger than the scent.

"Just a guess, but I'm thinking stealing is definitely frowned upon
in this place."

Evie's eyes popped wide and she braced against the wall to
steady herself. *The mission* stood before her wrapped in a white
towel. Her jaw unhinged. Smell and sound became secondary to
sight. She'd never seen anyone like him. Certainly not a man in
such an unclothed state—except, of course, for Ezra. But as Evie
dragged her gaze over him, she was having a hard time fitting Ezra
into his mold. From her crouched position, she saw wet wavy hair
that fell beyond his ears. The color was dark as pitch, darker than
Rachel Pruitt's. His features looked like something a blacksmith
would fashion—iron-like planes and a bold nose soldered together
by the sturdy angles of his cheekbones. His chest was as broad as
Revelations', though less pristine. It evoked visions of a centaur—an
untamed, Greek mythological creature, half man, half horse. Evie
had seen such beings in a library book. She'd hid the bold images
under a book entitled *Lessons on Gratitude*, taken from the shelf
above. At least a half dozen scars marred *the mission's* upper half.

Evie's brain defied the consequences, and her eyes followed the trail of hair that disappeared into the tuck of the towel. She felt her heart beat strangely, loudly, as if it were outside her chest. It alerted other body parts that shouldn't be considered in his presence.

"Geez, tell me you don't speak at all."

"What?" she said from her squatted stance. "I..." But as Evie rose, scraping her back along the rough wallboard, she realized how wildly distracting the whole of him was. Surely the first thing she should have noticed was his eyes—a dizzying color: blue-spruce evergreen, the stained glass in the meeting hall, the center of the passion flowers that grew at the edge of Good Hope's gate. Finally, she absorbed his words. "Of course I can speak."

"To me?" he said.

"I believe there are only two of us here." But it felt like more of a reminder to herself. She managed to unseal her gaze, all too aware of the precarious circumstance. Being there was wrong. Being there with a nearly naked stranger was unthinkable. She grabbed the leather bag. "Are you looking for this?"

"Uh, yeah..." He had the audacity to smile. "The, um... the undershirt too."

Evie had tucked the garment tight to her chest. They seemed at a standoff. The fire crackled from either side of them. Evie boldly shuffled forward. An unfamiliar awareness wove through her like a fresh breath of life. Evie tried to keep it in context—they were just two people in a room. And it wasn't as if a lightning bolt would ram between them—at least she hoped not. *The mission* met her halfway.

His mesmerizing irises lingered, tangling with hers, and a bob swam through his thick throat. Evie felt her cheeks flush and the whirl of heat intensify. As *the mission* claimed his belongings, his knuckles grazed her calloused fingertips. She jerked back her hand. Not because of the contact, but because her fingers were less than soft and perfect. *Only soft and perfect things should touch him...* And that, Evie supposed, was evil whispering directly in her ear. But looking into his eyes, she couldn't imagine evil feeling like this.

⁘

Disturbingly beautiful. It was the first clear thought to roll through Sebastian's head in weeks. He knew this because words like that had never rolled through Sebastian's head—not when faced with the opposite sex. Not when faced by anything. He drew a steadying breath, blaming the crushing imagery on his largely sedentary state and lack of human interaction. But as a few moments passed, the impression didn't subside.

It wasn't necessarily a pleasant feeling—more off balance—achy as his persistent pains. Surprised to find a woman there, Sebastian was more taken aback by her singular presence—a loud mix of innocence and a force to be reckoned with. He tried to brush it off. Maybe it was the fact that she'd so obviously broken the rules. Sebastian took the duffel bag from her and held it in front of the towel. She'd also managed to cause a full-on hard-on. Not even her conservative clothing could stop him from absorbing a figure to which he was instantly drawn. Sebastian shuffled backward. "I should get dressed."

"Dressed, yes..." she said, eyes saucer wide.

She was average height—which still looked small to him—and she wore no makeup. Long, thick hair was trapped in a braid, the braid falling over her shoulder with fringy loose edges framing her face. Her wide eyes were a soft shade of brown, a striking contrast to her blonde hair. He guessed the unkempt state reflected her day, though to him it came across as a tussle of sexiness. Sebastian had never seen a woman offer so much with so little effort. And this made him retreat another step. It was as unlikely as it was absurd. *Okay, take this as a reminder of how long it's been since you've seen a woman, never mind taken one to bed...* "I'll, um..." He motioned toward the bathroom.

"No. I'll go," she said. "I shouldn't be here."

Aside from Ezra's man-boy chatter, it was the liveliest conversation he'd had since arriving. Sebastian viewed himself as a solitary creature, but even a semi-friendly face felt good. Or maybe it felt good coming from her. "Do you have to?"

She glanced cagily toward the paned window. "I... I suppose I could stay a few minutes."

Inside the bathroom, Sebastian shuffled into his pants, pulling the sleeveless undershirt over his head while damning the ache in his shoulder. It was the quickest he'd moved since the Godfathers of the Night came at him with fists curled. Returning to the room, he found her focused on chores. Sebastian watched, deciding immediately that while perhaps necessary, he didn't like seeing her reduced to the role of maid.

"Stop."

The shuffle of a broom halted, and she gripped her small fingers hard around the pole, like maybe she'd use it as weapon if need be. On the other hand, he suspected she could hold her own and that pissing her off would not be to his advantage. "What... what's your name?"

He wanted to know. He needed to know.

"Evie," she said, though it was barely audible. She hesitated. Clearly it was not her place to ask. "And yours?" she said to his surprise.

"Sebastian... Christos."

"That's unusual."

"First or last?"

"Both."

"It's Greek..."

"I thought it might be," she said, her gaze cutting over him, lingering on his lower half.

"Yeah. My father..." He stopped, realizing he missed the nickname common to Andor and from the men around the docks. "Bash... some people call me Bash."

"Bash," she repeated. She nuzzled closer to the broom. "It suits you."

"Can you... would you mind telling me where I am... who you all are, besides the Fathers of the Right? Nobody will tell me anything."

Evie bit down on her lip, looking nervously around the room. "Well, I..." Her chest heaved.

It was information his guards were unwilling to share. Sebastian guessed input from her could end up in a public flogging—maybe for both of them. An urge bubbled inside him. More than he wanted to know, he wanted to protect her. "Never mind. That's okay. You don't have to say anything."

She inched closer. "Nothing. They haven't told you a thing?"

He shook his head. "Not even if we're still in Pennsylvania."

"You are," she said, her grip on the broom strangling. "You're about sixty miles outside Lancaster. Good Hope."

"Amish?" he said.

"No. Our lineage is Quaker. We have electricity... and a station wagon."

"I saw. I mean, that's how I got here."

"Where did you come from?" From the curious look on her face, it seemed like he should say Mars.

"Outside Philly. It's, uh... it's a long story."

"I... I don't need to know," she said, sweeping again. But she stopped just as fast, taking another step. "I mean I shouldn't ask."

"You're not. I'm offering. I was accused..."

"The police?" she said, reclaiming the step.

"No. I'm not in trouble with the police." Sebastian thought about how the truth would hit her ears. He stuck with basic facts. "The people I worked for. I was accused of stealing... *something*."

Her expression grew wary. "And did you?"

"I..." Sebastian's jaw slacked. "It's complicated. But I... I'm not a bad person." It felt like something he needed her to know.

A moment idled between them. "I'll believe you until you prove me wrong."

"Just like that?" he said, wondering if it was naiveté—which had to account for some of her—or an innate ability to judge right from wrong, maybe the good and evil in this strange place.

"When it comes to people, I trust my own mind." She shrugged her shoulders softly. "It's not something that's encouraged here. Were you ill when they brought you to Good Hope?"

"Ill? No. More like beaten within an inch of my life."

"The people who said you stole from them. They beat you?"

"Yes."

"And you were brought here to recover?"

Sebastian heard doubt. "Not exactly. Why do you ask?"

"Because the Fathers of the Right will keep you fed and sheltered. But this is not the place I'd bring a wounded man. We…" She swallowed hard. "They don't believe in medical intervention."

"That explains a few things."

"Not all of them."

She was smart and cautious, able to deduce that there had to be more to his presence. "My father," Sebastian said. "Somehow he knows these people… Your people."

"I've heard talk of that. The Reverend takes meetings—a group of men from outside Philadelphia. I've always wondered…"

"Wondered what?"

"Well… I shouldn't wonder anything." Evie looked between the door and Sebastian. "I should go. If they find me here…"

"If they find you here, what will happen?" If her presence put her in real danger he'd toss her out himself.

"Defiance isn't tolerated. That's something I know a little about." But she didn't move. "Then and again, I suppose I'm already here… aren't I?"

"And so far neither of us has turned to stone."

She nodded as if actually considering the prospect. "Your father and his people. I've wondered what the Reverend's connection is to them."

"That I don't know."

"So if you weren't brought here to recover from your injuries, and the police aren't after you, then..."

"I'm here because the people who said I stole from them want to kill me."

"Good heavens, what did you steal?" She sucked in a gasp.

Sebastian had clearly confessed something he should have kept to himself.

"I swear there's a good explanation." Evie stayed put, which told Sebastian that she continued to give him the benefit of the doubt. The simple closeness, her body to his, made his gut roll—a wave of crazy energy. Sebastian shoved his hands into his pockets. He didn't want to spook her.

"What... what, um, kind of place do you come from that people would want to kill you?"

The question plunged him into the moment. His world was more extreme than hers. "A place I doubt you'd understand. I... I'm sorry. I shouldn't be asking you for information. But no one's said more than 'Here's your lunch' and 'Take a bath' since I got here."

"And with good reason it seems." Evie bit down on her lip again, which had Sebastian thinking about things other than beatings and mob threats.

Her mouth was a perfect pout, lips full without lipstick, her skin glowing like the sun reached through her. The clothing she wore was beyond drab—a dirt-colored, out-of-fashion skirt and a pale-pink blouse—yet it only enhanced the long, white line of her throat, the buttoned collar clearly guarding what was beneath it. Part of him wanted to keep it that way.

She distracted the rest of him by asking, "The lunches. Did you enjoy them?"

"Huh?" he said, his wandering gaze meeting hers. "Yes. The food was all good but the lunches were the best."

She smiled.

"What?"

"I made all the lunches. Hannah made the breakfasts and the Widow Vale supplied your dinner. Spreading the work out will always lighten a task."

"Is that some kind of bible verse?"

"No," she said. "I believe it's common sense."

She appeared to have a lot of that. She also seemed willing to think for herself, a concept that wasn't too popular in this place. "I don't suppose you could tell me anything more, like if the brothers plan on keeping me here until Armageddon, or..."

"Mmm," she said, looking him over. "If it's Armageddon, I'd think you'd do better to worry more about your soul than the date. But no. I don't know anything. I'm sure Reverend Kane will visit soon. I suspect he's as anxious to see you go as you are to leave."

"Guess I don't fit in too well around here."

"He doesn't like outsiders—unless they've come to buy from the bake shop. But yes, I suppose someone like you would be of particular concern. We're not unfriendly, but the ways of our sect need to be protected. It's the reason the brothers haven't said much to you."

"You're right. They haven't been hostile... just indifferent. Except the one brother, he's been on the friendlier side. Uh, Ezra. Do you know him?"

"Ezra. Of course I know him." Her fingers fidgeted over the broom handle. "I'm going to marry him next month."

"You're— Marry... Ezra... Damn," Sebastian said with a heavy sigh. She skirted back on the curse word, maybe the reminder. Distance turned out to be a good thing as the cabin door swung open and a man ploughed through. His presence cast a shadow over the two of them. He was as tall as Sebastian and looked as stern as Andor dressed in black from head to toe. His hawkish gray gaze swung from Sebastian to Evie.

"Reverend Kane," Evie said, her voice raising an octave.

"What in God's name are you doing in here, girl? Or maybe we should consult the devil!" He forced himself between Sebastian and Evie, grabbing her by the arm.

Instinct drove Sebastian. He locked his hand around Evie's other arm and pulled her toward him. Whether it was surprise or Sebastian's strength, the Reverend let go. "Don't touch her."

"Touch her? She'll be lucky that I don't banish her from this sanctuary." He looked from Evie to Sebastian. "And how dare you speak to me like that. After I agree to take you in, store your sorry, sinful hide among my people." But he seemed more concerned with the girl's transgression, his voice booming. "Explain yourself this instant, Evie Neal."

Sebastian released her arm but remained on guard. No way was the lord and master of these religious crazies going to lay a hand on her.

"I, well... I was only dropping off his lunch," she said, pointing to the picnic basket that sat on the table. "I was going to leave it outside, and then... I, um—"

"Then I called for help," Sebastian said. "I, uh... I'd just gotten dressed. I was dizzy. I thought I was going to pass out. No one was here. I yelled and she heard me. I was just thanking her... Evie, is it?" he said, although Sebastian knew her name was stitched to whatever soul he had.

The white of her knuckles choked the broom. "I... Well, I..."

"Evie?" the Reverend said.

"It's what he said. I was putting the lunch outside for Ezra to bring in. I heard him call out and—"

The Reverend snatched the broom from her and Evie darted back. "And you decided to sweep up once you came inside?"

"I knocked over the broom when I grabbed for the edge of the fireplace," Sebastian said. "That's all. She picked it up. What's your problem? She didn't do anything wrong."

"She's here. That alone is wild disobedience in my parish."

Sebastian narrowed his eyes. He needed to think like these people. "And being a Good Samaritan, that wouldn't allow some leeway on disobedience?"

The look on Evie's face was fair warning that he'd crossed a line. In fact, he'd probably trampled it.

The Reverend didn't answer him, his tone beyond stern. "Go, Evie. We'll discuss penance later. Apparently, the time has come for me to speak to our *mission*. And I should say we'll begin with respect for authority."

She hurried toward the door. But with the Reverend's back to her, Evie turned. For as brief and innocent as it had been, Sebastian felt branded by the encounter. A breath rose and fell from her chest and her expression was full of wonder. But it was the flash of a nervous smile that he reacted to, Sebastian feeling his own heart beat as she disappeared out the door.

CHAPTER SEVEN

INSTEAD OF RETURNING TO ADAH KANE'S KITCHEN, EVIE FOUND HERSELF at the edge of the Wheaton's property. She wanted to be in a neutral place. Those were short supply in Good Hope. Her father's house was a poor choice—Gideon Neal, while nonthreatening, would only agree with whatever Reverend Kane postulated. Hannah was hanging wash in the yard, sunshine and fall breezes soaking into damp sheets. Evie paused near the gate, letting airy elements do the same for her. Perhaps her encounter with *the mission* would blow away on a breeze. It wasn't to be as Hannah peeked around the corner of a billowing wet sheet.

"Evie Neal, you look as if you floated in here on a cloud." She drew her hands to her waist. "It's about time Ezra put such a look on your face."

"Ezra?" Evie said, startled.

"Well, yes. I could make it out from the bedroom window earlier—you and Ezra on the path to the cabin. Surely he's the cause of that dreamy look."

"I..." Guilt clamped Evie's mouth shut.

"Evie?" Hannah said, coming closer. "What's going on? Tell me you've just come from the barn with Ezra. And on Tuesday morning!" She clapped her hands together, laughing. "I swear to you, if I'd half your spirit, I might suggest the same the moment

Tobias asks me to marry him. But you best be careful, the Reverend might read your mind by the look on your face."

Evie rushed toward Hannah and grasped her hands. "I wasn't with Ezra."

"What?"

"Hannah, I..." She pulled her friend along until they were on the far side of the wash line, out of earshot of another human being. "I met *the mission*. I spoke with him."

"But how?" Hannah asked, squeezing her hands tighter to Evie's.

"I went inside the cabin. I know I shouldn't have—that we're forbidden. But I only wanted to put clean sheets on the bed. He wasn't there at first. He was in the bathroom, which is why I thought it would be fine. But then he just appeared—like an angel... I don't know, maybe a devil, and... Oh, Hannah, there's something about him. Something dark and mysterious and fascinating all at once."

"I don't understand. Did he hurt you?" Hannah said, examining her friend from top to bottom. "If he did, Ezra, the Reverend, your father—well, he'll wish he'd never set foot in Good Hope."

"No, it wasn't anything like that. He wouldn't hurt me."

"How can you say such a thing? You just met him. You certainly can't know that about him."

"That's just it. I feel like I do. In fact, he lied for me."

"And that speaks in his favor how?"

"He defended me when the Reverend found us together."

Hannah let go of Evie's hands, cupping her palm over her mouth. She lowered it slowly. "Found you with him... inside the cabin?"

"Yes. We were talking. I know it was foolish, I'd gone in to change the bedding and... Well, that part doesn't matter. *The mission*, he's so different from anyone I've ever met. I couldn't take my eyes off him."

"That ugly, is he?"

"Hardly." Evie shook her head. "I'd say more brutally handsome— like a strong, wild horse. I don't know how to explain it. He's a jumble of things I can't sort out or put a name to. But that feeling you've spoken of so often..."

Hannah's expression grew more concerned.

"Bash. It's short for Sebastian," she said as if revealing his name might change the look on Hannah's face.

"It sounds like a good wild-horse name." Hannah crossed her arms. "And did you learn why the Reverend's brought him here?"

The question stopped Evie cold. The few details she'd learned had sounded unsavory. But an instinct to keep secret what Sebastian Christos had confided was stronger. "No," she lied. "Reverend Kane came in before he had a chance to say."

"Evie, I don't understand. Is this just about having defied the Reverend's rules... our rules? I've known defiance to put a warm buzz in your heart. But I'm not sure insolence explains the look on your face." She inched her gaze up and down Evie. "Or the way you're breathing—like you've run here from the cabin."

"I don't know either. But I do know I want to see him again."

"Are you mad? I'm sure the Reverend, never mind Ezra, would have something to say about that."

Evie pursed her lips, absorbing Hannah's warning—which was realistic. Before entering the cabin, her world had been orderly, defined. It still was. But glancing over her shoulder, she couldn't help but feel as if the world had grown a little larger.

"Evie, you have no business with him. See him for what possible reason?"

Evie's gaze ticked around the confines of the Wheaton's fenced yard. Then it moved on, locking with the sharp blue of the sky and a distant horizon. Evie had no valid answer, only a thrumming in her body that felt as welcoming as it did wild.

When Evie Neal left the cabin, the Reverend and Sebastian remained at a standoff. Sebastian held his tongue and temper as the Reverend paced around him, broom in hand. He didn't turn, waiting to be spoken to. He'd allow that much room for respect—not for the man circling him, but for a way of life he did not understand. Seconds later, Sebastian realized his mistake as the broom handle cracked against his weakened legs. He dropped to his knees, a curse word heaving from his gut. But the Reverend underestimated the fighter in Sebastian. He swung his aching body around, catching the broom handle as it came careening toward his head. "What the fuck is your problem!"

A new standoff ensued as each man held tight to a portion of the broom.

Eyes like two bullets narrowed at Sebastian. "You are my problem. Your presence. Your unclean life. Your language. Your ability to coax a young girl into a place she doesn't belong. I won't tolerate it. None of it. Not if I have to beat it into you."

"I explained why she was in here." Sebastian tightened his grip, thinking he could win the broom tug-o-war if need be. "What, exactly, would it have said about her if she walked away from someone calling for help?"

"It'd say she understands that my word is law—something I'd like to see more of from Evie Neal. I will win obedience from her."

"From the way she cleared out of here, I'd say she gets it. And she said that before you came in, that it was wrong for her to be here." The admission seemed to earn a point with the Reverend, who retracted the broom. Sebastian managed to pull himself to his feet. "Look, we agree that you don't want me here, and I don't want to be here. Obviously, I'm doing better. Despite the broom whipping," he said, eyeing the pole handle, which the Reverend still gripped. "I appreciate the food and shelter. Maybe I should be on my way."

"I wish it were that simple. I'd be pleased to turn you into the night, let you take your chances with the miles between us and what you might call civilization. But it seems you're to be my problem for some time to come. I've agreed to help your father by keeping you alive."

"How do you know my father?" Aside from the short fuse, Sebastian didn't see a whole lot in common.

"Business has put us in one another's path. Call it a necessary evil. The fact is I owed him a debt, and I'll keep my word. I said I'd do as he needed... and here you are."

"Business? What sort of business could you possibly have with my..." Sebastian's words trailed off, guessing an explanation wasn't going to come from the Reverend. That and he knew the only kind of business Andor Christos dealt in. Of course how it connected to this peculiar place he couldn't fathom. "You can't keep me here."

"And you have few options if you want to live. You'll stay—for now. But I'm working on a plan that will kill two birds with one stone. It will get you out of here—as you'd like, and it may benefit me. For now, it's all you need to know." He turned, heading for the door. "That and you'll not go near Evie Neal. Do you understand?" He glared at Sebastian. "Or next time, instead of a broom, it may be the business end of a shotgun."

"Why?" Sebastian said boldly. "Is she your property like everything else in Good Hope?"

"More than property, *Mission*." He stepped closer. "Soon Evie Neal will be bound to me for the rest of her life." He smiled, which could hardly be mistaken for a pleasant gesture. "Understanding the Fathers of the Right, it's beyond your heathen grasp. Stay out of our business and steer clear of our ways. You won't interfere with anything that goes on here in Good Hope. *That, Mission*," he said, pointing so fiercely it looked as if he'd pop the air, "would be where my loyalty to your father, and any Christos, ends."

CHAPTER EIGHT

Present Day

IT WASN'T THE DULL DING OF THE PLANE'S CABIN BELL THAT WOKE ALEC. It was the sensation of a serious boner beneath the blue blanket of an AeroMexico flight—someone caressing it. Alec blinked into eyes darker than his own. A sexy smile traveled from the hot dream in his head to the woman seated beside him. Then Alec remembered. It wasn't a dream. He and the woman had shared some cocktails on their delayed flight, the plane idling on a Philadelphia tarmac.

Once airborne, after the cabin lights dimmed, she'd asked in a thick Spanish accent if he'd ever made love to a woman in an airplane restroom. Well, no. But he'd fucked one or two there. His crass interpretation hadn't deterred her. Instead, his seatmate asked for a demonstration.

Alec obliged—what the hell, he'd seen the inflight movie. There was nothing but hours of mind-numbing air time in front of him. There'd been a condom in his wallet—always. Alec had returned to his seat first and the woman shimmied by minutes later, tugging at her skintight mini-dress. She'd trailed painted fingernails along his arm and mumbled something in her native tongue that sounded like satisfaction. From his inebriated state, Alec's mistake had registered. For the duration of the flight she'd be assigning labels to a thirty-five-thousand-foot fuck, one that he'd already marked *miscellaneous*. Her arm had looped through Alec's, and he suspected she'd decided their randomly assigned seats were fate. The worst part? There'd be no escape. That's what he got for thinking with his dick. Short of the parachute necessary for HAHO deployment—a high altitude op he gladly would have taken—Alec did the next best thing. He drank some more, making sure she did the same. From there, mercifully, he'd passed out.

Now he was conscious—partially. It was time to gather his wits and focus. From beneath the blanket, Alec guided the woman's hand back onto her own lap. "*No, gracias,*" he said, pointing as the plane touched down. "We're land... *Estamos aterrizando,*" he repeated in choppy Spanish.

The woman—whose name he couldn't remember—required no translation. He could see her mind flip from deciding what they'd call their kids to what she'd call him now. "*Cerdo!*" she hissed. *Pig...* Alec arched an eyebrow, having heard similar sentiments from other women. Damn, even Honor had tacked the epithet to him on occasion. But the woman's admonishment didn't stop there. She reached for the good-morning beverage on her tray—a direct hit.

Alec wiped away the sting of vodka, orange juice, and scorn as the aircraft landed. The woman was quick to exit, mashing Alec's foot with a stiletto heel. Before deplaning, a flight attendant handed him a hot towel. Upon retrieving it, the male attendant whispered to Alec, "For what it's worth, honey, if you'd fucked me like that— FYI, airplane walls are paper thin—I sure as hell wouldn't have thrown anything in your face."

It was one of the few times Alec Clairmont was at a loss for words. He handed the towel over, grabbed his leather duffel bag, and headed for the gangway.

Groggy and sticky, Alec blinked into the morning light of Bogota's El Dorado airport. It was noisy and crowd-filled. Adding to the confusion, he wasn't completely sure who he was looking for—other than Jess's ex-husband, Julian Silva. He scanned the people passing by, spying the woman in the mini-dress. She was bent at the waist, adjusting one high heel while her breasts spilled out from the swatch of fabric she was wearing. Most men looked—one concentrating so steadily Alec thought he might trip. But as the man looked up, Alec's stare hardened. He was the same man in Jess's wedding photos—the ones she insisted she'd mistakenly packed when moving into Alec's spare bedroom.

So this was Jess's ex—the man responsible for anger, tears, rogue containers of Haagen-Dazs and Absolute in Alec's freezer—Julian Silva. Tall and stylish, he also wore a smug grin, the kind Alec had wiped off the face of a guy or two.

Julian's gaze reverted to the woman in the mini-dress—the same woman Alec had fucked inflight. His perception matched Jess's take on her ex—a guy who had no ability to keep his pants zipped. According to his roommate, Julian's marital indiscretions had been the reason for their divorce. Alec put down his carry-on and scrubbed a hand over his still sticky face. Well, damn, weren't there a multitude of things wrong with that picture? Visually, mentally, Alec abandoned the woman in the mini-dress. As the man drew closer, Alec called out to him. "Julian? Julian Silva?"

He nodded. "You're Alec."

"Right," he said, "Alec Clairmont."

"Jess's roommate."

"Jess's roommate," he repeated.

Julian tipped his head and extended a hand. "Long, boring flight, huh? I've made it a few dozen times."

Julian's faint accent was well educated. It made sense. Jess wouldn't go for anybody who didn't challenge her. "Long, less some questionable entertainment. Any word from Jess?"

"No. But I'm not overly concerned. Not yet. The guide she's with, he works for me. The area she was headed to is remote. Armando knows the terrain."

"What are we talking about in terms of remote? Jungle, lack of people, native tribes."

"All of it, plus plenty of poverty. I spoke with Jess's editor at 3Cs magazine. He shared her story information with me."

"Interesting. I couldn't get a damn word out of him."

Julian shrugged. "I perhaps didn't mention that our divorce only needs to be filed back in the States. So as her husband..."

Alec nodded. Sneaky or necessary subterfuge? He supposed it didn't matter as long as Julian had secured good intel.

"Jess's original assignment was to see if she could confirm stories that have circulated through coastal villages for years. Stories about locals disappearing, ten and twenty at a time."

"Like some kind of under the radar, illegal immigration?"

"That's what I've heard," Julian said. "Personally, I think it's folklore—right up there with black magic and shrunken heads. Nobody gets out of that region easily—least of all by private jet." With that, Julian started moving through the airport's crowded corridor, Alec keeping stride.

"But a plane that could carry thirty or so passengers did go down last week. We have confirmation of that from the NTSB," Alec said.

"True. It's what started Jess on her journey here. The plane's disappearance and the lack of explanation for what it was doing here, Jess's editor wanted her to investigate the local stories and the missing aircraft."

"But instead of finding the present-day missing plane, she found the wreckage of the one my parents were on."

"About that... I'm curious. What were your parents' ties to this part of the world?"

Alec stopped in his tracks, deciding whether he wanted to answer. "My father worked for an international courier service. He piloted a small, private jet between the States and various locations on this end of the map."

"I see," Julian said, his gaze probing.

In return, Alec narrowed his. "Don't go there, man. My father wasn't a drug runner—I get the easy connection, especially with that route and this drug-rich landscape."

"Unfortunately, when it comes to export... Well, it is our number one commodity. Especially in the modern era of drugs, the unquenchable thirst for blow stateside and in Europe."

"I can't argue that. But I also knew my old man. Sebastian Clairmont was a lot of things—tough, a fighter, loyal to his family. I can promise you, the one thing he wasn't was a drug dealer."

"And I might not expect his son to have the most unbiased take on that." Julian started moving again.

Alec grabbed his arm, insisting on Julian's attention. "I'm only going to say this once: This is how it went down. My parents were already in country. Pop took a last minute assignment, moving small cargo from San Paulo to Colombia—there's nothing unusual about that. As we kids got older, my mother tagged along from time to time. It was an opportunity to see other places for free. They were adventurous. If you knew them, the scenario fits. But on that last flight, after their plane took off from Colombia, it disappeared from radar."

"And yet the wreckage Jess found is located farther west, an isolated island off the coast of La Carta. La Carta, in case you're unaware, is one of the region's most lucrative hubs when it comes to cocaine."

"Yeah. I know. Do you think I didn't do the research after Jess found the wreckage?"

"And that information doesn't alter your opinion?"

"Not in the least," Alec said, digging his fingers into the soft leather of the duffel bag. "Not if you knew my father. There's a reasonable explanation. Labeling him a drug runner because of the location... It's like saying he'd be guilty of murder if he drove past a jail every day. One thing doesn't have anything to do with the other."

Julian nodded. "Got it. No guilt by association. I've no problem giving your father... your parents the benefit of the doubt." He started down the busy concourse again.

"What about you?" Alec said, needing to regain the momentum, or at least establish that he had some. "What brings you back to the same drug-rich terrain? Jess mentioned you'd relocated back to Colombia."

"I'm undecided. I'm here while business is good. Anyway, it was only natural that Jess get in touch with me when she arrived in Bogota."

"Was it?" Alec said as they turned toward signs marked *salida*.

"Sounds like you and Jess shared a lot of personal information."

"Small apartment... back in Nickel Springs. I've overheard a few of your *exchanges*—witnessed the aftermath of others," Alec said. "I'll be honest, dude—the subject of *you* didn't bring out Jess's softer side."

"Well, you know Jess—a little drama goes a long way."

"Actually, I wouldn't describe her like that at all."

He pushed open a door, holding it for Alec. As he passed by, Julian said, "And you weren't married to her for six years."

Alec stopped and turned. "No, but I did live with her for a while—still do."

"And you're sure she sleeps in the spare bedroom?" Julian said.

"Positive—not that any other arrangement would be your fucking business."

Julian snickered, walking past Alec and taking the lead. "She was right—you are... *intense*. Take it down a notch, gringo. I thought your sole focus in coming here was the mystery of your parents' disappearance. Or is it something else drawing you to sunny Colombia? Believe me, I know that side of Jess too."

Julian was a shrewd manipulator, that much seemed evident.

"Sebastian and Evie, they've been gone a long time. Whatever Jess found will be there when I get there. But first I have to get to Jess. Any disagreement there?"

"*Ninguno.*" Julian said.

Alec glanced at his watch. "Okay, well, she's been gone for almost forty-eight hours with no communication. Shouldn't you be more concerned?"

"Lack of communication isn't a reason to panic. Not in the isolated region Jess headed into. Cell service is almost non-existent."

"Even so, is there a reason the authorities haven't been notified?"

"Did you miss the part about the isolated location? It's not really an option." Julian strode into a parking garage. "Just out of curiosity, did you happen to bring along your Superman military skills? That's not a bad traveling companion where we're headed."

Alec stopped, shifting the leather duffel bag to his other shoulder. "How do you know..."

"Jess, of course. She mentioned your glory days."

"Did she?" Alec said, not liking that intel from more angles than he could count.

"I heard you were a serious badass in your day—before you burnt out, bugged out... retired from life... whatever." Julian clicked the keys he held and the lights of a luxury SUV flashed. He smiled at Alec, cocking his chin at the vehicle. "I suppose when it comes to Jess *exchanges* go both ways."

Alec felt a flutter in his gut and one in his fist. It'd been some time since he had the raw urge to haul off and beat the shit out of somebody because... well, they existed.

"And just so you know, I'm not being cavalier with Jess's safety. I have asked some associates to look into the situation. Still, you're better off with locals on this op, Man of Steel," Julian said. "*La Policia* don't give a shit about an American woman and the whereabouts of her by-the-hour guide."

Julian wasn't without a point. Alec had been to enough remote regions to know that locals were the best bet. "*Associates?*" he questioned. "I never was clear on that—what is it you do here in the Motherland?"

"I'm in property management."

"Real estate?" Alec said, opening the door of the SUV.

"As it applies in this part of the world. Now do you want to get moving, or did you need to see my resume first?"

Alec slung his father's leather duffel bag into the back seat. "Let's just get busy finding Jess." *Maybe then I can figure out what the hell happened to my parents and how they ended up in La Carta—the cocaine candy store of South America.*

CHAPTER NINE

1977

Good Hope, Pennsylvania

AFTER SEBASTIAN'S ENCOUNTER WITH EVIE AND THE REVEREND, THE MEN returned to guarding him. Maybe it was his imagination, but they seemed more vigilant, sparse conversation growing even thinner. But Sebastian's clash with the Reverend had also provided a benefit. Sebastian realized he was back to full strength, or close to it. On the verge of stir crazy, he started doing sit-ups and pushups, running in place, which seemed like the only positive way to pass time. Nolan Creek watched with rapt attention, remarking, "If you truly put those muscles to work it would benefit you more, leave you twice as tired."

"Is that how you see it?" Sebastian said, shifting his sit-ups to an angle that hid him from the open hearth view. He'd rather not be Brother Creek's eye-candy, but he did feel bad about the way the guy chose to lead his life—using religion to conceal who he really was.

In between the calisthenics and the dry reading stamped North Good Hope Library, Sebastian also took to excessively long hot baths. It was his only chance to be alone. Alone with fantasies of Evie Neal. She'd managed to make her way into the tub with him where Sebastian relieved boredom with detailed fantasies of the chaste girl. He'd envision undoing the tight braid, unbuttoning the stiff wardrobe, burying their bodies into the bed's feathery mattress. He wanted to taste every part of her—starting with those pouty lips, making his way down a body that he'd thoroughly mapped in his mind. Despite her bulky skirt and a blouse that was an insult to her figure, the attraction was intense.

But Sebastian found he had more on his mind than sex. Other ideas filled in the edges of his Evie illusions. He wondered about the thoughts in her head—how she looked at the world, and how she might look at him. Could he ever evoke more than an *"I dare you"* fear from her? She'd only been in the cabin—or his life—for five minutes, but Sebastian couldn't shake her. She'd hit a switch in his brain, a signal that felt as vibrant as it was unclear. The days wore on, and he found himself more focused on Evie and less on his questionable future.

After the Reverend admonished her, what had become of the hypnotic Evie Neal? Worse, was she seriously going to marry Ezra Kane? Sebastian couldn't see it. By the time another week had passed, he felt his blood pressure rise. Evie Neal was too much fire for a guy who was like a lukewarm bath.

In the middle of a particularly long night, one where Evie had claimed every dream and wide-awake thought, Sebastian sat up in bed. Exasperated and riled, he hurled a pillow at the stone fireplace. The angle was just so, allowing Nolan Creek to lean and ogle him through the open hearth. "It slipped," Sebastian said, meeting the brother's fire-lit gaze.

He sunk back into other pillows, dragging a hand through his hair. He blinked into the beamed ceiling of a place that felt like a cage. This was nuts. This wasn't him. Sebastian rolled onto his side and closed his eyes. Even if he were given another five minutes with Evie, it wouldn't amount to a thing—well, anything more than a reminder of what he really was: a homeless thug running for his life, currently being held in limbo. He sighed. He needed to get a fucking grip. None of it should matter. Certainly not a woman—girl—whose life couldn't be more removed from his.

The thought brought him back around to Reverend Kane. Sebastian knew very little about the Fathers of the Right—mostly what he'd surmised. It hadn't left him too far from the word *cult*. They were no Manson clan—not prone to the crazed brutal events that had captured headlines less than a decade ago. Nor were they a commune, a trendy way of living he'd heard about. Mostly that happened in California and the Pacific Northwest. At the core, these people were traditionally religious. But even that description seemed sketchy, their lives and rules were crafted to reflect Duncan Kane's desires. The Reverend, Sebastian was sure, was about as holy as an old winter sock.

On a Sunday morning, having chewed the little information he had to bits, Sebastian spoke abruptly to Nolan Creek. "I'm going out—for a walk. Stop me and I'll knock you on your ass. So if that's been your fantasy, then go for it."

Nolan Creek looked up from his reading. Behind his glasses was a wide-eyed gaze. The look drew down Sebastian's frame, which only added to his determination. "I... I can't allow that. The Reverend, he'd... "

His keeper was a master carver, devout sect follower, and a pacifist. But Sebastian couldn't take anymore. He grabbed him by the collar, prepared to make good on his threat. He hauled back a fist that would pound forward with weeks of pent up frustration. He saw the pure fear in Nolan Creek's face and jerked him closer. Through gritted teeth he asked, "Is there anything you don't fear?"

"No. But I fear nothing more than the afterlife punishment that awaits me." He winced, bracing for the blow.

Sebastian let him drop back onto the chair. Walking out the cabin door, he spoke over his shoulder. "You've let me pass, Brother. You'll have to answer for it. Keep your mouth shut and I might come back."

Sebastian headed down the briar covered path. He jogged a few yards and stopped. After so many days inside, the daylight was piercing. He slowed to a walk, coming to the sect's town center. It connected to another dirt road—the way out. The unknown made Sebastian hesitate. How long until the Godfathers found him? What direction would he go? He'd overheard the brothers' talk. The closest town, North Good Hope, was more than twenty miles away. The isolated location was what Evie had said—interlopers were unwelcome. Standing alone, unattended, Sebastian felt like a prisoner of circumstance.

In the cabin there was no electricity or phone, but he remembered seeing telephone wires the day he'd arrived. Somewhere, there had to be a phone. But who would he call? Andor? He could demand to know if he had a plan. Or was dumping his son in this fresh hell the solution? Then Sebastian thought better of it. Maybe abandonment was a message, meaning Andor had washed his hands of Sebastian. He wasn't sure he wanted to know. Andor wasn't much of a father, he wouldn't call the two of them a family, but the idea of being completely alone gnawed at Sebastian's gut. He thought of his Uncle Paulos—but his father's younger brother wouldn't act without Andor's approval. Sebastian considered Bim. Bim was smart. He'd have solid advice.

With that idea in mind, Sebastian started toward the buildings— houses, barns, a couple of awkward storefronts. It looked as if the Reverend had built his own sovereign state in the middle of rural Pennsylvania. Right now, the place looked like a ghost town. There wasn't a person in sight. Sebastian heard faint singing. He squinted toward a distant building. It had to be the meeting hall—that was how the brothers referred to it. Sunday. Of course, they were all inside.

That was a good thing. Now was the perfect opportunity to find a phone. Sebastian moved deeper into Good Hope. Early October was in the air, and Sebastian noticed his breath as he walked. He'd tugged on a corduroy shirt that morning, a worn favorite he'd stuffed in the duffel bag. At the moment, he wished the shirt had a lining. Jesus, he hadn't even packed a coat.

At the third house, Sebastian stopped. He smelled cinnamon. He turned in a tight circle. Like their plain dress, dull conversations, and communal lives, the houses of Good Hope reflected order and uniformity, one mirroring the next. Each had an identical postage-stamp lawn and post and rail fence, though he managed to zero in on the one manufacturing the enticing aroma. A few steps and he could see through the front windows. Sebastian wasn't a peeping Tom, but seconds later his stare was pinned to a paned window.

Inside was Evie Neal. From where he stood, Sebastian had a clear view of a small dining room that led to the kitchen. He was surprised by how accurately his mind had mimicked every Evie detail—even the way she moved. She flitted about, tending to whatever was making his mouth water. Through paper-thin walls he could hear humming—something different than the voices he'd heard singing. He listened harder. The tune, some silly popular song—it'd played constantly in the pool hall.

But like their impromptu meeting in the cabin, Sebastian couldn't look away. Thoughts of finding a phone, even the desire to leave began to ebb. She stood out in this place of dull repetition. Of course, it didn't entirely explain the knot in his gut the second he saw her. He tracked Evie's movements as she reached to a high shelf. A bottle tipped, its contents splashing onto the front of her blouse. "Oh for the love of…" replaced the happy humming.

It was the most interesting thing he'd seen in weeks, and Sebastian was mesmerized as Evie stripped off the blouse. He was torn between staring and turning away. To his surprise, he did the gentlemanly thing and focused on his scuffed work boots, even stepping back. But his boot tangled in an evergreen shrub and while trying not to make a sound, Sebastian fell, landing flat on his back. When he looked up, Evie Neal peered down at him. She wore a slip and an awed expression. Her gaze canvased the street behind him. Cracking open the window, she said, "Hurry around back. It won't do either of us any good if someone sees you."

CHAPTER TEN

THE ONLY THING MOVING FASTER THAN EVIE'S FEET WAS HER HEART AS SHE raced to the kitchen door, flinging it wide. "I didn't know if they'd sent you away. I... I'm not to come anywhere near the cabin."

"Then I probably shouldn't be at your kitchen door."

A gulp wedged in her throat. "No. I don't suppose you should." Neither of them moved.

"Especially wearing... in, um, that..." His index finger trailed through the air in front of her.

Evie locked eyes with the cool green of his, and an idea about removing the space between them drifted into her head. She'd nearly forgotten her blouse-less state. "Oh... oh my gosh, how stupid of me," she said, crossing her arms over the slip. "I spilled cooking oil. Then I heard... " Evie darted away as Sebastian picked up the conversation.

"Uh, if it helps, you're still more dressed than most of the women on my side of the tracks."

Inside the laundry room, Evie grabbed a clean blouse and plunged her arms into it. Hastily, she worked the buttons and returned to the kitchen door. "Yes, well, we're not on your side of the tracks, are we?" He hadn't budged, still standing on the rear porch. "On the other hand, I suppose that makes us even."

"I think I'm still ahead. I was only wearing a towel."

Evie gathered her wits and the blush she felt rising. "What are you doing roaming about?"

"I was looking for a phone."

She opened the door wider and he came inside. Everyone in Good Hope was sitting in the meeting hall and Evie felt sure no one had seen him. Safely inside her kitchen, in the bright morning light, Evie allowed herself a lingering gaze. His strong frame was more mesmerizing than she recalled—and truth be told, she'd recalled it more than once. He looked better too—healthier. The fit of his T-shirt was snugger, outlined by an open corduroy shirt. It looked soft, like perhaps he wore it often. Evie inched her hand forward. The desire to touch it—maybe him—was vivid. She jerked back her hand and the forward thought. "We don't have a phone."

"You don't..." He tightened his wide brow. "Then why did you invite me in?"

"I don't know. I mean, you tripped outside and..." She moved her hands to her hips. "Why were you peeking in my window?"

"I wasn't. I mean, yes. I was. First it was the smell of whatever you're baking. And then I saw it was you inside—these houses, well, it's not like you can help but see in a window." Sebastian folded his arms. "Why aren't you at church with the rest of them?"

"It's the Widow Vale's birthday. I was asked to make cinnamon cake as a treat for after the service. She has no other family, so it seemed someone should... You have to serve the cake right away. It's best warm, and..." She pointed at the stove, but the gesture was weak. The heat pulsing between them was twice the temperature of the oven. "You should go."

"Right. Especially if you don't have a phone." He stepped toward the door but turned back. "You were humming a song I knew. A silly love song."

"Well, perhaps you think it's silly—"

"No. The name of the song, 'A Silly Love Song,' Beatles ex, Paul McCartney. Wings."

She knotted her brow tighter.

"Never mind."

Evie pointed toward the radio in the other room. "If no one is here, sometimes I listen to popular music. I just have to remember to put the station back before my father... My mother never minded, but he..."

"Your mother, she's not here."

"She's gone. She died last winter." Evie hadn't said it out loud to anyone—not since that fateful January night. There'd been no need. Everyone in Good Hope knew Elizabeth Neal was dead. Tears welled. "I'm sorry," she said, words at an impasse.

"Don't be. My mother's gone too—a long time." His fingertips came forward, but Evie was quicker, brushing at a lone tear. "I was never allowed any."

"Medical help?"

He shook his head. "Tears." Silence and the lingering scent of cinnamon filled the kitchen.

"Why are you calling someone?" she said. "To take you away?"

"It crossed my mind. I, uh, I need a plan. We both know I don't belong here. And it's not likely that I'm going to let Reverend Kane decide my fate."

"He doesn't decide—" Evie couldn't argue the point. "Who were you going to call? Your wife?"

"My... I don't have a wife."

"Oh. I see. You're like Nolan Creek then."

Sebastian's jaw dropped. "Like? Uh, no. Not if you're suggesting I'd like to date him."

Evie's brown eyes blinked into his, but she didn't respond. The thought was too bold.

"I wanted to call a friend—Bim. He's a doctor."

"A doctor?" she said.

"You sound surprised."

"It's just that... I've never met one. So, yes, that surprises me."

"You've never seen a doctor—not for anything?"

"No. I told you that. Reverend Kane... the Fathers of the Right. They don't believe in medical intervention."

"Yes, but I thought you meant... Well, I'm not sure what I thought that meant. Jesus, that's a little like playing God, don't you think?"

"They... we..." Evie struggled, lifelong rules dictating her explanation. "We leave it up to God's will."

"And it couldn't be that God saw to it penicillin was invented?"

It was amazing. Another person agreeing with the dark thought in Evie's head. Yet the doctrine of the Fathers of the Right ran deep. "It's not what we believe," she insisted.

"Sounds more like you don't believe in freewill. There doesn't seem to be much of that here—medicine, marriages, choices. How old are you anyway?"

"Nineteen. And you?"

"Twenty-four."

Except for widowers and Nolan Creek, Evie had never met an unwed man of that age. "How very unusual—don't you want to be married? To have children?"

"No," he said, shaking his head hard. "Absolutely not—especially the kids part."

"And you're sure you're not like Nolan Creek?"

"Will you stop. I'm very sure. Not like him, or any of them," he said, cocking his chin toward the streets of Good Hope.

"We're good people, Bash. At least none of us is running for our lives."

"Even so, your way of life... It *is* 1977." His hand brushed by the plainly furnished room. "If it wasn't for the oven, maybe the lamps, that radio," he said, pointing to the brown, square unit on a dining room server, "I'd think I'd fallen through a time warp."

Evie considered his point of view and reiterated hers. "Whatever our time, no one from here wants you dead."

"Yeah. That's true," he said. "You do know part of my secret, my reason for being here."

"And the rest?" she said, aware of the dangers bred from curiosity.

"The rest. It's…"

"I know. Complicated." Evie waited, tipping her head at his silence. "We lead simple lives, Bash. We're not stupid—you'd be wise not to make that mistake about me."

"I can see that," he said. "I won't—ever." Their gazes tied tight as a wild vine. "Do you have any of your own, Evie… *secrets*?"

"And if I did, I'd tell you because…?"

A smile edged into his rugged features. Ezra's grin was mischievous, *pretty*. This man's was so different—like the beauty you might find in a thick forest. Evie felt dampness in her palms, and each beat of her heart, the breaths in between. It was incredibly wrong—all of it. She shook her head, trying to clear the fog that had rolled in with Sebastian Christos. His smile faded, and her dreamy thoughts blurred. "I haven't told anyone the part of your secret that you did share. So if that's what you're standing here wondering—"

"I'm not. I knew… I had a feeling I could trust you."

"Strange. I found myself making the same claim about you to my friend, Hannah. I don't know why that should be. I don't know you, and you don't know me."

"I've thought the same thing. Why do you suppose that is, instant trust?"

He wanted her opinion. It startled Evie. When she didn't answer, he did.

"It'll sound as crazy to you as it did to me," he said. "But I keep thinking of two old souls inside two new people."

What a lovely thought…

Sebastian cleared his throat. "Of course, my old soul probably comes with a record and a warrant."

Evie laughed. "I can't imagine any old soul that couldn't use a little cleansing." She felt it so plainly, something wondrous pulsing off him and into her. But Evie also understood that was all it could ever be. "If it's what you want, I know where there's a telephone you can use."

"Right. A phone."

She turned toward the oven and clock. "The cake has another twenty minutes. If we hurry, we can go to the Wheaton's house. They have a phone—and a microwave," she said over her shoulder. "Everyone will be in the meeting hall for at least another half hour."

"Won't the door be locked?"

She looked queerly at him. "Why would anyone in Good Hope lock their door?"

"Good point."

"Just let me get my sweater." Evie felt him follow as she moved through the dining area, retrieving her sweater from the adjoining living room.

"That's your dress."

He pointed to a dressmaker's dummy. It wore her wedding dress, a modest white, floor length garb. The hourglass shape of the dummy—adjusted to mirror Evie's frame—provided the only adornment. She brushed her hand over the dangling cuffed sleeve. "Mrs. Wheaton, Hannah's mother, made it for me. I asked for lace at the neck," she said, touching the high buttons that assured its demure look. "It was thought to be too *revealing*." Evie touched the hook-and-eye buttons at the neck. "It's a fine dress. Mrs. Wheaton does splendid work."

"But you don't like it."

"Do you?" Evie asked, oddly interested in his answer.

"I don't know anything about wedding dresses. But I do think the bride is supposed to love it." He came closer, as if to get a better look. His green eyes cut from the dress to her. "Do you, Evie... love it?"

Nervously, she withdrew her hand from the dress, fingering a box of straight pins that sat on a nearby table. The metal pins rolled off her fingertips, plinking as they dropped back into the container. She stared at him. Sebastian Christos was wildly out of place next to the dress, perhaps her life. "I, um... I suppose. It's a perfectly fine dress."

"But are you in love with it?"

"The dress?" Evie said.

"The dress. Whatever comes with it."

She cast her gaze over the frock, wrestling with weak enthusiasm. It was particularly noticeable compared to the belly flutter the *mission* stirred. "Love doesn't have anything to do with it," she said pragmatically. "It's what I'm supposed to wear. It's expected. The simplicity of the dress is symbolic of our lives, the basic way we live... of the bride."

He frowned. "Simple isn't a word I'd try to dress you in."

Evie tucked a loose strand of hair behind her ear. "Then it's good you have nothing to say in the matter. A white dress, a pure wife—in God's eyes a right life," she murmured. It wasn't a bible verse, but one of Reverend Kane's many mantras.

Sebastian stuffed his hands into his pants pockets. "Right, I get it. White. Virgin—" He stopped as her eyes widened. "Purity," he corrected, "and all that."

Evie felt the push and pull of rules—the ones they lived by and the ones that could be broken. Every day the line grew fuzzier. "You'd think," she said, her whisper more sedate than the dress. "In my case, I suspect beige would do just fine."

She saw the shock on his face. Evie felt her own—admitting something so personal to a man who was no more than a stranger. *Or perhaps an old soul from another life...*

"Ezra?" he asked.

"Of course, Ezra. How could it be anyone else?"

He looked oddly relieved. "Ezra. Right. Besides, it's none of my business."

She'd never had such a forthright conversation—not even with Hannah. Evie turned fast, the sweater slipping from her shoulders. They both bent to pick it up. Crouched on the floor, eye to eye, their fingers tangled in the soft knit fabric. Evie wobbled and he reached, steadying her. "You're right, Bash. It's none of your concern. Not the dress... not Ezra."

"Not if you don't want it to be."

He barely braced her elbow, and all Evie could think was how it might feel to have that strong arm around all of her. She confessed a smaller desire. "I wanted a store-bought dress, from a shop in town. It's one of the few things we've disagreed about, Ezra and I. He's a sweet soul, kind, different from his father."

"Good to hear that much. And even if you don't really love—"

"You're wrong!" she insisted. "Of course I love Ezra."

"I meant the dress."

"Oh," she said, feeling her face flush. "Why would you think I don't love Ezra?"

"I didn't... I don't think that. Like you said, it's not my business. But since you walked into the cabin, odd things have been on my mind. Things I've never considered."

"Like what?" But Evie spoke again before he could. "Don't answer that. I ask too many questions. It's a terrible habit. My wandering mind, it gets me into trouble. I'm always thinking of things I shouldn't."

"Like what?" She hesitated and Sebastian prodded. "You can go ahead and answer."

"Aside from dresses?" Evie glanced at the one that hung over them like a dowdy chaperone. "Sometimes I dream about places other than here. Have you ever been anywhere, besides your home and here?"

"Uh, yeah. I've sailed to Greece, a few other ports in Europe."

"Greece? Good heavens." She swallowed hard, Sebastian fitting so snuggly into her fantasy. "You mean all the way across the ocean?"

He smiled wide. "Yeah. I guess I've traveled a good bit for someone my age, seen more than most."

"You do seem older—I'll say that. It sounds as if the life you've led has aged you."

"Maybe it's the old soul in me." They smiled and Evie glanced away. "Guess it's safe to say I've had a *worldly* education so far, if not a rough one."

She listened, unsure how to follow his thinking or his life. He'd experienced things, been to places Evie couldn't imagine. Her knees began to ache, but she didn't dare move. Not with Sebastian's face— his exotic life—so close to hers. "Reverend Kane doesn't approve of women traveling. Even so, I've thought about it... dreamed about it. But I couldn't really picture leaving here."

"If leaving here is what you want, maybe you ought to be shouting it."

"Honestly, as outspoken as I am, I'm surprised Reverend Kane still wants me to marry his son."

"Why should it matter what he wants?"

"Because... Well, Reverend Kane is our leader—he's anointed. He and my father, they agreed ages ago that..." And Evie stopped. She was making more the Reverend's point than her own. "How else would a life be lived, if not by the wisdom of elders? You wouldn't understand."

"You're right. I don't understand anything about this place. No doubt you'd feel the same way in my neighborhood. I don't suppose we'd have much in common in the real world."

"And which one of us do you believe lives there?"

He grinned again. "You're incredibly smart."

"For someone who's never been around the corner." She smiled back. "And in either place, I believe the one thing we'd have in common is bullheadedness."

"Another good point. But if you're asking about marriage, kids—having them or not—even what radio station you listen to, I don't think a person should have those things dictated to them. Not in the twentieth century."

"Not everything about this century is good."

"Like what? Doctors and retail?"

He surprised her, Bash zeroing in on the two things Evie had been openly bullheaded about. Yet his lack of belonging stuck out like a red dress in the meeting hall—something else Evie had seen in her dreams. Sebastian's presence made her too aware. The talk, the proximity, the lengthy conversation. The crouched position finally gave way and Evie dropped to her knees. She let go of the sweater. Sebastian held it for a moment, also easing onto his knees. She felt fringes of her hair breeze back as he draped the sweater around her shoulders.

"You look cold."

"On the outside... maybe." Her gaze moved from his bent knees, trailing up muscular thighs, past the waist of dark dungarees. She hesitated, looking at his leather belt, the buckle. But her line of vision narrowed as Sebastian's body drew closer. An urge to bite her bottom lip was strong. But it was too late, too busy, as Sebastian's full lips closed around hers. A tentative kiss turned to certainty—like the act had been waiting years to happen. Evie sunk her fingertips into the corduroy shirt—softer than she'd predicted—dead-ending into the solid mass of his shoulders. For the first time in Evie's life it felt like a wish had been granted—perhaps a prayer answered as Sebastian's arms encircled her.

Quick as the sweater had caped her shoulders, it slipped back onto the floor. From midway up, Sebastian's body pressed into hers, Evie feeling the parts of him that wanted to penetrate her. She gulped for air between kisses, glad to be on her knees. All of her felt wobbly—short on breath and good sense. But she didn't pull away as he moved his hands lithely over her, a heated sensation smoldering. She hadn't thought it was true—assumed Hannah had lied—that anyone could evoke such staggering emotion.

Evie indulged, hearing a hungry hum erupt from him. The sound caused her heart to pound and her body to demand. She felt his hand through the thick gather of her skirt, cupping around her bottom. An achy moan escaped her own throat as a desire beyond sunlight and air consumed her, drowning her in the moment. She was lucky to hear the kitchen door slam, her soon-to-be husband's voice cutting into a feeling entirely devoid of Ezra.

"Evie, are you here? My father was so busy blessing the Yeager twins he didn't see me sneak out the back. Evie?"

"Oh God," she said, detaching herself from Sebastian. She grabbed anxiously at the side table, steadying herself as surprise and passion nearly knocked Evie Neal to the floor.

CHAPTER ELEVEN

IN THE WEEK THAT FOLLOWED, EVIE SPENT MORE TIME IN THE MEETING hall than she had her entire life. She sighed, thinking that wasn't exactly true. But sitting in a pew with her hands in a prayerful vise, she guessed this time had been the most meaningful. She'd asked for forgiveness and she'd asked for guidance. She'd asked for time to turn back. On the evening before the day of her wedding, Evie concluded that God wasn't partial to providing last minute answers. Not to someone who only came calling when things got tough.

Had they gotten tough?

It wasn't as if she'd been caught red-handed kissing Sebastian Christos. Naturally, Ezra had been surprised to find Sebastian in Evie's living room. But the spilled box of pins had painted a credible picture about what they were doing, inches apart, on their knees. Ezra also accepted Sebastian's half-truths and reasons for being there: Brother Creek had fallen asleep. Sebastian had gone out walking. He'd decided to look for a phone. On that particular Sunday morning Evie was the only person in Good Hope Sebastian found at home. She'd been glad for irrefutable facts, continuing with the story: *"We were on our way to the Wheaton's house... He only wanted to make a phone call... I grabbed my sweater and knocked over the pin box... It was so clumsy of me..."* she'd said, the taste of lies and Sebastian in her mouth.

Perhaps Ezra hadn't questioned it because he'd been fine with the possibility of removing Sebastian Christos from their cloistered lives. As they rose to their feet, Evie kept brushing her hand across her mouth. In the mental midst of swearing she'd never look at Sebastian again, he'd caught her panicked glance. The look said *"Stop... Calm down. You're giving yourself away."* Evie was amazed at what a cool liar she could be. The only off part seemed to be her crookedly buttoned blouse, which Ezra never noticed. Evie had hurried toward the kitchen, away from them both. If Ezra had known his fiancée was dressed in little more than a slip when she'd answered the door... Or that only seconds before arriving at the Neal house, Evie had been locked in a kiss that felt as if it could will the earth to spin the other way... Well, their story might not have gone as smoothly. In the end, the only hiccup came when Sebastian said he no longer wanted to make a phone call, causing Evie to stifle a gasp.

Sitting in the front pew now, Evie sucked in another anxious breath. There didn't seem to be any air that would let her breathe easy. It was the least of what she deserved. The impending punishment would be rich, she guessed—God and man's.

"Here you are." Hannah broke into Evie's thoughts and nudged her way into the pew. "I've been looking everywhere for you!"

"I've been here for a while."

"And you find it surprising that the last place I'd look for you is the meeting hall?"

"Don't say that!" Evie turned, confronting Hannah's surprised expression. "I'm not a bad person. I've as much right to sit here as any of us."

"Of course you're not a..." Hannah leaned forward, her fair eyes and tiny features peering into Evie's face. "You look as if the weight of the world is sitting here with you. What in heaven's name is wrong?"

She couldn't. Evie opened her mouth and clamped it shut. "Ezra," she finally said. "I think it'd be better if he married Rachel Pruitt."

"What?" She laughed. "Oh my, wedding jitters from Evie Neal. Who would have ever thought? You've been betrothed to him since you could walk. My goodness," she said, her voice dropping to the tiniest whisper, "you've even slept with him. How can you not marry him?" She shook her head. "Granted, there's his father. I don't envy you that. But Ezra, he hasn't an unkind bone in him. And most important, Evie, he loves you, so I—" Evie reached, grasping Hannah's hand. "Evie?" Any lilt vanished from Hannah's voice.

"I'm not sure I feel the same about Ezra." She turned toward her friend. "I know I'd be a fool not to marry Ezra. He's everything you've said. He loves me—which is more than I can say for a lot of marriages in Good Hope."

"But?"

Hannah reached with her other hand, sandwiching Evie's in between. Surely she had to feel the cold tremble. Evie's brown-eyed gaze inched from their tangled hands. "I kissed him," she said as if she'd committed murder. "I kissed *the mission...* Sebastian."

"*The mission.*" Hannah's tone dropped to meet the gravity of the confession.

For the first time in a week, Evie didn't have to fight the thought. She kept going. "Last Sunday, in my living room. We were alone." She swallowed hard, a mix of spit and guilt.

"Evie, no." She tightened her grip around Evie's hand.

Why shouldn't Hannah be shocked? She'd been stunned to learn that Evie had had sex with the boy she was to marry. Until now, it was Hannah Wheaton's best-kept secret. A tentative nod picked up speed. Then, like any good friend, Hannah took up the cause. Her words brimmed with plot, as if deciding where to bury the body.

"All right. If you did kiss him, then he must have forced himself on you. That was it, right, Evie?" Evie's stark blink indicated the error in her assumption. Hannah didn't give up. "Ah, well, then, I know exactly what it was."

Evie leaned closer, anxious for an explanation other than the one her feelings offered.

"The devil. Pure and simple." Hannah nodded more deeply, motioning toward Reverend Kane's pulpit. "It's proselytization in the flesh—temptation delivered through the mouth of *the mission*," she insisted. "Think about it, Evie. The devil's made himself known, tried to make you trip on your way to the altar. Reverend Kane may be overwhelming at times, but this is what he's warned us about. Can't you see that? The guilt, the regret, the shame—"

"Hannah," Evie said, removing her hand from her friend's grasp. "Don't you think I've considered that? Guilt and shame, even fear. They've haunted me all week. And well they should." Evie looked from the solid wood pulpit to the stained glass window. "But the reason I'm sitting here.... What's not right, what makes no sense," she said, now wringing her hands tight, "is that I'm not the least bit sorry it happened."

CHAPTER TWELVE

HANNAH LEFT A SHORT TIME LATER. SHE WAS EXPECTED HOME TO WATCH her younger siblings—Mrs. Wheaton was going to sit with Nan Pffefer. Nan suffered a malady that grew worse by the day, some of the women in the bakery saying they didn't believe the once robust Nan would live out the week. Evie turned to the stained-glass window, which was an anomaly in Good Hope. The shiny, manmade object was the one thing Reverend welcomed into their plain lives.

Late afternoon sun shone through like a prism, but all Evie could see was the green of Judas's robe. It was the same green in Sebastian Christos's eyes. Evie closed hers, feeling tears between lids and lashes. What more did she need in the way of a sign? Betrayal, it seemed, came color coded. With fresh determination, Evie left the pew and headed toward the cabin.

Her mission was clear. This *distraction* would be confronted— swift and final. Nolan Creek sat outside the cabin whittling a hunk of hickory. With the harvest behind them, Brother Creek spent his winters making sweet carvings that they sold in the bake shop— crosses, decorative boxes shaped like leaves and doves. Evie stopped, smiling willfully at Brother Creek. And because lies were never spoken in Good Hope, Nolan easily believed hers—Reverend Kane wanted to see Brother Creek. Brother Ott would be along shortly to watch *the mission*. She knew Reverend Kane had gone to North Good Hope. Nolan Creek would wait obediently for his return.

Evie kept on her way, walking toward the potting shed and saying something about planting fall bulbs. One step closer to the shed than the cabin, Evie glanced over her shoulder. Nolan Creek had disappeared into the curve of the path. She scurried back, knocking lightly on the cabin door. No one answered. Evie pushed back her shoulders. *Nonsense. What would be the odds of catching him twice in a towel?* Yet, her shaking hand—one that Evie could hardly believe was her own—turned the white metal knob.

"Bash," she whispered, looking around the empty room. She heard feet hit the floor. Evie moved farther into the space, past the fireplace. At the edge of the bed, there he was, like a ghost. A ghost with no shirt.

"Evie. What are you doing here?"

"I, um..." For someone who'd come to say her piece, Evie was speechless. He was stunning, the sight of him seizing her senses. It made sense. Temptation was the problem. She was there to defy it. She took a deep breath. Evie hoped urges would pass, like a sneeze— necessary but quickly forgotten. Evie tried to recall the last time she'd sneezed. *See that...* She had no idea. *This will be the same... I'll soon forget him.* "I see you've not contacted your friend... yet."

"I, uh... I thought I'd wait out the week. Besides, to call someone I'd have to ditch my constant companions first. Where's Brother Creek?"

"Gone for now," she said. She cocked her chin at the book he held. "You're reading?"

"You don't have to sound so surprised."

"You don't strike me as the studious type."

"I was never much for classrooms, but books, they're... I don't mind reading. Nolan... Brother Creek brings them. Most aren't too interesting. But some are... *fascinating*. Kind of like other things in Good Hope."

"Other things?"

"Things I never thought of before here. Things I didn't know existed."

"I see." Skimming her gaze across his chest, Evie wondered about the scars. She wondered about so many things—like why being near Sebastian seemed to overshadow the rest of the world.

"Is that why you're here, breaking rules again to ask me what I'm reading?"

"No. Not exactly. Although reading..." She wrung her hands together. "It seems a discussion of the Spanish Armada would be a safer subject than any I might take up with you."

"French Revolution," he said, tossing the book onto the bed and stepping toward her.

Evie didn't move. But the closer he came, the more everything pulled her toward him. It was insanity. She barely knew him, and yet she felt safer—more alive—in his presence than with any other person.

"So if you're short on topics," he said, "let me pick one. Are you still marrying Ezra?"

"Blunt, aren't you?"

"I'm not much for f— No. If I've got something to say, I say it."

"And I can understand why you'd ask. What happened between us, at my house... It was..." Evie hesitated. The explanation sounded more rational when negotiating with God. "Hannah says it was the devil—in you or in me."

"In my pants, maybe." Green irises widened. They were an odd second to his smile, the divot in his chin.

"In your... I don't... " Evie wanted to say she didn't understand. But, in fact, she did. She dropped her gaze from his chest to an even less appropriate place.

"Evie." She flicked her eyes to his. "I can't explain what happened in your living room either. But in fairness, know I'm not that guy."

"What *guy?*" Evie wasn't sure she'd ever used the word.

"The kind who goes out of his way to kiss a girl—not like that. Not like you were the only one left—or maybe the only one I wanted. So as surreal as that whole scene was for you, know that it was just as crazy for me."

"Because I'm not that girl."

"I'm not sure what you mean."

"I've seen those girls—the one I'm not. They come into the bake shop from North Good Hope—painted faces and fingernails, more skin showing than you'd find on a stewed rabbit."

He cleared his throat. "Damn, you know how to take a visual down a notch."

But she kept talking, fingers flitting lightly over the collar of her blouse. "And their clothes—cut off dungarees and top-halves that expose... well, more than I would have thought the law allowed. That's the kind of girl you'd want to kiss in such a way."

"No," he said, a breath shuddering out of him. "The girl I'd kiss like that. I didn't know she existed. Not before you."

Evie sunk her teeth into her bottom lip, her attention rapt. "But you have to know, I'm going to marry Ezra tomorrow. It can't happen any other way."

"Why do you have to marry anyone tomorrow?"

"Why?" she asked, her eyes pulsing wide. "Because... It's what's supposed to happen. My father and Reverend Kane, and all the Fathers of the Right. It's unthinkable that it wouldn't."

Everything that wafted off Sebastian drew her in—a scent, the sound of his voice, the idea of touching him. It made her dizzy. *Steady yourself...* It was the only firm direction Evie heard in her head. She inched her hand forward—of its own volition—fingertips balancing on his hard chest. He didn't move, letting Evie discover, for herself, the things she wanted to know. Her reasons for coming to the cabin muddled. But there was no reciprocal touch, not as she mapped the coarse scattering of hair on his chest, moving past the stunning line of his collar bone and wide shoulders. Manly definition caused her to stare in a way that, otherwise, might be considered rude. She forged a path on Sebastian's body, examining... plodding... memorizing. His throat was rough—a mat of stubble that would, in another day, be a beard. The shape of his jawline was exquisite, a mix of steel and sweet invitation, a divot in his chin that softened him ever so slightly.

Finally, he reached. Not for her, but for the buttons on her blouse. As her fingertips passed over his lips, Evie slid her gaze downward. She watched the cotton fabric fall open as each button obeyed his command. She glanced farther, seeing the obvious tent of his cotton pants. She said nothing as their serious expressions tangled like briar branches. It was the only thorny warning her brain allowed. Evie absorbed what had to be Sebastian's practiced movements— *With who? Where? How many times?* She pushed it away. She didn't want to know. It only mattered that he was there with her now.

Sebastian unzipped her skirt. The garment dropped to the floor like a curtain's reveal. She slipped out of her shoes and stepped beyond the circle surrounding her. His strong hands led Evie away, drawing her toward him. The small room grew even tighter, and a moment later they stood poised at the edge of the bed. The fire crackled, the pop and hiss making Evie twist toward it.

"Look at me."

She did, dousing brimstone and other outcomes. Sebastian's lips pressed into hers, his hands running over the braid of blonde hair. She watched as he slipped the elastic off the end, untwining the plaited hair as deftly as he'd undone the blouse. Evie felt her long tresses set free, shuffling around her shoulders, Sebastian moving his fingers through it. "That's better," he said, the heat of his mouth grazing her ear. She longed for his mouth, his kisses more infectious than she recalled, urgent as fire, calming as needed warmth. Movements became more aggressive. He abandoned Evie's hair and drew her slip over her head. She let him. She'd never wanted anything so much.

With only the rapid beat of her heart in between them, Evie felt the clasp of her bra unhook. The action was as adept as his other skills. There was no hint of awkwardness as she slipped off the bra. Evie was absorbed in Sebastian's lingering gaze, feeling his hands move like a dance down her near-naked body. His touch to full breasts and hard nipples made her pulse race, every inch of Evie wanting more.

It was Evie's own desire that erased the last bit of distance. She guessed he knew better than to wait for a verbal cue. He laid them on the bed where Evie sunk into deep feathery softness. His body was a stark contrast—incredibly solid, easily overpowering if he wanted it to be. Yet she found trust to be present, whirling among the emotions he brought to the bed. The ropey muscles of his arms were a sensuous pleasure, and she dug her fingertips in as his hand reached between her legs. She gasped as he dismissed fabric, making contact—not with the place Ezra had sought out, not exactly, but higher. Evie's breath quickened to the point of fright.

He stopped—all that power withdrawing. "Wait." Sebastian's stare turned to a mix of concern and confusion. "I thought you said... Evie, tell me right now if it was just a story... if you've never..."

The dreamy daze ebbed. She crinkled her brow. "I wasn't lying. We... Ezra," she said, ignoring the shame that the sound of his name produced. "We've had sex." Sebastian nodded, wise enough not to pursue details. But his hand didn't return to where it had been, and Evie wrenched at its sudden absence.

"Don't... please don't stop." Boldness was, on occasion, to Evie's benefit. And perhaps to prove her claim, she reached, undoing the button on Sebastian's pants, then the zipper. She gripped her hand around the part of him that sprang forward. Her fingers danced over a sculpted velvety shaft—hard as stone. Every part of him was built so differently than Ezra—this too. Evie glanced fast. She said nothing, though he surely caught her startled look.

"Not, um...Not what you were expecting?" he said, kissing her again.

She smiled, shyness intervening. "I, uh..." She only shook her head. Thankfully, he didn't ask for an explanation, closing his eyes as he pushed his hardness into the palm of her hand.

"You keep looking like that," Sebastian said, kissing her harder, "tasting like that, touching me like..." He stopped talking, all his faculties clearly diverted. Evie let go, aware of the potential explosion of passion. It scared her—everything about Sebastian did a little, an awakening of all the things Evie wondered about.

But as she drew her hand away, connecting with a chest, hard as his maleness, Evie understood that what was about to happen had as much to do with her as it did him. Ideas connected. Sebastian skimmed off her underwear, all of him advancing with greater access. But again, the way he touched her—so intimately—it made Evie gasp—unsure of the moment, the pattern. Whatever feeling loomed, it was never a part of any encounter with Ezra.

"Evie, what's the matter?" he said, hand pushing her thigh open wider to him. He touched her again, making Evie aware of a pronounced wetness, like the first time—although that had been blood. It was enough to make her glance down—panicked. She saw nothing but herself, his fingertips, and a satisfactory smile on his face. "You can't tell me you don't want this."

She didn't answer, as the question didn't fit. In her experience, *wanting this* didn't seem to have much to do with her—other than as a necessary participant. This felt so different. Yes, she wanted Sebastian to kiss her. Yes, she wanted his touch. God help her, she'd go as far as to say she needed it. *But the act itself...* Clearly, Evie was missing something.

His smile abated. But Sebastian moved on, speaking with his body, his fingers tracing nipples that responded to his steady touch. His mouth took over the journey, Evie finding her fingers tangled in thick waves of inky hair. She forced her legs to relax as Sebastian nudged them apart. This time a finger slid inside her. It was closer to what she'd been anticipating, though what she might have called an intrusion now seemed inviting. As he pushed deeper into her, a second time, his thumb rose, making intimate contact. It was startling and unclear. She shoved his hand away.

Sebastian stared into her eyes, as if trying to read her mind.

Evie cleared her throat. "I... you can just, um... do it."

"Do what, exactly?"

Unable to muster the words, Evie captured an erection that hadn't eased. Sebastian succumbed to the message, swallowing hard and closing his eyes. As they fluttered open, she could see him struggling to focus.

"But don't you want..." Sebastian's drew a breath she could feel. His green eyes widened. "Holy shit. You've never..." He bowed his head, shaking it. "It figures."

Evie rose up to her elbows. For everything that drew her to Sebastian, the swearing did not. He held up a hand. "Wait. Just, um... just trust me here." He smiled. It was a grin that made her trepidation puddle. "Let me, um... show you something. Take you somewhere... else..." He kissed her deeply, Evie sinking back onto the pillow. "Don't think," he said in between the kisses. "I promise. It'll be all right."

Heeding the advice, Evie indulged in the feathery lightness of touches that grew more direct. His mouth cascaded down the side of her throat, across her breasts, coaxing the storm that brewed inside her. His fingertips trickled across the flat of her belly and Evie kissed him hungrily, holding Sebastian close. She felt yet another level of safety as his chest met with hers. Evie did as he asked, trusting him.

Preciseness drove his touch as he whispered odd words in her ear—something about going or coming. But it was drowned out by a giant wave as Evie was swept into a feeling she couldn't have fathomed. A sound emanated from her throat, a lusty gasp of pleasure. She dug her fingers harder into the muscles of his back. She wanted to claim all of him—she wholly desired the part she'd otherwise tolerated. Timing was also among Sebastian's honed skills and he kissed Evie precisely, perfectly, as the wave passed— *"a heavenly place"* was all she could think.

Evie's body trembled as she tried to right her mind. There was no clear thinking to be found—just the prospect of feeling him inside her. But Sebastian didn't seem to be in a rush, instead cupping her face, offering the most beautiful kiss—the kind that made Evie think of fairytales and endings that were really beginnings. "There," he said, looking triumphant. "Just so we're clear, that's the way it's supposed to work."

Inhibition intruded. Evie glanced away. But she was quickly drawn back, wanting to memorize every feature of his face. His existence seemed impossible—yet there he was, looming over her life, changing everything she knew. "And the rest..." she said, breathlessly. She tugged at his pants. Sebastian stood, shucking them aside. She was on her elbows again—his nakedness matching hers. He was incredible. It was all Evie could think as she looked up, Sebastian looking down over her. His body was beaten and chiseled, commanding and desirable. Evie sat upright, having dismissed ideas about getting it over with... only wondering how they might stay this way forever.

He reached, not to her, but inside Evie's head. "What... what are you thinking?"

She knew of no way to verbalize feelings he evoked—something physical, but not. Something intangible that grew stronger by the second. The urge riding her, it didn't feel unnatural, but it was uncommon. The flat of Sebastian's stomach was even with her face—more scars, some clearly newer. She kissed them, feeling his breath quicken, startled by the tender contact. His unlikely trepidation gave her confidence and small kisses floated from his battered ribcage downward. A scent of maleness grew stronger as the shape of his body led her from a perfect vee, beyond muscular flanks, to the center of him. Evie moved her mouth and hands in a graceful motion, dropping—without thinking—onto her knees.

"Evie... Jes—" He stopped, a guttural hum pleading out instead.

She glanced up to see one arm brace against the nearby wall as his other gently guided her head.

What happened next, Evie did not know what to call it, but it clearly pleased Sebastian as the kissing advanced and much of his erection disappeared into her mouth. The coaxing movement of his hand wasn't forceful but encouraging. His hardness grew stiffer, the salty hint of liquid hitting her tongue. She didn't want to stop, even as he lost a bit of control—his words and grip growing more potent.

"Christ, Evie, if you keep... I..." The strain of his voice caused her to pause. She looked up into his face as his hand tenderly touched her face. "In the bed," he said, jerking his gaze between it and her. "I... I want to make love to you in the bed. Not this way... not this time."

She smiled. But as Evie began to rise, embracing the lovely thought, the moment snapped like a whip. The cabin door flew open. The small room was enough that Sebastian's bare bottom—Evie on her knees—were visible from the entrance. Brother Creek's voice penetrated through. "Oh dear God help us..."

CHAPTER THIRTEEN

As the first seconds passed all Sebastian thought was how this was worse than any beating he'd suffered. Evie scrambled backward, hiding from the wide open view. He stood naked, a full frontal, as Brother Creek looked on. From his stunned stance, Brother Creek seemed frozen or maybe overly focused. Steadily, Sebastian said, "You want to give us a minute?"

It had to be pure shock as Brother Creek complied, going outside the cabin.

A minute? Sebastian scrubbed a hand over his face. He needed a fucking few years. Evie was a mess, trembling so hard she couldn't get her clothes on. She wasn't crying—at least not outwardly—it read more like terror, almost hyperventilating. Sebastian yanked on his pants. In the meantime, she'd managed everything but the blouse. "Here, let me..." He picked the white cotton garment up from the floor and she snatched it away.

"Don't touch me!"

"Evie," he said softly. She struggled with the blouse, like a cat in a sack, turning it right side out, unable to steady her aim long enough to get an arm into it. "Evie, stop." She did, her flushed face looking desperately into his. "That was bad. I get it—really bad." Her lips looked even poutier than usual, and Sebastian had to force himself to stay on track. Shame on him—he was still distracted by the idea of kissing her. "But maybe... maybe in some crazy way it's better that it happened."

"Are you mad?" she said, the first tears spilling over the rims of her eyes.

"No, but after the shock wears off it might be a wakeup call. Whatever's happening here," he said, shifting his arm between the two of them, "it should tell you that marrying—"

"You *are* mad," she decided, resuming her fight with the blouse. "Hannah, she was right. You are a devil. Brother Creek, walking in like he did, if that wasn't a sign—"

"Listen to me." He grabbed the blouse, demanding her attention. "It wasn't a sign. It was horrible timing—this crazy, unreal world you live in. Don't let them do this to you—don't let their rules decide what you want."

She huffed even harder, shaking her head.

"Evie, was there anything going on here, before my keeper showed up, that wasn't your own free will? What was about to happen, what I said... Did that feel like evil?"

She blinked blankly at him.

"If that's true, if it's what you think—in your own head—I'll tell Brother Creek I forced myself on you. I swear, Evie, you won't be to blame."

Sebastian swallowed hard at the out he'd given her. Beatings, public humiliation, his hard-ass life, he could survive any of it. The idea that he would force himself on her—it made him feel worse than the seedy life he'd led. A breath, more fraught than the last, trembled out of her. She moved a trembling hand over her throat and gathered her thick hair, hauling it over one shoulder. She was searching for a comfort zone, the familiar braid that should be there, not the out of control cascade of hair.

"But it was so..." she said. "How will I ever..."

Sebastian took a chance and pulled her to him. Evie didn't resist. She held on tightly, skin to skin. Sebastian felt pure terror pulsing off her. An equally nervous breath shuddered out of him, but for an entirely different reason. Whatever was rolling through him, because of her, he'd never felt that for another human being. "I know," he said, kissing the top of her head. "What just happened, I'm sure we scored a new high for Good Hope's top-ten commandments not to break."

In between the tremors, Evie dug her fingers in tight as if searching for solid ground.

"We'll figure it out. We'll explain—"

"Explain how?" she said in a pitchy whisper. But as Evie spoke her arms moved tighter around him. "You're going to provide a reasonable explanation as to why I was naked, with *the mission*, the day before I'm to marry the Reverend's son?" She inched back, her face streaked with tears. She had a point. "How will you ever make this right?" Evie cupped her hand over her mouth. "Oh, dear Lord, Brother Creek, he's probably already gone to tell the Reverend or Ezra." She started for the door.

"Evie, wait!" He rushed past her, peering out the window. "No. He's there, just pacing. Maybe the shock made him forget how to get to the main street." Sebastian turned, looking at Evie, who stood beside the fireplace. The flickering light washed her in an innocent glow, and Sebastian was nearly crushed by a wave of guilt.

If his sorry ass hadn't landed in their world, Evie would marry Ezra Kane tomorrow, convinced she was happy and fulfilled in this strange life. Sebastian approached, not saying anything. Instead he mechanically helped her into the blouse. She let him. He tried to read her mind, but his own was too overwrought. What was the best way out of this? Evie had watched as he unbuttoned the blouse. She watched now as he re-buttoned it. Sebastian forced calm, going steadily at the task. But confidence didn't help. It was no good as her tears splashed onto his hand. "I promise you, Evie. I will make this right."

"Short of rendering Brother Creek mute, I don't see how."

Their gazes met and a rush of anger coursed through Sebastian. No one should have this kind of power over her. Glassy tears reflected the firelight, reflecting him.

"You don't understand," she said. "Where you come from, maybe this would be *horrible timing*. Here it's... It's beyond unthinkable— What I was doing, me on my knees... I don't expect I'd do such a thing with Ezra."

And Sebastian had to bite down on the inside of his cheek. *All right, so that was another first for her...* But it also forced him to pay attention to the rules of this stunted way of life: conduct, virtue, and the very thoughts in your head. All of it was subject to judgment, making what happened tantamount to treason. He furrowed his brow. *And that wouldn't be exclusive to getting caught naked with the opposite sex...* Sebastian glanced over his shoulder. "Evie, listen to me. Right now, no one knows but Brother Creek. Maybe we can keep it that way."

"Oh, Sebastian, you don't know him. He clings to the Reverend, looks for his approval at every turn. Why do you think he's been your main companion? The Reverend knows he'd report the slightest misbehavior. I'd expect the only thing stopping Brother Creek is how to describe what he saw." Her face reddened and she pressed her palms to her cheeks as if trying to contain her own actions.

"Maybe," he said. "Or maybe we can catch him off guard too."

"What are you talking about?"

"Wait here." He squeezed her shoulders. "And try not to panic."

"What are you going to do?"

Sebastian plucked his undershirt from the end of the bed and pulled it on. "I'm going to have a man-to-man talk with Brother Creek."

"And say what?"

"I'll explain later. Just... just trust me. Can you do that?" She hesitated then nodded. She was counting on him. The responsibility felt greater than any he'd ever assumed—for Bim, for refugees, for his father or the Godfathers of the Night. Sebastian couldn't stop himself from kissing her. It surprised him when she didn't pull away, instead sinking into the kiss. It was a warm, snotty mix, Sebastian pausing to brush tears from Evie's face.

He almost said the hell with it. Why not pack their things and leave Good Hope together? But as the kisses wound down, looking into her fearful expression, Sebastian counted the reasons that couldn't happen. It was too much too fast, demanding Evie Neal trade an entire life—everything she knew—for a man she'd known a week. And not just any man, but one whose life had a price on it. In all the new turmoil he'd nearly lost sight of the old. Right now she was in trouble—he wouldn't put her in danger. Sebastian aimed for a confident smile. "Hey, do you happen to have a handy verse about truth?"

"What?" she said, looking queerly at him. "Why?"

⸺•◦••◦•⸺

The first moments alone with Brother Creek mimicked their time together—waves of tentative silence. Sebastian felt it from the second he'd arrived—men who'd wanted to ask questions but found themselves bound to obedience and order, their righteous lives. Right now, Sebastian was betting everything on that mindset. "Why, um... why don't we jump to the end game, Brother Creek? What do you plan on doing about what you walked in on? Because while I couldn't give a rat's ass what you say about me, Evie Neal is, sadly, at your mercy."

"As she should be," he said anxiously. Nolan Creek's fair skin was white as milk and he continued to blot his face with a handkerchief. He held his glasses in the opposite hand, using them in pointed confrontation. "Perhaps Evie Neal should have considered that before she *sunk* to such perverse behavior."

"Perhaps you should consider knocking next time."

"Humor? You're going to try and make that disgusting spectacle humorous. Why am I even talking to you? We'll let Reverend Kane deal with this. I've observed enough when it comes to you." He turned, heading down the path that would take him to the center of Good Hope. "I assure you, *Mission*," he said over his shoulder, "it's not difficult to envision you indulging in such shocking behavior."

"Interesting point," Sebastian yelled. "Exactly how many times have you envisioned it?"

Brother Creek took a few more steps and hesitated. He turned. "I don't know what you mean. I've done nothing but what's been asked of me."

"Maybe. But while you've been *watching* me, I've noticed plenty about you—works both ways, *Brother...*"

"If you've words to say, *Mission*, speak in something other than innuendo."

"Look, it's nothing to me, and I'm sure you have your reasons for living like you do—maybe a solid wall is better than temptation. Your choice. I get it. Even in 1977—never mind this backward place— that's a tough hand. It wouldn't fly in my neighborhood, that's for damn sure." Brother Creek drew closer, paying scrupulous attention to Sebastian. "But here's the thing. While the Fathers of the Right wonder blindly why you don't marry the Widow Vale, I have a pretty good clue. So does Evie."

He folded his arms, a snicker sputtering out of him. But he didn't dismiss Sebastian. He didn't move.

It strengthened Sebastian's hunch. "'*Then you will know the truth, and the truth will set you free.*' Isn't that how it works?" he said, quoting the scripture Evie had supplied. "You're so keen on truth, Brother Creek, go ahead... Go paint a full color picture for the Reverend. But if you do, I'll do some enlightening of my own. I saw you. It wasn't Evie's state of undress that had your eye—it was mine."

He gasped as if Sebastian had spat fire, snarled flames. "I don't know what kind wicked lies you'd be willing to tell to save that wretched girl, but—"

"Would they be lies, Brother Creek?" Sebastian shrugged, moving closer. "I think that's the bottom line here. They may be labeled lies. You're right. It's not likely that the word of *the mission* and girl who they'll call a whore will be taken seriously. But if I've figured it out and Evie's done the same... Well, there has to be doubt among the others. Do you want us to fuel it? Out you onto the streets of Good Hope?"

"Are you implying..."

"I'm not implying anything. You're not into the Widow Vale because that's not the way you're wired. It's your business—unless you do something to make it mine. Think about it. What you saw in there, it'd only be one more secret you have to keep."

Brother Creek continued to blot his moist face. While not overly proud of his scheme, Sebastian couldn't think of another way. Judgment, it seemed, would not come in a yes or no as both men were alerted to Reverend Kane's voice. He and another man came around the curve of the path. Bolting crossed Sebastian's mind. His cagey glance moved to the cabin door. *Not without her...* Sebastian breathed deep, using his considerable height and frame to stand his ground, maybe to shield her.

"Brother Creek, what is *the mission* doing outside?"

There was a pin-drop silence, only the caw of a crow piercing from above. Sebastian stepped forward. The option of knocking his keeper unconscious wasn't lost on him. It would be a delay.

"Reverend," Nolan Creek said, fiddling with his glasses, nearly poking himself in the eye as he tried to put them on. "Brother Neal. I'm surprised to see you here."

And bad fell to worse as Sebastian realized the other man was Evie's father. He blended into the Fathers of the Right like all men. Brother Neal looked complacent and dutiful, dully dressed. But Sebastian also had to admit he saw slivers of Evie. He shoved his hands in his pockets, burdened by emotion—dislike for a man who so blindly followed the Reverend and compassion for Evie. She was probably peeking through a window, doubly mortified by the sight of her father. The walls were thin enough that she could hear the conversation.

The Reverend's gaze never left Sebastian. "Gideon and I, we were speaking about moving Evie's things to a cottage behind my house. It's where she and Ezra will live—nearby."

"We'll miss her, Evie's brothers and I," Gideon said. "But that's the beauty of our community. She'll never be more than a few houses away."

"Mmm, true," said the Reverend. "Our houses will be one as Evie becomes part of mine."

Sebastian knotted his brow, the statement disturbing and possessive. Reverend Kane zeroed in on Nolan Creek. "My reason for coming here was to put you in charge of moving Evie's things. Since your aversion to marriage is so clear," he said, "see to the matter during the ceremony." Sebastian drew a hopeful breath— the in-passing remark might read like an omen.

Brother Creek didn't respond, and Sebastian watched his keeper's mental tug-o-war.

The Reverend continued. "But it seems a more pressing matter is at hand. Brother Creek, you haven't answered me. Why are you defying my order? What is *the mission* doing outside?"

"Reverend Kane, you should know..." Sebastian's hopeful breath deflated, prepared to pounce. "I have to tell you..."

"Go on," he said, striding closer.

"The reason *the mission* is outside... It's because I found..."

Every muscle in Sebastian tensed. *Fuck it... Just take him out, better those consequences than...*

"I defied your order, Reverend, because when I arrived, I realized *the mission's* quarters bordered on filth. It hasn't been properly cleaned since he came to be with us. I knew you were busy with Ezra and Evie's wedding plans. I took it upon myself to ask a couple of the women to come by and clean."

"Did you?" the Reverend said.

"Forgive me, I did. But I also knew you wouldn't want women in his presence, so I brought him out here."

Evie was quick to back up the explanation. A broom batted against the cabin window, ruffling the curtain. "I see," the Reverend said, his stare evaluating. "Next time, consult me first, but it seems *the mission* won't be with us much longer—not in Good Hope." The news piqued Sebastian's attention. "I'll send Brother Wheaton to take over. When he arrives, come to the meeting hall. I need to speak with you about *the mission's* future."

"And *the mission* doesn't get a seat in that discussion," Sebastian said.

"When I'm ready. Until then, reflect on the cleanliness of your surroundings."

Sebastian didn't pursue more questions—not in that moment. He just wanted them gone. That much went his way. The Reverend and Gideon Neal did an about face and retreated toward the center of Good Hope. Sebastian and Brother Creek were left standing in the shadow of a giant elm, the fall sun a fireball. Sebastian squinted and glanced sideways. "Thank you."

Nolan Creek turned. "For allowing you to blackmail me?"

"Right. Sorry. But I couldn't let you do that to Evie. As much as you don't want these people to be your judge and jury, I won't let them be hers. Can you understand that much?"

He offered a timid nod. "I understand what it is to feel things that God and the world would consider a heinous sin. To be banished to Hell for giving into wicked desires."

Sebastian glanced again, wanting to say, *"Sorry you have to look at your life that way..."* But right now Evie was his sole focus. "Will you let me talk to her—alone?"

Nolan Creek folded his arms and stared into a waning sun. He nodded again. "I'll give you five minutes. Not a moment longer."

Sebastian didn't waste a second, darting back inside. Evie stood by the fire, the broom in one hand, bracing her other arm against the mantel. "Are you all right?"

Her harried gaze cut to his. "Evie…"

He came across the room and took the broom from her grip, tossing it aside. She fell into Sebastian's embrace. "It's okay. He didn't give anything away."

"How?" she said.

"Brother Creek has his own secrets—he'd like to keep it that way." She nodded slightly, gazing past his shoulder. She was still shaken, but there was no time to ease her past it. "Evie, listen," Sebastian said. "Time is not on our side. I…" Holding onto her shoulders, he gave her a gentle shake. "Evie." Her doe-eyed stare traveled back to his. "Tell me you'll call off this ridiculous wedding. Tell me— whatever this impossible thing is between us—that it's enough to stop you from marrying Ezra. For me… But mostly for you."

"I…I wouldn't know where to begin." She blinked, finally engaged in the moment. "How could I do such a thing? I'm not talking about the Fathers of the Right, or blindly doing what they say. But how can I do that to Ezra?" She broke from Sebastian's hold, dragging herself a few feet away. "He's been nothing but kind and caring for…" She turned. "For forever. I'll be the first to admit Ezra deserves better than me, but I don't know that it's kinder to break his heart."

"Evie, trust me. Break his heart." The look on her face said the remark was as callous as it had sounded. "Not exactly how I meant that to come out." He glanced toward the door, picturing Nolan Creek counting off the minutes. "Answer the question, Evie. The one you've been avoiding since I asked it at your house. Do you love him?"

Her answer surprised him. "I don't *not* love Ezra."

He didn't say anything but turned toward the fireplace, pressing his hands into the mantel. For a second Sebastian thought about putting his fist through it. He felt like a fool. Whatever feelings had rolled in, wild and unexpected, it wasn't any more than that. Not for her. Sebastian was no more than a glimpse at a world she'd forever disavow. But a moment later, her hand touched his back—feathery light. While the fire danced in front of him, it didn't compare to the warmth she generated. Her touch widened as Evie's hand became her whole body, clinging to him, her arms claiming his chest. Sebastian covered her hand with his, squeezing, all of him bracing for good-bye.

Her thoughts sounded whispery but sure. "What I feel for Ezra, it shouldn't be questioned. It's the way a bride should feel on the eve of her wedding because what I feel for him is real and comfortable and warm. It's like a placid pond with a lovely view." He bowed his head deeper and dropped his hand from hers. "It's true. Ezra and I, we should go on from here and live an equally lovely life. It's what I've believed since I was old enough to be taught things. And it would happen just that way if..." she said, her embrace tightening, "if I hadn't lived the past week. But I have, Bash."

He straightened his spine, turning. He had to touch her, fingertips fluttering over her cheek. Evie cupped her hand over his. "As much as honor and good sense tell me to reject you, I can't. I don't know how something grows so strong in only days. Not compared to something that's been nurtured and planned for years. But what I feel for Ezra...it's *nothing* like what I feel for you." She pulled in a tremulous breath. "So when I leave here... Yes. It will be to tell Ezra that I can't marry him."

CHAPTER FOURTEEN

Present Day

Alec and Julian drove for more than an hour. The buildings of Bogota faded, the scenery growing rural and rough. Modern buildings gave way to shacks, poverty overtaking the cityscape. Before the setting changed completely, Julian pulled the SUV up to a duplex. It was the nicest building they'd seen for miles. "My last property in Libano. I use one of the units myself from time to time. Final stop before heading onto Jess's last point of contact."

"So a bathroom break?" Alec said.

"Something like that."

Walking through a swirl of dust, the two men made their way to an end unit. An iron gate guarded the door, and Julian turned four separate locks. Alec's instinct said it was a tossup—indicative of the crime rate or what Julian kept inside? He glanced around: two teenage boys idled about twenty feet away—neither looked friendly. A heavy-set woman hurried along dragging two toddlers and a grocery cart behind her. The air was thick with heat, poverty, and the smell of desperation. Inside the duplex the temperature dropped twenty degrees. Alec thought of Jess and his parents—it was a bad spot on the globe to get stuck without water or protection from the elements.

"I'm going to change. Do the same if you want," Julian said, his glance sliding over Alec. "I'll be ready shortly." He disappeared into a bedroom and shut the door.

Alec plucked at the sticky neck of his T-shirt. He'd nearly forgotten the screwdriver thrown at him that morning. He scraped a hand across his jaw. Shave. He wanted to shave. Before heading into the bathroom, Alec helped himself to Julian's refrigerator and bottled water. He multitasked, getting out his cell, drinking water, and unzipping the duffel bag, searching for jungle-wear, he supposed. The cell signal wasn't great, but the phone connected. "I'm here."

"And where is here?" Aaron said on the other end.

Alec moved toward the blinds, peeking through slats and barred windows. The boys had moved on from their post as sultry heat lingered in their place. "Far as I can tell, about a hundred miles outside anywhere you'd wanna be. We're heading toward the coastal area where Jess was, but there's some nasty terrain between it and us."

"Okay start with the 'we' and 'us.' You mean Jess's ex, you're with him."

"Yeah. Julian. Can't really give you the 411—"

"Because he's in earshot or because you're not sure."

"Both. How are things there?"

"Cool... Fine," Aaron said. "Listen, Alec, I spoke with Jack Preacher. He said he can clear me to come down there. Tossing my parole is just paperwork at this point. What do you say?"

"I'd say good luck finding me in this fucking hole. Stay put for now, Aar. Let's not do that to Ruby—not this second anyway."

"I hear you. And no matter what she says, I know she appreciates that."

"So the honeymoon continues, I take it."

"A honeymoon less a marriage—sure. But one thing at a time. You know?"

"Not really. Never aspired to your *fate*."

"Yeah, I get it. More like Pop. Not the marrying kind, even after five kids."

Alec didn't say anything right away.

"You still there?"

"I'm here. Aar, why do we think it was Pop who never wanted a trip to the altar? Do we know that or is it some lame ass, Neanderthal assumption? I mean, we know Pop's work kept him away. Mom had to be more grounded—what the hell, she had us kids 24/7," Alec said. "Their non-marriage wasn't a secret, but they were vague about a reason."

"I remember it as more of an excuse, the effect of 70's communes and free-spirited living."

"Yeah. But if you lay it out, nobody was more committed to Mom than Sebastian Clairmont." Alec glanced out the window again. "Most of the time..."

"What do you mean 'most of the time'...?"

Alec hadn't even realized he'd said that part out loud. "There were gaps. One time, Pop was gone for longer than usual. I was what... five, maybe six? It was before Honor and Jake came along."

Silence crackled through the line. "Well, then we know Pop had to be home at some point," Aaron said, laughing.

"Copy that. But as Julian and I were driving, I was thinking about a conversation I had with Pop years and years ago. I was getting ready to go on my first tour abroad, and he opened up a little about traveling, about different places. Eventually, he talked about where Mom was from... somewhere in Pennsylvania."

"Sounds right. I mean, we know her mother died years ago. All she ever said about her father was that she didn't have a relationship with him. But we don't know much else, do we?" Another pause snaked through the line. "Geez, now that you say it... did we go there once as kids?"

"Yeah. We did. It was a cabin," Alec said. "But I wasn't sure if it was in Pennsylvania, or the place Mom was from—or if they were the same thing. Not until you just said that." Alec's gaze moved around the condo living room. He closed his eyes. "I remember a trip—it was just Mom and us. She had a friend there. Damn. What was her name? Helen... Harriet..." Alec dragged his hand through his hair. "Shit, Aaron, you know I don't do names."

"Particularly the 'H' ones." It was a snarky reminder of *Hazel*, the last woman to roll out of Alec's bed, and the name he could not recall. "Hannah," Aaron said. "I think it was Hannah. Mom used to talk to her on the phone."

"That's right. Hannah. And that cabin in Pennsylvania, it was cold as shit." Alec remembered that part more clearly—mostly because the only time he'd been colder was bobbing in the Pacific during BUD/S training, treading water for six solid hours. But in the same mental frame where he saw the cabin and stone fireplace, he also saw the image of a tall, craggy-faced man. "Aaron, do you remember a nasty son of a bitch. Some kind of clergyman..."

"No idea. If you're vague on it... my memory is even vaguer. But what does any of that have to do with a plane crash that happened years later on a different continent."

"Nothing... yet. But if you're trying to put together a puzzle, every piece helps." Alec turned toward the bedroom door, which was still closed. "Do something for me. See if Jack Preacher will give you an assist. Find out if he can trace the closest cell tower to Jess's last call. I'd like to know where it was made from."

"You got it. And Alec..."

"Yeah?"

"Be careful."

"Always my first rule, bro."

Alec wasn't keen on having to depend on Julian for information, direction, or his personal safety. He had no firearm—airline regulations making that an absolute certainty. It was also a fact about which Julian had to be aware. Jess's almost ex emerged from the bedroom. Both men had changed, though Alec didn't have time for the shave he'd wanted. Julian had traded his sleek city image for jungle-ready, a bandana knotted at his throat, hiking boots, and a holster at his waist. Alec wasn't surprised when he opened a safe, tucking a Glock 20 into it. A gun like that was no casual weapon. "Just a precaution," Julian said. "Can't be too careful where we're headed." At the condo exit, Julian grabbed a wide brimmed hat with a bandana tied around the bond. "Sun's a bitch." He tossed the hat to Alec.

"Thanks..." *But I'd rather have one of the other guns you've surely got locked in that safe...*

The village road narrowed and poverty opened up wide. Jungle didn't give a fuck about socioeconomic status—neither did desert. Alec knew Middle East countries, this part of the world, not so much. But he understood the lure. Desperation bred like flies. People wanted out of places like this, making the prospect of covertly relocating bodies—human trafficking—big business. He suspected it might have something to do with the local stories and the plane crash Jess had gone to investigate.

In the heyday of his military service, Alec had participated in drills off the Caribbean coast. It was the ocean opposite of where they were now. A real-life emergency had thrown Alec and his SEAL team into action, rescuing a US cargo ship taken hostage by Haitian pirates. Considering the potential for blood and bad karma in this place, Alec guessed his experience might come in handy. Otherwise, he'd be at Julian's mercy. It was the last place Alec Clairmont wanted to be.

The SUV navigated ropey mountainous terrain, jungle paths that would make most people lose their lunch. It made Alec glad for a seaworthy mindset he could call upon at will. As they drove, Alec envisioned Jess navigating the rough landscape with a guide—a man she'd only met that day. And who knew what lay ahead, topography or local terrorists? Hanging onto the SUV's handrail—an amenity more likely meant for accommodating dry cleaning—Alec tightened his grip. He reassured himself. Jess could take care of herself. She was the most no-nonsense, solid woman he knew. If not for the unlikely personal insights—Haagen-Dazs, Absolute, and late night crying jags courtesy of his driver—Alec would swear that Jess's vulnerabilities were nil. He pasted a sideways glance on Julian.

Of course, he did know about those things.

"Up ahead... La Carta," Julian said. "It would have been where Jess and her guide rented the boat that took them out to the island."

The mountainy jungle had been a tunnel and they exited on the other side, rolling into a searing sun and blue skies. It felt like humid resort weather, less the obvious lack of amenities. The road was a mix of broken asphalt and rock, the landscape dotted with native housing—shacks, a fishing village from what Alec could ascertain at a glance. They passed a few rickety storefronts. No cell towers were visible. He checked his phone—no service. Then he checked his text messages. There was one from Aaron.

Preacher confirms-Jess's last call to you made from western Libano

Processing the intel, Alec looked cagily at Julian. Jess had called from his duplex. His gut hadn't been off—Julian Silva wasn't sharing everything he knew. He dragged a suspicious gaze over his escort and onto the town's dilapidated thoroughfare. Running water and reliable societal rules seemed iffy—swarms of dirty, barely clothed children wandered about and dusty sidewalks were filled with people who looked as if life had wrinkled them. For as capable as

Jess was, Alec didn't like the odds on possibilities and outcomes in this place.

"Let's walk down to the waterfront, see if we can figure out where they rented a boat," Julian said, parking the SUV.

The two got out and Alec followed, taking off the wide-brimmed hat and wiping his sweaty brow. He let it hang by the strings, down his back. He wasn't surprised when street urchins flocked like seabirds, asking for spare change, offering child labor in trade. The same occurred in all impoverished countries he'd traveled. Alec shooed them away. It would incite a riot if he so much as tossed a quarter into the road. What he found more disturbing was the faces of the adults—particularly the older men and women. They gawked, mouths gaping, as if they'd never seen a white guy from the States. Rumblings of native language grew louder. Alec couldn't make it out—a dialect he didn't know.

"You seem fucking popular," Julian said, striding in front of him.

"Yeah, I get that impression." The locals were definitely pointing, and not at Julian but at him. The villagers that lined the shack-like storefronts followed along. None approached, though clearly curiosity drove them.

Julian turned. "You sure you've never been here before?"

"Positive." But as Alec scanned the growing crowd, he caught a glimpse of himself in the side-view mirror of a parked van. *No... not me...* Just as a connection clicked, an elderly woman lunged toward him. She grabbed onto Alec like he was a long-lost son.

"*Eres tu!*" she cried over and over again. "*Pensamos que habías muerto.*" A man that belonged to her, or she to him, pulled her away from Alec. Watching them recede, Alec read shock and awe on their faces. From around his neck, the older man drew a crucifix to his lips and kissed it.

Julian turned, poking Alec hard in the shoulder. "Don't fuck with me. What's with the Christ-like reaction? These people know you."

"I think they're confused," Alec said tentatively. "Not me. My father. I..." He glanced once more in the side-view mirror. "I look like him. *Eres tu...* That translates to 'It's you,' doesn't it?"

"Yeah," Julian said. "It does."

"And the rest of what they said?"

Julian hesitated. "It means *'We thought you were dead.'*"

It was tough for Alec to feel things. He knew this about himself. Years in the military—shit he'd rather forget—a personal history that didn't read much better. Cutting off emotion had allowed him to deal, to survive where others failed—alcohol, PTSD, deep wells of anger usually channeled onto the wrong place or person. He'd fought, hanging onto mental toughness that rivaled his SEAL experiences. Alec had refused to succumb to deadly emotions. In exchange, it had made *this* his life—a detached state of being that meant he could function.

But now, facing an entire village that mistook him for the father he'd dearly loved and lost, seeing their Lazarus reaction, it caused Alec to draw a shaky breath. It was a place even his tough mind was unprepared to go. The inside of his mouth felt like one of the many deserts he'd crossed, his ears filtering the odd dialect. He still didn't understand it, but he could make out one word they repeated. *"Sebastian..."* Alec's gut clenched and his heart pounded—two things strictly forbidden from his life.

"If nothing else," Julian said, "I'd say you have confirmation about the plane. Clearly your father had an association with these people. From the reaction, I'd say it was god-like. Be glad it's not the other way around." In his frozen stance, Alec felt like a statue erected in Sebastian Clairmont's honor. Slowly he turned, taking in awestruck faces, tears, and pointing fingers. He tried to muster a mouthful of spit. There was nothing. *God-like. In this forsaken place? What the hell does it have to do with my father?*

"I...I need to know more. We need to talk to them," Alec said. "There's got to be information, about my parents... about Jess."

But on the mention of her name, Alec's ears retuned. Beyond the immediate chaos he heard a woman with an American accent shouting—first in Spanish, worse than his, then curse words in plain English. Both men stepped in the direction of the yelling.

"You listen to me, you sorry motherfucker!" she shouted. "You can't keep me here. I'm an American citizen. And you can bet your sorry Colombian hide, when I do get out of here, the State Department will hang you by your misguided, native balls, you stupid—"

"Jess," both men said at once, ploughing past the onlookers and into a building marked *Carcel*.

Inside a jail that looked as if it'd been dropped from an old West movie set there was a single holding cell. Inside the cell was Jess. She looked sweaty, and dirty, and pissed off, but she appeared to be in one piece.

"Oh thank God!" she said as Alec and Julian came through the door.

As both men rushed toward the cell, a deputy with a semi-automatic weapon stepped into their path. Two sets of hands went up. From there Julian shimmied left where he dove into a heated conversation with another officer. This man wore the shiniest badge, epaulets on his shoulders, telling Alec he was in charge. "Are you all right?" Alec yelled.

The guard turned, snapping at Jess, clanking his weapon against the bars. It fired a round—accidentally it seemed—bullets spraying into the plaster ceiling. Julian yelled louder—so did the guard's boss—both men pointing at Jess. The chaos alone was life-threatening and Alec held up his hand in a calming gesture, shouting, "Calm down, brother" in Spanish. Diplomacy was the only weapon at Alec's disposal. Jess scooted to the back of the cell and sat on the filthy cot mattress. Her wide-eyed glance darted from Alec to Julian to her jailers.

Aggressive dialogue continued to Alec's left. After a few moments, he couldn't take it any longer. "What?" he said, nudging Julian's arm.

He didn't turn but signaled for Alec to be quiet. Alec waited, mentally using the moments to pace out an exit strategy. He mapped the jails interior, devising the best way to overtake at least two jailers while commandeering their weapons. It would be risky but not impossible.

The rapid verbal exchange going on next to him slowed. Julian was now doing most of the talking. There seemed to be an amicable exchange of "*Sí*" and "*¿Podría usted por favor, mi amigo?*" It ended with the senior officer nodding, retrieving a key. Alec put his strategy on hold. Peaceful solutions weren't often an option for Alec—not by the time SEALs had been summoned. But, if possible, he was all for a diplomatic resolution. As the officer approached the cell door, Julian leaned over. "Seems Armando, her guide, was wanted on some drug and larceny charges. There was a pretty good bounty on his head. They assumed she was a partner in crime."

"Didn't you say her guide worked for you?"

Julian shrugged. "Consider where you are, man. It's not like hiring a white-collar guy from Omaha with a degree from Michigan State, not in this place."

Alec didn't like what he heard, but was unsure if he could argue it. His attention was averted as the cell door opened. Cautiously, Jess walked out and past local law enforcement. Alec and Julian stood side by side. But Julian took a firm forward step and Jess responded, meeting his embrace. Alec felt the muscle in his jaw lock tighter.

Julian cupped his hands around Jess's dirty face. "You're okay?"

She nodded, gripping onto his arms.

"Thank God." He kissed her, full on the lips. The action was unexpected and Alec retreated a step. "Let's get you out of here." Julian turned, the length of his arm capping Jess's shoulder, holding her close.

But she didn't move, not right away. "Alec," she said.

A tear had cut a dirt-streaked path on her cheek. Alec didn't like it. Whether they were in Nickel Springs or this place, Julian Silva seemed to result in more harm than good. "Uh, here... take this." Alec yanked the bandana from the band of his hat and handed it to her.

"Thanks." She wiped it over her damp, dusty face. "It's good to see you."

"Better to see you," Alec said. "I... we were worried."

"For a minute there, so was I." On Julian's prompt, she started toward the door but stopped and looked back at Alec. "I'm fine—really."

"Good to know," he said, thinking of the conversations they'd had in the past six months—maybe more so the ones he'd overheard. "I'm fine" weren't words he associated with Jess Donnelly and Julian. "Let's, um... let's get the hell out of here."

The threesome exited into the sunny impoverished setting. But instead of focusing on his surroundings, the thing Alec normally memorized in a place like this, he was aware of his breathing, maybe his heartbeat and tightly set jaw. Following Jess and Julian, he huffed. *Relationships... Wives... Marriage... It was all nothing but trouble.*

CHAPTER FIFTEEN

1977
Good Hope, Pennsylvania

EVIE HAD PICTURED SCENARIOS THAT WOULD COMPLEMENT HER WEDDING day. Fall colors, the smell of crisp leaves, a ceremony in the fading sunflower field. The sun glinting off Ezra's blond hair and his lagoon-blue eyes shining. The images had been sublime. Arriving at the gate of Ezra's house, Evie righted the visions. She gripped her fingers around the braid she'd neatly redone and tipped her chin upward. Sebastian wasn't to blame—not for all of it. Reality should have woken her months ago. The same moment Reverend Kane deemed the sunflower field an inappropriate place for their solemn ceremony. The wedding would take place in the meeting hall. End of discussion. Evie had turned to her father, who insisted the Reverend had a right to choose. Ezra, to her disappointment, had objected even less. "Evie, what does the place matter?" he'd said, unwilling to challenge his father. "The point is we'll be married when it's over."

Her marriage to Ezra was no more than a task, a means to an end.

Focused on those realities, Evie knocked on the Kane's front door. Adah greeted her, smiling as if everything was fine—as if tomorrow her son would marry the girl he loved. They exchanged pleasantries,

Adah saying how she looked forward to having another woman in the house, especially while Ezra was away on mission trips. Another point, Evie thought, as Adah guided them through the simple rooms. *Ezra will be gone for chunks of time... How much of my life is to be spent with Ezra, and how much in the Kane house?* While her heart ached for Ezra, Evie knew she did not want that to be her life. It brought her back around to Sebastian—the man who'd lit the dark fissures of her mind.

Was it good? Was it right? Evie sighed. She supposed resolutions had to be handled one at a time.

As Adah prattled on about canning her ginger-carrot slaw and wild-grape jam, Evie absorbed none of it. Her mind stayed on Sebastian—the moments before Nolan Creek interrupted—the words he'd said, the command of his touch, the things he made her feel. Evie closed her eyes and leaned into kitchen table.

"And when the steam is perfect, the sweetness can't be described. It's like nothing you've ever tasted..."

Yes, that's exactly the way it was...

Evie sensed a hand on her arm—a womanly touch. She opened her eyes, feeling dizzy, her thoughts unprotected.

"Evie? Are you all right, dear? You look terribly distracted." She blinked, focused on a face that mirrored Ezra's. "Well, of course, you're distracted. You're getting married tomorrow, and here I am, going on about jam!" Adah reached, pulling Evie into a motherly hug. The manly scents of Sebastian Christos were trounced, replaced by lavender soap, a hint of ginger.

"I... I'm sorry, Mrs. Kane—"

"Adah—I thought we agreed you'd call me Adah. I know it's... *irreverent*, but I understand that 'Mother' would be far too hard for you. So, Adah, yes? I can't very well have a new daughter calling me Mrs. Kane."

She was so kind, so genuine, so like Ezra. Evie swallowed hard, her glance cutting to the Reverend's vestments. They were pressed and waiting for tomorrow. "Adah," she said, trying on the adult version of her life. "I need to speak to Ezra. Is he here?"

"He's in the garden."

"Could I talk with him—alone?"

Adah looked confused, as if Evie had asked to make wine instead of jam out of her grapes. But she recovered, smiling. She glanced at the front window, which offered a full view of the meeting hall. "Reverend Kane isn't here. I suppose it would be all right. After all, you'll be married to Ezra this time tomorrow."

She sucked in a breath, processing Adah's reaction if she knew the truth—not about Sebastian, but the fact that she'd already slept with her son. Was anything in Good Hope what it seemed? Evie felt exceedingly exposed. She hurried, leaving Adah Kane in her kitchen with her slaw and simplicity. Ezra stood with a garden hose, watering the last of the fall vegetables, cauliflower and butternut squash. Spying Evie, he dropped the garden hose, and a terrific smile broke over his face.

"This is a surprise. What are you..." He rushed toward Evie but stopped and changed paths. Darting to the spigot, he shut it off. "Comes out with such a force. It wouldn't do to have a flood the size of Noah's Ark, not the day before our wedding."

She smiled weakly at his innocent joke. "Ezra, I need to speak with you. It's important."

His light expression faltered, and he peered past her shoulder. Taking Evie by the hand, Ezra led her to the edge of the yard. On the Kane property line was an outbuilding, converted to their future living space. "Come inside," he said, twisting the knob. "I have a good idea what's been on your mind."

"What's been on my mind?" Evie said, wondering if he'd been reading hers.

"You've been distracted, upset all week. Don't think I haven't noticed, Evie. I know you."

"That's true. But you couldn't possibly know..."

"Well, I've taken a reasonable guess."

He looked her over and the sting of guilt drilled deeper. Was it that plain? Could Ezra sense what she'd been doing less than an hour ago, how much she wanted another man?

"Like I told you, months ago in the barn, it'll be fine." Ezra clasped her hands, swinging them outward, like children playing a game. "After tomorrow it will hardly matter. You'll be my wife, and no one will question—"

"Ezra, what is it you think you know?"

He said nothing aloud, his gaze traveling cautiously to her stomach. "Remember what I said to you about Abigail Strand's baby. A ten-pound baby after a six-month marriage, I shouldn't think—"

"Ezra!" she snapped. "I'm not pregnant." *In fact, I've come here to tell you I can't marry you at all—because of Sebastian... because of this life...* Evie squeezed her eyes shut. Compared to that, pregnancy felt like a minor detail. "Ezra, no," she said, halting the swing of their hands. "I'm not... It has nothing to do with that."

"It doesn't?" he said, his face a mix of disappointment and confusion. "Then what brings you here, looking so beautiful and nervous?" He laughed and whispered, "I know it's not the wedding night." Ezra let go of her hands, brushing his through the air. "You haven't even said a word about the paint."

New paint. Evie hadn't noticed the smell or the fresh shade of beige on the walls. It was a Fathers of the Right tradition. When a couple married, their first home was prepared by members of the community. Families donated items—furniture to kitchenware, setting up housekeeping for the bride. Evie glanced around the space. It was interchangeable with all the homes in Good Hope. A burlap-colored couch was a spare that belonged to the Pruitts. Scatter rugs were strewn about, braided by the women of the sect, and an army of second-hand kitchen supplies lined the countertop. It was underwhelming and extraordinarily real. On a side table, on a sturdy metal easel, sat the only color in the room—a delicate painting of the sunflower field. Evie touched the picture's frame. "This is beautiful, Ezra."

"You weren't supposed to see it until tomorrow. I thought since you didn't get the setting you wanted for the wedding, I'd paint a vision you can keep forever."

"That's so like you." Her fingertips fluttered over the hazy watercolor image—Ezra did have a talent with a paint brush. *Such a short time ago, everything had looked so different.* Evie blinked her damp eyes at the picture, which came into focus. "Ezra," she said, spinning around. "My timing is awful, and what I need to tell you.... Well, know that it's as hard to say as it will be to hear."

A stiff smile edged onto his face. "If something has you this upset, Evie, and I've no clue what it is, then I think you'd better tell me—now."

For a second time that day, there was no knock, just Nolan Creek speaking as he appeared in the doorway. "Ezra, your mother said you were out here." His eyes cut to Evie. "She, um... she didn't say Evie was with you."

"She gave us some time to ourselves. Evie and I, we were about to discuss something important." He turned and his voice was different—thicker. And for the first time, Evie heard the hint of a man. "Give us a moment, Brother Creek. I'll be right out."

"I can't do that."

Evie's heart pounded, waiting for Brother Creek to renege on his agreement with Sebastian. He narrowed his eyes in her direction.

"Your father," he said, looking to Ezra. "He has an errand for you. Brother Pruitt is in the meeting hall. He'll tell you the details. You can speak to Evie later—for the rest of your life, if you like."

She knotted her brow at words that sounded like a promise.

"Go... *Now.* Reverend Kane has not had a good day, and I wouldn't be the one to try his patience."

As quick as Evie had heard the faint inkling of a man, it vanished. Ezra reached for her hand, squeezing Evie's fingers, which were cold and shaking. "I'll be back. We'll finish our talk." She smiled as she always did when Ezra was coming or going. Evie smoothed the front of her skirt, watching until Ezra disappeared into the house.

"I take it you've not done anything foolish yet?"

"Brother Creek, maybe it would be best for all of us if you let me see this through."

"I can't do that," he said. "And not for your sake, but ours—all of us."

"My reasons have nothing to do with other sect members. Why should my feelings matter to anyone other than Ezra?"

"So I'm right. That's what you're doing out here. Tell me, is this a new habit of yours—cozying up with men behind closed doors to wreak havoc?"

A week ago, Evie might not have challenged any man belonging to the Fathers of the Right. Not today. Evie drew on her newfound resolve. "Brother Creek, if you care at all about Ezra, you'll let me do this my way. It isn't your concern."

"You're wrong, Evie. Nothing is that simple in Good Hope. Anything to do with preserving our ways is my concern. If you don't marry Ezra—whatever your reason, you'll shake this community to its core. If you refuse to be Ezra's wife and stay here, how will that work? Look at the fuss and curiosity caused by my refusal to marry—and that's to a woman seen as a simple match. It's not a proclamation Reverend Kane's been asserting for years. Worse, if you were to leave here, leave Ezra behind... Conceive what they'll think? I can't let that happen. This year alone we've been weakened by the abandonment of three families. I can't have the Fathers of the Right crumble around me. I can't lose this place."

"Why? Are you so afraid of what's beyond our walls?"

"I am." His mouth twitched, the tiny movement conveying gut-wrenching fear. "God help me, I've been tempted." He drew a handkerchief from his pocket, dabbing at his upper lip. "If you must know, I've succumbed."

"I'm not sure…" Evie tipped her head, trying to absorb the inference. She recalled his pleading prayers. "Brother Creek, how is it you've…"

"Those trips I've made with the Reverend to Philadelphia. There's an area—inner city, a place he's never been. While the Reverend's taken private meetings, I've gone off on my own, a place where one finds other men who…" Evie covered her mouth with trembling fingertips. Nolan Creek's speech dropped to a covert whisper. "*The mission*, he said you knew this about me."

"I suspected," she said. "Although that's different than knowing." She batted her eyes at him. "I suppose shock is as present as air today." Silence teetered, Evie processing his candidness. She guessed there was comradery in dark secrets. "I'm sorry for whatever your troubles are, Brother Creek. I don't wish you any ill will—but maybe it's better to stop hiding. Maybe there's something to be said for following your heart or your instinct or simply what you're made of."

He shook his head vehemently. "Here, in Good Hope, it's not a remote consideration. Out there… out there it wouldn't be openly tolerated. But none of that matters nearly as much as how God would smite me."

It was a lot to take in, but it didn't change Evie's mind—not about Sebastian. "I can't marry Ezra to save your way of life. You can't expect that I would."

He nodded, blotting his lip again. "I thought as much. I know you're a willful girl." Brother Creek stuffed the handkerchief in his pocket, but his whole body stood firmer. "Then I'll ask you this, will you marry Ezra to save the life of *the mission*?"

CHAPTER SIXTEEN

AFTER EVIE LEFT THE CABIN, SEBASTIAN PACKED AND UNPACKED HIS duffel bag. The street-savvy, headstrong parts of him said to get the hell out of Good Hope. Take his chances. The rational parts wouldn't let him leave without Evie—or maybe it was the irrational parts. Sitting on the edge of the bed, he rubbed his hands over denim-covered thighs. He thought about what he and Evie would be doing right there, in that bed, if Nolan Creek hadn't walked in. If this bizarre place wasn't wedged between them. If only he had more time. The thought hit a precipice as the cabin door burst open and Reverend Kane came through. His movements were serpent-like—too silent for such a large man. His followers were blind to everything, including his physical approach.

He glanced at the duffel bag. "Good. You're thinking about leaving. That will facilitate the discussion."

"Yeah, feels as if I've overstayed my welcome."

"You flatter yourself, *Mission*, if you think you were ever welcome."

"Right. Either way, I've healed up enough to take my chances outside Good Hope. It's a big world—the Godfathers can't track every corner. They haven't found me here."

"Thanks only to my silence, which I wouldn't be quick to dismiss."

"Meaning?"

"You've wondered what my connection is to your father."

"I've got a good idea. I may not know you, but I know Andor. If you're doing business with him, somehow... some way, you're tied into his drug scene."

The Reverend stretched his arms out, shifting them in a vague gesture. "Good Hope was meant to be a self-sustaining, inclusive community. Years ago, it became apparent that our survival could not be maintained by way of farmers' markets and quilts sold at county fairs."

Sebastian furrowed his brow. "So you deal drugs to supplement your income?"

"I do not—" he boomed. The Reverend turned, avoiding Sebastian's glare and stoking the fire.

Sebastian remained on guard. It could be that the Reverend was contemplating striking his unwanted, all too aware guest with the hot steel rod. He guessed Duncan Kane saw himself as a courier, like Andor—hardly the image of an actual dealer. That guy bore a deep scar, slick attitude, and no morals. Drug dealers looked nothing like his father or a man cloaked by a robe and religion. Sebastian shook his head at the absurdity.

The Reverend spoke directly to the burning logs. "The Fathers of the Right provide a discreet, unassuming point of exchange for product." He looked at Sebastian. "If anything, our role was ingenious. So unlikely it's diverted law enforcement for years." Removing the iron from the fire, he dug the glowing tip into the floor.

"You miserable fuck," Sebastian said, unfazed by the weapon he held. "You pious trader—anointed leader, my ass. You're worse than Andor. He was only responsible for a son. You? You've got one hand in the lowest end of society, the other around the throat of your devout followers. That's a hell of a scam, Duncan," he said, deliberately employing disrespect. "All your missions to South America, you weren't spreading the word—you were picking up contraband."

"I'll not discuss the details of my means or motives with you, *Mission*," he said, narrowing his eyes. "And I'll certainly not be judged either."

"If it helps you sleep," Sebastian said. "But here's what's not adding up. If you're running drugs into the States, why divulge such a damning secret to me? There must be a reason."

"Several," he said without hesitating. "I've been communicating with your people. There's news, and it doesn't bode well for you. Your Godfathers have done further backtracking. That last drug shipment wasn't the first to be altered. Apparently, for the past year, consignments were tainted. None were as glaringly bad as the one that put a price on your head or caused them to beat you within a breath of your life. Just the same, there is now a documented trail of tainted product being delivered to Greece—product that traces back to you.

"Confirmed first-rate goods," he said as if speaking about imported silk from the West Indies, "that I personally delivered to your father. It turned substandard by the time it arrived in the Port of Piraeus. You," he said, poking a finger at Sebastian, "were the only man with access. It's clear to the Godfathers—and to me—that you substituted the product I delivered, selling the real goods for personal profit." He shook his head at Sebastian. "Greed, I assure you, it is a sin."

A small smile pushed onto Sebastian's face.

"You find this amusing? Then you're willing to forgo any more claims of denial?"

"And admitting anything to you would benefit me how?" Sebastian said.

"How much do you value your life? Share with me the location and profit of your vast income. My continued protection will be worth it."

"I'm not telling you a damn thing—mostly because there's nothing to tell."

"Where's the money hidden, *Mission*—in a bank, under a rock?"

"There is no money. It's gone," he said. "Every dime."

The Reverend moved closer, his hair parted in the middle, a dull grayish-brown. Pock-marked cheeks filled the basins of his narrow face. Sebastian watched a thin smile emerge. "How convenient... and unlikely. For whatever you are, you're not a drug user—that would have been evident weeks ago. So what's become of your ill-gotten gains?"

"I'm telling you, there's no money. If there was, don't you think I would have used it to vanish the moment I could walk farther than the john?"

"A point I've wholly considered. Why do you think you've been guarded day and night? If you did slip away, I suspected your first stop would be the treasure you're harboring. It's been more than a month—and nothing. Time's up."

"You can't take what's not there."

"Clearly, from the near squalor of the life you led, you haven't spent it."

Sebastian shrugged. He no longer saw a point in hiding the truth. "Missions, Reverend. Isn't that what you're supposed to be all about? I became aware of a situation where dirty money could be put to good use. Simplest terms, I stole from the rich and gave to the poor—helped out a friend and his many relatives."

"A Robin Hood scenario?" His stare turned examining. "You surprise me. I didn't see benevolence on your short list of virtues."

"Interesting. I thought it would have been first on yours."

"Again, your judgment is irrelevant." The Reverend's stare didn't waver.

"If you don't believe me, I could point you to a relocated, third-world village of over one-hundred people. They're currently adjusting to life in the United States."

"But even if such a story was true, you wouldn't share the details."

"Not likely. Not with you. You'd just have them deported. So I guess that leaves us between a rock and a hard place. Trust me, Reverend. The transportation might have been free, but getting them out of their terrorized homeland ran an easy six digits—about the going rate for several kilos of high-grade cocaine, fresh off the farm in Colombia."

"Worth a beating that nearly cost you your life?"

"Not everything went according to plan. I took a risk. I paid a price."

He nodded. "It's not cowardly—I'll give you that." His gaze ran the length of Sebastian's frame. "If what you say is true, then the money is gone. That's unfortunate. With a profit to share, I might have come to your aid. At least shuttled you out of here with your life. If it isn't true... Well, it hardly matters. I can be patient. It seems you'll be under my watch for some time to come, just not in Good Hope."

"And why is that? Why the fuck wouldn't I just take off out of here?"

"As you noted, your risk wasn't without consequences. I'm afraid that continues. The Godfathers of the Night on this side of the world are now in debt to the homeland faction in Greece. They're a powerful group. That beating you received—you're aware of their penchant for retribution."

Sebastian grazed his hand over his stomach, the ribs that finally did not feel tender to the touch.

"Your father..." The Reverend removed an envelope from his jacket pocket.

"You saw Andor?"

"Earlier today. Other than asking if you were alive, he didn't ask much."

Sebastian shrugged, feeling an old punch to the gut.

"He sent this, concerned that you might find my persuasion lacking."

Sebastian took the envelope. His name was scrawled on the outside in his father's handwriting.

"Your Uncle Paulos... the other men you're friendly with on your freighter, their families—something that may influence you more—are in real danger. The Godfathers are owed money—a lot of it. My guess is you have a solid sum in your head."

About 150K, give or take a few grand... The bargain price of moving Bim's village to safety... After skimming off the top for more than a year, Sebastian made the near fatal error of trading the entire last shipment of drugs for a lump sum—there was no choice. The remainder of the Sudanese village, women and children, were on the verge of being slaughtered by the newest and most heinous group of warlords to invade the region. Bim had called it genocide. What Sebastian had done previously, moving people in twos and threes, multiplied to forty times that number. They were desperate people pleading for help, out of terror, out of options. Sebastian had made some inquiries in the Port of Piraeus. Money talked, and he was able to contract safe transport for Bim's village out of the Sudan. Vinny and a few other crew members had helped secure their passage aboard the freighter. And now, because of Sebastian's actions, their lives were in danger too.

"*Mission*, are you listening?"

Sebastian looked from the floor to the Reverend.

"After intense negotiations, I've helped all parties reach a settlement in terms of payback."

"I'm not moving one more shipment of drugs. I won't go back."

"No worries there. You'd hardly be trusted with product that has a street value. More importantly, times have moved on and we're seizing the day. I'm sure you've heard my followers talk. Our missions to South America have become quite involved. We'll continue to make trips there to spread the word. However, the scope of merchandise has changed, along with the flow of goods. Instead of being a safe courier for transfer out, we'll be bringing another commodity into the country."

"You're going to supply drugs to the largest drug producing country on the planet?"

"You need to catch up, *Mission*. Although, like my followers, you haven't been privy to current events."

"Current events?"

"Rebels are running rampant in what were our finest distribution points. It's greatly inhibited courier routes. Guerilla forces—in numbers that grow by the day—are waging war over formerly profitable territory. And what they're in need of more than anything is weapons."

"Weapons... guns?"

"Precisely."

"And how is it I fit into this scheme?"

"Twofold. Your father assures me that you're skilled in overseeing our travels by freighter. When we dock, you'll assist in helping guide our goods off ship—trunks of needy items for the infidels, clothing, educational supplies, food. I'm told you're very good with customs officials. We'll supply the religion."

"And your charitable offerings," Sebastian said, plugging in the pieces. "They'll likely have false bottoms. Trunks and crates filled with weapons." Sebastian snickered—it wasn't *not clever*. "Brother Creek, Brother Wheaton, your own son. They're up for making those kinds of trades—dealing with mercenaries and lawless guerillas, exchanging guns for money. You'd risk their lives like that?"

"Don't be absurd. Their only mission is to spread the word of the Lord. They'll have no knowledge of any side dealings. They never have. It's what makes you so valuable and expendable all in the same thought. I wouldn't risk the lives of my followers or son, not beyond ordinary mission work and God's will. I do, however," he said, striding silently toward Sebastian, "have no trouble risking yours."

CHAPTER SEVENTEEN

"Do you understand what I'm telling you, Evie Neal?"

She nodded at Nolan Creek, clamping her hand to her mouth.

"The *mission* is in more danger now than ever before. The Reverend is the only person who can or is willing to save him. He's going to employ him by taking him on our South American callings. He's confided to me that he can guarantee the *mission's* safety and keep him out of harm's way."

Having listened to Nolan Creek's grim tale, Evie blinked back tears as the gravity of the circumstance sunk in.

"It wasn't easy for me to decide. I had to stand before the Reverend and agree that it is a good and righteous thing, to save a man so willing to pull a young woman into his clutches. So I've come to warn you. If you go through with this, if you leave Ezra because of *the mission*, safe harbor and pity will be the last thing the Reverend offers him. That's the way of it. You've made it clear you don't care what happens to the rest of us, but—"

"Brother Creek, that's not fair. You can't lay that responsibility at my feet."

"And yet, there it sits," he said, pointing as if Evie's legs were weighted in cement. "It's why I bring you this counsel. If you'll not be swayed by our souls, consider what will happen to *the mission*. Think very hard, Evie, and separate what's a sinful desire and what's right. I've been doing so since I found the Fathers of the Right. It's possible."

Evie balled her hands into clammy, tortured fists. She could barely fathom the circumstances or the story Nolan Creek had shared. Unless Sebastian accepted the Reverend's shelter, he'd be a dead man. "You... you're sure he'll be safe? No harm will come to Sebastian if he does what the Reverend says, stays in his employ."

"All that's come before you today and this is what concerns you?" He snickered, putting on his hat. "Ezra, he's some kind of lucky man."

"I am indeed—and I praise the Lord for His gift."

Ezra stood in the doorway. Evie startled as if she'd seen a ghost. She turned away, rushing to the kitchen, feigning interest in a hand mixer.

"Brother Kane. You're back. I'll be on my way." Nolan Creek's voice traveled the short span between living area and kitchen. "Since I won't be at your wedding, I'll offer my good wishes now, Evie. I know it will be a perfect day."

Evie didn't respond as the two men traded places and Nolan Creek exited. She put down the mixer, fondling a set of green, glass mixing bowls—a gift from Adah. "It's so like your mother, so sweet of her to part with these."

"My father said he'd buy her a new set next time he goes to North Good Hope. It made her happy for you to have them." Ezra, who'd come into the kitchen, slid his arms around Evie. "Before, you were upset about something. Now I find you having a love affair with kitchenware I know doesn't mean that much to you. Are you going to tell me what's wrong? You seem more upset than when I left. Did Brother Creek say something bothersome?"

She turned in his arms, unable to hide wet lashes. "He only reminded me how important tomorrow is," she said, her voice cracking. "The reverence of the occasion. That's all." While she kept still, a whirlwind brewed inside Evie. Everything she'd been taught and warned about was being challenged in one dizzying, frantic afternoon. She clung to Ezra. It hadn't been a lie. The feeling was familiar and safe and lovely.

Why couldn't she be happy for that? Clearly, it would solve every problem. While the rest of Evie tried to rally those feelings, her heart was the lone dissenter. It ached wildly for feelings Ezra could not evoke. And now, after knowing Sebastian's touch, Evie's awareness was acute. Yet dwelling on it helped no one. "Ezra," she said, her voice beaten to a whisper. "Tell me something. Would marrying me make you truly happy?"

"How can you ask such a thing? Marrying you is the only thing I've ever wanted." He tucked her tighter to him. "I know we've had a few spats of late. I know you're a strong thinker, Evie. God help me, it's one of the things I love most about you." Ezra eased back, his face as solemn as hers until he smiled. "That's when it's not driving me completely mad, challenging the very way we live. I think we can agree that obedience is not your strongest virtue."

Evie looked away.

"But as long as we're married... It's true. Being your husband, nothing would make me happier."

Guilt and gratitude came with his embrace. But mostly the hug kept Evie from looking Ezra in the eye. "That's kind of you," she said, yielding to the rules and rituals of the Fathers of the Right. "I'll work on that, I promise. Clearly, for every reason under the sun, being your wife is what I'm meant to do."

⁂

Sebastian read the letter from Andor. He crumpled it, sending it airmail across the cabin. Brother Wheaton looked up from his readings, though he didn't respond like any normal person asking, "Hey, what's wrong?" In this tight-knit place of communal living, Sebastian was decidedly alone. He walked to the window and peered out. That got a rise out of Brother Wheaton who, unlike Nolan Creek, stood, prepared to meet a challenge. It dulled Sebastian's impulse—which was to find Evie and get the hell out of there, together. Going about it rashly wasn't a smart idea. Sebastian turned. The balled paper sat on the floor. He shot a frustrated look at Brother Wheaton and retreated to what had become *his side* of the cabin. Smoothing the crinkled pages, Sebastian reread Andor's note. Bottom line, if Duncan Kane had been unconvincing, Andor's letter stressed the gravity of the situation. He moved his eyes over the words.

"Gios, it took much effort to negotiate this peace with the Godfathers in Greece. It no longer matters whether you are to blame for the loss of product and money. But understand that only you can repair it. If not for me—which I suspect would not convince you—think of the others, your Uncle Paulos, his family, and Vinny's, men on the Diamatis who are your friends. Innocents who will pay if you are weak in reply. I know this much about you, gios: I have no influence but loyalty does."

Sebastian slumped onto the edge of the bed. The mattress was feathery, the irony rock solid. Who would have thought he'd end up with a worse problem than when he arrived in Good Hope? Busted ribs and no future suddenly didn't sound like such a raw deal. He dragged in a breath and looked at the duffel bag. Reverend Kane's strengths were about control. When it came to his followers, clearly the man had never done much actual snooping. If he'd only searched the leather bag he would have found a bank book tucked into a side pocket. It wasn't a fortune—most of the money had gone to relocating Bim's village. But Sebastian had been wise enough to put a few thousand aside. He'd kept it in anticipation of trouble, though this exact situation hadn't crossed his mind. The money could get him moving. Get him—and now Evie—somewhere else.

He touched the letter, which lay beside him, and thought of the wild chain of events that had led him here and to her. Evie was the anchoring peace in a sea of chaos. He considered Bim. Bim who was smart and trustworthy and indebted to him—not that Sebastian had planned on asking for repayment. But now... He considered the bank book again. Bim understood the rigors of acclimating to a whole new world. If Evie was willing, maybe he could work it out. Hell, if she refused to marry Ezra, what life would there be for her here? Sebastian couldn't leave her in Good Hope, not under that circumstance. Nor could he take Evie with him to South America. But Sebastian could arrange to keep her somewhere safe until he satisfied the Godfathers or found another way out.

He spent the rest of the night honing his plan and waiting for his chance. It came the next morning. Brother Wheaton left and Brother Ott took over. He was an elder member of the Fathers of the Right, and the one most likely to doze off. Sebastian made a short excuse about taking a long bath. By the time he ran the tub full, he could hear Brother Ott snoring. It was almost too easy, retrieving the duffel bag and slipping out the cabin door.

It was Saturday, but the main street of Good Hope looked like it did on a Sunday, devoid of life. He'd overheard enough talk to know that the bakery did its biggest business on Saturdays. Sebastian approached the shop. Dust and confusion swirled. There was a sign in the window: Closed for Wedding. Sebastian looked toward Evie's house, sprinting the short distance. As he peered through the window he only saw a naked dressmaker's dummy. Bells chimed. The meeting hall sat on a diagonal, farther down the street. Sebastian swallowed dry air and hope as he began walking, then running, taking the front steps of the meeting hall three at a time. At the door, he hesitated. He pressed his ear to the wood. There was no sound. He eased it open, slipping inside. Glancing around the dim vestibule, he faced another set of doors. They opened. A boy, about five or six, came out. He blinked up at Sebastian, startled by a stranger in his small world. Sebastian squatted, pressing a finger to his lips. He whispered, "Is everyone inside?"

The boy's eyes were full moon wide. But he relaxed, smiling at a man who surely had to be one of them. He whispered to Sebastian. "I have to go to the bathroom." The boy started toward a set of stairs but turned back. "Mother says it's okay if I miss the part where the man and wife are to kiss."

With an iron weight sinking into his gut, Sebastian managed to rise. The door to the inner sanctuary hadn't closed tight. He inched it open and ducked inside, standing in a shadowy corner at the rear of the meeting hall. The angle was as unforgiving as the reality in front of him. Evie faced Ezra, wearing the gown she did not love. But her hands were in his as all eyes were lowered in dutiful prayer. All except Evie's. She stared past Ezra's bowed head, her eyes steady on a stained glass window. Sebastian looked toward it, an unlikely green hue dominating. A stronger energy, maybe a longing for what would never be, drew her gaze to Sebastian's. In the midst of her public wedding, the two shared a private moment. He shook his head slowly, feeling the heart she'd unearthed shatter. While his expression had to read as devastated, hers was resolute, determined. A sudden flinch conveyed the bride's only outward ambivalence. But Ezra sensed this too, and Sebastian watched as he tightened his grip around her hands. His fair head rose and he smiled at Evie, who looked back just in time to say she would be Ezra's wife.

CHAPTER EIGHTEEN

Present Day

MARRIAGE. Alec continued to mull over the manmade institution from the balcony of his La Carta hotel room. Partly because he'd been listening to one rekindle—Jess and Julian sweet talking each other on the balcony below. And partly because *not* being married always made Alec think of his parents. Nowadays tying the knot was optional, back then, not so much. He sipped a cup of strong coffee, wishing he'd pressed his parents for more of a reason when he was twenty or twenty-two. *"Come on, Pop—what gives? Five kids and a forever gig between the two of you, and yet...?"* But back then, it wasn't something a guy that age spent time thinking about—it was just a fact, like they lived in the Dutch colonial on Lakeshore Drive.

Alec turned his attention to the early morning street scene, which differed considerably from a sedate Nickel Springs setting. Vendors came to life, putting out their wares—everything from live chickens to a tobacco stand. Packs of unattended kids roamed the congested thoroughfare, merchants shooing them away. From his fourth-story point of view, he saw an inviting beach and azure ocean. If it weren't for the remote access, the place had all the makings of a top-notch resort. He pressed his arms into the creaky rail and sighed—a land developer he wasn't. Alec's senses traveled downward, drawn again to Jess and Julian's voices.

After securing her safety from the La Carta jailers, exhaustion had overtaken the three of them. They'd decided to call it a night— at least it's what Julian had pushed for and won. Alec let it go. It was late. The island would have to wait until morning. Another reason he'd backed off—Jess. Alec suspected she was more shaken up by her jail time than she'd let on. She had to be. It was the only explanation for her quick acceptance when Julian suggested they share a room. At the rail, Alec heard laughter. He almost backed off but instead found himself caught up in old-fashioned eavesdropping.

"It makes me happy to see you smiling this morning."

"Freedom will do that. Thanks again for coming, Julian."

"Did you think I wouldn't? Here, more coffee."

"She'd rather have tea..." Alec murmured. It's what Jess made when things weren't right—a bad cold, a bad day, a worse than usual phone fight with Julian.

"I... Well..." she said. "Before yesterday, our last conversation wasn't our best."

Alec tried to translate a lingering silence.

"Maybe not that part, but these past few hours...Definitely not the behavior of two people on the verge of divorce."

Alec heard laughing... *giggling*. Jess didn't giggle.

"But, Julian, maybe last night—*us*—was just reflex."

"Or maybe she was scared..." Alec said slightly louder.

"Reflex?" Julian said. "Nobody makes love like that out of reflex. You wanted it. You wanted us."

There was another patch of silence—but Alec knew that one. It was Jess weighing her words. She was a careful thinker.

"I wanted what we had six years ago, Julian. No part of my travel plans for *3Cs* magazine included coming here to sleep with you."

"Maybe I'm just the culture, customs, and continent you can't get away from," Julian said, riffing on the magazine's full name. "It appears—"

"We have unfinished business."

"Exactly," Julian said. It was followed by another pause, one that also required no interpretation. "So how about letting me demonstrate another custom?"

Alec realized how hard he'd been gripping the balcony rail. A rotted piece of wood gave way. He let it go. Jess's personal life was none of his business. He retreated—mentally, physically. The tight vintage square footage was dated, a worn out room with a turquoise floor, chipped paint showing bare wood. Alec felt cornered, unable to escape what was going on under the paint, under the floor, under Julian. *The hell with this...* It was Jess's mistake to make.

On a vigorous run through La Carta, Alec headed up a scorching trail that led to the outskirts of town, five, maybe six miles. From the edge of lost, he stuttered to a stop. Heaving deep breaths, Alec checked the compass on his watch. He pinched his eyes closed, all parts of him numb—only the slight pulse of heat-inspired nausea. Opening his eyes, he guessed his roommate and her almost ex might be ready to get to work. It was all that mattered.

Alec jogged back at a slower pace, passing by the *neighborhoods* of La Carta. Electrical lines were spotty and outhouses were common. Time had forgotten this place—maybe forsaken it. Except for a few hit-and-miss satellite dishes, it looked like hellish poverty. Glorified shacks passed for houses and emaciated stray dogs wandered in droves. Between the edge of the town and bungalows was a school. It looked large enough to accommodate the urchins he'd seen wandering the streets. He supposed a truant officer was not a priority here. The building looked dated, though well-built compared to everything else. He watched for a while, still catching his breath.

A woman led a group of children to a play area. There was plenty of equipment, but it was worn, the asphalt busted like its benefactor had long since vanished. The kids didn't seem to mind, swarming swings and slides like happy bees. Their teacher pushed one swing, then the other. She was dressed in a longish skirt and long-sleeved blouse that seemed counterintuitive to the oppressive heat. Her hair was braided, wound tightly to the back of her head—even from the distance Alec could tell she wasn't Latina. He continued to stare. Alec understood burkas, mandated cultural clothing, but the woman's looked more like something from a different century.

Alec's military observations faded to civilian ones. He wasn't watching, he was remembering. A woman dressed exactly like her had once pushed himself and Aaron on swings. His mother was there. In the back of his mind, the thrill of the swing gave way to an argument—a vicious, thundering fight. Someone hurting Evie. Alec struggled to grasp the memory. The clergyman was back, dressed in vestments, his pockmarked face stern. Alec could picture Aaron—who was three, maybe four years old—reaching for Evie. But she couldn't get close to him—like there was a fat object in the way. The recollection was old, sandwiched between stronger military memories that Alec spent most of his mental energy trying to keep subdued.

As he stood on the side of the dirt road, an impulse shot through him. Alec wanted to ask the teacher if she might fill in his blanks. Her clothing, if not her presence, seemed tied to the bits and pieces of his childhood memory. Then Alec thought better of it. His shirtless, sweaty appearance would scare the hell out of her. Aside from that, even from this distance, he could see she was young—probably younger than him. He sighed. Surely his elusive memories wouldn't mean anything to her. He glanced at his watch and jogged back to the hotel.

An hour later, Alec, Jess, Julian, and a hired motor boat captain were bumping through a rough ocean. Alec's gaze stuck mostly to the blazing horizon. In between, the two people standing beside him kept registering as *a couple*. The shoreline of La Carta grew smaller as an island came into focus.

"See, I told you," Jess said. "It's thick as a rainforest, devoid of people. When I started questioning the locals about my investigation—*3Cs* tip on a recent plane disappearance—this," she said, pointing, "is the story they wanted to tell. It took some back and forth to establish that they weren't talking about a plane that vanished last week but more like a dozen years ago. The locals talked about a husband and wife with a lot of reverence. I don't know if they were missionaries or what, but some of the village elders spoke about a school connected to the couple."

"I saw the school," Alec said. "It's on the edge of town." He looked toward the island and back at La Carta. His parents' plane, the oddly dressed woman on the playground, and his vague memory, it all seemed to link—though, admittedly, the missionary part didn't add up.

"Nobody knew anything about the missing plane I came looking for," Jess said over the hum of the motor, "but the subject set off a barrage of stories. To me, it sounded like local legend. My translator relayed stories... or maybe it was just hearsay about the couple and their plane. They said it might have gone down on that island. But what struck me as really strange is that for an island not too far from the mainland, nobody knew much else.

"That's when I learned why it is no one's ever gone in search of any plane or the couple—years ago or now. It's been rumored that..." Alec turned, facing Jess. She swallowed hard. "Well, the island, they call it Isla de la Muerte."

"Translation?" he said.

"The story goes... Listen, Alec, I'm sure it's native talk, but the villagers claim..." She quieted and looked toward the horizon of Isla de la Muerte.

"What, Jess? Just say it."

"Alec, remember where you are. The stories I heard, they were told to me by people who still believe in rain gods. Theories varied about what happened to the man and woman, starting with a plane crash, and ending with..."

"With...?" Alec said, grazing his arms through salt air.

Jess leaned against the bulkhead and Julian's arm moved around her shoulder. Goose bumps rose on her flesh and Julian took over the explanation. "Isla de la Muerte—it means Island of Death. The area where Jess found the plane crash, the island was said to be inhabited by an ancestral tribe that practiced cannibalism."

Alec gripped the frame of the boat's windshield to stay steady on his feet. It felt like his seaworthy legs might come out from under him. His glance brushed warily with the hired captain. Alec tugged at a bandanna knotted at his throat and locked his eyes on the island.

They anchored the boat offshore. Alec weighed his words as Julian checked his weapon. Insult or safety? "You know," Alec said, opting for safety, "I've got serious real world experience discharging a weapon."

"We're fine." Julian tucked the gun into his waistband, squinting up at Alec. "So have I," he said. "I can handle it. Here." He opened a cargo bin. Inside was a machete. "Can you handle that?"

Alec picked up the medieval instrument. Definitely not his weapon of choice. It made Alec wish he'd spent the morning scouring the streets for a firearm connection instead of a heat-filled jog. Surely he could have scored a gun. He was irritated, having allowed something other than the mission to influence his actions. The threesome trudged through knee-deep water and onto shore.

"This way," Jess said. After a few hundred yards, the necessity of the machete became apparent. Alec took the lead, cutting through thick jungle. He followed the vague path made two days before by Jess and her guide. Sunlight dappled the green forest, hit-and-miss light peeking through. It was eerily silent, less the caw of native birds and the swish of falling fauna.

"It's just a little farther. My guide was one of a few who could confirm an old wreck. He said the father of a friend came out here years ago to investigate."

"And?" Alec said over his shoulder.

"He never came back."

All three stuttered to a stop and cagey glances passed from one to the other.

"In my guide's opinion, the man was swept away by a sudden storm," Jess added. "He wasn't a believer in the village rumors. Considering the odds, sudden storm is far more likely. Anyway, it didn't take us long to—"

Forward motion ended in a manmade clearing. Alec's sweaty grip pulsed around the handle of the machete. The scene depicted Jess's photo, but the live version held more impact. His breath quickened and his mind was rushed by images of his parents— scenes more vivid than home movies. He felt fingers lock around the back of his arm. "Alec, are you all right?" Jess said. Julian pushed past them, moving closer to the wreckage.

"I, um..." Why the fuck hadn't he told Aaron to come with him? Aaron was good at dealing with live-wire reactions. There was no containing this. He looked from the scene and into Jess's hazel eyes. "It just can't be good, you know? I mean, not knowing for years was rough. But if I have to go back and tell them..."

"Let's take it one step at a time, okay?" Jess said. "And I, uh... Well, I know it's not like you to need anybody—for anything—but should you find yourself in that place... I'm here." Jess's hand slid down his arm, squeezing the fingers that weren't wrapped around a machete.

"You sure about that?" It was all Alec could get past whatever the hell was in his throat.

Julian called Jess's name, which seemed to answer the question. "Of course," she said before moving toward her ex.

Time and the jungle had overtaken the ruins. The plane had married with the landscape, vines and native plants hugging twisted metal. It made the whole sight look like a modern art exhibit. Alec took charge, like he always did—Middle East, home, or here. He quickly boarded the plane, the cockpit's door missing. There were no human remains, just as Jess had texted. Empty crates and dirt were most obvious, a cracked control panel and windows.

Backtracking from the cockpit through the interior, Alec examined the cabin floor. It was dark—small but without seats. This plane had been meant for cargo. A hole in the upper shell allowed spears of sunlight to pierce through, a thick overgrowth of vines strangling daylight. Between his hands and the machete, Alec cleared it away. With better light, he could make out a faint trail. Dark steady spots on the cabin's floor. He followed them to the plane's exit and hopped down. Jess was in his path.

"What?"

"Blood stains. They go from the cockpit to here." He continued to follow the trail, which was more like streaks—as if a bloodied body had braced against the plane while moving along. On the tail section were the markings Jess had discovered. In a fairly neat order, scrawled in blood, were initials: S.C., E.N., followed by his name, Aaron, Honor, Jake, and Troy's.

Julian stepped up to the plane, brushing his hand over arrows that jutted from Honor or Jake's names to the initials E.K. It was hard to tell what, precisely, the arrows pointed to. The line moved shakily between the names of Alec's siblings. Julian ran his hand harder over the dirty hull and Alec fought the urge to tell him to get his hands off his parents' plane. Julian glanced back at Alec, looking intrigued by the plane's bloody, cryptic message. "Jess explained about your siblings names on the plane, but who is E. K.?"

"I don't..." Alec didn't want to have this discussion with Julian. "K... Kane," he said, irritation jarring a memory. "Duncan Kane." The whole name popped into his head, matching the clergyman he'd recalled earlier that morning.

"And who's Duncan Kane?" Jess said.

"Connected to E. K.... maybe? Total speculation, but Duncan Kane was some kind of preacher that ties to my mother's past. I'm not sure how. Her personal history, before my father, it's always been... *sketchy*."

"As a kid, do you remember anything about this area, talk of it, or coming here?" Julian asked.

"No... I don't." Alec struggled for a memory—but it was too old, or he'd been too young. Now he wished he'd approached the teacher in the village, asked questions.

"If you ask me, those arrows," Julian said, pointing, "read like a clue."

"If it is, it's kind of a vague one," Jess said.

"That or the person who left it was out of time... or blood," Alec said, swallowing hard. He didn't want to give Julian any credit, but he agreed. The arrows, the initials, it did strike him as a clue left in haste. When Alec didn't say anything else, Julian walked away, examining other parts of the plane. "Evie and Sebastian," Alec said, "nothing about them was... *traditional*. Their relationship—in a lot of ways they belonged to each other like no two people I've ever seen. Even as kids we could see it, the emotional bond. On the other hand, there were moments... spans of time completely out of sync with that feeling. None more striking than the fact that they were never married."

"That's quite an observation," Jess said.

"In what sense?"

"Aside from the fact that I've never heard you use the words 'emotional bond?'" They traded confounded stares. "Those are pretty vivid observations coming from a guy who generally sees in black and white."

Jess's words hit hard—that she said them, that she knew him so well. Alec wasn't comfortable with either fact. "Yeah, well, this whole thing dumps me on a path way out of my comfort zone."

"I get it," she said, relenting. "But there is another option here.

You can make a different choice, Alec."

"Like what?" he said wiping dirt from his hands. "Hop a flight to Rio, plant my ass in some white hot sand and pretend this doesn't exist?"

"Not so extreme. But you don't have to see this through. The outcome, it might be more than you bargained for. It might be something you can't—"

"Handle?"

"I'm just saying I feel responsible. If I hadn't discovered the plane... Look, I'm sure not knowing what happened to your parents has been torturous. But if learning what *did* happen to them is even worse..." In Jess's motionless stance, Alec saw internal squirming. "For as tough as you are, Alec, sometimes I worry that you're a heartbeat from losing it. I don't want to be the person who pushes you off that cliff... or," she said, displaying sentiment he refused to acknowledge, "causes you that kind of pain."

"You can't protect me from the truth, Jess. I don't want you to. I get it. What we learn may be extremely gruesome. But if any Clairmont is going to bear that, it's going to be me."

She nodded, forcing her voice lighter. "Oldest child syndrome?"

"Or shortest straw. I'll let you know."

———◆◆◆◆———

On a map, Isla de la Muerte spanned about a fifteen-mile radius. Alec had walked a portion of it, the group staying on the east side of the island. The wreckage held the only signs of a human presence. Other than blistering heat, the island appeared to pose no other threat. Regardless, Alec understood that didn't mean one hadn't existed years ago. Back on the mainland, he contacted the NTSB. They would pick up the physical end of the investigation.

Alec spoke with Aaron, relaying facts. The two agreed to keep speculation about possible cannibalism between them. Both brothers felt strongly that the grisly theory wasn't something they wanted to dump on Jake or Troy, especially Honor. It wasn't that she couldn't handle it—Honor was as tough as any Clairmont. But there was an instinct to protect the only girl among the *Tribe of Five*. Right or wrong, Alec knew Sebastian Clairmont would have done the same thing. From there the brothers formulated a plan. Alec would learn whatever else he could in La Carta. Aaron would work the angles closer to home, trying to unearth their parents' curious past, particularly Evie's.

First on Alec's list was the town where he fought folklore and a language barrier. The boat captain, who spoke English, accepted a crisp hundred-dollar bill to interpret. Julian and Jess had gone in a different direction. It was fine. He preferred to be on his own. An hour later Alec and the guide questioned an older woman who'd gasped audibly upon spying Alec. She told them about a couple—a man who clearly resembled him (except for the eyes)—and a pretty blonde woman. She poked a crooked finger at Alec, accusing in broken English, "You are him with her eyes..." He gulped at a description of his parents that would result in a spot-on sketch of Alec Clairmont. Other villagers chimed in, offering thickly accented confirmation, saying "*Sí Sebastian*" then "*Evie.*"

Alec wanted all the clarification he could get. "Sebastian... Sebastian Clairmont?"

The villagers looked from one to the other, hesitating. "No... Christos... Sebastian *Christos*..."

The surname meant nothing to Alec. Lastly, he plucked a photo of his parents from his shirt pocket. He'd been saving it. The photo was the ultimate confirmation, the older villagers leaving Alec with no doubt.

Sometime later, Alec had cobbled together a story: In the mid-seventies and into the next decade guerilla rebels had terrorized the region. It was a dangerous period of political unrest, native factions fighting for control over the drug-filled landscape. The villagers told

Alec that initially Sebastian's presence only enabled the violence. But over time, his mission had changed, arming a separatist group—one that had ultimately wanted peace. With Sebastian's help they were able to take back La Carta and the outlying land. After the violence waned, Sebastian's visits didn't stop. They changed as he brought medical supplies, a doctor, food and, eventually, a woman with him. His benevolence raised his status among the people of La Carta to almost god-like.

It seemed their travels were random—sometimes just Sebastian, sometimes with Evie, who they took to be his wife. All agreed their assistance in the aftermath of a forgotten, war-torn region was lifesaving. They'd even funded the school Alec had seen. He was amazed by the stories he heard. None of it matched memories or the things his parents' talked about. As far as Alec knew, Sebastian Clairmont's employment history was exactly what he'd told Julian: he worked as a pilot for an international courier service. In his downtime, his father worked in Nickel Springs as the caretaker of the old Rose Arch Inn.

But as a village elder picked up the story, speaking about one trip in particular, emotion swamped Alec. He wanted to run, but instead he was stuck in the middle of fucking La Carta, listening to a family history about which he hadn't a clue. Via Alec's translator, a man said that at one point they hadn't seen the woman for more than a year. When Evie did return with Sebastian, they had a son with them—an infant. The couple made many trips and the baby turned into a toddler. A few years later, Evie appeared to be pregnant with another child. Looking at the dusty streets of the village, Alec guessed it probably didn't look too different thirty-plus years ago. Maybe he'd been wrong about his assumption that he'd never been to La Carta before.

The villagers went on to tell him that the woman's visits grew less frequent. Alec did some quick math. By the time his twin siblings came along—Honor and Jake—toting four children over rough terrain, in this surely never-safe place, was improbable at best. Then, according to the locals, about a dozen years ago, the couple had made one last visit. They'd arrived and left by a plane that Sebastian piloted. They never returned again. Tales began to circulate, talk of smoke rising from the island the same night Evie and Sebastian's plane left La Carta. The island with a hauntingly horrific reputation.

It matched Alec's timeline but not the explanation the NTSB had provided. The government agency had informed the Clairmont children that Sebastian picked up a last-minute courier assignment from San Paulo to Bogota. The authorities told the *Tribe of Five* that their parents' plane had vanished from radar after leaving Colombian airspace. Endless, mountainous terrain, thick rainforest, bad weather that night, it had seemed more likely than not that the plane would never be found.

At the time his parents' plane was lost, Alec had been on the other side of the world with his SEAL team, about as distant and detached from home as a person could get. He didn't even know they'd taken a trip. Not until the stateside call came, informing him that while he stood in a warzone, his parents' plane had disappeared. In a mind-numbing haze, Alec had soaked up the support of his SEAL brothers while packing his gear to return to Nickel Springs— emergency family leave.

After hearing all the stories he could absorb, Alec ditched his translator. He wanted to pursue his other lead alone. By the time Alec made it to the gate of the school it was late afternoon. He thought no one was there. But a door was open and he went inside. Alec counted off ten classrooms. They were abandoned, adding an eerie vibe to the scene. It put Alec on guard. He turned a corner and peeked into the last classroom. The walls were painted minty green, the room filled with desks. The woman he'd seen earlier sat behind a larger one. He knocked.

She didn't look up but reached into a drawer. A second later the woman was pointing a gun at him. "What do you want?"

"Whoa!" Alec said, both hands flying up. "I was just looking for whoever's in charge."

"Because?" she said, the gun aimed steadily, like she'd have no trouble firing it.

"I'm from the States... New York. I'm looking for information."

"What kind of information?" she said, rising, though the gun didn't lower.

"About my parents. Look, could you put the gun down? I just want to ask few questions."

"You may be new, gringo, but I've been here long enough not to take strangers at their word."

"Isn't that kind of crazy, keeping a gun in your desk drawer... *in a school*?"

"It's safer than what these children face day-to-day out in the streets." She shrugged, still holding a steady aim. "I keep it locked during school hours. Feel better?"

"If you'd put it down I would. I just wanted to ask—"

"What's your name?"

"Alec Clairmont."

"Alec—" Her expression changed.

"Yes, Alec," he repeated. "Why? Does it mean something to you?"

She didn't reply but lowered the gun, which Alec took as permission to inch forward. He did but mapped a line of defense if needed: desks, chairs, and a globe. He noticed that it said USSR, not Russia, an indication of the classroom's age. He proceeded in slow motion, taking a mental inventory of the teacher. She looked to be in her mid-twenties, definitely younger than him. She was pretty enough with fair eyes and caramel colored hair. Her round nose was freckled from the sun or maybe just the effect of no makeup. "Like I said, I'm just looking for information—my mother, Evie Neal. Sebastian Clairmont," he said, going on a hunch. "Do those names mean anything to you?"

She shook her head, but her eyes never left him, her hand still gripping tight to the gun.

"I saw you earlier this morning. What, um... what's your name?"

"Kiera... Blyth."

"Kiera," he repeated. "You're from the States?"

"Yes."

"You're a teacher here?"

"*The teacher*," she said. "Though today was the last day of school. I've been on mission here for nearly two years. I was sent... Well, my parents thought it best if I... What exactly is your question?"

Maybe it would be better if he got right to the point. "The way you're dressed... It reminded me of something from my past. As a kid, I visited a place where the women were dressed like you. That's a huge coincidence for a three-thousand-mile span, wouldn't you say?"

"We believe in a modest appearance."

"Who?" he said, cocking his chin at her.

"The Fathers of the Right. My community, my people."

"A religious group?"

"It's one way to describe us. La Carta has been part of our mission for years. There used to be many of us. Now... now it's just me."

"Just you? They sent you to a place that requires you keep a gun in a drawer... alone?"

"I can take care of myself."

He doubted that. She might be packing heat, but he didn't sense the survival skills that came with someone like Jess. "That doesn't answer my question. Why are you here alone?"

"Our mission leader has diverted more and more funds over the years. But I'm not privileged to know his specific agenda. The school was once a priority. Not anymore."

"Mission leader? Who's that?"

"Our Reverend... Well, he's not the sect's reverend any longer. He coordinates mission trips abroad, charitable work."

"His name wouldn't happen to be Kane, would it?"

She didn't reply, her small brow furrowing.

"Look, I'm just trying to find out what happened to my parents. They were on a plane that crashed on an island off La Carta about a dozen years ago. My mother might have been associated with the group you mentioned, the Fathers..."

"Fathers of the Right. I don't know anything about your mother."

Alec took that as a direct lie. "But you do know a Reverend Kane." He also suspected her silence was an admission. "On the side of the plane there were names, initials. Most of them belong to my family, my brothers and sister—my parents. One set of initials was different. E.K. Does any of that mean anything to you?"

"E.K.... written on the side of a plane wreck?" She paused. "E.K. That... well, it could be Ezra Kane, the elder Kane's son. He's our current sect leader in Good Hope—in Pennsylvania. He pleaded my case with my parents, my father in particular. The younger Reverend Kane didn't want me to come here. He thought it too harsh a punishment."

"Punishment for what?"

"I don't see how that's your business."

"Just trying to get a feel for your Fathers. Are we talking grand theft auto or drinking moonshine behind the church?"

"Again, not your business. Just things that aren't tolerated in Good Hope. And it's not a church, it's a meeting hall." She hesitated. "Regardless, you'd be caught in a heartbeat if you drank behind it. However, there is an alcove in the basement where they keep the old, high-back piano. A bottle of Wild Turkey is easily hidden in the top."

"In other words no one's found it since you were sent here."

And they were back to silence.

"So, Kiera, this Ezra Kane, is it possible that he knew my mother? Maybe they were friends... neighbors?"

"Friends?" She shook her head. "No, I don't believe *'friends'* describes what they were to one another."

CHAPTER NINETEEN

April 1979
Good Hope, Pennsylvania

OUTSIDE OUR DAILY BREAD, EVIE BOUNCED A FUSSY BABY ON HER HIP.
She rummaged around the interior of a carriage, looking for a hat.
The spring air was chilly and growing damper. She didn't want to
cause him more discomfort—baby Benjamin had been an irritable
red-faced, fighter-fisted infant from the moment he was born.
Hannah, who'd worked the Wednesday afternoon bakery shift,
joined Evie. She reached to the hat and secured the ties in a firm
bow. The baby continued to cry. Evie was about to ask if her friend
had pocketed a bakery treat when the rare sound of a car engine
interrupted. The community station wagon turned the corner. It
was followed by a second car—a van.

"What in the world," Hannah said. "Reverend Kane, he insisted
the brothers wouldn't be back for another week." She looked
perplexed, glancing between the wailing baby and vehicles.

"That's what Adah told me. It's what Ezra's last letter said." Evie
shuffled a few feet forward, boosting the baby. Ezra had been gone
nearly two months this time. Shortly after their marriage, Reverend

Kane decided the time had come for his son to take up missionary work on a more regular basis. Evie shifted the inconsolable baby to her other hip.

Men poured like holy water from the station wagon and second vehicle. Dressed alike, it was hard to discern one from another and Evie strained her eyes searching for Ezra. Colum Ott, Timothy Yeager, Daniel Pruitt, Jonah Neal, Evie's own brother, all came into focus. On this mission, the Reverend had sent the majority of the sect's younger men on a ship that sailed to South America, even those who didn't normally partake in outside mission work.

Evie determined Ezra was not among them and the usual mixed emotions snaked through her. They were feelings that had followed her back down the meeting hall aisle and into her new life. Being Ezra's wife meant being aware of what she did not feel. She'd prayed that would change. It had not. In the past eighteen months, she'd told herself, again and again, it didn't matter—a good friend made a better husband than most. But living in Good Hope without Ezra was equally strange, like the loss of a limb—or perhaps a crutch. Evie had become increasingly dependent on her husband's warm smile and what he felt for her to carry them through. The men filtered toward the women. Watching them, Evie reassured herself that she'd done the right thing for everyone on that numbing October day.

As months, then a year passed, she'd caught snippets of conversation not meant for her ears. Snippets that had validated her choices. Ironically, Sebastian Christos sailed aboard the same ship as her husband. Under Reverend Kane's protection he'd been kept safe from harm—just as Brother Creek had promised. And marrying Ezra, it appeared to have given her young husband what he wished for most. Both men had benefited and Evie tried to be satisfied with that. The baby she held cried louder and she shushed him, jiggling Benjamin in vain. He grabbed tight to her braid with his pudgy hand, the snappish tug reminding Evie where her attention belonged.

"I wonder why they're back so soon," Hannah said, touching the baby's cheek. She walked alongside Evie, pushing the baby buggy.

"If something were wrong, wouldn't Reverend Kane have alerted us?"

"I'm sure all is well," Hannah said. She smiled, moving past Evie as Tobias Blyth came toward them. Hannah had married him only a month after Evie's own wedding. His proposal had been imminent. Evie guessed he'd been waiting for her and Ezra's marriage to pass—the fuss of their conscript marriage overshadowing anyone else's news. Hannah had been ecstatic on her wedding day, beaming up and down the aisle. Evie had sat alone in a pew, wallowing in feelings of envy, the touching ceremony so removed from what she'd felt during her own. Days after Hannah married Tobias she confided to Evie that their wedding night was everything she'd dreamed of. Everything Evie's was not.

In fact, Evie had gone from playing along to outright pretending, feigning the emotion her husband could not evoke. She smiled at the baby who'd quieted to gulping hiccups and tucked his bib tighter. Evie glanced around a suddenly bustling Good Hope—while there was a burst of energy, nothing in it seemed to belong to her. Such was the life of Evie Neal. *Evie Kane...* No matter how hard she tried, Evie could not get comfortable with the name. It was like an ill-fitting blouse, the constricted feel cutting into her, forever present.

Hannah hurried to her husband as Reverend Kane approached Evie. He moved like a thunder cloud, his dark vestments and looming frame rolling in. When he left earlier in the day, he'd made no mention of returning with the men. Of course, it would not have been the Reverend's prerogative to share his plans. He stared disapprovingly at the baby, who'd begun to wail again. "I see he's not improved."

"Not hardly," she said, thinking things she shouldn't—like how Benjamin might benefit from medical intervention.

"He'll outgrow it," the Reverend said, cupping the baby's red cheek. "The Lord will see to better health, I'm sure of it."

"It would also be nice if He could see to a full night's sleep for his mother's sake." The Reverend's gaze pierced Evie and she changed the subject. "Ezra?"

"He's not with us. His mission was going well, and it continues. Another matter disrupted the efforts of the men. It was God's will that I bring them home ahead of schedule. They flew in a few hours ago."

"Flew?" she said. "On an airplane?"

"No, on eagles' wings. Yes, on an airplane. It was, uh..." There was an unlikely hesitation. "A necessary evil," he finished. "I thought you'd want to know that Ezra is well. He's in a completely different part of the country—far from where the brothers were carrying out their mission. The political climate called for an expedited retreat."

"Expedited retreat?" she said. "Is it unsafe? I know the area is unsettled, but you never said anything about the mission work being dangerous."

"All mission work comes with risk. Don't be foolish, daughter. And I'll ask you to hold your tongue there."

Evie skirted back at the Reverend's sharper tone. She recalled the sting of his hand the night her mother died.

"You won't question Fathers of the Right work, and you needn't be concerned. Ezra will sail back in a few weeks, on schedule."

Evie didn't speak. She only jostled the baby harder, his cries conveying her frustrations.

"Go. There'll be many hungry men for supper. We'll eat together in the fellowship hall. It will enhance our sense of community, women seeing their husbands, sons and brothers safely returned by my hand." He brushed past Evie, his arm knocking against her shoulder. "And add one extra." The collision had spun Evie halfway around. She turned, facing the Reverend. His gaze burned past her head, in the direction of the vehicles. "Circumstance dictated I return *the mission* as well—I suppose we've no choice but to feed him."

Evie whirled the other way, swinging the infant so hard he spat up. Looking toward the van, a last man exited. Through the cool evening breeze, the scattering men embraced their wives and mothers. Evie saw through the physical matter as if it wasn't there. Her gaze picked up where it left off a year and a half ago, locking on the forbidden frame of Sebastian Christos.

It was done.

It was long over.

It had barely happened.

These had been the thoughts Sebastian repeated over an ocean and more recently as he was shuttled onto an airplane bound for the States. Upon arrival at the cabin, Brother Ott had left him at the door with a lantern, a note from Reverend Kane, and more freedom than he'd ever been allowed in Good Hope. The note said to come to the fellowship hall if he wanted to eat. He hadn't eaten since the day before. But his stomach had quieted on arrival, filling with an ache that crushed emptiness. It was there the second Sebastian saw Evie. *Evie and a baby.* At first he had no intention of going to any fellowship hall; surely he wouldn't be missed. He'd eat tree bark or squirrel. He'd starve. He crumpled the note and threw it at the cold fireplace.

A rising moon shone outside the cabin window. Thinking of Evie had been one thing. Reality was too much—or so he realized as old wounds split wide, bleeding out at the sight of her. On the ride from the airport, Sebastian convinced himself that avoiding Evie was the best way to handle the situation—he'd only be in Good Hope a few days. Sebastian snickered, his head bowing to the moon. Avoid her? How fucking stupid. How about having to face Evie *and* the crying baby attached to her hip? "Maybe the good Reverend does have divine insight to punishment," he said to the moon.

Sebastian turned away from the window. In front of him was his former prison—hell, clearly it still was. He opened the leather duffel bag and dumped its contents onto the bed. Touching a clean T-shirt, he could think of nothing but the day Evie had turned up there, the fear and wonder in her face. He could still feel it. Those same fears had collapsed days later, igniting into binding heated passion. Now, looking at the fireless hearth, Sebastian knew he needed to bury his feelings with the rest of the spent ashes.

He headed into the bathroom and took out the mirror, which was precisely where he'd left it. He stared into his tanned, seaworthy face, and a full beard. "She's probably forgotten it happened... or is just damn sorry it did."

Enough. This wasn't him. "To hell with her," he muttered.

Sebastian pressed his arms into the cool, ceramic sink, his lips pursing. He didn't mean that. He wished her nothing bad. Not even her fair-haired boy of a husband who'd spent his first sail south with his head hung overboard. Thankfully, it was a large ship and Sebastian stayed with the crew. It had allowed him to steer clear of Ezra as well as the brothers that sometimes made the journey.

Staring at his bearded reflection, Sebastian was pissed off to find himself still stuck in this mess—the Reverend's web. But if his plans worked out, things would soon change. Keeping that end game in mind, he got out a razor. If he wanted to eat—and Sebastian decided he did—basic needs were a priority. Nothing would keep him from functioning, not even Evie Neal. *Evie Kane... Evie Kane who now had a child...* Even if her feelings for him had been real, that mind-blowing fact made her marriage irrevocable. Evie would never leave the father of her child. Sebastian was sure of it.

He absorbed his unclean appearance and features turned rugged by whipping winds and the lurking dangers of his *job. Get over it... You're not that man—not to her...You never had a chance...* It'd been nothing but a crazy, fucked-up fantasy—one he'd made the mistake of living off for more than a year. It was time to let go. Sebastian ran water in the sink and started scraping away the rough exterior. He'd get through the evening, clean shaven, and with a decent meal. Fuck the obstacles. He'd prove to himself he was that much of a man.

Compared to the cabin, the comfort level in the fellowship hall dropped considerably. What did he expect? Anyone who wasn't a card-carrying member might as well glow green. Women physically avoided him while the men begrudgingly acknowledged him. Lively conversation turned to a dense hum, the way you might whisper about lurking evil. Sebastian ignored it. He'd come for food and he headed straight for it, taking a plate and reaching blindly for whatever was in front of him.

"You're still alive."

Brother Creek stood next to him.

"Very observant."

"I'd wondered. The Reverend hasn't spoken your name since you left. It's like you were never here."

"Guess it worked out for you."

"I can't deny that." Nolan Creek nudged him along. Sebastian hesitated. In front of him was a cheesy casserole with a delicate crust, a tasty dish he recognized.

"Please. Go on," Brother Creek said. "Help yourself to her food. But understand nothing has changed. That's all of her you'll get."

"I don't know what you're talking about," he said, keeping emotion in check. He took a large scoop and moved down the line.

"Good. See there." He leaned close to Sebastian. "Lust never lasts."

He turned sharply toward Brother Creek. "Are we talking about you or me?" Sebastian headed toward an empty table. Brother Creek sat down across from him and Sebastian understood why. Better to befriend a man who knew your deepest secret, especially since all Evie Neal matters had been settled. Sebastian kept his eyes on his plate and his mind on the food. But he couldn't keep his gaze there forever, eventually scanning the room's perimeter.

"I must say. I'm amazed you made it through unscathed. I assume whatever work you handled for the Reverend wasn't an easy task."

"You honestly have no clue," he said, teeth ripping into a biscuit. "Some close calls, but once I found my rhythm, made the right connections... Until yesterday, it all went your Reverend's way."

"He's a man of good deeds, even if his servant must be a heathen." Nolan Creek poked his glasses tight to his face, squinting at the open collar of Sebastian's shirt.

Sebastian touched a newer scar. "Knife fight outside La Carta. An inch farther and you would have gotten your complete miracle. But they sent me to do the dirty work, right? I was probably lucky to have come ashore with my balls intact."

Brother Creek widened his gaze.

"I'll rephrase. I'm lucky not to have been taken hostage by rebel forces or have my head blown off. More palatable?"

Nolan Creek cleared his throat and reverted to his plate.

It gave Sebastian a moment to steal an informational peek. Evie stood in a corner, her profile to him, still holding the baby. Every so often he swore her glance darted in his direction. Better sense insisted otherwise.

Sebastian needed to kick memories to the curb. The ones he'd so foolishly expanded upon. He hadn't forgotten a thing, silky, honey-colored hair that looked as if the sun's rays wove through it. The contrast of her velvety brown eyes—they lit with a curiosity that made him forever wonder what was on her mind. Sebastian forced food down his throat and shifted in his seat, physically stirred by more intimate images. How powerful it had been to kiss Evie, the softness of her mouth on his. Her arms gripped steadily around his body as her lips grazed, more timidly, along the beaten, scarred skin of his chest. The fantasy-like, hypnotic surprise as she'd taken him in her mouth. How seconds later—if the man seated across from him hadn't interrupted—Sebastian would have made love to her. He closed his eyes. If things had happened that way, would it have been enough? Would Evie have left Ezra at the altar? In the deepest recesses of his mind, no matter how the facts told a different story, Sebastian believed it to be the truth.

He dragged in a breath. He needed to get his head around said facts—crying baby included. He looked at Evie again. No doubt she'd immersed herself in motherhood, relieved that she hadn't given into him or the thought of a life so incredibly different from the one she lived. He stabbed at a piece of meat, but irony put a sour taste in his mouth. Sebastian had navigated through life-threatening situations. Yet he was unable to control something as simple as a glance, which kept drifting toward her. But as Evie handed the infant—who continued to cry—to another woman, his glance turned into a stare. "The baby," he said.

Brother Creek glanced over his shoulder. "Ah, the Blyth child. Sad little fellow. Hasn't stopped squalling since the moment Hannah Blyth gave birth." He dipped his biscuit in gravy, settling his eyes on Sebastian. "No. Much as I'd like to tell you otherwise, the child isn't Evie's... nor Ezra's."

"But they've been married..."

"Long enough to produce two children—and they should have. So comes the punishment, *Mission*. Can't you see it?"

Sebastian leaned in, waiting to be educated.

"Her heinous sinful actions. The Lord has seen to it that she's being rightfully punished, left barren." Nolan Creek looked piously at Sebastian. "Though I don't see how it's fair to young Ezra."

Sebastian narrowed his eyes. "And you think that's why they don't have children, because of what Evie and I..."

"Could it be any clearer?" Nolan Creek's voice dropped to a whisper. "And you wonder why I seek the protection of this community. Think what would happen to me if..."

Shaking his head, Sebastian's back hit the chair. The power of twisted conviction—it was mindboggling.

He spent the next hour sitting at a rear table, listening. Eventually he'd tipped his chair to the wall, tucking his corduroy jacket around him. He propped his feet on the chair in front of him. Rain pounded outside, encouraging him to stay put. The group seemed to have forgotten his presence, regaling stories about Algar, the village they fled outside Colombia. He listened to their version of the events. Apparently the men were deep into their missionary work—converting the infidels—when they had to flee because of hurricane weather rising from the west. Sebastian stifled a snicker, running a hand around the back of his neck—sort of amazed it was still attached to his head.

It had been more like an uprising of terror from the west. A faction of guerilla forces with a thirst for murder had broken free from a government prison camp. They'd slaughtered two villages in the path of Algar where the Fathers of Right prayed and provided a solid cover story for the Reverend. Thanks to Sebastian's warning, they'd escaped with no minutes to spare. It was maddening. Not a single man realized their *work* was subterfuge. Not one suspected Sebastian and the small band he'd hired were there to handle the treacherous exchange of weapons for cash.

Finally, he had enough. Sebastian slipped out a side door. If his plans worked out, in a matter of weeks, this would be a bad memory. The rain had nearly stopped, reduced to an eerie mist. Walking through a fog that slowed him, he crossed the narrow alleyway between the meeting hall and the next building. As he stepped blindly forward *"Bash"* pierced through the elements—the weather and his mood. He turned into what felt like some kind of crazy fucked up dream. Evie emerged from the mist. "I... Well, at least I thought you'd say hello before leaving."

She kept coming. When she stood inches away Sebastian reminded himself how they were really worlds apart. "Hey," he said dully. Turning, he flipped up the collar of his jacket and forced footsteps toward the cabin.

"Wait."

Just keep moving... Do not make this mistake...

"Please..."

He slung his neck back. *Fucked if I do... Fucked if I...* Like his glance, Sebastian's will was unable to deny her. He pivoted. "What?"

"It's..." Her fingertips stretched toward him as if she was seeing a ghost. Well, damn, who knew what they'd try to spook you with around here. A balled fist retreated to her chest. "It's good to know you're all right. That you're safe."

"Alive, you got it. Is that all?" Sebastian shook his head, swearing her gaze had gone glassy. "If you're worried that I'm going to say anything about... Don't. I'm no more threat to you than I am Brother Creek. I'm not going to tell anyone—"

"Tell...? No," she said. "I never thought for a second you'd—"

"Evie. What is it you want?"

"You're so angry."

Sebastian stuffed his hands harder into his jacket pockets and swung the coat open wide. "What can I say? You leave a lasting impression." For someone who'd taken such a chance, coming out there to find him, she seemed to have seriously little to say. It was unlike Evie Neal. "I don't get it. What? Do you really want to have a 'Hi, how are you' conversation?"

"I've worried... wondered," she said, swapping words. "That's all."

"Before or after your wedding?" There was no point in talking. "You don't get to do this, Evie." Sebastian stepped toward her and Evie moved back. "You don't get to ambush me on the edge of your world because you can get away with it while they all sit inside."

"That's not what I'm doing."

"Then why didn't you speak to me in there? I've been sitting in the same room with you for the past two hours. Or maybe you only saw me as I left."

"Of course I saw you!"

In her voice, he heard wild frustration.

"Do you think it was easy being in there, Bash?"

"I don't know what to think, Mrs. Kane. In the regular world you'd be a fucking cock tease. Here... " Her expression startled and he immediately felt guilt. *Damn her...* "Exactly. You can't handle the language, never mind the fact. Evie, just go back inside where you belong."

"You're right. I can only behave as I've been taught. Except, it seems, when you're around."

"Honesty and keeping your word, that's what you're all about. It's all you know. I'm not sure why you'd want me to tell you that's a bad thing. I can't imagine what you want from me."

"I told you, I wanted to see if you were..." They both knew it her sad attempt at a lie. "Fine. You're right. I seem bound to the truth." She shrugged her shoulders. "Let me share mine. To start, the jolt of having you back in Good Hope is still sinking in. I never thought I'd lay eyes on you again. I spend every day living with that truth, so you'll forgive me if it turned out to be a startling error." She blinked fast, swiping at a tear. "Do..." Evie's words jammed as if the truth was having trouble finding its way out. "Do you think I got out of bed this morning expecting to see you? Isn't it enough that I get into it every night thinking of you?"

"You..."

Evie clamped her hand over her mouth, the other following as if needing to double down on her admission. Her glassy gaze turned to steady tears. Her hands dropped. Sebastian didn't think, he just moved. He kissed her. It was wickedly powerful, her body collapsing into his embrace. An achy mewl rose from her throat as one kiss connected to another. But he could feel her knotted fists kneading hard on his shoulders. It seemed to be the only part objecting. It was a furious struggle of passion and penance as Evie pushed away from him.

"I didn't..." She shook her head. "I swear I didn't come out here for that either."

"Like hell you didn't."

Evie brushed a hand across her mouth, lowering a shame-filled gaze. If Sebastian was angry before, he was furious now—with her, with himself. "I shouldn't have come back here. You walked away from us once, Evie. That's enough for me. Go home." He motioned toward the meeting hall. "Go back to your people. Do what's right in your mind."

"And that's exactly what I did, Bash. You've no idea."

"Not true. I've got the Evie Neal scars to prove it. Seriously, go," he said, his eye roving her like they'd met in some skanky bar south of Philly. He knew she felt it, crossing her arms over her chest, clinging to her own shoulders. "Go. Before I turn into your worst fear, before I forget who you are, where we are. Before I just take what I want." Her breath caught visibly on the last warning. He needed to finish it. "Go wait for the husband you don't love. It's what you chose."

CHAPTER TWENTY

At three a.m., Sebastian stared at the cabin's beamed ceiling. It was a change, even if it didn't seem to move time. He'd spent hours staring into the embers of a hot fire. He'd tried to sleep. It was futile. Every time he closed his eyes Evie was there—beautiful and bound to a life she was destined to lead.

He rolled over and forced his mind on more hopeful things, like extricating himself from the Reverend's grip. He'd followed orders and repaid a chunk of the Godfathers of the Night debt, but Sebastian had also begun to formulate a plan B—an exit strategy. He'd be damned if the Reverend and Godfathers would be the only ones to benefit from his dubious actions. Over time, he'd put his knowledge of plotting and thievery to work by inflating the price tag of the weapons he delivered, often collecting double the profit.

It wasn't without great risk—the guerilla marks he swindled could have killed him at any moment. But knowing he'd lost Evie, having to travel on the same ship as her husband, gave recklessness new meaning—at least when it came to Sebastian's own life. He pocketed a little of the money, like he'd done with Bim's Sudanese cause, but mostly he put the profit in the hands of separatists that wanted peace. That part had taken a while, forming trustworthy alliances, defining the good and evil that surrounded him in South America. Until six months ago, it had gone according to plan. Even if there hadn't been an obvious way out, at least Sebastian wasn't entirely aiding the enemy. Then, on a dark fall night, during a delivery of weapons to a northern faction, Sebastian was captured. Not by guerrilla forces, but by U.S. government officials. They'd been working undercover, sent to intervene in hopes of ending the South American conflict. Initially, Sebastian thought that was it. Best case scenario, he'd go home by way of an American military prison.

But as he'd sat handcuffed to a chair—day two of a brutal interrogation—he realized it wasn't going to go that way. His American captors wanted information. Then they'd just want him dead. Who would know? Who would question it? He'd be another nameless casualty in the anarchy of this South American mess. His own father would assume he'd finally managed to get himself killed—by guerilla forces, by a Godfather hitman, by fucking the wife of the wrong villager.

Sebastian had sat slumped in the chair, pulling air past badly bruised ribs. In that moment, he'd decided he was done. He was ready to give into the idea of this being a fucking fitting end to Sebastian Christos. Beaten into the hazy fog that surely preceded death, Sebastian had choked down a bloody wad of spit—maybe a tooth. A handgun had just been introduced to the conversation, placed on the table. It sat between Sebastian and his fate. Then the government agents had left him to think about it. Sebastian had been trying to hang on to a silent, dignified end.

A new agent came into the room. Through bleary swollen eyes Sebastian gazed up at a strapping frame and serious expression. In the moment, he'd been curious: How bad would a fresh punch feel? The agent's swagger confirmed that he owned the same hard-ass attitude as his colleagues. But as they made eye contact, Sebastian realized his anger wasn't directed at him. SAM14—the agent's operative name— was furious with Sebastian's captors, men who were his subordinates.

Even so, Sebastian had been wary of an eleventh hour showing of good cops/bad cops. He could guess the end to that movie.

Hours into a conversation with SAM14, Sebastian had begun to change his mind. It took him a while to gain any trust, make the connection in his mind. Where had he witnessed this same viable breadth of honesty? Where had he learned that trust was a real character trait? Through his pain, sipping the water then whiskey SAM14 had provided, Sebastian knew where he'd learned it: Evie Neal. He'd let his guard down an inch at a time. And as imminent doom waned, an idea had occurred to Sebastian. He'd ended up making a counter offer to SAM14 and eventually striking a deal.

Anarchy had hold of South America—a frenzy of drugs and weapons and money and killing. The South American setting was more lawless, but the action wasn't so different from the Greek mafia back in the States. What about organized crime? Did his own government have any interest in what Sebastian knew about that? It turned out they did. Once SAM14—which stood for Surface to Air Missile (the 14 being how many SAM14 had recovered from rebel forces)—was convinced Sebastian's information wasn't bullshit, they'd hammered out terms. An alliance was formed. It had worked out better than Sebastian might have hoped. Six months later, he remembered thinking, "Hell, I'm alive…I'm not going to jail." In time, SAM14 became Sam. To this day, Sebastian didn't know his real name, but he'd come to trust the man, even calling him a friend.

The two worked in covert tandem. Sebastian continued to go about his business, but with one adjustment. After completing the arms deals and based on Sebastian's intel, American forces swooped in, confiscating the rebel warriors and weapons. It gave them jurisdiction as the weapons were being supplied by an American-based outlet—namely Sebastian and the Godfathers of the Night. It was Sebastian's hope that eventually the Greek mafia's power would be neutralized and his freedom ultimately earned.

The single piece of information that Sebastian had kept to himself was Reverend Kane's role and the Fathers of the Right. Twisted as it was, he wouldn't involve men who had no idea of their true mission. Ignorance would not be an excuse in the eyes of the law. But Sebastian couldn't bring himself to implicate Good Hope, imagining the community in ruins, turning into the lead story on the six o'clock news. As much as the exposure might push Evie into his arms, Sebastian couldn't destroy her life that way. He didn't want her by default.

Lying in the bed, in the cabin, Sebastian slammed his sleepless body into the mattress again. Even in the midst of a covert mission—one that couldn't be more distant from Evie Neal—she managed to be at the center. Rain had begun to fall again and a familiar ping rose off the tin overhang on the cabin door. He sat up. Pinging sounded like tapping. Definitely knocking. He rose from the bed, but Sebastian refused to allow hope to cross the cabin floor with him. He opened the door, aware that hope had come along regardless. He knew this because his heart started beating the second he saw Evie's rain-soaked face.

Evie rushed inside and to the edge of the fireplace. She didn't look at him, staring hard into a glow of smoky wood. "Tell me I can be here and we can just talk. Please. Promise me." She wondered if she might get through this without eye contact. In fact, a blindfold might be a fitting solution. In her head she'd been able to handle Bash. She wasn't as sure about the flesh and blood man. He was already invading her senses—sight and smell. Earlier, the sound of his voice had sunk hard into her heart. Light flickered from behind, his shadow looming as he lit a lantern. Evie clung to mental fortitude. This could be no more than a necessary conversation. "Just promise me," she repeated, "We'll only talk."

"Back in the alley," he said. "You and I, we determined there's nothing to talk about."

"That's not true." Evie's arm flared out, fingers splayed so stiffly they trembled. Her unbraided hair fell forward, droplets of rain hanging like tiny globes of water on golden strands. "I do have something to say. I can't let you leave here again thinking of me the way you do."

"Evie," he said and she pinched her eyes shut. Instead of anger, she heard compassion. "You don't have to do this. You don't have to explain. I hate it, but I get it. Good Hope is your life. I know why you married Ezra."

She spun so fast her skirt licked the fire's flames. "No you don't."

"Yes, Evie…I do. You married Ezra because it's what they planted in your head since the moment you could understand words. I'm no brainwashing expert, but I can put that much together. I never had a chance, and there was never a choice."

"Of course there was a choice," she said, surprised by her own conviction. The wet shawl draped loosely about her and Evie shivered, tugging it tighter. "Before I left you that day, I'd stood right here and said I was going to tell Ezra I wouldn't marry him. But you think I changed my mind the second I stepped away from you. You think what I felt wasn't strong enough, that it couldn't compare or compete with my life here."

"Isn't that what happened? Not only did you marry Ezra, you stood at an altar and looked me right in the eye while you did it. That's a damn convincing message."

"I…" Her mouth gaped, confounded by her own actions. How could she ever make him understand? "I… I see why you would think that."

"Great. So we're on the same page." Sebastian drew his hands to his waist. "And what? You snuck out of your bed, came by in the rain to twist the knife?"

"You couldn't be more wrong."

"Doesn't sound that way."

"Bash," she said, finally meeting his eyes. The green was as intense as she remembered—as if his eyes belonged on a wild animal. "I knew they were sending you away. Brother Creek told me."

Sebastian's mouth bowed. "And that helps how? Did it make your decision easier? Thanks, Evie, but I'm not sure sharing or this little visit is helping."

"Just listen," Evie said, pressing her hands into the space between them. "Brother Creek warned me that day, after I left you. He said you were in even greater peril than when you'd arrived in Good Hope. Did you not confess to me that your life was already in jeopardy?"

He nodded.

"Brother Creek said things were worse, that the best chance you had at survival was to accept Reverend Kane's offer of protection. That traveling aboard a ship would keep you out of harm's way."

"Protection? He told you that was the plan?"

"Told me it was the only way to keep you alive." She saw a look of confusion on Sebastian's face. "It appears to have been the truth," she said, waving her hand at him. "You're alive. You're... *here*." Evie stepped closer to the flames, which seemed a safer choice than him.

"Evie..." His lips pursed. "It's not untrue, but it's also not exactly the way it happened... or the deal I took. He, um... he left out a few details. Think about it. Nolan Creek had his own motivation for getting me out of Good Hope and your life. Why didn't you come to me, talk to me before... " He inched closer. "Jesus, Evie, I had a plan."

"A plan?"

"Yes. A plan. Though it doesn't matter now."

Evie could still see it, the pain he felt the day he left Good Hope. "I knew how I hurt you, marrying Ezra with you as my witness. I'd settled it in my mind that you'd hate me for the rest of your life—or for however long I mattered to you. I never thought you'd come back. I never thought I'd see you again."

"Seems like the joke's on us."

She glanced at his sinewy frame. It was a face and a body that every part of Evie but her dreams had denied.

"So after everything, here *we* are. Any idea what I'm supposed to do with that?"

"No," she said, determined to finish the conversation. "I only know I can't let you leave Good Hope again believing I willingly chose Ezra over you. But in the alley, when you..."

"When I kissed you," he prodded.

"When you did that," she whispered. "I... well, it seemed..." Evie ran her fingertips over her lips. "It seemed as if nothing has changed for you. Is... is that true?"

He frowned harder and nodded his head slightly.

From beneath the shawl, a tremulous breath heaved from Evie's chest. She shouldn't have asked. It was better to think of him as having taken countless, faceless women to bed, though too painful to imagine that Sebastian might have fallen in love with just one. She nodded back. "Then I was right to come. I owe you this much. I can't live the rest of my life letting you think that marrying Ezra was what I wanted. It was a choice, and one I don't regret. No matter what else it's done, it's kept you alive."

"Evie..."

Sebastian brushed a stray lock of hair from her damp face. She needed to go, but Evie couldn't move. *Just let me be with him... just for a moment...* The feel of his fingertips on her face was so heavenly, so real. She reached, pressing her hand hard over his and drawing it tighter to her face.

"Your marriage to him, to Ezra..."

The tears from the alley welled and she squeezed his hand more firmly. "Ezra, he's a good person," she said, closing her eyes. "I can't stand here and tell you he treats me in any way that would disparage him. It's done, Bash. I can't change what is. I won't—"

"But you don't love him."

Her eyes fluttered open. "It doesn't matter."

"The hell it doesn't."

"It would be wiser for me to lie. I should tell you I've fallen madly in love with my husband."

"It's not in you, Evie. You're not capable of that kind of lie," he said, his thumb brushing through a stream of tears. "I'm not sure how you've lived it for the past year and a half."

"Nights spent in a precarious bed, days reassuring myself it was best for everyone. But you're right. I don't love Ezra in that way." She shrugged, fighting a fierce weight. "Surely there are worse lies to live."

"Tolerable," he agreed. "Maybe even doable... if it wasn't for one thing."

"What's that?" she said, lost to the touch of his hand, knowing it was all she'd ever have of him.

"The fact that you're in love with someone else."

"I..." She released his hand, but he was quick to grab hold of it. "I've waited... I've prayed for the feeling to leave me, like an illness or the winter. But the moment I saw you tonight..." She shook her head. "It was more powerful than ever. I don't understand how that's possible, I—"

Sebastian gathered her into a furious kiss. Reason and honor jammed on contact. Evie felt the shawl slip from her shoulders, felt compelled to kiss him back. Her closed fists from the alley opened, fingers digging longingly into his shoulders. It was the reality of a million dreams. Then she pushed away. "You promised. You said we could just talk."

"I didn't promise you a damn thing." Sebastian hands wove through her hair as a gentler kiss met with her forehead. He tipped her chin upward, insisting that their eyes meet. "Tell me you don't want this, Evie. That you don't want us. You stand here and say it."

"It... it doesn't matter what I want. I made a vow. It can never be undone, you know that. What we feel doesn't give us permission to—"

"The hell it doesn't," he said, all but shaking her by the shoulders. "You're no more bound to Ezra than I am to a life without you. Circumstance is keeping us apart—not a vow you made out of fear."

"We see it differently."

"Let me show you another point of view."

He was so close Evie's tears barely fit between them. Inside, every part of her whirled. She couldn't control the onslaught of emotion. Sebastian kissed her again and Evie felt the undoing of rules and the promise she'd made. That life seemed powerless in the confines of the cabin. Sebastian claimed her—his mouth, his hands, his mind. Passion erupted, more manic than the storm outside.

Working the buttons of her blouse, Sebastian slid it and her skirt away, all of it falling at his command. He kicked the garments aside, and a warm flush settled over Evie as his gaze grazed her barely clothed body. A last moment of trepidation flashed through her mind, and for a second they were silent. She bent her neck forward, her head burrowing into his chest. Their hands twined together. "God help me," she whispered. Her breathing was so wrought, so unsteady, Evie thought she might pass out.

"Evie," he said huskily. "I'm half out of my mind for asking, but if this is only going to end up driving you further from me. If it makes things worse..."

For better or worse, it no longer mattered. Evie answered, not with words but actions. Her trembling fingers moved down the buttons of Sebastian's shirt, stripping away the last of her apprehensions. She pressed her mouth to his chest, washing his hard body in delicate kisses. As she undid his belt buckle, Sebastian unhooked her bra, saying something about how simple, white cotton never looked so sexy. Evie smiled shyly. *Sexy* was not a word she'd ever considered in this regard. Sebastian cupped his hand around her bottom, and he drew her body to his, his hardness pulsing between them.

"Let that be the slightest indication of how much I want you."

Evie inched back, stroking her hand over the velvety smoothness of a taut erection. She remembered the way she'd pleased him once before, thinking it would happen again. But Sebastian seemed to have other ideas, steering them toward the feather bed. The back of her calf met with the mattress, and Evie realized she was trembling. But he was right there, steadying her mind and body. "Do you know how many times," she said, "in how many ways I've thought of us... Had to think of us to get through..."

"Don't say it." The softness vanished and Sebastian pulled her close. "I don't want to know how you thought of us to get through nights with him. And I promise you," he said, letting go and shucking aside the rest of his clothes, "no matter what's in your head, what you might be telling yourself, this will be more than a sacrificial memory."

Evie wasn't sure what he meant, but the time for questions had passed. A moment later they were on the bed. Sebastian loomed over her, Evie studying the hard body and muscular frame of her would-be lover. Sebastian was a captivating sight but also a telling story. She wanted to know about all the little scars—knife fight or beating? She saw a new mark on his neck, a fresh scar. Had she come closer than she'd feared to losing him forever? But he was there now, and she responded to reality, locking her arms around his broad shoulders. She buried her nose in the scent of him—a soapy, brawny maleness, suntanned skin that tasted of unholy adventure.

His mouth moved along her body, his tongue circling her breasts, delicately suckling each one. The tenderness of his movements surprised her, his hands drifting in between her legs. It was all so natural, the way her body encouraged his, legs shifting apart and inviting the deft entry of his fingers. She gasped at the exquisite intrusion, anxious to know how it would feel to have all of him inside her.

But he kept on a downward progression, Evie feeling a flutter as his mouth passed over her belly and a wave of luxurious sensations overtook her. A moment later, their eyes locked from a curious angle with Sebastian's mouth buried deep between delicate folds of flesh. Her heart raced at the intimacy while a building of sweet tension overtook her. A growl of satisfaction emanated from his throat.

She reached for him, but her hand dropped, digging deep into the tangle of sheet, Evie tumbling into a valley of passion. She couldn't breathe, she lost focus. She nearly panicked, needing to know Sebastian was there. That this wasn't an indulgent dream—the kind that had woken Evie over and over only to find him nowhere but her imagination. The feeling was shattering, and she could barely catch her breath as his mouth began a reverse journey, shushing her with kisses that trailed across her stomach and breasts. Longingly, she touched him, admiring his black wavy hair, the breadth of his body as it made love to hers. She whispered, "I'm not sure I can take much more of that..."

He smiled, which Evie saw as a rare thing, perhaps meant just for her. "You can, Evie," he said, poised over her. "You will."

Evie traced his chin with her fingertips, her brow wrinkling as she touched the new scar. But as her eyes met his, she bit hard into her lip anticipating what came next. While she'd dreamt of the tiniest details, she did not envision anything so defining. Her gaze skimmed from his chest to his shoulders and the strain of muscles in his arms as Sebastian pushed into her. As his steely shaft drove into her, Evie slipped into a new hollow of emotion, though it was the shared feelings that captivated her. This was sexual and powerful and what she'd longed for, in her mind and in her heart. Her body was merely awarded the physical pleasure as Sebastian's thrusts grew more aggressive. When his mouth kissed hers, Evie was startled, the taste of herself as unlikely as the scene. He hooked his arm around her leg, opening her wider to him. Evie's heart thundered as her fingers dug into his muscular back.

"Evie," he whispered. "I can't come... I shouldn't..." His eyes closed as if talking took any reserve strength.

She only pulled him tighter. "It doesn't matter—not for me. Nothing will happen..." She didn't finish the thought as Sebastian succumbed to her suggestion. Evie felt the tremor of pleasure consume him as he came with a breathtaking shudder.

CHAPTER TWENTY-ONE

AFTERWARD, THEY TALKED FOR HOURS. NOT ABOUT THE FUTURE OR anything that required Evie to commit to leaving this life, or more to the point, her husband. Sebastian had to trust she'd come to the right conclusion. Instead, he told her a version of his life for the past eighteen months, working on the South American bound freighter and explaining that he served as the brothers' liaison, negotiating the locals and rough terrain. He didn't speak of real dangers or Reverend Kane's deceitful role. Sebastian didn't want that bastard anywhere near the bed they lay in.

Evie reciprocated with what he guessed was an edited version of her life, not speaking of Ezra but only of her life in Good Hope. It probably wasn't too far from the truth. While Ezra sailed often and was gone from Good Hope for stretches of time, Sebastian had only thought of his homecomings. Each time Ezra disembarked in the Philadelphia port, Sebastian watched from the deck. The fair-haired slip of a man who would go home and make love to his wife. The thought sunk hard into his head, and Sebastian held tighter to Evie. Would she wake up tomorrow and see herself as nothing but Ezra's adulteress wife?

He'd forced the thought away and made love to her again—more intently than before, enough to make Evie cry out his name. When exhaustion finally overcame Sebastian, a smile crept onto his face—

the moment sleep wove through him and Evie whispered, "I love you," into his dreams.

When the sun rose, Evie wasn't beside him. He wasn't surprised she was gone, only that she'd slipped from the bed unbeknownst to him. Sebastian wanted to make certain she got home safely, undetected by the watchful eyes of Good Hope. Instead, it was a brisk April breeze that went with him to breakfast. Apparently, during planting season, morning meals were communal. Evie was late to the fellowship hall, a fact that didn't go unnoticed by Reverend Kane and the others. Sebastian fought the urge to grab her by the hand and run like the devil from Good Hope. He kept his distance. The two traded glances as she hurried about her chores. Brother Creek poked Sebastian in the back.

"Reverend Kane says to make use of you while you're here. You'll work with the brothers today, planting."

Sebastian swallowed down scrambled eggs and home fries. He guessed keeping the brothers alive wasn't enough to earn him room and board. "Fine. But my farming skills are a little nonexistent."

"If you prefer, there's fencing that needs mending."

He wiped his hands on a napkin and sipped the last of his coffee. "Lead the way." As the two men left, Sebastian and Evie traded a fast glance.

Nolan Creek leaned in and whispered, "I think I might have been wrong about lust. I think keeping you and the young Mrs. Kane apart is best for all of us." He held the door as Sebastian passed through. "Perhaps best for her husband more than anyone."

⸻◦•◦•◦⸻

Evie had been late to breakfast because she was unable to move from the chair in her and Ezra's cottage. She'd dressed but hadn't bathed. The scent of Sebastian had soaked into her skin, and she refused to wash it away. The guilt she'd anticipated had risen like the sun with her. She hadn't been wrong about that, but not entirely right. While there was guilt there was no regret.

After breakfast, Evie returned to the chair, immobilized. She didn't move for hours, watching shadows shift in the tiny cottage. Time had faded into early evening when Hannah showed up. She demanded to know why Evie had been late that morning and where'd she been all day. She quietly replied, "I've been here," and Hannah grew more concerned. No member of the Fathers of the Right spent an entire day in solitude, not without a serious reason or at the Reverend's direction. If it was neither, Hannah jumped to the conclusion that Evie hadn't felt well. Perhaps a sign of morning sickness, she suggested, giddy at the prospect.

It was the only point at which Evie felt truly ill, no longer able to listen to the plot for a life she didn't want. Solitude and reflection had run out of room, and Evie took a deep breath. She confessed everything to Hannah, whose shock, Evie thought, might result in a heart attack. When it didn't, the two women sat staring at one another. One stunned by the unlikelihood of what had happened, the other trying to formulate a resolution.

"Evie..." Hannah said, stopping and starting for at least the fifth time. Her hand rose to her mouth again, her skin so pale Evie still thought she might faint.

She forced herself out of the chair. "I know," Evie said, turning in a tight circle. "It's the best and worst of everything possible."

"I can't even imagine..." A dazed Hannah blinked at Evie as if she didn't know her.

"Do you think I'm awful?" She turned away again. "Of course I'm awful," she said, tugging at her long, blonde braid until it hurt. "Trust me, I've not been sitting here all day excusing my actions." Deeper guilt pulsed through Evie and she moved farther from Hannah. "I should beg for guidance, seek a way to make it up to

Ezra. Forget Sebastian exists." Evie shut her eyes as the next thought came. "Maybe it'd be best if I just waited to burn in Hell." She was rambling now, though she supposed it was a fact.

She startled as Hannah touched her back. "Surely there's a way to be forgiven."

Evie turned, a knot in her throat that felt like a noose tightening around her neck.

"I can't claim it's right...what you've done. I can hardly believe you did it—confessed it to me. But if you feel for *the miss*—for Sebastian," she corrected, "anything like what I feel for Tobias, then I know some of what you mean. I sat with you in the meeting hall the day before your wedding. I did nothing to help when you told me you didn't love Ezra... that another man... Well, this proves I'm not a very good friend. But I never thought it would come to..." A breath rose and fell from Hannah. "Oh, Evie, what are you going to do?"

"I don't know," she said, hoping for the kind of wisdom Hannah Blyth wasn't capable of delivering.

"Pray, maybe," she said, taking Evie's hand in hers.

A voice boomed from the doorway. It wasn't preceded by a knock. "Good to hear it's prayer that has you both huddled together," said Reverend Kane. "Still, do neither of you have a task to keep your minds and hands busy? Who's caring for your child, Hannah?" He glanced about. "From the quiet I assume he's not here."

"My mother is minding him. Evie and I were talking. I worried she wasn't feeling well."

"Then we share similar thoughts. It's part of why I came by."

Hannah moved swiftly toward the door, following the implied direction. Out of the Reverend's view, she smiled empathetically. It made Evie's nerves prickle, wondering if the Reverend, indeed, had eyes in the back of his head. He might have been looking out his bedroom window last night—she hadn't thought of that. Perhaps he'd watched Evie as she'd slipped from her lover's arms and into her own house. She fidgeted, hands wringing. It might be even worse. Had he seen Evie go to the cabin—listened at the door as she made love to a man who wasn't her husband, the Reverend's own son? Perhaps their righteous and stern leader had known all day, letting Evie languish before pouncing.

A shaky sigh wove out of her. Ominous dread was the least of what she deserved.

The silent screaming moment lingered. Evie didn't dare think of Bash—at least she tried. The Reverend finally moved, circling her, his all black attire and commanding presence swallowing the space. She grimaced, wiping damp palms down the front of her skirt. "Is there something I can do for you, Reverend?" He faced her and Evie wondered what she always did: How was it possible that Ezra was even his son? She trembled inwardly, unsure how long she could keep steady on the outside. Usually steps ahead of his flock, the Reverend seemed oddly unaware of Evie's state.

"And was Hannah Blyth right? Are you feeling unwell?"

"I woke with a headache," she said, telling the smallest lie she guessed the conversation would produce. "I'm sorry about this morning. I'm not often late."

"Late in what sense?"

Evie's brow crinkled. It pulled tighter as the hint of a smile curved around his mouth. "Are you finally pregnant?"

"Excuse me?" she said, flummoxed by the question. That he'd ask such a thing or she'd be expected to answer. But in the same instant, Evie realized her father-in-law had no clue about Sebastian. A second shaky sigh seeped from her gut. "If I were, I'd certainly tell Ezra before you. But since I haven't seen him in months, it's not a conversation we'll be having anytime soon."

"Good," he said, stepping toward her.

"Good?" she replied.

"I've been praying, Evie, asking God why it is you and Ezra have no children. My son's been present enough to see to it."

"I..." She stepped back, finding herself flat against the wall of the small cottage. "I don't want to talk about this with you."

"Nonsense. Every subject in Good Hope is my concern. Particularly those closest to me." He drew tighter, grazing his hand against her cheek. "You know this."

Evie brushed the feel of his touch away. "You have your answer. If that's all you wanted to know..." She looked toward the door.

"Hardly. In fact, we've barely broached what I've come for. You see, I've finally been given answer, Evie. I understand your situation and what's to happen here."

"My situ... I think you should go."

He reached with his long fingers, gripping her chin. "Go? Go from where? My property?" he said, his eyes roving Evie. "When you married my son, you became his property. And Ezra has no property that isn't mine. Serious, prayerful counsel has made this clear to me. I was only uncertain, exactly, what to do about it." The Reverend eased his grip on Evie's jaw, his coarse thumb running the length of her throat. "You've no children by Ezra—and he's had sufficient opportunity. Yet the Kane bloodline needs to continue. That is a certainty. Adah is gone for the evening. You're alone."

"I don't... What are you saying?"

"I'm saying that the Lord told me that I'm to be the instrument."

Evie filled with shock and fear—the beauty of last night clashing with the twisted moment. His hand moved lower, groping her breast, and Evie struggled as his body pressed hard into hers.

"Feistiness suits you, Evie. Compliance comes so easily to most women. God has truly offered me a conquest. The reward will be that much richer when I have your obedience."

Evie recalled the slap from years before. The pious coldness Reverend Kane delivered as her mother lay dying. She realized how he justified every behavior—she'd be damned if he got away with this one. Evie slammed her knee upward, catching him hard in the groin. The stunned expression on his face, the swear words spewing from his mouth—the Reverend's very human reaction. She'd never seen anything like it, not from him. His ashen face reddened as he staggered back. But it wasn't enough to elude his grasp, and Duncan Kane recovered, grabbing Evie's blouse. Fabric tore as he forcefully spun her about.

"You'll not escape my mission, Evie. It's God's will." He had her by the hair, making his point by striking her hard across the face. The sting was reminiscent, Evie tasting blood. Spittle hit her face, coming from his mouth the way it did when he preached furiously from the pulpit. Evie tried to wrench away, but his grip was like an iron cuff. The Reverend's mouth was over hers. Could God truly be so vengeful? It seemed possible as Reverend Kane pushed her into the cottage wall. He groped beneath her skirt, his icy hand meeting with her bare skin. Evie shuddered, inside and out, wondering if this was punishment for betraying her husband and her life in Good Hope.

CHAPTER TWENTY-TWO

Present Day

ALEC SAT ON THE EDGE OF HIS HOTEL ROOM BED THINKING EVERYTHING about his parents' past seemed to hit a wall. He'd begun to wonder if their life together had been as complicated as their deaths. Right after Kiera made the curious statement about Evie's connection to Ezra Kane, she'd clammed up, told him to get out. And because she was waving a gun at him, leaving seemed like a reasonable suggestion. He'd try again tomorrow. Kiera Blyth definitely knew more than she was saying. Alec was only in his hotel room a few minutes when there was a knock at the door.

"It's me."

He opened it. Jess was on the other side. He knew that look, even the smell. She'd just showered, his nose filling with *sunset vanilla*—at least it's what the label said on one of the many bottles that had invaded his apartment shower. Layers of curly, blonde hair were already drying in the heat. Inwardly, he squelched other information—like the fact that forcing her hair straight took an hour and serious swearing. But she liked to wear it that way sometimes. He stepped back, clearing personal space. *Home...*

Since they'd arrived in La Carta the concept had steadily

deteriorated. Even friends who shared a living space felt like shaky ground. Jess brushed by him wearing a skimpy, black dress and an attitude.

"Julian went into town. He'll be back shortly."

Alec didn't reply, still staring at the dress. He didn't like it. Not here. For her capable, independent state, Jess looked best in the cargo pants she usually wore on assignment. Maybe the casual flowy skirts and flip-flops she'd wear on the weekends. The sexy dress conflicted with both images, but he supposed that was the point—looking hot for her almost ex.

As roommates, she and Alec had spent time together by default—open Sundays and holiday Mondays. They were good at being singular creatures in the same living space. There'd been trips to the supermarket and a flea market that Jess had dragged him to once—a place where he'd had a surprisingly good time. On occasion, she'd gone with him to the Clairmont house for dinner—nothing big. Nothing planned. Now, Alec dragged his gaze over what he perceived as a rather *planned* appearance.

"Are you going to answer me?" she said. "Did you learn anything from the schoolmarm?"

He hadn't realized she said anything beyond noting Julian's whereabouts—like he gave a shit about that. "Bits and pieces. Despite the schoolmarm's evasiveness, she did admit to a connection between this group in Pennsylvania and my mother. She called them the Fathers of the Right."

"Sounds like a panel on Fox News."

"Or worse—religious extremists."

"It's not the same thing?"

"Whatever. It doesn't make sense. My family wasn't big on religion. I'd say my mother was more spiritual than anything, but it wasn't something she forced on us. Evie Neal definitely didn't fit with what I saw today. And Kiera Blyth—that's the girl... woman...

teacher's name—she's holding back."

"Interesting."

"What's that?"

"You remember her name."

Alec narrowed his eyes. "If she has relevant information about my parents, I would have remembered her shoe size."

Jess let it go.

"I'll take another pass at her tomorrow. As it was, I was on the verge of getting myself shot."

"How would you…?" He guessed she dismissed it as Alec being flip, moving on. "Why don't you let me talk to her tomorrow? Maybe having a woman there would put her at ease."

"Maybe. And no offense, but I do have experience talking with hostage takers and those taken hostage. I can handle her."

"Fine," Jess said, holding up a hand. "Far be it from me to get in the way of Alec Clairmont in action. If you don't want my help…"

"It's not that."

"Then what?" she said. "You've been standoffish—or more like pissed off—since you broke me out of that jail. Aside from the reason we're here, which I get is difficult, what gives Alec?"

"Nothing."

"Bullshit," she said, eyeing him in a way that only Jess could. "I know detached, unemotional Alec. This is detached, unemotional Alec with a nasty chip on his shoulder."

He shook his head, turning away. "Can't help what you're imagining. Isn't what's going on with my parents enough?"

Jess folded her arms, tipping her head at him.

"Look, aside from coincidence, my parents aren't even the reason you're here. Not because of what's happening to me or my family."

"Thanks, Alec. Ankle-deep thoughtfulness, as usual."

"Sorry," he said, glancing toward the open balcony, the blankness of the dusky sky.

"Maybe things didn't start out that way, but how could I not be involved? We're hardly strangers, and if you don't mind me saying, your hard-ass attitude is bordering on ungrateful."

"Ungrateful?" he said, his voice rising. "How am I being ungrateful? I would have said more than 'thank you' when we got back to town—maybe bought you both a beer—but I couldn't fit it in before you and Julian took off. Sorry if figuring out what happened to my parents is cramping your sex life."

"Oh, that's rich coming from you." Jess stiffened her shoulders, folding her arms tighter. "You're seriously going to pitch a fit over Julian? Get real. You forget, I pay rent to live in the land of casual, no-context sex. A place where I have to negotiate around whatever piece of ass you drag back to our apartment after some bodyguard gig."

"So what?" he fired back. "You seem content enough fucking your almost ex-husband."

"What does that have to do with anything? And it's not like I'm fucking him directly across the hall in an apartment with paper-thin walls!"

"No, just one floor below me."

"Fine, Alec. You've got me there."

He backed up a step, but it was the confirmation of Jess and Julian sleeping together that created real distance.

"And just so we're clear," she spat at him, "until you've waited in said hall, while some strange woman flushes whatever she's flushing, then passes by you without so much as a 'Hi, I'm the skank du jour,' before slamming your bedroom door, you really don't have much to complain about!"

"I didn't know it was such a strain on you. What do you care anyway?"

"I don't," Jess snapped, turning toward the door but pivoting back. "Maybe it was just the shock of realizing that Alec Clairmont hype was, in fact, reality."

"Hey, you have no right being pissed off at me for discovering that I'm exactly what was advertised. You rented a room, Jess—not a piece of my life."

"No arguing there." Her glare cut like a razor. "I guess it was the confusion of those faint glimmers."

"Faint glimmers? What the fuck does that mean?"

"Moments where letting your guard down didn't seem like the worst thing that could happen to you. You know, Alec. A real life. The thing you avoid at all costs."

Alec shoved his hands into his pockets. A constricting six-pack of abs grew tighter by the sentence. It was true. Aside from his family, Jess was the only person who caught parts of an Alec he preferred not to let breathe, never mind acknowledge. The fact she'd said it out loud—or maybe that she noticed—totally ticked him off. On occasion, he could do the casual weekend thing. But he couldn't do this. "Enough," he said. "If we don't learn anything more by tomorrow, I'm headed back to the States, picking up the investigation there." Alec walked to the balcony, below was the dimming street. "Great," he said, glancing back. "You can put your dress into action. Julian's on his way in." He faced her and Jess narrowed her hazel eyes. Among his survival skills, Alec was particularly adept at being a complete bastard if need be. "Would it make things even if I came down one floor and waited outside your room while you fuck him?"

Jess stormed past, thrusting the door open. It slammed, flakes of ceiling plaster snowing down on Alec's head.

⸻

He didn't feel like food. Booze, on the other hand... Finding the liquor mart in La Carta was a no-brainer. Sitting in his room, Alec was a quarter of the way through a bottle of tequila when there was a knock at his door. It had to be Jess. Rumblings from the room below had dissipated. He'd guessed the two had gone out for sustenance afterward. Yeah. The chipped turquoise painted floor was that thin.

Jess had brought a guy home once since moving into his apartment. Upon realizing it, Alec left, spending the night in Aaron's old room. He'd thought he was giving them privacy. Downing another shot, Alec assured himself that short of finding another hotel, liquor was the best way to do that now. The knocking grew more intense. No doubt Jess had gotten to the *"count on it"* fight with Julian. She wasn't on the verge of divorcing him without reason. The guy was a prick—definitely in Alec's opinion and in Jess's when she was seeing straight. Why she'd lost sight of that since arriving in La Carta... well, go figure.

Positive that vindication was on the other side of the door, he let her knock again. *No need to rush the shoulder to cry on...* Not that Jess really ever did that. One more passionate knock penetrated. Alec hauled himself out of the chair, striding confidently across the room. Righteousness seemed to sober up his half-crocked head. He swung the door open, unable to smother an "I told you..."

"Hello... Alec, right?"

"Uh, right." Confidence faltered. On the other side of the door was Kiera Blyth. "What... How did you find me?"

"La Carta is a small place. Strangers stand out. You left a pretty good trail in the village today."

"Like I said, I'm looking for information."

She didn't wait for an invite but helped herself to the inside of his room. Her clothing was different from earlier—still a simple blue dress, but more in tune with the climate, definitely her figure. Her brown hair was no longer braided but fell in full waves past her shoulders.

Kiera cocked her chin at the nightstand. "I see you found the liquor store."

"I'd offer you a drink, but I'm guessing you don't..."

"Then you'd guess wrong."

Right... the Wild Turkey...

She flashed a smile at him. "I'll help myself." She poured a full shot glass and downed it. She winced a bit as the liquor rolled through her throat. "It's been a while."

"The booze?"

"The everything."

"Meaning?"

She poured herself another shot but only drank half.

The tequila he drank felt apparent again, off-kilter numbness weaving through his body. Kiera approached, offering him the rest. What the hell, it was his booze. He downed it. "So exactly what are you doing here?"

"How much explanation do you need for this to work?"

"I mean here. In this godforsaken hole. Did you rob a liquor store back home, kill somebody?"

"Much worse."

Alec widened his eyes.

"They caught me with a tube of lip gloss, earrings, and a bedroom floorboard filled with trashy romance novels."

"You're kidding, right?"

She shrugged. "The fact that they also caught me naked with the Pruitt boy might have had something to do with it."

Alec half smiled. "More than once?"

"No, but he was the fourth boy." She stood so close her breasts brushed against his chest, the faint smells of perfume and lust wafting off her. He supposed her story didn't matter. Kiera inched her fingers in between them, starting a *tough-to-misinterpret* unbuttoning of his shirt. "How about we skip past the part where my presence surprises you?"

"Presence I could get my mind around..." He grabbed her hands as they reached for his belt buckle. "This..."

Standing on her toes, she kissed him before he could get another word out. "After you left, I couldn't get the idea of fucking you out of my head. Do you want to spend more time asking stupid questions?"

Alec thought for a second—then he didn't and released her hands. Fuck it, boldness was certainly in her wheelhouse, everything from pointing a gun at him to wrapping her hand around a... He closed his eyes. Clearly his dick had no issues with the offer. Alec had handled his share of aggressive women—but mostly in bars, backstage at rock concerts. Never missionaries. He didn't even care for the position. It made him ask, "This, um... this seems a few light years out of schoolmarm character."

She shrugged and shimmied his pants lower. "I asked around. I understand the woman you're traveling with belongs with the other man."

Alec's jaw clenched along with his stomach.

"Ah, that's not a fact you like."

He shook his head. "Not a fact that affects me—can't speak for her bad choices."

"Fair enough." She kissed him again, and this time Alec kissed her back, his hands moving through her hair. "I also heard you were alone."

"Doesn't mean I'm lonely."

"Really?" she said, her mouth grazing his jaw as her hand caressed a hard as hell dick. "How else do you describe you and a bottle of tequila in a room that, I know for a fact, doesn't get *pay TV*?"

"My choice."

"Choices are good. Assume I'm here to add to the selection." Her mouth, her body, felt like a warm tropical indulgence. When she dropped to her knees, taking him in her mouth, it all seemed like temporary consolation. Escape from the reasons he'd come to this godforsaken piece of the world right down to his fight with Jess. Alec burrowed his hand into her hair. Forgetting this way held more promise than tequila, plus the bonus of no hangover. She rose again, as if the blowjob was just an appetizer. It was ample enticement. Alec's hands were on the dress, then under it, skimming the supple skin of her thigh. She wore silky panties that were at extreme odds with the clothing she'd been wearing earlier. He slid his hand beneath the barely there fabric, cupping her ass.

Kiera pressed her body to his. "Earlier, whatever you thought..." she whispered. "A lot of that is true. I am the schoolmarm you met..." She inched back and smiled.

He didn't return the gesture.

"That's what you thought, isn't it?" she said. "Schoolmarm?"

"Seemed logical, while this seems..."

"More like a fantasy?"

He blinked at her. No, actually, this fantasy hadn't crossed his mind. But it sure as hell seemed to be describing hers. Like the woman on the airplane, Alec didn't debate the offer. In fact, as Kiera slipped back onto her knees, any conscious reasoning went to hell. Damn. It beat the hell out of the mood he'd been in before she showed up. Alec dove into the moment, leaning just enough to deposit the shot-glass onto the table. His breathing turned lusty; another minute and days of frustration were going to explode in her mouth. She must have sensed that he was at a precipice because she rose to face him. Alec's instincts took over.

The simple, blue dress had a simple zipper down the back. The schoolmarm stepped out of it, Alec quickly shedding his clothes. Suddenly he didn't want the blowjob. He just wanted to fuck her— hard. Directness was to both their advantages as Kiera discarded her undergarments. It worked for him. Alec wasn't in the mood for foreplay pleasantries. A furious exchange of groping and kissing ensued. Breathy gasps dominated as the two fell onto an already messy, unmade bed. Alec's mouth trekked down Kiera's body the way it did other women—urge providing a solid substitute for feeling. Pale, hidden from the sun flesh, met with his anxious mouth. He might have labeled her body virginal, but she'd clarified that possibility. A moan of pleasure pulsed from her throat as Alec indulged in erect nipples, Kiera encouraging him with every inch of her body.

Sexual scents filled the air, overtaking perfume and the taste of booze. Alec dragged his mouth across her stomach and hipbone. Her back arched as Alec slid a finger inside her. She gasped tense but pleasurable sounds, all of Kiera telling him that whatever her story, she had no qualms about the one playing out here. Seconds later, she caught him off guard by becoming the aggressor. Kiera lurched forward and gripped him around the shoulders, kissing him hard.

"Fuck me... just fuck me... now," she insisted.

A warning went off in Alec's head, but it was too easy to ignore as Kiera kissed him again. He reached to the nightstand and his wallet. Alec tore open the condom wrapper, sheathing himself. The two of them were stretched across the short side of the mattress, Alec pushing her long legs apart. He glanced upward, making the error of eye contact. This was meaningless sex. They both knew it. And Alec, he didn't have use for any other kind. But in her face, awash with raw desire, Alec saw something troubling. It was something that did not belong in this room—a vibe that was overtly vulnerable. Alec didn't respond to it, not in any human way. Instead he jerked his head to the right.

She obliged, turning over and shuffling to her knees. Yeah. She definitely knew this routine. He didn't hesitate and thrust into her, the ambiance reverting to the fuck she'd come for. Other than the physical act, the only other contact was minimal and necessary. Kiera seemed to get his disinterest in intimacy, touching herself as she cried obscenities of satisfaction. It was the grand finale Alec needed, clutching the pillows beside them as the moment came full circle for him.

The directness with which Kiera had ambushed his room spiraled along with the manmade passion. Alec didn't even offer her a drink as she dressed, relieved that she didn't appear intent on hanging around, or worse, spending the night. As she struggled with the zipper on her dress, Alec pretended to be busy straightening the bed covers. When she got as far as the door, he guessed he'd dodged any bullets marked personal. But as he turned toward her, the scene unraveled.

"Tomorrow," she said, her hand on the knob, "when you leave... I'd like for you to take me with you."

"Take you with me?" The panicked feel of *"you jackass..."* shot through Alec.

"Yes. I know you came here to figure out what happened to your parents. But you're missing some big puzzle pieces. My guess is you're headed to Good Hope, Pennsylvania. I want to go home. You can get me there. If you do that, I'll take you to someone who can tell everything you want to know about Evie Neal and Ezra Kane."

CHAPTER TWENTY-THREE

1979
Good Hope, Pennsylvania

Reeling from the Reverend's grasp, Evie raced like fire down the path that led to the cabin. She stopped at the wooden stoop. Panting hard, she pressed one hand to the doorframe, steadying herself. With the other, she touched her puffy lip, glancing at the torn blouse sleeve. She stepped back, feeling colder than the spring ground that met with her bare feet. The moon lit her bloody fingertips, her mouth throbbed. She cupped a hand over it, thinking she might be sick. Evie focused on gathering her wits—separating in her mind what had nearly happened with the Reverend and her vow to Ezra. By the second, everything she ever knew kept changing.

Then Evie almost retreated. If she went inside the cabin, if Sebastian saw this, neither Ezra nor the Reverend would matter. He'd never leave Good Hope without her. Evie blinked into a well-lit night and down the path. Then she faced the cabin door. She realized it wasn't a choice. The only thing to do was to accept what was. Evie turned the metal knob. The door swung wide. At the same time, so did the bathroom door. Sebastian came out wrapped in a towel. He smiled. "We have to stop meeting like..." Through fading light, Evie's tousled state registered and he charged across the cabin floor. "What the hell happened?" His wide eyes turned fearful. Sebastian touched the corner of her mouth, his fingertips coming away bloody. "Evie?" he said, looking at her blouse sleeve, ripped from its seam. "Tell me who... Not Ezra? Did he come back?"

A thousand thoughts whirled, but Evie couldn't hold onto a single one long enough to speak. She thrust herself into his bare chest. The moment his arms where around her, Evie knew she belonged there. In all of Good Hope, in all her life, she'd never felt so safe.

But Sebastian's breath grew as uneasy as hers. "Evie, tell me what's going on. *Now*..." But he didn't let go, his hand pressing hard to the back of her head. "If it wasn't Ezra..." Then he pushed away, holding her firm by the shoulders. "The Reverend. He did this."

She nodded, wet lashes fluttering.

"Because he found out about us?"

"No. Because he wanted... *the same*." Her explanation was small and unclear. But she saw Sebastian grasp every word. His face lit with fury. He grabbed his pants from a chair and yanked them on. Turning for the door, Evie caught him by the arm, the muscle so tense it was like gripping an iron beam. She found her voice, screaming for him to stop. "You can't... Don't! It will only make it worse. Nothing happened."

His gaze careened over her. "Nothing happened? Let me get you a fucking mirror. Enough, Evie! And he won't get away with it, not this."

"He didn't," she said, scrambling to find calm. Hysteria would only incite a vengeful hunt. "I... On a side table, there was a painting Ezra made for me. It sat on a metal easel. I grabbed for it... struck him with it. The Reverend, he fell to the floor, and before he could get back up I ran... *to you*."

"Because it's where you belong. I should have never let you go back there. I'm sorry if that's what it took to prove it."

"Maybe not." Evie shook her head. "Do you... Well, do you think it's punishment for what you and I... because we...?"

Sebastian scrubbed a hand over his face. "Tell me you don't really believe that."

"In my heart...no. In my head..."

"That's where we're going to start, Evie—in your head. I've kept quiet because I didn't want to be the person to unplug everything you've ever known. But you need to know a few truths you won't find in Good Hope. Maybe now," he said, his gaze trailing over her, "you'll believe what I'm about to tell you."

They sat near the fire, one chair facing another. Sebastian did most of the talking. Evie heard stories she would have called lies from anyone else. Stories she might not have believed before today. She didn't want to hear the harsh facts—not even from Sebastian. But as he revealed his true mission, the criminal means by which the Reverend earned money, and how Sebastian was working to thwart his efforts, Evie knew that every word was a new gospel.

Sebastian Christos was a ruffian by trade, a man who'd done dubious things. But the more he spoke, the more it was apparent he'd done so for a greater good. He was untamed and unpredictable. His future was as shaky as snow in a globe. Despite it all, Evie knew an honest man sat before her.

When he was done, he leaned back in the chair. Evie held the towel he'd been wearing, dabbing at her lip now and again. It had stopped bleeding some time ago. Mostly she'd been wringing the towel tighter with each unnerving detail. Sebastian's focus shifted from an explanation and onto the torn blouse. His jaw was rigid and an angry breath sucked into him. She wanted to cover the mark on her arm, and Evie tried adjusting the sleeve. It kept falling, a welt rising like a wax seal—official validation of the truth, she supposed. "It will be fine," she said.

"Which part?"

The question was direct and the answers made her shudder.

"Tell me what you want, Evie." He leaned forward, pressing

elbows on his thighs, hands clasped in front of him. "Right now and for the rest of your life. Because if even one part is left up to me..." Sebastian sat back again, calmly finishing the thought. "Reverend Kane will need more than a prayer when I get through with him."

"I don't want to talk about him anymore." Evie had settled that much in her mind. "I don't want to think about what he's done or the corrupt ways he's misled good people." She closed her eyes, realizing the impossibility of convincing anyone in Good Hope of what Sebastian knew—the stories of *the mission*. The depravity was almost too much to comprehend, let alone resolve.

But in the wake of devastating truths, she felt at peace. Evie knew what she wanted, which was to shut everything else out. In all her life, she'd never needed anything so badly nor been able to reach for it so readily. Evie stood, met by an odd longing—the desire to erase a false life. With Sebastian seated in front of her, she began undoing the pearl buttons of her ruined blouse. He seemed to know this wasn't for him or even meant as a lure. He folded his arms, watching as if bearing witness.

She discarded the garment by dropping it into the fire. Flames lapped around it until the blouse was no more than a fiery glow of fabric and freedom. Still sitting, Sebastian's eyes locked with hers. Evie unzipped the skirt and let it fall, nudging it aside. It was then the air and their twined gazes turned more sensual. Evie tugged the tie from her hair, fingers spinning through the braid as if undoing her life. Yellow-gold waves capped her shoulders, and Evie guessed this was the woman Sebastian wanted to see. A half step forward invited him to reach.

He drew her body close to his, but he did ask, "Evie, are you sure?"

She answered by unhooking her bra. He didn't wait for more words, suckling each breast as her fingers wove through his thick dark hair. Breathing was more about desire as his mouth moved from one side to the other. She felt his fingers loop around her underwear. In a single fluid motion, the cotton fabric slid downward and Evie stepped out of it. When he touched her, Evie's body trembled, and his fingers reached to the nub of flesh that ached for all of him. He tugged her closer, and Evie stood, straddled over either side of his seated frame. Sebastian pushed the chair back, knocking it over as he dropped to his knees. His face pressed into her mound and Evie had to grip the fireplace mantel to keep upright. That exquisite thunderous tremor built within her and Evie fought it, wanting Sebastian inside her when this happened. But she couldn't or didn't know how to find the words. She dug her hand into his shoulder. "It has to be together," she said. "It has to be more powerful than anything that's happened today."

She peered down and he glanced up. "It will." She had no control over this part of Sebastian, and as his mouth filled with her, his hands braced her body.

"Please..." But she was lost to him and the moment as he literally kept her from collapsing as she came. "Bash ..." tore from her lips and Evie couldn't imagine anything more consuming. But as he rose, she sensed more of a beginning than closure. He never broke contact with her body, unfolding his tall frame until she had to look up. She was grateful for the support of his body as it held onto hers. Evie pushed past the sting of her mouth as he kissed her... again and again. But it wasn't enough for either of them. Sebastian's hands roamed anxiously over her as she unzipped his pants.

Immersed in more emotion than Evie thought possible, she slid in his arms, turning her back to him. It was only to gain her bearings, temper, the pace. It did no good. Sebastian took sweet advantage, caressing her breasts, his touch slightly less gentle. Evie tipped her head to the side and Sebastian alternated kisses on her neck with words.

"I... I've seen other men love people... *women*. Watched how they behaved, the things they'd do for them. I never thought I'd feel that... I didn't know it was in me."

Evie's lungs filled—no, it was all of her—as the last of the coldness inside her warmed. She understood the weight of his confession because she felt it too. She tilted her head back and closed her eyes.

"But I have to tell you," he said, nuzzling her neck. "I hope this is all of it."

"Why?" she said, a small smile invading her bruised lip.

"Because to feel anything more would be the end of me, Evie Neal."

She absorbed the name. It was who she was. But the thought drifted off as Evie felt the physical half of his claim press against her. As Sebastian reached past the flat of her belly, his body tried to inch hers right, toward the bed. Her only response was to hold her hands to his as they mapped her body.

"Evie," he said, warning in his voice. "If we don't take this down a notch... I might not think about this in ways that work best on feather mattresses. You don't know what you're asking for, how I want to..."

"I think I do." She drew his hands to her mouth, kissing them. "I want to know."

A deep breath pulled into him, as if weighing how he wanted to go about this. Urge won out, and Sebastian steered them toward the table at the center of the room. "Put your hands on it." She followed the instruction. His mouth met with her spine, a silky touch compared to the brashness of his voice. Sebastian nudged her legs apart, and Evie had to brace her arms firmly into the table. It was what she wanted, the power of Sebastian taking her completely as he thrust into her. She'd never envisioned such a provocative pose. It was a wildly heated moment, unfathomable desire and curious small talk.

"Jesus, Evie... I never... Never thought this could be..."

"About anything but us."

"Yes... exactly. Us." A sound vibrated from her throat. The force with which he moved inside her was delicious and a little dangerous. "Sorry," he said, "we can slow it down."

"No!" she said, reaching back with one arm, making contact with his warm skin. But she had to let go, hold firm to the table. It was all so dominant—Evie couldn't imagine a more defining act. Small talk dissipated, leaving momentous breaths that conveyed Sebastian's desire until all of it spilled into her.

In the hours afterward, neither spoke about time. Evie didn't want this to feel like the life of a butterfly—beautiful and fleeting. Neither talked of what was outside the cabin door—which he'd locked by jamming a chair under the knob. Instead, Evie and Sebastian took refuge in the cabin's amenities. Now that Evie had him so close, she was willing to wash the rest of the day away. Sebastian said he had the perfect cure. In fact, he claimed to have worked out that exact scenario countless times in his head. He smiled at her confusion, and Evie watched as he filled the giant cast iron tub. She climbed into it, Sebastian joining her. Sinking into him and the warm soapy water, Evie thought she'd never been anywhere more enticing. "Do you think it's possible," she said, resting in his arms, "to make love in a bathtub?"

"Do I...?" Avoiding the bruise on her arm, Sebastian's body wrapped tighter around hers. "Isn't that what bathtubs are for?"

Evie laughed.

Sebastian didn't, telling her to turn around. "Just about what I thought," he said, gently guiding her until she straddled him.

It was a snug fit but an appealing one as Evie found she rather liked the in-charge angle. His erection throbbed between them, Evie's soapy hand stroking the hard shaft. He let her take the lead, kissing him deeply, longingly, moving herself over him. As she did, Sebastian took over, guiding himself into her. Evie gripped his shoulders, their foreheads bumping as the tight confines made the motion more teasing—rather subdued compared to the scene at the kitchen table. But with the subtler movement came another delectable sensation, and Evie wanted to ask if there was a handbook for all the things she didn't know. All she could do was kiss him, amazed to discover that even in water, a fire could light.

With his hands wrapped around her back, Sebastian's eyes fluttered open. "Definitely exceeding my imagination."

She arched her back and a look of surrender fell over him, demonstrating to Evie that even subtle sex was an awe-inspiring thing.

"Do you have any idea how often I've thought of this?" he said.

She shook her head, kissing his cheek, his mouth.

"Then you probably don't know this is the moment I tell you how much I love you."

⬦

This time, as dawn approached, they lay in the bed together. Sebastian was wide awake, a thousand thoughts keeping him on guard. Evie had slept for a few hours. But looking at her, he was able to push the problems away. She'd never belong anywhere but with him. He caressed her arm, narrowing his eyes at the bruise. It surprised him when Evie opened hers, staring, as if maybe she'd been thinking too. But her words didn't match the thoughts that filled his head.

"If I could have a wish," Evie said sleepily, "it'd be for a son with exactly your eyes."

He blinked, the motion of his hand halting. "What did you say?"

She sat up and righted her words as if they'd spilled accidently like a glass of milk. "I'm sorry," she said, pulling the sheet past her breasts. "I shouldn't have said such a thing. Of course you wouldn't think of..." She glanced over her shoulder. "Our worlds, they're very different. Aren't they?"

"Evie..." He sat up too and kissed her shoulder. "I can't argue that. But it's not even about... Look, it's not something I've ever thought about—not in a good way."

She twisted her body, looking at him. "How else would you think of it?"

"Well, for one, not at all—except how to keep it from..." Sebastian puffed air into his cheeks, letting it escape. He'd been so cavalier about sex between them. "We should have talked about... I'm sorry. My fault. I didn't think..." He dragged a hand around the back of his neck. "Of course you're not doing anything to prevent..."

"I told you, I can't... Well, I knew nothing could happen the first time, but obviously there's been sufficient chance since—"

"Wait. What couldn't happen the first time?"

She didn't look at him, staring at the fistful of sheets she'd gathered. "Getting pregnant. It can't happen the first time you have sex."

He widened his eyes. "Uh, Evie, yeah it can."

"But Ezra said..."

"And he took his sex education class where? Listen to me..."

Her mood turned antsy, Evie tucking a length of hair behind her ear and pulling her knees tight to her body. He considered the gentlest way to pursue a necessary conversation. Sebastian doubted she had a clue about how *not* to get pregnant. The fact that she hadn't gotten pregnant, he guessed she might be right. Maybe she couldn't have children. "It's fine. I'll take care of any precautions." He brushed his shoulder against hers. "Seems when it's just us, most everything slips into place, but we will have some hurdles. We can talk about kids and eye color another time. Does that work?"

"Of course... you're completely right," she said, though her gaze looked everywhere but at him. "Speaking about children...It was a foolish thought for a million reasons, never mind saying it aloud."

He shrugged. "Since you mention it... And just so you know," he said, trying to get the blush to fade from her face. "With eye color come all the Christos traits. We're not a walk in the park. You might want to think about that."

Evie hugged her knees tighter and turned her head, peering hard at him. "So far I seem to be doing all right with that walk."

Sebastian pulled her to him, their bodies easing into the pillows. "You do have a flair for untamed. But how about we focus on first things first? What happens when that sun comes up hauling reality along with it?" Snuggling into the feather mattress, they both looked toward the fireplace's spent ashes.

"My blouse," she said. "I suppose we could begin with you loaning me a shirt. I'd think wearing it down the main street of Good Hope should make a statement."

"Is that what you want, a grandstand show?"

"No," she said, her blonde hair brushing against him. "But it's what the Reverend deserves. Of course, how we'd convince anyone else...That I have no idea about."

"I might. Let me ask you this," he said, broaching a new subject. "I have to go back to South America, at least a few more trips. I explained to you about Sam, my contact there. I made a deal—I have to keep my end of it. But how would you feel about leaving here with me?"

Evie reasoned it out. "I won't be able to convince anyone of what you've told me. Strange as it will be, I don't believe I can remain with the Fathers of the Right or in Good Hope." Her hands squeezed over his. "Wherever you are, it seems like I should be there too."

He sat up, Evie following. That wasn't exactly his plan. "Evie, you can't come with me to South America. But I have friend in Philly. His name is Bim, he's a doctor. He'd do anything I ask, you could stay with him until—"

"Leave here *and* leave you?"

"I know it sounds daring... complicated. But I know Bim. He'd take good care of you."

Her head shook harder with every word.

"It's the best way out. Maybe the only way."

"You'd want me to stay with strangers? No. I won't do it. I can't."

He studied her anxious face. He got it. She'd never been beyond the library in North Good Hope or bought a dress in a store. She'd never lived among people that weren't exactly like her. From every angle she faced a huge learning curve. "Okay, but you can't stay here. Not after what happened with the Reverend. How long until you wake up one night and find him standing over your bed? You don't think keeping his son at bay has been part of his plan—at least subconsciously? Frankly, I'm surprised it's taken this long for him to..."

"You give me little credit, Sebastian Christos. Do you find me so frail and weak? You don't believe I could outwit him, fend him off?"

"Not my point. And I prefer not to test the odds. If you think for one second I'm leaving you here to..." He shook his head. "Do you find *me* that frail and weak?" he said, overcome by protective instincts. "It's not happening, Evie. You're done with this place."

To his surprise, she agreed. "Maybe so. But I also won't stay with your friend. If you're going to South American, I'm going with you."

"You're going... Don't you think taking on the outside world should start on a smaller scale, like maybe the mall?"

"Not if South America is your destination. Besides, you're not the only reason I need to go—"

"Evie, stop. You're not coming with me, not for a thousand reasons. If you think I'm taking you from Good Hope and delivering you to the jungle... There's no way." She tried to object, but he wouldn't let her get a word in. "You'd be blown away by my neighborhood back in South Philly, never mind a radical foreign country. You'll stay with Bim."

She was silent, though it didn't strike him as obedience—not like the women of Good Hope. She folded her arms across bare breasts, her face stoic. "Are you quite through?"

"With this decision... yes." Sebastian folded his arms behind his head, elbows splayed wide as he sunk into the pillows.

"Good. Then you'll be quiet so you can hear how it will work." His wide blink met with her brown-eyed stare. How had she ever managed for so long in this oppressive life? "Since I don't know the difference between what's in a mall or South Philadelphia or the jungle, I suspect that part won't matter. And it's not even about what I want, Bash. I have to go with you."

"Because..."

"You haven't considered every part to this problem."

He knotted his brow.

"If I wore a wedding ring, I suspect I would have twisted it raw on my finger by now. With all that's happened, have you forgotten? I am married to another man."

It wasn't that he had. But right or wrong, he saw Ezra Kane as nothing more than an unfortunate nuisance. Evie's burning glare said she wasn't seeing quite the same thing.

"For whatever Ezra's father has done, Ezra deserves none of it. You know where he is. I want you to take me to him. I have to tell him face to face—about us, about what his father has done. If I can't honor my marriage, I will honor the bond we've shared since childhood. I owe him that." Sebastian tore his hands through his hair as her determination came clear. "I won't leave here any other way, under any other agreement. Think about it, Bash. I *can* get out of this bed and go back to my life here. Don't doubt me."

"I've already said my piece," he said, refusing to move from his prone position. "You're not staying here at the mercy of that bastard."

"Then I'd say you have little choice."

"Be realistic." He sat back up. "I don't doubt you'd do anything—including outright murder to avoid the Reverend. But look at your arm... your mouth. Dumb it down to physical size and will, eventually he'd..."

"I'm sorry if this feels like blackmail. I should think it's going to feel worse for me if I have to go through with it. But unless you agree to take me to Ezra, I don't see how else I leave here. That's the way of it."

He sighed, weighty and unsure. "You picked a fine time to assert your independence, Evie."

"I suspect you might want to get used to it."

CHAPTER TWENTY-FOUR

GETTING THEM OUT OF GOOD HOPE WAS EASIER THAN EVIE ENVISIONED. So many men returned from Colombia the rental vehicle had been a necessity, the keys left in it. Racing against dawn, Evie slipped back inside the cottage and packed a few things. On her way out, she stopped, righting Ezra's painting and the easel, which lay on the floor. Reverend Kane was nowhere in sight, the Kane house dark. But passing by her father's house there was a jab of ambivalence. If her mother were alive, would she be doing this? Evie looked toward Sebastian, who waited by the van. The outline of his frame was unmistakable, even in shadowy darkness. Uncertainty faded. Not even her mother could change her mind or how she felt. As for Gideon Neal, since Evie married Ezra her father had become more like a distant relative. Chances were he'd see nothing wrong with her father-in-law's perverse means of extending the Kane bloodline. *"Go Evie... if the Reverend deems it God's will..."* She shuddered and she did go, passing by her father's house. In her mother's death and Evie's life, Gideon Neal had been no more than a complacent bystander.

"Are you ready?" Sebastian asked.

It sounded more like, *"Are you sure?"*

Daylight was a rooster's crow away. Lights turned on in the Blyth and Pruitt houses. Evie knew their day before they lived it—a repetition of actions, blind devotion, and conformity. She didn't want the same. Too overwhelmed to speak, she nodded at Sebastian. As they left the confines of Good Hope, roads quickly turned unfamiliar. Excitement, expectation, and a dollop of fear drove the pounding in Evie's heart.

Sebastian explained that they would sail to South America aboard a ship. It was scheduled to leave later that day. On the outskirts of Philadelphia, seabirds circled, squawking from above. "The harbor," he said, "it's not far from here." He smiled and reached over, squeezing her hand. "I need to make a few stops first, including returning this van." He parked and the two got out, the swell of traffic and people unnerving Evie. She held tight to Sebastian's hand as they went into several places of business.

The first was a bank, and Evie didn't ask as Sebastian came away with a large sum of cash. From there, he suggested her clothing was ill-suited for traveling by land or by boat. They walked down another busy block, Evie glancing from stranger to stranger, people who came in a myriad of colors, all looking so different from one another. Sebastian stopped at the entrance to a storefront. One woman came out, then another. Each looked like a fancier version of the women she'd seen in North Good Hope. They carried several shopping bags. "Uh, this should work," he said. A revolving door took them into a ladies' clothing shop, its whirling spin indicative of Evie's new life.

Inside, she perused rack after rack of readymade clothing, the choices of fabric and fashion dizzying. After a few turns around the shop, Evie was overwhelmed and confused. Everything was such an unknown. Panic flickered. *If shopping for clothing is a mistake...* Just as her breath bordered on hyperventilating, a woman with sky-high hair, the color of angels' wings, came to Evie's aid. "What a beautiful young lady you are. Pastels would be perfect on you."

Evie said nothing, and a few moments later it was likely the saleswoman thought she was a beautiful deaf mute. She didn't say a word, only accepting outfit after outfit as the woman led her into a room where the purpose was to try on the clothes.

A short time later, Evie peered into a long mirror. The most full-length reflection she'd ever seen was her glassy image in the window of a hardware store in North Good Hope. The saleswoman looked decidedly pleased as she and Evie absorbed the astonishing result. She'd never worn trousers, let alone blue jeans. She didn't know how to respond when the saleswoman insisted that hiding her figure was a sin.

"Sweetheart, I don't know who convinced you high-buttoned collars and bulky skirts were in this spring, but trust me, they were just jealous."

Evie reached toward the reflection, unsure if it was her own—the way her breasts filled out the tight-fitted material, a pale-pink T-shirt and denim hugging her backside and legs. Sebastian was leaning against a wall when she came out of the dressing room. He stood ramrod straight, the awed look on his face matching hers.

"A transformation, I should think," she said softly.

"Only on the outside." His gaze met hers as Evie looked in yet another mirror. "Don't hate me for saying it, but I'm a fan."

Several purchases later, they left the store and made their way to the dock. He asked Evie to wait in the van while he talked to the ship's captain, described as "a guy he knew." Evie suspected there would be pieces of Sebastian that would not be explained, questions she shouldn't ask. She looked around streets she'd never walked on, volumes of people taking up the sidewalks—more than she'd ever seen in one place. The men carried square cases and many of the women hurried along in high-heeled shoes and tightly tailored suits. Other types of people caught Evie's eye—a man who appeared to be sleeping in a cardboard box and a few feet away another one with a metal cart selling food. Between them was a police officer, none seemed interested in what the other was doing. In Good Hope, it was difficult to find a moment in the day where one's life went unnoticed.

Evie looked in the direction Sebastian had gone. As he reappeared through the thick of strangers, the breath she'd been holding eased. Not long after they'd settled their business and the van was returned, they boarded the ship. Sebastian whisked her below deck and through a maze of narrow corridors, finally unlocking one of the many doors they passed.

A hum of nerves wove through Evie, her eyes darting around the cool metal clad hallway. On the opposite side of the door, her nerves eased, pleased to see a bed and bath, though there was barely enough space to turn around. Sebastian apologized for the small simple room. Evie didn't answer, reassured by the close quarters. He said the trip would take six days—he'd prefer it if she stayed mostly in the cabin. "It's safer. What goes down up on deck... well, let's just say it's not a cruise ship."

"Cruise ship?" she asked.

In the early morning hours, Sebastian did take her up on deck, when most of the crew was still sleeping. Awed by the vastness of the ship, Evie marveled at its smallness compared to the ocean. She admired the way Sebastian fit so comfortably into every aspect of his seaworthy existence. He'd been out of his element in Good Hope—or so this proved—his confidence apparent on board. On the ship's deck, Evie turned away from him and looked east into a rising sun. The air was chilly and fresh until an acidy aroma intruded. She turned. In the drugstore, a place filled with bottles of medicine Evie could not name, Sebastian had bought several items, including cigarettes. He stood at the rail, pursing a smoldering stem between his lips. Evie frowned but said nothing. A moment later he tossed the cigarette overboard and cleared his throat. "Compared to what you're doing, quitting shouldn't be all that tough."

Another day passed and the glassy ocean turned rough, sloshing them about like a toy boat in a tub. Romanticism turned queasy. Everything, in addition to Sebastian's eyes, went a little green.

Lying in the bed, the only quick movement Evie made was darting to the closet-size commode—a space where a person couldn't even fall on her knees to reach the toilet. But Evie was quick to recover, adjusting to the rough ocean. Sebastian said he was impressed by her sturdy sea legs.

"But I thought you liked the jeans?" she said, pointing to the pair that had been draped over a chair for two days. He seemed to find her remark funny, though she wasn't sure why.

"Feeling better?" he said the following morning.

"Much. Thank you." Evie had opened the port window, and the fresh, salt air blew back her hair. She was on her knees on the bed, staring, still amazed by how the ocean met the sky the way it did the land. She was grateful for the chance to see it and angry that it'd been kept from her. But as Sebastian cozied up next to her, brushing his stubbly face against Evie's smooth cheek, those emotions ebbed. His powers of persuasion were like a potion. He embraced her shoulders, kissing one. Evie's glance cut sideways. The contrast of his strong hands on the delicate fabric of her nightgown was mesmerizing.

While on their Philadelphia shopping spree, the saleswoman had brought the nightgown into the fitting room. "Honey, if you're going traveling with him, I might suggest this..." Evie had only touched the silky, white fabric, not trying it on until the first night on the ship. Sebastian had come into the room carrying a tray of sandwiches and soup. He'd sloshed the soup everywhere as he shoved it onto a table.

"Are you trying to kill me?"

"What?" she'd said, panicked by what sounded like disapproval. He'd stared as though he couldn't comprehend the Evie in front him. "The woman in the store said you'd like it." He hadn't said much else, but an hour later Evie knew the saleslady had been correct.

She closed her eyes now, facing the sea breeze and basking in Sebastian's touch—something she'd begun to look for in her sleep.

Her mind drifted between him and the open air, Evie sure it was the most perfect state of being. The nightgown had a delicate elastic yoke, mimicking something like what Evie would have liked on a wedding dress. He nudged it down, exposing her shoulder. She liked the way the garment obeyed, giving Sebastian what he wanted and she needed. As the days had gone by, his touch grew surer—a sense of permanence. He pushed the gown lower, exposing her top half. Evie saw the sun on her breasts and felt the wind against her skin. With nothing but sea for miles, she hardly minded the exposed view. "Do you want…" she began.

"Just don't move." His voice was husky, a tone she understood. The fact that she wore no underwear only boosted his motivation. Her glance caught a glimpse of his T-shirt flying off, his solid erection pressing against her. She moved her legs apart. Sebastian reached around, his fingertips floating down her belly, touching Evie in a way that seemed like a second language to him. She tensed at the contact, gripping her hands around the rail that anchored the bed to the wall. "I have to confess," he said, his words a hot, penetrating whisper. "Sometimes I think about fucking you. *Just* fucking you." She widened her eyes then closed them, her teeth sinking into her bottom lip. "I had to tell you," he said, his hardness beckoning. "Do you think that's awful of me, Evie?"

While the language would take some getting used to, she couldn't deny a desire the rough words evoked. "I think," she said, placing her hand over his, the one kneading her breast, "*sometimes* it may be best that way."

"Damn, another thing we agree on." His actions took her breath away. And it was a different Sebastian that drove himself into her with unapologetic force. There were no sweet sentiments, his touch coarser as it ran the length of her back, his teeth nipping at her shoulder. Evie was awed by the brusque behavior—using words she wouldn't ordinarily say, asking for more, not less. Sebastian accommodated and the reward was ultimately Evie's. She came before him, a wicked combination of rough touch and edgy language, things she reminded herself to ask him about later. As he reached a shuddering climax, Evie was the one left empowered and pleased. The second after he came, ragged and breathless, an even gentler Sebastian returned to her and softly kissed the shoulder he'd nipped. "Thank God, for you, Evie."

She smiled, which he could not see, thinking perhaps he'd learned through curious means, something about heavenly gratitude.

CHAPTER TWENTY-FIVE

1979
South America

THE SHIP HAD BEEN A SAFE HARBOR FOR EVIE AND SEBASTIAN—A respite from reality. On Saturday morning land appeared, small on the horizon, and growing thoughts of Ezra began to edge into Evie's mind. On the bed lay her clothing choices. Sebastian watched as she wrung her hands, vexing over them, fingering one of the skirts she hadn't put on since leaving Good Hope.

"Everything else will be a big enough shock," he said. "If it helps, I don't care what you're wearing when you tell him." He didn't wait for her answer but left the cabin, a nudge to Evie that she needed to decide for herself.

A short time later she stood on the deck, smoothing the front of a simple, brown blouse. It went well with a hip-length cloth coat that the saleswoman had called a "safari jacket," supposedly a popular fashion statement. Sebastian had taken a more practical view, insisting it would be good protection where they were going. Evie had wanted to put on the A-line skirt, different as it was from the bulky gathered skirts she'd worn for years. But that seemed counterintuitive to the terrain Sebastian had described.

Docking the massive freighter was a lengthy orchestrated event. Evie watched as the last of the ship's lines were secured and men on shore and off scurried about, tending to various tasks. She squinted at palm trees and noticed moist warm air that differed greatly from Good Hope's climate. The more distant landscape was veiled in green-covered mountains, and Evie grasped Sebastian's point about the terrain. The jeans she'd chosen were not only figure-hugging but now practical. Evie folded and unfolded her arms, her steps fidgety and nervous. Sebastian waited near the gangway. Her jumpy insides calmed as he locked his arms around her.

"Ready to do this?"

"As I'll ever be. How far did you say Ezra was?"

"A few hours south. This way." He tugged her by the hand, heading down the ramp. "Hopefully not a long enough ride for you to change your mind."

She stopped and Sebastian looked back. "Not hardly." She pulled in front of him.

"Evie, wait." She turned. Sebastian dropped his leather duffel bag to the ground. "Better do this now." He unzipped the duffel bag and withdrew a yellow envelope. "Listen to me—*carefully.*" The serious look on his face put one on hers. "It's an extreme precaution—but a necessary one. If anything happens to me... if you find yourself alone here, open this. There are three letters inside. One is for you. The others will get you out of here. You'll need them. Don't hesitate. Just do what it says, exactly what it says."

"Bash, I don't want to—"

"Evie." His tone quieted her objection. "This place is full of more evil than you've ever been warned of, it's dangerous. Please. Just do it. Promise me, if you have to, you'll follow the instructions."

She nodded, tucking the envelope into her satchel of belongings.

"Good," he said, gathering their bags and her hand.

For as comfortable as he was on the ship—and despite his

warning—the foreign place suited Sebastian. Evie was amazed at the number of people he knew in the dock area, many approaching, calling him "Bash," expressing their obvious delight at his return. The fear he'd instilled in her ebbed. Most people looked curiously at her, and after the second or third acquaintance she noticed that Sebastian offered no explanation about his new companion. Even more telling, not a single person asked.

As they moved from the busy port into a parking area, the mood that accompanied his friendly greetings dissolved. Sebastian's grip grew firmer, never letting go of Evie's hand, the same way his eyes never released the distant perimeter. At a glance, he remained relaxed, but Evie sensed a wariness that wasn't present in Good Hope or aboard the freighter. A man with darker skin than she'd ever seen led them to a large boxy vehicle. "Sam says this one." He handed Sebastian a set of keys. "He also said to tell you that if you wreck another Jeep, it's coming out of your hide."

"Maybe remind Sam that one mangled, government-issued vehicle is a small price to pay for a couple dozen live Marines."

They shook hands, the dark man's face going somber. "He knows this, Bash... He knows." The man reached beneath the back of his earth-colored jacket and handed Sebastian a gun. Evie couldn't stifle a gasp. She knew rifles—every home in Good Hope hunted game. The solid, black handgun was so small in comparison but looked far more menacing. The man's expression turned skeptical. "Since you're here," he said to Evie, "I assume it means you're as jungle savvy and capable as him."

Sebastian tucked the gun into a belt holster that Evie hadn't noticed. "Let's just say if I'm in need of a prayer, she's my best bet."

The man laughed. "Right. Because he'd be a fool to bring you here otherwise."

Between the gun and foreshadowing, Evie's insides fluttered. *And to think a shop in Philadelphia was overwhelming...* But she was there because she'd demanded it, and Evie cocked her chin at the Jeep. "It's fine with me if you drive."

Sebastian smirked at the bold, albeit needless, remark.

"No worries, Edwardo," Sebastian said. "If she proves to be as land worthy as she is seaworthy, I'll be running to keep up with her."

No one said anything else as they departed. Miles down a road that slipped from civilization to a barely there path, Sebastian finally spoke. "Starting to wish you'd never left Good Hope?"

A bump jarred Evie from the seat, her head hitting the canvas roof. She grasped the purpose of the handrail. "Probably not near as much as you wish you hadn't brought me in the first place."

Sebastian steered the Jeep to an abrupt halt. Then he reached, yanking Evie into a ferocious kiss. He pulled away just as fast, and Evie brushed her fingertips over her stinging lips, wanting more.

"If we weren't on the edge of a jungle filled with land pirates, unpredictable native tribes, rapists of varying degrees, I'd fuck you again, right here, right now." He sucked in a breath and drove back onto the path. "So don't ask me about me wanting you here again. One thing has nothing to do with the other."

Evie tucked a sweaty thatch of hair behind her ear. She said nothing as the sun faded to shadow and the road narrowed even more. Sebastian didn't look her way again. His gaze was fully engaged, like a hawk scanning for prey. The rest of the ride was rough but uneventful. An hour later thick brush and a bare bone road receded. It delivered them to a village—rows of shacks lined a landscape more isolated than Good Hope, certainly more uncivilized. A few beat up cars moved through the streets. Chickens ran in between them, moving faster than any vehicle.

But the village wasn't completely foreign, looking something like the pictures she'd seen in mission magazines. Now that Evie had a glimpse of the outside world, she tried to connect it in her head—how being in this pin-size spot served God and the greater good. It seemed the places between Good Hope and Philadelphia alone housed enough infidels to keep one busy. Why here? And then it made sense, Sebastian's explanation of the guns and money and drugs motivating Duncan Kane's trips, not missionary work.

A bearded man emerged from a clapboard structure. Evie squinted. Even with facial hair, his thin frame and fair appearance was like a fingerprint on her mind. Her husband looked terribly out of place among the dark-skinned people, though many approached, talking to him. He moved along like Ezra, serene and chatty.

"So here we are," Sebastian said. "Otava. Also known as the fucking middle of nowhere."

She glanced disapprovingly.

"Well, it is," he said to the coarse description. The two sat in silence fifty yards away from Ezra, the weight of what Evie was about to do sinking in. "I knew this would be hard."

Her wary gaze met his.

"But if being here suddenly makes it seem more like impossible... if you can't go through with it..."

"What?" she said, shrugging at Sebastian. "You're going to tell Ezra you ferried me from Good Hope to here for a conjugal visit?"

"Uh, yeah. I guess not."

Ezra spotted their vehicle, one that clearly didn't belong. He hesitated, as if assessing before starting toward it. Grasping the handle, Evie thrust the door open, feet landing steady on the dirt. She moved forward and Ezra stopped completely. Sebastian's door slammed, the three of them positioned just so. It made for a precarious triangle. But instead of surging toward his wife, Ezra held his ground. He didn't move from the point of his sharp angle. While her presence should have been the biggest shock, Evie saw something more in his reaction. Possibly her strange clothes or unbraided hair. She drew closer. His expression didn't change. Evie didn't see the expectant joy with which Ezra had returned to Good

Hope after months away. Sebastian moved along too but several paces behind.

From a dozen feet away, Evie called out to him. She hesitated, waiting. There was no reply. "Ezra," she said again. She moved faster. Sebastian was close, but not quite beside her. The second she was within arm's length of Ezra, he reached out and delivered a powerful, head-snapping slap. It knocked Evie off her feet, a dirt-covered hand rushing to her stinging cheek.

She heard "Jesus Christ..." as Sebastian shouted the words, shoving Ezra and picking Evie up in one fluid motion. "Are you as fucking twisted as your old man?"

Propped to her feet, Evie couldn't gain her bearings—the raging sun from above, the pulsing heat from the slap. Teary-eyed, she blinked at Ezra, his sunburned face surrounding pools of blue eyes. She'd never considered that he'd do such a thing. All the years they'd been friends... But he wasn't a friend. He was her husband, and she guessed the slap clarified what he knew. Evie touched her mouth. It was the second time in a week her fingertips came away bloody. "Ezra..." she whispered. For what it was worth, he appeared equally shocked by his action. Villagers had stopped, a circle growing around them.

Ezra's glare moved to Sebastian. "Get your hands off of her."

"Why? So you can take another swing?"

"Because she's *my* wife. What she's done..." He eyed the onlookers and came closer. "It's between Evie and me. My father was right about everything. If I'd used a firmer hand, taken control from the start, she might not be standing before me, the shameful, damned woman she is. This is what I get for letting her think freely. Letting her influence the way a marriage should be handled."

Clearly, the Reverend had gotten to his son before Evie could. While the facts were bad, while she'd been unfaithful to her husband, Evie could predict the version of things that had been filtered into his head. "Ezra, listen to me. Whatever your father's told you, it's not the way it happened.... Not exactly."

He snickered. "Are you going to stand here and tell me you've not crawled into his bed like a common slut—like the whores I've seen on the streets here and in Philadelphia?"

"Shut your mouth before I shut it for you," Sebastian said. "And I swear to you, *Brother*, it'll be a hell of a lot more than a slap."

"I knew in my gut. My father should have never allowed you sanctuary in Good Hope."

"Too bad your gut didn't have the balls to ask why he did it."

Ezra ignored the remark. "And to think I was only concerned how you might touch a community. I was naïve. I never thought you'd be so immoral as to touch another man's wife. Does it mean nothing to you that she belongs to me?"

"Do you hear yourself?" Sebastian said, incredulous. "She's not a possession. Wake up, *Brother*, she's not your property."

"Sebastian," Evie said, touching the tense muscle of his arm. "It's all right."

"*The mission's* point of view doesn't make him right. We all understand there's a world beyond the Fathers of the Right— unclean, easy lives. Part of thinking for yourself means having the strength *not* to follow the masses."

"I'm hardly the masses," Sebastian said. "And she's entitled to choose whatever she wants."

Ezra sucked in a breath. "So do you deny sleeping with him? Letting him touch you like..." He frowned deeply. "You must be so very proud of your *choice*, Evie. You've not only turned your back on everything you've been taught but happily spit on our marriage in the process."

"It's not that simple. Yes, part of what I have to tell you will be hurtful, but it's not the only reason I've come... or even the main one. I need you to hear what I have to say—about the Fathers of the Right and—"

"Lies," Ezra said, shaking his head. "You'll tell me nothing but lies. And you think I'm stupid enough to listen. You're right. I did speak with my father, but I also spoke with yours and several of the elders, Charles Ott, Nolan Creek."

Sebastian slung his head back. "Great... all the monkeys in the circus."

"At first, I argued. I defended you, Evie. I said *the mission* must have kidnapped you, taken you against your will. They didn't convince me so easily. I trusted you more than that. Then Nolan Creek spoke up. I wanted so badly to call him a liar, to reach through the phone and throttle him. Call him names worse than he called you—"

"I could suggest a few," Sebastian mumbled.

"But in the end," Ezra said, "all I could do was hear them. Listen to how Brother Creek found the two of you together the night before you married me. As he said the words... the disgusting sin-filled words, all I could think is, 'Why would he lie?'"

Evie closed her eyes—the answer so complex the argument was lost. Duncan Kane and his clansmen had done a fine job of protecting their stake in the world and in Ezra. Evie swiped at her tears, her hands smeared with dirt and blood and guilt. Her husband wasn't completely wrong. And no one but Evie was to blame for setting the stage. It was true. She'd done a terrible thing because she loved another man. She stepped away from Sebastian, shirking his hold.

"Evie?" Sebastian said.

With a more complacent Evie in front of him, Ezra went on. "You're right to lower your eyes to me. It'll be some time, if ever, that you can look at me again. As it is, Father suspected you might try to contact me. I admit, I never thought you'd do anything as brazen as to show up— and dressed like you are..." He jerked his hand toward her, but Sebastian was right there. "Tell me, *wife*, did you come this distance to rub your filthy life and flimsy clothes in my face? Isn't it enough to know you've made a fool of me and forsaken everything you know is right?"

"Exactly. Everything from the way I dressed to what I was taught, the rules we all blindly follow." She stared silently for a moment. "I was never given a choice, Ezra—nor were you—about our lives or who we want in them. If you won't listen, then I can only tell you how sorry I am to have hurt you like this. For whatever else they've filled your head with, you need to hear that much from me."

"Evie," Sebastian said. "This isn't doing anybody any good. Let's just go."

"No," she said, stepping farther from Sebastian. Both men looked startled. "Please, Bash. I need... I want to talk to Ezra alone."

Evie glanced around the shack Ezra called home. The inside was tidy compared to the rest of the village—theological books on a shelf, a bible on a bedside table, a neatly made bed—a quilt his mother had sewn. The plain surroundings seemed more customary to both. They must have as Ezra looked at Evie's bloody mouth, looking a little queasy himself. From a basin of water, he rang out a cloth and handed it to her. "I am sorry." His blues eyes glistened and he blinked hard. "A few days ago the last thing I might have imagined is striking my wife. But a few days ago, I could not have envisioned the story I've been told." Ezra thrust his hands to his slim waist and his gaze to the shack's wooden floor.

She dabbed at her tender mouth. Evie did not think Ezra could deliver a harsher slap than his father. She was wrong. "I, um... I'm not sure where to start. I know how it must sound, Ezra. I don't..." She stopped. A modicum of obedience might be best given the circumstance. "What is it you'd like to know—other than what you've been told?"

"I..." He closed his eyes and tipped his fair head toward the thatched roof. "God help me, Evie... I just want to wake up and have it all be a horrid nightmare." Tears spilled down his face, and her own eyes welled at his pain. "Other than what's now obvious, I want to know if you slept with him before you married me."

She was surprised by his directness. "No. Not before he returned to Good Hope with the brothers. But I'd also not stand here and lie. It did nearly happen the night before I married you."

"And am I to be grateful for that?"

"No. You shouldn't be grateful and I shouldn't be forgiven. But you should also know that after we were married, I tried, Ezra. I tried to forget him, to make our marriage work. I prayed so hard. I committed every part of myself to being your wife."

"Then why didn't it work?" His face was perplexed, like a child confounded by a rainy day. "Why couldn't you just do as you were supposed to... as it was proclaimed by my father and our entire community?"

Evie stared, her bleeding mouth agape.

"Say it," Ezra demanded, archaically, as if waiting for Evie to say, "witch."

"I don't..." Evie had dishonored so much that a reasonable explanation seemed out of reach. "Because what I feel for him is different than what I feel for you. I'm sorry. I don't know how else to say it." They were the gentlest words she could muster. Evie moved toward him. Ezra held out his hand, rejecting any offer of comfort. "Ezra, understand, it's not a him or you question. I've known you all my life. Except for the past twenty minutes," she said, pressing the cloth that still came away bloody, "we've been close. We've been the best of friends."

"We are married," he said, though it sounded more like a warning. "You made a vow before God. You're bound to honor that, Evie—no matter what he's told you."

"He hasn't told me anything. We haven't even discussed... I insisted that Sebastian bring me here so I could talk to you myself. If you meant nothing to me, if my life in Good Hope were as false and sinful as they've told you, ask yourself why I would have bothered with this journey?"

"You've come to ask for what I'll never agree to—an annulment of some sort. Our marriage is irrevocable. You know this. If I'm to live with that fact—so are you."

"I'm aware." It was something she'd not yet shared with Sebastian. Evie didn't know if it mattered. Sebastian had been dumbfounded by the mention of children. She suspected marriage might result in the same reaction—a topic that was not part of the things he wanted. "It's not why I came here. Though I am curious, this is what you want? To be married to a woman who openly chooses another man? I'm thinking of you, Ezra. You deserve someone who—"

Ezra's stare burned into hers. "No matter what you've done... what you've *chosen*," he said, his tone filled with contempt, "I am bound to you forever, Evie. As you can see..." He glanced at her flat stomach. "God has seen to it that any union—unholy or otherwise— will bear you no reward. Even if I am to suffer the same fate, loving you unrequitedly, I take solace in His punishment."

Evie had no easy answer for that and she moved on. "Ezra, it's not my wish to hurt you. I can't say that I don't love you." It drew a hopeful glance from her husband. "But I don't love you in the way..."

"In the way you love *him*."

It was the bravest thing she'd ever heard him say. The swell in Evie's throat wouldn't let her swallow or agree out loud.

"And may I ask your plans?" he said. "You'll what? Go off with him—live in some unthinkable state of sin, just wait to burn in Hell. It's what will happen. You have to know that."

"Maybe," she said. "But at least I understand the truth I'm to live on Earth. There's nothing good in anything I've come to tell you. But also know I couldn't leave Good Hope and let you go on living so blindly. You're right. I'm not here to ask for a divorce. I'm here because as much as you deserve honesty regarding your wife, you deserve no less when it comes to your father. You need to hear the rest of what I've come to tell you."

CHAPTER TWENTY-SIX

Ezra had refused Evie's version of life in Good Hope. She'd done her best to convince him that Duncan Kane and his missions were not what he and the other brothers believed them to be. She considered having Sebastian offer his input, but it only would have hardened Ezra's denial. Her husband had flinched. But Ezra remained unconvinced when Evie told him about his father's anointed sexual advance. But knowing him so well, Evie thought she'd seen a flicker of doubt. And that's where they'd left it. At the edge of Otava, Ezra staring icily as his wife left with her lover.

They'd gone on to the town of La Carta—a place Sebastian seemed to know well. In a small hotel there was a room waiting for him. Exhausted, they'd dragged themselves across a turquoise-painted floor and fell into bed. Sebastian didn't touch Evie that night, or the next, only to hold her close as she cried out of guilt and out of answers for a promised life that would never be lived. Rain had poured down since they arrived, adding to the bleak mood. In the gloomy days that followed, silence fell like a fog between them. Evie saw the bad weather as a good thing. It gave them something to discuss.

Neither broached the obvious: What, besides downpours, their future might hold. But without asking, Sebastian seemed to understand that the undoing of Evie's marriage wasn't to be. Lying in the bed, she looked across the brightly painted floor and out to the balcony. Sebastian sat there with a cup of coffee or a shot glass of something stronger, for hours now, a distant stare his only companion. Evie accepted that she was unwittingly the cause of immense suffering when it came to both the men she loved.

On the fourth morning, just as she wondered what would come next, Sebastian received a phone call. After hanging up, he told Evie he'd be gone a few days, possibly a week. Then, rather bluntly, Sebastian stated there was no "way in hell" she was going with him. If she fought him, he promised to put her in the Jeep and take her back to her husband in Otava. It illuminated the danger of Sebastian's *mission*. When she asked exactly where he was going, he said, "To work. It's why I'm here." An hour later a soaking wet courier showed up at their hotel room. He brought an envelope and a damp duffel bag of weapons—just a sample of the truckload Sebastian would deliver. Like the vendors on the street below, apparently it was wise for Sebastian to be familiar with his wares.

"Good luck, Bash," the courier said. "I fear you'll need it on this one."

Evie stood on the balcony, rain falling heavily behind her. It sounded like the beat of a war drum. Sebastian didn't answer, only hustling the messenger out the door.

"Tell me you'll come back," she said.

"The envelope I gave you at the dock. You remember what I told you?"

"I remember."

"Evie, I know you've been upset, but you need to understand, things may not get better from..."

"I'm fine," she insisted. "There are a lot of new realities to adjust to. Your purpose here, despite our visit with Ezra, it's the part I've feared most. I take it my fall from the fold hasn't thwarted my father-in-law's activities."

"Seems not," he said, crouched over the contents of the bag. He examined weapon after weapon—smaller handguns like the one Sebastian now carried everywhere they went and larger weapons that made the rifles in Good Hope look like toys. "I have a job to finish. I won't lie to you. It's dangerous and the outcome isn't a guarantee. But Sam—the Delta Force operative I'm working with—there is an exit strategy. After I get through this run, assuming I get through it..."

Evie sucked in a breath as the rain fell harder.

"I'm going to push for an end to this. That I have something to... That I have to get back because..." He dropped a last gun into the bag. It hit the floor with the clank of rattling metal. "Jesus, Evie, you haven't said a word... well, nothing that matters since seeing Ezra. Before I go... It would help if..."

"Help if what?" Evie's thoughts emerged from the haze of rain and moodiness. If she could do anything to assure his safety, there was no question.

He stood. "I was in Good Hope long enough to learn how life works. The things that can be undone and... Well, those that can't."

She nodded, confirming that both understood the situation.

"So we're a little stuck. I can't ask what I really want..."

"What is it you want to ask?"

"I wanted to ask..." A breath filled his broad chest. It was nervous compared to his exchange with a mysterious courier toting a sack full of guns. "If things were different, know that I'd ask you to marry me."

Sebastian's solid frame, his strength inside and out, and all Evie could see was the glassy green of his eyes. She hurried across the turquoise floor, thrusting herself into his arms. "Yes. If I could... absolutely, yes, I'd marry you."

It was a long, aching silence before the two finally made good use of the lumpy mattress. Sebastian didn't leave an inch of skin untouched, Evie watching their hands link as rays of sun overcame the gloom, streaming in through the balcony. Again and again, she looked at their sunlit hands as Sebastian made love to her. She kissed him, fervently and often—making up for the previous days. There was no mention or use of the condoms he'd insisted on after those first times in the cabin. Evie wanted it that way, nothing between them. As his strong body overtook hers, in ways that Evie knew would forever leave her breathless and fulfilled, she looked once more at their tangled hands. Heated from the moment, warmed from the sun, Evie took it as a single sign. Perhaps hopeful rays of sunlight would be the only blessing their union would ever receive.

———

Nine long days later, Sebastian returned. Tension faded from his body when he saw her. In turn, Evie gasped at a sizable gash above his right eye. Better than the eye itself, he told her. She didn't ask but only stared at other random bruises. He tried to deflect her attention, telling Evie about the successful raid. After delivering his weapons, but before he could exit the scene, SAM*18* and his Delta Forces swooped in. Together they'd killed many rebel forces, Sam's team taking others into custody. Evie stopped him. She said she didn't want to hear of any more killings or those who'd come to kill. She only wanted him to know how relieved she was he wasn't among the dead. On the nightstand, Sebastian noticed the envelope he'd given her when they docked. It remained sealed, but clearly she'd been thinking about it.

Needing a change of scenery, Sebastian suggested they sit on the balcony. He was appreciative, if not surprised by a fresh bottle of tequila. She didn't drink any, only shrugging as she pushed the bottle and glass toward him. He filled it, asking how she'd come by the liquor.

"In town, of course," she said. "I walked around a lot, met some of the people... learned a bit of Span—"

"Stop. You walked the town?" He hadn't thought to insist she stay put while he was gone. Sebastian assumed it was understood. "Evie, you can't do that. This isn't a safe place. A million things could happen—these streets, the people, they're unpredictable."

"That's nonsense."

He blinked at her firm reply.

"Oh, I'm sure there's danger. But those I met, they're lovely people, Bash. Poor, in need...hopeful," she said, crinkling her brow. "Most of them are Catholics, which was interesting. I even bought you a gift from one." She left the balcony, returning with a small fabric pouch. "I thought it would look handsome on you—and it put a few pesos in the woman's pocket."

He opened it, smiling at her thoughtfulness. The last time someone bought him a gift, he thought it was a model airplane. Maybe he was ten. Inside the pouch was a length of leather, a native stone attached to it.

"It's an unpolished emerald." She popped up from her seat and insisted on fastening it around his neck. "There," she said, admiring her gift and sitting again. "It's perfect. Your dark hair, your eyes... your face, when it's not been beaten to such a state."

"Thank you. It's not something I would have bought for myself," he said, running his hand around the rugged piece of jewelry. "But, Evie, back to my point. Those streets are dangerous, and you can't just—"

"You're being overly cautious. They're just people. In fact, I thought a great deal about what the Fathers of the Right could accomplish *if* aiding locals was their true mission. The people... Maybe not the ones you've come into contact with, but here in La Carta... They only want basic things—schools for their children and decent food. Not these heinous wars that drugs have brought to their country."

She passionately went on to tell him a story of a woman villager whose husband had been murdered by guerilla forces. She'd been left with no money, no hope, and six children to feed. Sebastian listened as Evie cleverly laid out a strategy for delivering more than God's word to a desperate population. He was impressed, Evie shrugging at his surprise. "Don't be so shocked. I've spent twenty-one years listening to how missionary efforts should work."

But Sebastian was also grateful that her adventurousness hadn't resulted in more than deep thinking. "Anyway," she said, finishing her story, "for all that's not right in Good Hope, no one would let another starve." Evie was saying something about giving the woman money to buy food when the cut above Sebastian's eye began to bleed.

More like gush.

"It's just not stopping," Evie said, pressing a second blood-soaked cloth to his head. "Maybe if you were to lie down. That's what the brothers did when they bled from head injuries—kicked by a horse or not moving fast enough from the swing of the hay bailer."

"I don't think lying down is going to cut it," Sebastian said, a hissing sound seething through his teeth. "Sam wanted me to come back to basecamp, see the in-country medics, but that would have taken two more days. There's a good doc in town. I've seen him before. Maybe we should go," he said, looking at a cloth that now dripped blood.

"To a doctor?" she said.

"Yeah. I don't think the gash is too deep. Head bleeds are the worst, but..." He stood, seeing two of Evie. "Hold on." He sat again, focusing on one of her. "Forget me. I just thought of something else. You've never had so much as a vaccination. You've been walking around this place for a week, interacting with people. What the hell was I thinking, bringing you to the middle of the fucking jungle? Do we have one more washcloth? We're going to see Doc Sanchez—*now*."

Sebastian's bleeding head became secondary, wooziness forgotten, as he whisked them from the hotel room and into a taxi. It took them to the other side of town. The taxi dropped them in front of a building that was nicer than most in La Carta.

"This is where the doctor is?" she asked.

"His office, yes. Dr. Sanchez—he's a good man. He took care of a deep leg wound, some shrapnel, about a year ago. And my neck," he said, grazing his hand over the new scar he'd worn back to Good Hope. "US support partially funds his practice, so it's a few thousand grades better than what you might expect in these parts."

"Since I've no expectations, I suppose I wouldn't know whether or not to be impressed."

Pressing the bloody cloth to his forehead with one hand, he gripped Evie's shoulder with his other. He swore he felt a slight tremor as she marched ahead. Her bravery ran deeper than his own. He'd only put his life up for grabs—she'd traded hers for the uncertainty of his. As they sat in the waiting room, Sebastian considered the life-changing, precarious things Evie had navigated in the past weeks. The only regret he'd witnessed was her culpability in hurting her husband and the man she loved. Evie waited at his side, glancing curiously around the space. For as much as Sebastian trusted Dr. Sanchez, there was still a woman with a chicken in a cage seated across from them, a man mumbling in Spanish, who clearly hadn't bathed since his last visit.

Sebastian leaned, saying to a skeptical Evie, "It's a little different in the States." Dr. Sanchez emerged, greeting Sebastian. He ushered them into an exam room where Sebastian took pride in introducing Evie to someone for the first time. "My... my, uh, better half," he said. "Evie—"

"Neal," she replied, shaking the doctor's hand.

"Evie... my pleasure." But he quickly turned his attention to Sebastian, making a fast medical assessment. "Hmm, not near as bad as the leg... or the neck," he said, examining the wound.

"That's what I figured, but the bleeding wouldn't stop, so..."

"So here you are," he said, shaking his head. "I won't ask, amigo. But know that every time you turn up, merely needing stitching, I thank God."

From the other side of the exam table, Evie smiled and said, "I do the same thing."

She didn't flinch as Dr. Sanchez shot him full of Novocain and proceeded to sew up his forehead with seven neat stitches. "It's not too deep. When this one heals, it won't be much for your collection."

"His collection?" Evie said.

"The scars," both men said.

"That's good," she said, "since this one is on his forehead. Some of the others, especially the one on his left hip..." Her words trailed off as she stared sheepishly at her folded hands.

Sebastian and the doctor exchanged muted looks of amusement. Admittedly, the levity felt good. Then Sebastian's tone shifted. "Doc, while I have you here. Evie doesn't come from a background of good medical care, or any for that matter."

"She's not from the States?"

"No, she is. It's, um... it's a long story. We had to make a hasty exit to here. Since then it's occurred to me that she's never had any immunizations."

The doctor's expression also sobered. "Surprising—and not a good thing in the States, but here in particular—typhoid, malaria, yellow fever, even polio. You're susceptible to any of it without proper immunization." Evie looked concerned and the doctor reached across Sebastian, patting her arm. "No worries, senorita. You look perfectly healthy to me. I'm sure we're not too late. Let's do some history, and we'll make certain you are prepared for the less pleasant aspects of my beautiful country."

Evie wanted Sebastian to stay, and he listened as she answered medical questions with some difficulty, not understanding others at all. Sebastian insisted they draw blood from him first so she knew what to expect. Evie only remarked that it wasn't so bad as she took her turn. When a nurse handed her a plastic cup, Sebastian wasn't as sure how to convey that request. A perplexed Evie said, "You want me to what?"

Explaining as best he could, Sebastian guided her to the restroom. "Trust me. It's all just standard op."

With that part over, the two returned to the waiting room, Dr. Sanchez would rush the results. Sebastian grew concerned as they passed the hour mark. Finally, a nurse asked him to come to the exam room. "I'll be right back," he said. Evie smiled as he stood, glancing between him and a woman with a goat, who'd replaced the woman with the chicken.

A short while later, Dr. Sanchez left him and alone in the room Sebastian paced the floor. Seconds later, a nurse opened the door and Evie came inside. "En aqui, por favor," she said, pointing to a chair.

"Bash, what's wrong? First they bring you back here, and now to look at you—your tan has gone white. Clearly something isn't good. Was it your blood? I'm not so naïve. I know it can detect horrible diseases. If you're ill—"

"Evie, sit," he said, also pointing to the chair. She did, looking up at him with a worrisome face he hadn't seen since he arrived or she'd left Good Hope. He sat on the doctor's stool, wheeling it up to her. "Dr. Sanchez wanted to talk to me first because he sensed... Well, he thought... After you'd explained your lack of medical history..."

"Bash, is it me?" she said, swallowing hard. "Am I sick?"

He closed his eyes and took her hand in his. A smile pushed into the hollows of his cheeks, not minding at all the ache of a bruise. He opened his eyes. "Evie, you know how you insisted that the reason you didn't have any children was a punishment from God?"

She nodded.

He squeezed her hand tighter. "Baby, I have some pretty strong proof it wasn't a punishment... and I don't think it had anything to do with you."

CHAPTER TWENTY-SEVEN

Present Day

ON THE FLIGHT HOME, ALONE IN THE RESTROOM, ALEC STARED INTO THE mirror. For as much as he saw himself, he saw Sebastian Clairmont—Evie's eyes, maybe a shade darker. He took pride in being the eldest, though he hadn't thought of it often in recent years. The trip to South America provided clues but no real answers about Evie and Sebastian. Why a crashed plane and no bodies? What were Evie and Sebastian's real ties to La Carta? And most of all, why did they leave the initials E.K.—scrawled in blood—on the side of the plane? Alec renewed his vow to find the truth. He owed them that much and more. It was as firm as the vow he'd taken with his Navy SEAL brothers, another chunk of his sequestered, seldom visited past.

He returned to his seat, feeling more in touch with a SEAL mission than he had in years. Alec tucked his hands neatly in his lap, ordering nothing stronger than club soda. Four middle seats were the only tickets available. Jess and Kiera were sandwiched in between himself and Julian. He shifted in his seat, looking past Kiera. Julian's hand rested on Jess's bare knee. He breathed deep. *A skirt.* It figured with Jess's usual *"I'm working"* cargo pants packed in a suitcase. It seemed his roommate had altered her assignment.

He settled back, purposely avoiding Kiera's gaze. In the hotel lobby she'd shown up with a large suitcase. Alec had offered a curt explanation to a bug-eyed Jess: "She's coming with us."

When the flight landed in Philadelphia and they deplaned, the rows of exiting passengers separated Jess and Alec from Kiera and Julian. "Enough punishment," Jess hissed from behind him. He knew she was standing on her toes—that much shorter, the sound that close. "Our last scene wasn't our best, but would you explain why the schoolmarm is continent hopping with us?"

His inclination was to say, "As soon as you explain why Julian is doing the same." But he skipped over that demand and shared basic facts. This was about nothing but the mission. In exchange for an airline ticket, Kiera had promised to unearth the parts of his parents' past that now appeared a well-guarded secret. Jess poked him hard between the shoulder blades. "Fine for now," she said. "But so we're clear, Lieutenant Commander, don't think that's the end of this." He half turned, surprised by her boldness. He got it. Jess's use of his rarely mentioned military past and rank were meant to convey a pissed-off mood. Too bad. She greatly undershot what it'd take to provoke the same from him. Alec kept calm and didn't engage as the foursome spilled into the crowded airport.

After customs they approached baggage claim and logistics forced Alec to be more forthcoming. Jess said something about Julian arranging for transportation. Did he want to do the same? "We're all set," Alec said, poking at his phone. "Our ride is inbound."

"Your ride?" Jess said.

"Yeah. Go with him," he said, cocking his chin at Julian, "or come with me. Whatever. But it was time for some Clairmont reinforcement on my end."

The airport doors split wide and Aaron walked through. Among the *Tribe of Five*, he was Alec's closest mirror image. But as Aaron plucked off sunglasses, the green irises struck Alec in an unusual way. What if his brother had been the one walking the streets of La Carta? Surely the villagers would have deemed him Sebastian Clairmont's ghost. *Or Sebastian Christos...* Whoever the hell he was. Questions loomed and the unknown fate of his parents dug deeper into Alec. He shook his head. He was doing it again—feeling shit.

Comfort also slipped into the mix as Aaron wrapped his brother in a giant hug. It irritated Alec—how bad feelings had to exist to make others matter. But the embrace said a lot, including a silent acknowledgement. The wreckage had been officially identified by the NTSB. It was the plane their parents had been on. But only Alec and Aaron knew about the grisly cannibalism story that went with the Isla de la Muerte.

"Good to see you, man," Aaron said.

"You've no idea." He held on a little longer, the same way Aaron did the day Alec had picked him up when he was released from Biddeford Correctional Facility.

"Reinforcements," Jess said. "Can't say I'm surprised." She and Aaron exchanged a quick hello, and Jess made a brief introduction to Julian. He left them, saying he needed to check on his transportation arrangements.

Aaron probably felt the stare as his brother turned toward Kiera. "Oh my gosh," she said. "There's two of you!"

"Uh, yeah. And that one," Alec said, pointing to his brother, "couldn't be more spoken for. Aaron, this is Kiera Blyth."

Her smile dropped like an iron weight. "Story of my life." She released the handshake Aaron offered and pointed to her suitcase as it dropped onto the baggage carousel.

Alec reached for it.

"If you don't mind waiting a few minutes, I need to use the ladies' room." Her gaze flicked over Aaron. "You're sure?" she asked, doing a slow three-sixty as she ambled away, dragging her luggage.

"You've no idea." Aaron crinkled his brow at his brother as she disappeared into the crowd.

"Explanation please?"

"Long story short, she's tied in with the place we're headed to. Bringing her was my only way of getting more information, maybe a foot in the door. And Ruby is...?" He was surprised she wasn't with Aaron.

"She just got the gig she wanted in Nickel Spring's ER," Aaron said. "Her first shift is tonight. It was either quit before she started or stay behind. Honor was slammed at Abstract Enchantment, and it did seem like a good idea if Ruby hung around in case..."

"In case we do get to the end of this thing and the news is not good... like you can't make it up, remote jungle island, not good."

"Something like that," Aaron said.

"Let's hope it doesn't go that way." Alec breathed deep, thinking about a worse outcome for their parents than simply dead. He changed the subject. "But I'm guessing you're already missing your other half."

"Like crazy—but, for now, here's where I belong. So details, bro. What gives with the girl on a heat-seeking mission for a hot date?" Aaron pointed in the direction Kiera had gone.

"Uh, yeah... heat-seeking," Alec said, thinking of last night's furious fuck. "We may need an interpreter... maybe an ambassador. She's our best bet."

"And what else is she, Alec?" Jess said, butting into the exchange. "I saw her in the hotel lobby last night. I can spot an Alec Clairmont target a hundred yards away, though in her case it seemed more like a done deal."

"No shit?" Alec said, deadpan. "Why? Did she glide through the lobby smoking a cigarette, looking satisfied?"

"More like a *just been fucked* rumpled vibe. Call it the unwanted data from my forced study of Alec Clairmont in his natural habitat. I've probably seen the look more than my byline." They traded smirks.

"But I was surprised when she turned back up today with luggage in tow. Usually your bedmates aren't given a last call warning, never mind an invitation to travel. What was it, Alec? Love at first fuck?"

"Cute, Jess. I'm amazed you noticed anything, so tied up with your own one-on-one business. Either way, it's not the reason Kiera's here."

"Not to deny that it happened, of course."

"Uh, guys," Aaron said, "how about you either take the insults outside or cut to the chase?"

"Fine," Jess said, her stare burning through Alec. "Why would you need either an interpreter or ambassador on this side of the map?"

"Kiera was more or less banished to La Carta by her parents, who are members of the Fathers of the Right."

"The group you had me ask Jack Preacher to research," Aaron said. "I have a complete dossier in the car. They're hardcore, imbedded in a minor slice of Amish country, a place called Good Hope. But according to Jack, their MO is more customized religion than anything mainstream. How, exactly, it connects to Mom—definitely Pop, I have no clue."

"I'm not sure either, and that's where Kiera comes in. In exchange for the transportation, she's promised to enlighten us. And another thing, I'd be willing to bet somewhere in Good Hope we find that cabin we both remember."

"I've been thinking about it," Aaron said. "I definitely remember an argument. But I also can't figure out this feeling of being terrified and not being able to get close to Mom—like I just couldn't."

Alec took a step back. "Weird. I have the same memory. Geez, you couldn't have been more than three, maybe four, and you remember that?"

"I guess so. Tells you how impressionable whatever went down was."

Jess looked between the two brothers. "Huh. It's hard to picture either of you as helpless little boys."

"Unfathomable as it is, we didn't arrive in the world as adults." Alec narrowed his eyes and Jess narrowed hers right back.

"What is going on with the two of you?"

Neither Alec nor Jess answered.

"Anyway, this Good Hope is like a small, sovereign state. And the group, the Fathers of the Right, they've used religious freedom as their means of avoiding government radar for years—at least that's the cliff note details in the info Jack provided."

"You did your homework. Good man."

"Didn't want to disappoint big brother," Aaron said. "So what's your plan, to infiltrate this place with one of their own?"

"Something like that. Nothing too heavy handed. I was hoping— between you and I—we could use some Clairmont charm and persuade these Fathers of the Right to talk."

"Pfft..." Jess snorted a laugh. "Well, possibly Aaron..."

Alec ignored her. "If we work the right angles, who knows what these people can tell us about Mom?"

"Could be a plan," Aaron said. "But to be honest, I have to side with Jess."

"About what?" Alec said.

"The charm factor." He looked his brother up and down. "It's not really your strong suit, which makes me doubly glad I sent for extra help. Charm is inbound," Aaron said, pointing. "Complete with a fucking camera ready smile."

"Meaning?" Alec said.

As Aaron spoke, a bubble of noise erupted from the other end of baggage claim. Whispers turned to gasps and gasps into shrieks of delight. High pitched squeals pierced through, growing louder. *"Oh my God! It is him! It really is Jake Clairmont!"*

The threesome turned, Alec and Aaron rolling their eyes at the wave of adoration flooding their way. Security, normally on alert for airport trouble, found themselves working crowd control. Fans had ID'd one of Hollywood's hottest stars as Jake, and youngest brother Troy, tried to make their way to Alec and Aaron.

"Uh, better go help these guys out." Alec switched to bodyguard mode and quickly identified the sergeant in charge. He made a fast friend by mentioning his military past and the fact that Jake Clairmont was his brother. Then he bulleted instructions. In seconds, security guards shifted metal gates, corralling the perimeter of one baggage claim carousel. Alec, Troy and Jake—who was lucky to lose only the hat off his head—slipped into the isolated center.

Jake plucked aviator sunglasses off his face, which only incited louder cries of adoration. His eyes weren't green like Aaron's, nor were they blue like Honor's—something in between. "Great," he said to Alec, pointing at the opening from which luggage emerged. "Now the only way out is through the baggage carousel."

"Sorry, bro," Alec said, pulling his brother into a hug. "Happy to shove you through first." It was standard-op *Tribe of Five* humor. "It was the best I could do on ten seconds notice."

"Yeah. I get it," he said, scanning the mob. They gawked at Jake like an animal in a cage—maybe the hottest attraction in the zoo. He looked back at Alec. "Troy and I laid pretty low on the flight in, but it all came apart once we got off. I should have planned ahead, but coming was a quick decision." Jake looked at Aaron, who he hadn't seen in seven years. "Damn. A public floor show wasn't exactly how I thought we'd do this." Alec could almost see the lump in both brothers' throats.

"Yeah. But we get to do it."

A long, hard hug ensued between Aaron and Jake—Jake who'd last stood at his brother's sentencing, everyone sure that they'd be old men by the time any public meeting took place again. Alec was still reeling from the unraveling of his brother's fate, and he suspected Aaron was doing the same. A glance passed between Troy and Alec. "How you doing, little brother?"

"Can't say I'll be relocating to Utah anytime soon, but watching Jake work was cool. I stayed out of trouble, if that's what you're asking."

"I'm not," Alec said. Then he play-slapped his youngest brother's shoulder. "Well, maybe I was curious. Anyway, I'm glad nearly all of us are here."

Jake's arm hung loosely around Aaron's shoulder. "Honor and Aaron have been keeping us up to speed. If we're on the verge, or even on the trail to finding out what happened to Mom and Pop... Well, I told them to film around me for a while."

"You can do that?" Jess said.

Jake smiled at Jess, who he met when she'd once interviewed him—an offbeat assignment for the investigative photo-journalist. Alec had been helping out with bodyguard detail. Jake had actually introduced them, a photojournalist and ex SEAL working the opposite ends of stardom. As it turned out, one of them needed an East Coast place to crash. The other had a spare bedroom.

"The producers didn't love it and the director had a meltdown," Jake said, answering her. "But I told them there was a family emergency. It's a movie." He grasped Alec's shoulder with his other hand. "I may live it a few thousand miles away, but you guys are my life."

A ruckus, separate from the fan buzz and flashing smart phones, caught Alec's attention. "Damn, hang on a second." He hustled over to the sergeant. "She's with us," he said as Kiera made a failed attempt to gain access. The sergeant and Alec's gaze skimmed over Kiera as she walked toward the group, wheeling her suitcase along. On the plane, she'd worn a short floral print sundress. Alec had noticed because as much as he tried to avoid it, her bare knee kept leaning into his. She'd returned now in the bulky gathered skirt and long-sleeved blouse buttoned high at the neck. Her long hair was neatly braided. Alec supposed the change in costume was deliberate, maybe even helpful. It drew curious looks from all the Clairmonts and Jess. "Kiera's going to give us a hand with the information we already have. Isn't that right, Kiera?" Alec forced the question, feeling he'd delivered on his end. It was time for her to start talking.

She was preoccupied, looking curiously at the fawning crowd. Then she looked at the Clairmont brothers, who had doubled in number since she went to the restroom. She was fixated on Jake. But what person wasn't in this insane square footage?

"He's Jake, isn't he?" she said, pointing.

"Yeah. But let's work on getting us out of here. I'll get you an autograph later," Alec said. He started for the sergeant, planning an exit strategy.

"What would I want with his autograph?"

Something in Kiera's tone made Alec pay closer attention and he turned back. "Lots of people do. He is Jake Clairmont."

"Movie star extraordinaire," Troy said, laughing. "Maybe she'd rather have a lock of his hair."

"Shut it," Jake said.

"I wouldn't know anything about movie stars," Kiera said, which made sense to Alec. "But I do know Jake is the one with a twin... a sister."

They stood frozen in a circle, the world buzzing around them. "That's right" Alec said. He took a step closer. "How do you know that?"

"There are letters from your mother to mine. I shouldn't have read them, but I did," she said. "In them she talks about Jake. But the parts about your sister and her father, I believe that's what you've come to Good Hope to learn about."

CHAPTER TWENTY-EIGHT

1984

Nickel Springs

IN THE SUMMER OF 1984 VACATIONERS WERE FEWER IN NUMBER AT the Rose Arch Inn. It was a change from the two previous years where guests had crammed into the popular, upstate resort. This was both good and bad. Evie worked less hours preparing meals for the dining room, but it left her with more time to think and to worry. Sebastian hadn't been back for nearly five months. He'd never been gone so long. For two months there'd been no word at all, not a speck of information. Usually Evie received message at the caretaker's cottage where they lived on the property. They were short notes from Sam, saying that Sebastian was safe or indicating when he'd be home.

From Evie and Sebastian's first trip to La Carta to the two sons now playing on the edge of Lake Butterfield, they'd been whirlwind, adventurous years. The serene setting almost served as a façade—or just impossible to find if you were looking for Sebastian Christos. After completing his work with SAM22's Delta Forces, Sebastian was offered a government job. It came with specialized training, honing the street-smart skills on which he'd survived. Then, two years ago, Sebastian earned a pilot's license, though he didn't talk much about how it affected his work. "An international courier service," he'd said to Evie. "If anyone asks, that's what I do, pilot a Cessna that delivers documents and small cargo to various destinations south of the equator."

The violence of South American guerilla forces had declined, but it was still a turbulent, drug-rich landscape. With Sam as his handler, Sebastian had proven himself to be a valuable asset. Evie couldn't say she loved his chosen profession, but she understood Sebastian's need to be of service. Reluctantly, she had agreed to his precarious job—informant, courier, government security detail. He'd also been adamant about properly providing for his soon-to-be family, and Evie found it difficult to argue his desire. Several years removed from those choices, she sat lakeside now in an Adirondack chair, admiring the best parts of her life with Sebastian—Alec and Aaron.

While Sebastian settled into his government role—home for spans of time, gone for others—he and Evie had also spearheaded a different project abroad. They'd taken it upon themselves to redirect the efforts of Reverend Duncan Kane. Part of bringing Sebastian's initial mission to a close included telling SAM22 about the Reverend's involvement. In turn, Sam had wanted to make the Reverend answer for his crimes. Sam, who Evie had never met in person, wanted to raid Good Hope, publically outing the Reverend and pulling back the curtain on the sect's unsavory activities. Distraught by the idea of destroying a common life Fathers of the Right members truly believed in, Evie objected.

She had a better idea.

Instead of exposing the Reverend—so messy and public—why not make him pay by implementing the good he'd purported? There were willing men in Good Hope and Sebastian to help oversee much needed charitable efforts in La Carta. With Sam's assistance, it had panned out better than Evie anticipated. The way Sebastian had told the story, Reverend Kane was whiter than angels' wings when faced with the prospect of exposure and prison time. He'd readily succumbed, going on to play the role he'd professed. Under Sam and Sebastian's watchful eye, Reverend Kane used the Fathers of the Right to draw attention to the needs of La Carta and other villages. His appeal attracted the aid of honest charitable organizations—some religion based, some not. Sam, who wielded significant power, had been so impressed he'd secured matching government aid. Education, food, and decent medical help had made progress combating the drug-related means by which most people in La Carta survived.

As for Good Hope, Evie had never gone back, though she did exchange letters with Hannah Blyth. It was her sole link to everything she'd left. Evie was at peace with it. Her life was in Nickel Springs—a government chosen spot where Sebastian and his sons were given the last name Clairmont. SAM22 had promised and delivered a great deal, but he was wary of Sebastian's Greek mafia ties and enemies he might have made in South America. After Alec was born, he'd insisted on a fresh start and a blank life. Sam had even provided official credentials bearing the last name Clairmont. It was a secret, Evie supposed, her sons would accept as truth. She wasn't sure how she felt about that, though she never discounted the necessity. She often promised herself that years from now, when they were adults, she would tell her sons the whole sordid story.

In an effort not to tell a complete lie, Evie symbolically chose to use Neal. She never quite lost sight of the fact that she remained married to another man. She'd contemplated it now and again—going to Ezra, asking for a divorce. But she could never get past the turmoil it would create. She and Sebastian never spoke of it, their lives too complicated and delicately balanced to risk unwanted attention. The facts drew a reverent breath from Evie, who half smiled at three-year old Aaron. He stood on the muddy shoreline, waving a stick in her direction. Evie waved back, his green eyes sparkling just as she'd wished for and brighter than the lake water.

As the afternoon wore on things grew quiet. Maybe too quiet. Grace had come by, a trustworthy teenage girl who worked prep in the kitchen. When things were slow she'd help Evie with the boys—a reprieve she didn't mind. Aaron had fallen asleep, napping in a nearby pup tent, Alec and Grace fished from a rowboat a few feet off the dock. Evie was on the verge of dozing in the chair. A lazy June breeze floated through and the crunch of a branch stood out. In a split second Evie was on her feet. She didn't look up but scanned the ground for something larger than the stick Aaron held earlier. Darting a few feet forward, she snatched up a fallen branch, prepared to swing.

"Evie?"

The voice belonged to a stranger. They led a solitary life in Nickel Springs. Aside from Grace and the Rose Arch staff—who didn't make trips to the caretaker's cottage—visitors were not rare but unheard of. The intruder came toward her—a solid looking, sizable man in a dark suit. Evie backpedaled toward the tent, gripping tighter to the branch. She wished she'd agreed to the dog Sebastian had wanted to get on his last trip home. Something large, something like a German Shepard or Rottweiler. Two boys were enough to manage, she'd argued. And forget the gun he'd once tried to leave in her possession. She wouldn't hear of it. Now, Evie thought, she would have been wiser to listen—at least about the dog.

"Evie, it's all right," he said, holding up his hands. "It's me. It's Sam."

Evie was no longer so naïve. She didn't know his voice. She'd never seen a picture of Sam. He might have fit Sebastian's vague description, but so could fifty other men. He stopped several feet away, clearly aware of her uncertainty.

"I swear, it's me... SAM24 at last count. Thanks to Sebastian we've removed every ill-gotten surface to air missile clear to the edge of the rainforest."

She guessed it was supposed to be a show of proof. Then she remembered what real proof would look like. "Take off your shirt," she instructed.

"What?"

"Your shirt—if you're who you claim to be, take it off."

He nodded, unknotting his tie and discarding the suit jacket. Hurriedly, he unbuttoned a white dress shirt. He tossed them all onto the lakefront lawn, lastly yanking an undershirt over his head. Evie glanced at the water. Grace's flummoxed expression stared back. Without being asked, the man turned his muscular frame. Evie could have easily lunged forward, cracking him across the head with the tree branch. Instead, she swallowed hard, not especially prepared for the seams of fleshy scars that crisscrossed his back.

Sebastian had confided stories of Sam's military past, his government life—among them a near-death lashing at the hands of the Northern Vietnamese. "Sam," she said, dropping the branch. A flood of fear released and Evie moved toward him. He turned around, retrieving his clothes. But as he pulled on his undershirt, Evie stopped midstride. If the man who handled Sebastian—a person who operated in secret, with whom she'd never had a conversation— stood on her lawn... Well, it couldn't be for any good reason.

<hr>

Two months later

Evie's initial reaction had been to walk into Butterfield Lake and reunite with Sebastian and her mother. Two small boys would allow no such reaction. Sam had done his best to explain, telling Evie that Sebastian had missed his last three check-ins. It was the reason she hadn't received the usual updates via the courier. Then, about a week ago, Sam and his team received distressing news accompanied by stunning photos.

A group of civilian workers had been taken hostage. They were on assignment, south of Bogota with AmeriTex, a large, stateside corporation contracted to help rebuild Colombia's embattled infrastructure. According to Sam, Sebastian's last mission had been to run recon in the area, help provide security. It had been considered a *soft* assignment, low risk. "After AmeriTex, Sebastian was out of there, on his way home," Sam had said. An attack on the workers was a complete surprise. It wasn't even guerrilla forces but a violent gang bred from the streets of a war-torn region. They'd wanted money from AmeriTex in exchange for their employees' lives. Sam didn't know if Sebastian had been identified as a government agent, but he assumed as much from the intel he'd finally received.

"What intel?" Evie had asked.

Photographs.

At that point, Sam had given her a choice. Evie could take his word for it or she could look at the pictures herself. For two days Sam patiently waited, spending time with Sebastian's sons. Evie finally said she was ready to see the photos. She'd sent the boys off with Grace, a visit to the local zoo. At the cottage's kitchen table, Sam slid a folder in front of her. She opened it. The quake to Evie's chin was immediate, the urge to vomit nearly overtaking her.

Sebastian was chained to a pole, so bloodied she hardly recognized him. In truth, she was able to identify the leather band and emerald stone around his neck better than his face. But she knew the body, the scars, she knew it was him. From the pained expression on his face, she also knew he was alive. Evie clung to a glimmer of hope. Then Sam slid another photo in front her.

"The, um... the higher ups at AmeriTex didn't inform us of the ransom demand—not until it was too late. They thought keeping it under the radar would keep their guys safe. They paid the ransom—

the thugs shot every one of their employees, all twenty-five. Dead men don't talk. They can't identify their captors. I'm so sorry, Evie."

Library book images from World War II clicked through Evie's head, bodies from Nazi prison camps lying in a heap like discarded shoes. With trembling fingers, she traced the open eyes of one man in the pile, his arm twisted at an awkward, unreasonable angle. If the picture had been in color, she might have lost her mind right there. The green of Sebastian's eyes stared lifelessly. It would have been the end, it would have been too much. "And where... where is he now?" she'd quietly asked.

Sam hesitated.

Evie looked up to see him blink back tears. "Sam?"

"Afterward..." He cleared his throat, having to stop for a moment. "Afterward, the gang responsible for the whole heinous scene, they burned the bodies and building to the ground."

When Sebastian was away Evie was lonely, but she never felt alone. In the weeks following that changed. The Rose Arch Inn was a beautiful place, but because of their covert lives friends were no more than acquaintances. Evie thought of the envelope Sebastian had left her years ago. *"It's an extreme precaution—but a necessary one. If anything happens to me... if you find yourself alone here, open this."* Evie tore into the envelope as if the contents might tell her how to resurrect a dead Sebastian. Inside were two letters and a document. The document would put her in touch with Sam—no longer necessary. One was a letter to Evie. Reading it, a piece of Sebastian returned to her, the letter filled with emotion he was more likely to convey physically than verbally. It was a treasure amid deep tragedy. The second letter was for Bim and about Bim, the friend he'd wanted Evie to contact stateside. She considered Sebastian's direction, but circumstance was different than when he'd given her the envelope on the freighter in Cartagena. She wasn't penniless, naïve, or stranded in the harsh landscape of a foreign country. While Evie read and reread the letter from Sebastian to her, she put away the one regarding Bim. Taking her grief to a stranger was too awkward, though Evie did feel the need to express her sorrow to someone.

Soon letters to Hannah became phone calls and phone calls a lifeline to another human being. Her old friend listened to Evie's story, stunned and sympathetic. It didn't take long for the calls to become a daily ritual. The conversations were more detailed than Hannah's letters, telling Evie that much had changed in Good Hope. It was a less harsh, a more peaceful life. Ezra had been responsible for this. He was now their sect leader, essentially having switched roles with his father, who still led South American missions. The last part, of course, Evie already knew.

More weeks passed and Hannah asked Evie to visit—the other way around wasn't possible. "You know it'd be frowned upon, Evie—even a simple trip to a lakefront cottage. Tobias would never allow me to go alone, and he wouldn't be willing to come with me." Evie supposed not everything in Good Hope had changed. Overwhelmed by grief and two sons who required more energy than Evie had to give, she finally agreed. She hadn't yet told her sons about their father. Aaron was too young to understand. Evie wasn't sure how she might handle what was sure to be Alec's catastrophic reaction. He'd so idolized *Poppy*. But the boys were used to long absences and that bought Evie time. For now, when Aaron climbed onto Evie's lap, asking why she was so sad, she'd only answer that she missed "Poppy," the curious name Sebastian's sons had fallen into all on their own.

When Evie arrived in Good Hope, Hannah was more than welcoming. Evie had no plans to visit anyone else or to make her presence known. It set needed boundaries for the trip. Initially, there was terrific comfort in being with Hannah. She was someone who at least knew of Sebastian, able to picture the man Evie spoke about. And she did talk about him—telling Hannah about their adventures in South America and settling into a more domestic routine in Nickel Springs, saying that she wouldn't change a moment of it.

Evie was surprised but unaffected when her father and brothers turned up at the Blyth's door. "I couldn't very well *not* tell them you were coming," Hannah admitted. Her father and two brothers, Christian and Jonah, sat like ducks in a row on the sofa. Evie felt a modicum of sadness—her own flesh and blood evoked no more than acquaintance-like emotion. "You look well, daughter," Gideon said, as if he'd seen her yesterday. They never mentioned Sebastian or offered condolences. Gideon Neal did not acknowledge his grandsons, other than to glance peculiarly at the boys. Even with a more peaceful life, Evie understood the strict rigors of the Fathers of the Right doctrine. She was an outcast, as were her sons. Cruelness would not be permitted but acceptance was forbidden. It was the gray lens through which the Fathers of the Right responded to interlopers.

Still, the time with Hannah was a good thing. Evie had only planned to stay two days, but two became four and four nearly a week. Hannah and Tobias had three children now—Benjamin, the eldest, still sickly—thin and pale, intolerant of most foods. More than once Evie had to bite her tongue, tempted to take the boy to a doctor herself. She wondered if she stayed long enough, perhaps she might broach the subject with Hannah. Thankfully, their two younger sons were healthy boys, making fine playmates for Alec and Aaron. Tobias was tolerant of Evie, but she suspected it was in deference to his wife. Hannah had likely put serious effort into coaxing her husband into the civil behavior. Pleasant as it all was, Evie knew it couldn't last.

At the week's end, it was time to move on. Two women from the sect had come by under the pretense of baking Hannah a peach cobbler. They spoke to Evie, but it was as if they were testing the waters, as if they might consider allowing her back into the fold. Evie wanted nothing to do with that. She wasn't sure about Nickel Springs, but she was certain Good Hope was not where they belonged. Evie was folding the boys' clean wash, preparing to pack when Hannah tried to convince her otherwise.

"Summer has almost a month left. The weather is beautiful. We could fix up the cabin. Why not stay a while longer?"

"I can't," Evie said. She'd thought of the cabin—she was ambivalent about seeing it. "I need to figure things out. I need to do what Sebastian would have wanted."

"Perhaps he'd want you to stay somewhere where people care about you."

Evie smirked. "Here? In Good Hope? You think this is where Sebastian would like to see us? I doubt that. I, um… I was thinking of contacting Sebastian's friend, Bim. It's what he asked me to do if anything ever…" Her words trailed off. "I mean, it would be difficult. I don't know Bim."

"A stranger? Seriously, Evie? You'd consider turning to a stranger before trusting people you know. Those who'd look out for you."

"That's a bit of a stretch. I'm a curiosity, someone to whisper about… I'm not one of you." Evie folded another small T-shirt. "Besides, other than you, who in Good Hope truly cares about me?"

"Your husband, I would think."

She'd said it so fast, like an unexpected gust of wind. "You promised, Hannah. You swore to me you would not bring Ezra up."

"I'm sorry, but I can't see you leaving here with two boys and no one to care for you. I think Sebastian would agree with that much."

"And you think he'd want Ezra to be that person?" It was an absurd conversation. No one could take Sebastian's place. She wouldn't dare let anyone try. The suggestion only heightened Evie's determination to leave, and she continued with her preparations. Begrudgingly, Hannah helped—packing suitcases, packing the car.

During Evie's visit, Hannah had done a poor job of hiding her awe over her friend's capable qualities: driving, single parenting, and the willingness to be on her own. As Evie counted the cash in her wallet, Hannah watched curiously—women of the Fathers of the Right carried none. It was one of many markers that denoted the discrepancies between Evie and Good Hope. Tomorrow she would go back to Nickel Springs, to the caretaker's cottage. From there... well, from there Evie didn't know.

As it often did, fate decided what came next—without warning and sooner than Evie expected. At two o'clock that morning, she found herself at Hannah's bedroom door, calling out. A dizzying fever had gripped her—a stabbing pain in her side. The next few hours and into daybreak were a blur of cool cloths and vomiting, Evie begging for the keys to her car. Even in her hazy state, she knew Good Hope was the last place an ill woman should be. She called out for Sebastian. The only reply was Hannah's strained voice, reminding her he was gone. The pain—physical and emotional— was ravaging, as if one were battling to outdo the other. Evie's last lucid thought was to wonder which one might kill her first.

From there she'd slipped into an unlikely childhood memory, maybe a dream, running through a high, back field in Good Hope with Ezra. The two of them tumbled down a giant hill. The light was dim, the weather fall-like. They tripped and rolled, their bumpy descent safer with Ezra by her side—a side that pulsated with an angry pain as they careened to the bottom. With a jaw-rattling thud, they'd landed on tree roots. Evie forced open her eyes. There was no hill, only the blue of Ezra's eyes staring down into hers. She blinked, assaulted by light and odd beeping sounds. The sharp pain was gone. "Ezra," she whispered. "What... where are we?" She tried to sit up but made no progress. Ezra touched her shoulder.

"You shouldn't move." He looked jittery, eyes darting like an animal out of its habitat.

"The boys..." She struggled against his hold.

"They're perfectly fine." His grip grew firmer. "They're with Hannah. It's you I'm worried about—though not near as much as last night."

"Last night? Ezra, tell me right now what's..." Evie drew her hand to her forehead and saw an IV in her arm. Her gaze moved right to a blood pressure cuff. A woman walked around Ezra to the other side of the bed. She wore a white coat.

"Excellent. You're awake. I'm glad to see it—and a little relieved. I can't fathom why you'd wait so long to seek treatment. Another five minutes and... Well, I don't mean to be maudlin, but we might not be having this conversation."

Evie heard Ezra's voice. "I... I went as fast as I could the moment... well, as soon as I knew I needed to bring her here."

"Yes, but a hundred miles an hour down the interstate? You're lucky that cop was sympathetic. It's why we have ambulances," the woman scolded.

"I didn't think of it," Ezra said.

Evie tracked her gaze to him, seeing him swallow hard.

"She had a fever of 104, vomiting, and a stabbing pain in her right side." The woman shook her head. "Did you think she was going to miraculously recover from appendicitis without medical intervention?"

Evie crunched her forehead and pounded her fist against it. She looked at the woman. "I... he brought me to a hospital?" She looked incredulously at Ezra.

"Lancaster General, in the nick of time. Your appendix nearly burst." She glanced at Ezra. "Reckless and heroic as it was, you can thank your husband for saving your life."

CHAPTER TWENTY-NINE

1984

Good Hope, Pennsylvania

AFTER THE FOG OF ANESTHESIA WORE OFF, EZRA REMAINED AT EVIE'S SIDE. She was convinced he was a dream. Finally, she asked her reverie a question: "Ezra, a hospital? The Fathers of the Right, more than anything, you don't believe..."

He appeared shaken by his own actions. Ezra's eyes—edged in tiny crow's-feet—though just as blue, moved around the foreign setting. "God help me, you have that power over me, Evie. Clearly, I would do anything to keep you alive."

She blinked, tears running down her face. "Even after... After all that happened between us?"

Ezra reached, covering her hand with his. "Vengeance isn't mine. You should know that. I can't say I know how to explain it to my parishioners, but that doesn't seem to matter much right now."

Evie turned her head, looking out the hospital room window, but she didn't let go of Ezra's hand. It was too soothing and she was too grateful.

After being released from the hospital, Evie agreed to return to Good Hope. There wasn't much choice with two energetic boys and her body still on the mend. Initially, she stayed with Hannah, where Ezra visited every day. But as soon as Evie was up and about she asked to move to the cabin. She'd been hesitant before, but now she felt sure. It was more fitting than anyplace she'd been since Sam had delivered the devastating news about Sebastian.

As she recalled, the cabin was rugged but manageable. The boys thought it was a wild adventure and the aura inside brought Evie some peace. It coaxed a smile from her, watching Alec and Aaron dart about, repurposing the place where she'd fallen completely in love with their father.

Hannah and Ezra were her only visitors, Gideon Neal coming by once. It was an uncomfortable social call, her father remarking as he left, "I don't know what it is about you, daughter. I understand that you never fit comfortably here—especially after your mother passed. But your presence in Good Hope, must it always result in such an upheaval to our lives? First, there was your inexplicable desertion—a cross I've had to bear. And now your ability to get a good man like Ezra to turn a blind eye to a core belief. I still cannot grasp that he took you to a hospital."

Evie didn't reply as he left. She supposed Gideon Neal was incapable of making the connection: his ability to have a conversation with his daughter was only thanks to Ezra's blind eye.

While seeing Hannah was easy, Ezra's visits took more effort. At first there were serious subject matters, Evie saying she planned to tell the boys about Sebastian soon. Ezra nodded. "It will be difficult. But when you do, if you want me here, you only need ask." Evie thanked him and switched to small talk. Soon wasn't today. She listened thoughtfully as Ezra spoke about his rise to the role of leader, and how he felt oddly comfortable in that capacity. Evie said she wasn't surprised at all. Ezra had a gift with people—reverent in his beliefs but compassionate, something his father had sorely lacked.

It was the bridge to a lengthier conversation about his father. On his next visit, Ezra told Evie that after he'd returned to the States, he'd confronted Duncan about Evie's accusation. "I asked him, Evie, if he ever touched you... if he ever said it was his divine right to..." Ezra went on to say that his father had vehemently denied every word. But he'd brought it up without malice toward Evie, which told her that Ezra doubted Duncan Kane's innocence.

As for his father's role as missions' leader, Evie assumed Ezra didn't know any more than the next person in Good Hope. He only spoke of the "fine work" and "benevolent efforts" his father now coordinated in South America. Evie nodded at his simplistic impressions. She decided it best that those thoughts be Ezra's truth. He didn't believe her back in Octava, and he wouldn't now. He certainly wouldn't believe that until Sebastian and Sam thwarted Reverend Kane's efforts—drugs to gun-running—his father's actions were criminal and insolently unholy.

Ezra also did not need to hear that it was Sebastian who kept tabs on Reverend Kane's activities. Sitting outside on the cabin step, Evie inhaled a shaky breath. Reality had slithered back in. Of course, Sebastian would no longer be able to make certain of Reverend Kane's doings or anything else. Ezra went on to tell her about the subtle ways in which he'd changed the Fathers of the Right. It was still a strict doctrine, though more tolerant with telephones in almost every home and certain jobs outside Good Hope permitted. "My father has done well since going abroad. In turn, I seem to serve the people of Good Hope to their satisfaction." He hesitated, prayerfully folding his hands. "It's to this end, I've been thinking... Well, since you've come back... I mean nearly from the dead, I've been considering other changes in Good Hope."

"What sort of changes?"

"It has to do with... for example, the Yeager's daughter. Her vision isn't good—she's been to the prescription specialist—you know seeing glasses are permitted."

Evie nodded.

"They say glasses won't correct the matter, though apparently drops to her eyes would. And then there's Benjamin Blyth—ill since the day he was born, which you know."

"I do," Evie said softly. "I've often thought how treatment might help whatever his lingering illness is."

"And that's just it. I'm no longer sure God wouldn't allow an earthly hand in those matters. I'm considering advocating... *encouraging*," he said as if trying the words on, "some medical intervention."

Evie didn't speak, treading carefully. "I can't disagree with you, Ezra. But I realize what a huge decision that would be."

He smiled at Evie's healthy, sun-kissed appearance. "Seems I've already made the decision. Continuing to let others suffer would be the travesty of the lesson." Ezra changed the subject, talking about the four marriages he'd officiated that year, the seven babies due before next spring. Numbers were up in Good Hope. But as Evie listened, she did wonder about his happiness.

"Ezra," she said, interrupting. His mouth closed midsentence. "I want to know something. Are you fine with this life? I mean, yes, you have the community, but you're such a good person. Well, I wonder... Don't you ever get lonely?"

Anguish flashed across his face, and Evie guessed he understood what she meant. *Tell me, Ezra... Did it ever repair itself, the heart that I smashed into a million pieces?* And for a moment, Evie couldn't make eye contact, wondering why he would choose to sit on the same step with her, never mind save her life.

He spoke with great care, in a way that defined Ezra. "It's not that I don't have regrets. It's not that I've forgotten." He looked toward Alec and Aaron. They were immersed and unaware, sailing a plastic boat in a nearby mud puddle. "But since you left... *this life*, I've done my best to have one. What were my choices?" Then he laughed, which felt terribly out of sync to Evie. "Can we agree that you would have made a woefully poor minister's wife?"

"But all this time, there's been no one else? You haven't wished..."

"Ah, you know better than to ask about wishes. And no. There's not been anyone."

She nodded, tucking her knees tight to her chest.

"While sect members don't speak about it—at least no one does to my face, it's become a symbol of sorts—the strength one person can muster, even in the aftermath of complete devastation, utter loss."

"Well," she said, staring at her sons. "I can appreciate what you mean."

After a month in Good Hope, Evie made new plans to leave. She felt stronger, more so than when she'd arrived. Evie focused on the artificial mindset she lived in when Sebastian was gone. It was methodical and mechanical. Sometimes she'd move forward a day at a time, sometimes only an hour. Now, it would just be forever. Waves of longing continued. Sadness scratched at her like a million grains of sand. But with Alec and Aaron as her priority, Evie was compelled to go forward.

On her last night in Good Hope, she built the first fire of the season. The temperature had dipped like it sometimes did in September, and the boys had complained of the cold cabin. She'd let them go to Hannah's for the night. But Evie admitted it was also selfishness. She wanted the space to herself. She'd gone into North Good Hope earlier that day to buy a few things for the trip back to Nickel Springs. She'd also bought a bottle of tequila, the kind Sebastian drank. She hated the taste and the nasty sting at the back of her throat. But one sip also had the power to deliver Sebastian to her—even if it was just for a few seconds.

Evie took a bath in the tub where she'd made love to Sebastian, the water cooling twice as fast with one body resting in its cast iron embrace. She put on a simple, white nightgown and climbed into the feather bed. Rain began to fall, hitting the tin overhang. It was too reminiscent. Alone there, Evie felt more sorrow than she thought one person could bear. She'd made a mistake. She threw back the covers and got out of bed. She needed to get Alec and Aaron—it didn't matter if it was close to midnight. She wanted them with her. But as she stepped into the fire lit path, on her way to the door, it opened. Ezra was there, not wearing vestments but tan trousers and a button-down shirt. He was soaked.

"It's raining."

"I heard. What are you doing here? It's so late."

"I need to talk to you. In the morning you'll be in such a rush to leave. Evie, I've held my tongue. So much time has passed. I understand that nothing can be the same." Evie thought she should get him a towel, but he seemed unaware of his dripping state. "Let me say that again. Nothing was ever what I thought, so 'the same' doesn't come into question here."

"Ezra, are you all right?"

He was speaking fast, odd for Ezra. "No, Evie, I'm not—and I need this said before you go. I know you're not a big believer in God's plan, so I won't try to force any such idea in your path. I'm all too aware of how that can backfire. But I want to suggest something, and I want you to hear me out."

"I have to get the boys..." She started past him. He grabbed her arm but released it immediately. "I need them with me."

"It's late. You'll only frighten them. Haven't they been tussled about enough?"

"Why would you care about... They're not your sons." They stood back to back, a half step apart—as if reprising some childhood game.

"No, they're not. But I could love them as if they were. You know that, Evie. I could be a good father to them."

Evie stepped back, looking Ezra in the eye. "They have a father," she said steadily. "I'll see to it they never forget him."

"I would help you do that too. But a ghost can't raise boys. While

I might have blamed you for our lack of offspring... It seems clear that I was wrong. I'll never have my own. I'd do right by them, Evie. I swear it."

She shook her head. "Here? In Good Hope? Not likely—not ever."

"That's why you need to listen. I've thought it through—carefully. But if you leave here tomorrow—"

"Ezra, you can't be serious? You want me to stay here and do what...?"

"Be my wife," he said. "Which you already are."

She'd nearly forgotten.

Evie dragged her fingers through her hair. "Ezra, I can see how you'd work that out in your mind. And I'm grateful for everything you've done—you saved my life. But..."

"Evie, I'm not asking you to come back to Good Hope." Ezra inched closer. He touched her cheek. Evie didn't move. Like his hand over hers in the hospital, it was soothing. It had felt that way since she was a girl. "I'm fully prepared to leave this life. The Fathers of the Right, they will survive without me. But I'm not sure I can survive without you—not twice. We can go wherever you like. To this Nickel Springs or New Mexico or Rodeo Drive in California. I don't care. Not as long as you're with me."

Evie didn't know if it sounded mad or like a plausible theory.

Ezra cupped his hand tight to her cheek. "Hear what I'm saying. But know the choice is yours."

She blinked hard—he had changed.

"There is something to be other than alone for the rest of your life, which is what I know you'll do."

Evie opened her mouth to object. She didn't. He was right about the last part. Alone was the only option to Sebastian. Evie approached the suggestion from a different angle. "You can't mean that, Ezra—not about leaving Good Hope. Your life is here."

He lowered his hand from her face and squeezed her fingers. "I do mean it. And I need to tell you something else—no matter what you decide. I can't lay my head down one more night, not without saying how sorry I am. Sorry for striking you in Otava. I hate myself for it, and I need you to know that."

She squeezed his hand back. Old feelings of love and friendship coursed through Ezra's touch, sinking into Evie. She closed her eyes. "I know you are, Ezra. It was an awful moment—for both of us. But what you're suggesting now, it's not how you behave. It's not what you do. You can't—"

"I assure, you, Evie. I can. And if you agree, I will. I've loved you my whole life. Much has happened in that time, but the fact hasn't changed." Ezra stood there, firelight flickering off his wet clothes and melted dreams. "Don't you think I've had opportunities? Don't you think women—believers as they might be—have offered me their bed? Some quite bluntly... Rachel Pruitt rather often."

Evie inched back. How obtuse. It had not occurred to her. Unlike Nolan Creek, Ezra would be the ultimate prize in this extraordinary place.

"I said no to all of them."

"So you were waiting... hoping something like this would happen to me, to Sebastian?"

"No! Of course not."

And because Evie knew Ezra so well, she knew it was the truth. "Ezra," she said, letting him pull her closer. "Please don't put me in this position. Time and death, they can't make me fall in love with you—not like that."

He was undeterred. "You once told me that you did love me in some way. Was that untrue?"

"No," she said, more easily than she thought possible. "What I feel for you has always been something good. Something genuine. Something peaceful."

"So if it's not an ocean of passion, and yet we find ourselves adrift,

I can accept that. Evie," he said, waiting until her eyes met his. "I should be happy to be with you on any terms. You do love me in some sense. You just said it. We are married. Your sons have no living, breathing father. Give me one valid reason it can't work?"

"I... I don't know... Because..." A breath shuddered out of Evie, but she clung to Ezra's shoulders, her fists full of his shirt. It was like grabbing onto a solid thing—a place where the hurt wasn't stabbing. Before she could respond, Ezra's mouth met with hers. It was a physical nudge, and Evie slipped toward his suggestion. The kiss was sedate, so unlike the command of Sebastian. But Evie didn't stop the quiet advance. Ezra kissed her harder, which was hardly like kissing a stranger. Then he held her close. Evie stared at the fire's flames, her emotions filling with something other than grief. Willingly, she waded into feelings that were not sadness and loss.

Ezra led them toward the bed. He spied the bottle of tequila and Evie didn't know what to say, other than *"One more drink might help..."* She shrugged. "It's not my habit, just my memory." She didn't touch the bottle, but she did wonder what Ezra might taste like if he downed a swig or two. Without the aid of alcohol, he kissed her again. Evie kissed him back—in part because she didn't want him to speak. She didn't want to talk about anything that mattered. God, least of all she didn't want to think.

At the edge of the bed, Ezra slipped the nightgown over her head. His face looked as awed as it had in the barn all those years ago. He was still fully clothed and Evie hesitated, her fingers poised at the buttons of his damp shirt. "Ezra, I can't promise anything. It would be wildly unfair of me to—"

"Just give us this night." He kissed her again. "That's all I'm asking for now. You can decide anything more later."

He ran his hands lithely over her body. Evie shivered at his touch. Her stare was overtly conscious, Evie making certain she understood what was happening. A fair-haired man stood before her, his build slight. She did not have to raise her chin to look him in the eye. His irises were a beautiful lagoon blue. Not the green of a spruce tree or the center of a passion flower. He did not elicit desire, just friendly, familiar warmth. It was the kind of love that might get you through. She continued, focused on gratitude. Hastily, she unbuttoned his shirt, unbuckled his belt. She kissed him in a way that would make him feel like her husband. Ezra deserved this and Evie would do so because it felt good to think of someone else. They lay together on the bed where Ezra reclaimed what he'd so painfully lost. And for that, Evie was glad—able to offer him something as simple as her body. It didn't matter. She was no longer using it in that way.

And for her part, Evie took advantage, wrapping herself in human comfort that Ezra gave so freely. Evie made sure her eyes stayed open—concentrating. If Ezra could look inside her head, Evie wanted to be sure of what he'd see—himself, the two of them in a bed. Ezra was gentle and pleasant—a more mature version of that anxious, happy boy. He was all the things he'd been when she was nineteen but little more.

As a lover, he hadn't improved—though, of course, he'd admitted to having passed on the opportunity to learn. Evie didn't coax him or give him cues. She wasn't interested in making a better lover out of Ezra Kane. As the act itself approached, Ezra brought humor to what had to be his tense, emotion-filled moment. "I think I recall how this parts works."

"There's nothing wrong with instinct guiding you."

He smiled, his face lit by the fire, poised over hers. "You keep looking at me—so intently. Why?"

Evie swallowed hard and answered truthfully. "Because it's you."

Minutes later, Evie buried her nose in his shoulder, Ezra's skin infused with the scent of starch, the clerical collar that so often rode his neck. She let go long enough to swipe fast at tears she couldn't stop, that she did not want him to feel. He might not have noticed anyway, so overcome by his thundering moment of pleasure and tears of his own, inadvertently mixing with hers. Ezra held her face in his hands and kissed her once more, whispering in her ear. "I'm certain that was different for me than it was for you—but I also know it was meant to happen."

Not long after, Evie pretended to be asleep, and it didn't take long until Ezra was snoring softly. He was used to sleeping alone and did not reach for Evie. She was thankful for this. She'd willingly gone to bed with him, but the instant it was over Evie knew it was all she could do with him or for him. Inside the cabin, a long stretch of darkness finally gave way to dull, gray light—rain still teemed. Evie opened her eyes and stared at the wall. She felt Ezra lean over her. Instinctively, she recoiled as he touched her arm. His body stiffened, drawing away from hers. He sighed deeply—painfully. "Should I take that as your answer?" She couldn't look at him, nodding her head against the pillow. Contemplative moments of quiet passed, like waiting for a last breath. She could tell he was debating further argument. "No matter what I've said, there'll not be another night like this one, will there?" And the last breath came, languishing from Ezra's gut. He rose from the bed. There was the quiet rustle of clothes being gathered, pants being zipped.

"I understand if you hate me," she whispered. "If you banish me from Good Hope forever, I could hardly blame you. I almost wish you would."

He pressed his arms into the feathery mattress, causing her to roll slightly toward him. "You've had enough pain, Evie. I won't add to it—not if you truly can't see yourself to even halfway of what I've offered. As for hating you, I'd think you'd know by now God has made that impossible. I'm not sure why He allowed me last night. Understand, while I'd prayed for a different reply, I'm not sorry this happened."

Ezra kissed the side of her head and as always Evie was comforted by his touch. As he walked to the door and left, she almost yelled for him to come back. It was raining. It was cold. She didn't want to be alone. She would do it—Evie would live her life as Ezra's wife if it brought him happiness. Hers no longer mattered. But as daybreak widened, Evie knew it would be the cruelest fate of all.

She let an hour pass, then another, finally getting out of bed long enough to put her nightgown on and restart the fire. She could see her breath in the cabin. Standing near the edge of the bed, she stared at the bottle of tequila. Evie gripped its neck and guzzled— the kind of drink meant to erase things. She gagged and the sharp tasting liquid rushed back up her throat. Thunder boomed. "By all means," she shouted. "Do it! Let lightning strike." Evie kept the booze down and collapsed back onto the bed, a shivering ball of human suffering. At the moment, she couldn't even be a mother to her sons. Evie hit her lowest point, crying so hard for so long, she thought her tears might catch up with the rain.

Nature dominated with a thrashing downpour and gusty winds. She didn't move, not when branches cracked overhead or as a steady leak dripped down the side of the stone fireplace. She didn't stir when the fire died. Between gulps of air, which Evie seemed doomed to take, she brushed her hand across the label of the tequila bottle. She wondered how much it took to get truly drunk. But her attention was distracted, the sound of a door opening. Surely Hannah wondered what had become of her. The boys must be looking for her by now. She threw back the covers, grasping at an idea about functioning. Aaron and Alec couldn't see her like this. Evie stepped from the bed, hoping to dash past whoever had come into the cabin.

It was five steps to the bathroom. On the third, she froze. Evie looked toward the figure that had come through the door. She clawed at the hair that hung in her face, hampering her view. Her legs quaked, unable to support her. There was nothing to hold onto, except Sebastian, who rushed forward just in time to catch her.

CHAPTER THIRTY

Present Day
Good Hope, Pennsylvania

ALEC HAD NO STATE-OF-THE-ART OPS GEAR, BUT HE HAD FLESH AND BLOOD Clairmont brothers. Together he guessed they wielded a presence equal to Sebastian's. The thought allowed him to approach Good Hope like a SEAL on a recon mission. A half-hour inside in the target zone, Alec extracted what he'd call *mid-level intel*: the place was a world unto itself, not unfriendly but reserved, and he probably shouldn't have said "you're fucking kidding me," so loud.

After that, he channeled his Middle East manners. It was necessary in environments that operated under strict customs. If you wanted to get along, if you wanted information, you'd better get on board. The Clairmonts and Jess weren't the only outsiders walking the streets of Good Hope that Saturday. It was an advantage. They blended. Not even Jake, who had to invest in another hat before leaving the airport, stuck out. Kiera explained that the bake shop/ice cream parlor attracted tourists, people who'd spend money before going home to the Internet and their complex lives.

"Eating sounds good to me," Troy said.

"It's not a bad idea," Kiera agreed. "My presence is unexpected. Six of us showing up at my parents' door at once will not be helpful."

"Copy that," Alec said. "Jake, why don't you, Troy, and Jess hang back, have—"

"No way," Jess said. "I didn't come this far to eat an ice cream cone."

Alec was surprised she'd come at all. She'd had a tense exchange with Julian in the airport, which seemed standard to him. Red-faced, she'd stormed off, informing Alec, "I'm going with you."

She continued to make her choices clear. "I get that you've *got this*, Alec. But an investigative journalist might not be a bad asset, considering."

"You're right." Her mouth had been poised to argue and she clamped it shut. "Jake, maybe you and Troy can shake down the locals. Use that charm or your acting skills—whatever works. See if they have anything of interest to add."

"Good luck with that," Kiera said. "They won't share anything with outsiders—not unless it can be scooped into a cone or tied in a pastry box." She smiled at Troy. "Even good looking boys can find themselves *hard up* in Good Hope."

"They can try, can't they?" Alec said, his patience wearing thin. Since she'd seduced him in his La Carta hotel room, Alec had regretted his Kiera choices. True. They wouldn't be standing there without her assistance. But she also impressed Alec as the type who liked to push buttons, stir the pot—the type he liked least of all.

When the foursome finally arrived in the Blyth's living room, Alec hoped it would signal the end of Kiera's involvement. If Tobias Blyth was shocked to see Kiera and three strangers he hid it well, calling her "daughter," nodding at him, Aaron, and Jess. Alec stood with this hands tucked behind his back and disregarded the fact that he'd aggressively fucked the man's daughter less than twenty-four hours ago. Aside from the paternal meet and greet, Alec was having a hard time nulling out the family visuals—the sex-kitten that had clawed her way into his bed, versus the sedate, dowdily dressed girl in front of him. She attributed her sudden presence to "God's will," which her father seemed to accept as sufficient reasoning.

Aside from that there wasn't much information to process. Plain was the décor of choice, beige walls, simple furniture, braided rugs, and a corded phone on the wall. There was a small television, and Alec did note a Lancaster newspaper. The Blyths seemed to be living on the cusp of yesteryear and now. Tobias Blyth had just said he needed to get back to the meeting hall and prepare for tomorrow's services when a woman came down the stairs.

"Do we have company, Tobias? Millie Pruitt said Rachel's son might come by to ask Sarah if she'd like to walk to services with him to..." Clearing the staircase, she stuttered to a halt. Hannah Blyth first looked at her daughter, who she hadn't seen in two years. But her gaze was quickly seared to Alec and Aaron. "Lord have mercy on my soul," she said, a hand flying over her heart.

Varying degrees of shock and awe followed. It came from Hannah Blyth, who first hugged her daughter and went on to identify Alec and Aaron without introduction. And it came from the Clairmont brothers, who grappled with the story Hannah told. At first it'd been a whirl of questions and answers, most of it centering on what they'd come for: information about Evie. Hannah, it seemed, was the Holy Grail of knowledge, filling in many blanks. She was clearly cautious, but after Alec told her about the crash site and cryptic initials on the plane, Kiera's mother was more forthcoming. The brothers were engrossed as the woman told a bizarre tale about a man they called *the mission*. He'd turned up in Good Hope in the fall of 1977 and turned Evie Neal's world upside down. His name, she told them, was Sebastian Christos.

Alec thudded his back into the chair, absorbing the same name he'd heard on the streets of La Carta. It was the first solid connection between his father and this place.

"Christos... That's Greek," Jess said. Alec and Aaron traded glances as if looking in a mirror, applying heritage to features that fit an ethnic description.

Hannah Blyth went on to explain that she and Evie had been good friends, the two of them growing up together, their families devout members of the Fathers of the Right, which she described as a singular religious organization. "Of course, things were different back then. Our ways were quite fundamental, overtly strict. Your father was an outsider to say the least. From what I know, he was sent here for protection—protection from what... Well, Evie never said." Hannah stared at her folded hands. "But... I will tell you, if there is such a thing as love at first sight, I believe it describes what happened to your parents."

Alec and Aaron added the little they knew about family history. Evie had told them her mother passed away years ago, and that she no longer communicated with her father. She'd never said why or mentioned brothers of her own. It was a piece of information that struck Alec as clandestine, telling him how many layers there were to this story. Hannah nodded as if she'd been witness to it all.

After that the conversation took a more curious turn. "Years after Evie left Good Hope with Sebastian," Hannah said, "she made two distinct trips back. Sebastian wasn't with her either time. The first visit was unexpected. It, um... Evie came here because she thought Sebastian was dead. We all did."

"Dead," Alec repeated. "You mean dead before the plane crash?"

"Indeed. More than a decade or more before that tragedy." Hannah didn't elaborate, which only added to Alec's frustration. He started to interrupt but Jess nudged him with her elbow.

"Please, go on Mrs. Blyth. We're grateful for anything you can share."

It took all Alec's willpower to embrace silence.

"Evie's second visit came less than a year after her first. It too was out of sheer hopelessness, desperation. You boys stayed with me both times. You don't remember?"

Alec and Aaron offered their vague recollections, stressing that no memory answered their questions. "If I hadn't discovered Kiera in La Carta, the school," Alec said, "we would have never found Good Hope. Neither of our parents ever mentioned it." At that point Kiera did interrupt, smiling coyly and excusing herself. She wanted to see her six brothers and sisters. Obviously large families were key to Good Hope's survival.

"Speaking of siblings," Hannah said, "the five of you, you're all well? Over the years, I've wondered... prayed for you. Your mother kept in touch with me until... well, until the end. Short letters mostly. After your parents disappeared we followed the story in the newspaper. In one of her last Christmas letters, she referred to you as the..." Her fingertips fluttered to her forehead. "I can't quite recall..."

"*Tribe of Five*," Alec and Aaron said at the same time.

"That's right... *Tribe of Five*," she repeated.

"Most of us are here—"

"Here? In Good Hope... today?" she said, her monotone speech spiking.

"Yes. We left Troy and Jake at the bakery," Alec said. "We didn't think all of us turning up on your doorstep was the best idea."

She smiled, but Alec read it as more nervous than genuine. "Your other brothers. And your sister, Jacob's twin. Is she here?"

"No," Alec said, not having heard anyone call Jake "Jacob" since Evie had last said it. "Honor's at home in Nickel Springs. She didn't make the trip."

"She runs an inn—Abstract Enchantment," Aaron offered, the place surely burned into his mind. "She's a chef, a very good one."

Hannah nodded. "It doesn't surprise me. I wouldn't have given a nickel for any quilt Evie might have sewn, but she truly had a gift with food."

"That's for sure," Alec said, recalling meals he hadn't thought about in ages.

"I saw them once as infants," the woman said, circling back around. "Honor and Jake. Even then, you could see how the boy resembled the two of you... Sebastian. And the daughter... She was different, fair and blue-eyed."

"Still is," Aaron said, trading a look with Alec.

"Evie was awed by her." Hannah took a breath, staring at Alec and Aaron. "Well, I believe it was probably the femininity after so many boys."

"Might have been. Anyway," Alec said, trying to steer the exchange. "We've learned a lot recently—places that our parents were deeply connected to but the reasons don't add up."

"Beyond that, why was any of it a secret?" Aaron said. "What, specifically, do you know about La Carta—other than it seemed like a great place to banish your daughter to?"

"I'm sure our methods seem harsh to an outsider, but Kiera's father... the elder Reverend Kane, it was their belief that true missionary work would benefit Kiera," Hannah said. "Other than a place where Fathers of the Right work is carried out, I don't know what you mean."

"With all due respect, Mrs. Blyth, I don't believe you. I think you know a great deal about La Carta—going all the way back to a time when our parents were frequent visitors. So we're clear, I'm not leaving here until I get some answers."

Hannah was silent, as if weighing her options.

Go ahead, think it through, lady... But I swear, you will tell me... Why did you call my father "the mission?" What was he doing in Good Hope? Even better, why did everyone think he was dead? And the plane, those initials... what does it all mean...? Alec had to bite his tongue to keep from bombarding her with questions.

"Wait there," Hannah said. She returned a few minutes later with a large envelope. "It may give you some answers. I don't know that it will solve the mystery of your parents' disappearance."

Alec's urge to tear into the envelope was too great. He put it in Jess's steadier hands. Inside the large envelope were three smaller envelopes. The first contained a letter from Sebastian to Evie, dated April 1977. There was also an official government document, calling out the moniker *SAM14*, a phone number, and a long series of letters and digits. There was a third smaller envelope with the word "Bim" written on the outside.

The three of them reached for the letter from Sebastian to Evie. It looked as if it had been read a thousand times. Hannah prefaced it. "It's an old letter. It was written before all of you were born, not long after Evie left here. From the gist of it, I think they were at sea, traveling from the port in Philadelphia to South America."

"Okay, maybe fill us in on that part. Why were they traveling to South America?"

"Our mission work, before we embraced air travel, men used to sail out of that harbor. I do know your father was employed in some capacity on large sailing ships." She took a deep breath. "Evie, she had her own reasons for wanting to go with him. Anyway, the letter, it's not the sort of thing a member of our sect would put on paper."

Alec read the first few lines—then he couldn't read anymore. That part of him, the small space that allowed for human emotion was already maxed out. Instead, he watched Jess's face. It told the story, shifting from scrupulous reporter and softening to something else as she bit down on her lower lip. "Oh my..." she said in a whispery tone Alec didn't recognize.

Aaron read along, clearly at a faster clip, maybe skimming. He leaned back in his chair. "Jesus," he said. "That's a lot for man who wasn't big on words."

"I didn't know your father well," Hannah said. "I had mixed emotions about Evie's decision to leave here with him. There are countless reasons she should have stayed, some binding."

"Like?" Alec said.

"For one, Good Hope was her home." Hannah touched the corner of the letter. "We... the Fathers of the Right, we're her people. Isn't that enough?"

Alec leaned forward. "My perspective differs. Especially being a member of the *Tribe of Five*. Lucky for us she left... Otherwise, none of us Clairmont kids would exist. Would we?"

Hannah opened her mouth then pursed her lips tight. She cleared her throat and continued. "After Evie's second visit," she said, jumping time, "when Sebastian came for her... I don't think she needed those papers anymore. I never read the letter until after they vanished. I didn't think it was proper. After I did... I must admit, I had a better appreciation of their relationship. Sebastian, he would have moved heaven and earth for her—and that's not something we profess to do in Good Hope."

Jess slid the letter back into its envelope and Alec was relieved. He was able to make a more pragmatic assessment about the other pieces of information. He picked up the paper bearing a government seal. "Okay, this is more than a little curious. It's CIA..." Alec said, picking up the paper bearing a government seal. "SAM14... interesting."

"Can you decipher it?" Aaron asked.

"It reads like a code name, but I think it's also a clue. SAM—capped like that—stands for Surface to Air Missile. The number, I don't know... maybe a count. All special ops branches of the military do that with high value targets—keep a count, assign ownership."

"Weapons or bodies?" Jess said.

"Both," Alec replied casually, looking over the information. "Surface to Air Missiles would have been a popular commodity around this time period in South America. The place was a hotbed of guerrilla rebels. The US Government spent lives and billions trying to keep SAMs and drugs out of the hands of opposing military factions. In the late seventies into the early eighties, places like La Carta would have been greatly affected. And I'll go as far as to surmise this: Pop's love letter might offer some personal insights. But this document," he said, shaking the paper at Jess and Aaron, "tells me more. He was in deep with the government. I'd guess that SAM14 is a call sign for his handler, and the phone number a point of contact—maybe in case Mom needed it—remember, we're talking pre-cell here, pre-internet. Communications options were limited. The series of numbers and letters, I'd bet it's a code verifying who she was and her clearance for access."

"Wait," Aaron said, shaking his head. "You're talking, like, spy scenarios. Pop worked for an international courier. Some of it was government related, but it wasn't classified."

"Says who?" Alec shrugged. "You just learned you have two uncles you didn't know existed. Consider what else we don't know." Alec looked at Hannah who avoided his gaze.

"Alec, come on," Aaron said. "Pop didn't live your life. He piloted and delivered international documents and small cargo."

"I don't think so," Alec said, suddenly surer of the source of his hard-ass Navy SEAL wherewithal. "I think *international courier* was a clever cover for what he really did."

"My gosh, I can hardly wait to see how *Bim* fits into the picture," Jess said, reaching for the smaller envelope. It turned out to be a second letter, also dated April 1977. It spelled out a stateside connection for Evie, somewhere she should go if Sebastian didn't return. *"I know you didn't love the idea when I suggested it, Evie. But if anything happens, if I don't make it back—from this assignment or the next... go. Sam will be good for money and getting you back stateside, but he won't be able to help beyond that. I trust Bim. You should too."*

"Now what do you think?" Alec said to Aaron. Bim's name was followed by an address in Philadelphia, along with his medical credentials.

"He was a doctor?" Jess said.

"He was a friend of your father's. I don't know anything more about him, other than Evie chose not to seek him out when she thought Sebastian was... *gone*. I've told you everything I know," she said.

"I don't believe that," Alec said. "You haven't begun to explain the two *distinct* visits my mother made back to Good Hope, let alone how or why she thought our father was dead. And we haven't even gotten around to the bizarre initials left on the side of their—"

"Alec," Jess said, grabbing his rigid arm.

She was right. Alec could see the startled look on Hannah's face. She was close to telling them to leave. He backed off, speaking in a gentler tone. "You said the first time Evie stayed a while. I do remember bits and pieces of being here. I remember swings and a pond."

"And a cabin," Aaron added.

On the mention of a cabin, Hannah sucked in a sharp breath. Alec exchanged a fast glance with Jess, whose look back said she saw the same.

"Could we see the cabin, Mrs. Blyth?" Jess asked, her request respectful and soft. "It may not tell us anything, but you never know. It is years later. Don't you think Alec and Aaron, grown men, have a right to know about the past—especially if we're unable to figure out exactly what happened to Evie and Sebastian?"

"You pose a complicated question, Jess... Is it Jessica?"

She smiled. "Only if you're my mother."

"Mmm, mothers. We're an interesting lot. Sometimes we know our children better than they know themselves. As for the *Tribe of Five*," she said carefully, "they're not mine. And I'm not sure I'm wise enough to provide the proper answers. But fine. I can't see the harm in looking at a dusty, rundown room and a bath."

The four of them walked single file down a winding path. There was no choice, the dirt trail was nearly overgrown with brush. "No one has used the cabin in years. Our Reverend, he doesn't like anyone to come here."

"Why's that?" Alec asked as they regrouped at the door.

"I expect the memories it holds are too extreme for our modest lives."

"Good or bad memories?" Alec asked.

"A strong amount of both. He's away today. It's the only reason I've agreed to this."

"Difficult man? Violent temper?" Alec asked, tuned into the Grim Reaper image cloaked in black.

"Our Reverend? Heavens no," said Hannah. "He's a good man. Kind. I shouldn't wish to upset him. That's all."

"Why would talking about my mother upset him?"

Turning the doorknob, Hannah didn't answer. The dusty, cobweb-filled cabin felt like a sealed tomb, its insides airless. They left the door open, but the warm autumn day did nothing to combat the stifling setting and dark corners. Alec's head pounded, and he began to sweat. It wasn't like him—this was hardly enemy territory. Even then, he knew how to breathe easy. It had often been the difference between staying alive or ending up dead. This feeling was more personal, and it connected to the cabin. Images pounced, his mind filling with the past. He remembered. The man in the black cloak came at his mother, Alec's small fists beating him as he screamed for the man to stop. Aaron clung to the edge of her shirt, holding a Teddy bear.

"Alec," Jess said, touching his arm. He yanked it away and took a turn around the room. It was all so vivid. The argument incredibly fierce. Alec focused on the stone fireplace. He closed his eyes. Aaron's voice cut in, but the sound only clarified a memory, the reason Aaron couldn't get to his mother—the object in the way. She'd been extremely pregnant, her face exhausted and fearful. A younger Alec was terrified as the Reverend screamed at Evie, shaking her. "*They're mine...*" Alec whispered.

"*They're...* Alec, what are talking about?" Jess said.

"The Reverend who was here that night, he was yelling at my mother, saying *'they're mine...'* over and over." Alec looked at the hearth. It was still there—an iron poker. As a boy, he'd grabbed it, ready to defend his mother. At that exact moment, the scene in his head shifted, jaggedly, like stones tumbling down a hill. The fear that filled a younger Alec had bottomed out as Sebastian Clairmont pounded through the cabin door.

"What's going on here?"

An unknown voice penetrated from behind Alec, the abrupt timing knocking him off balance—at least mentally. He spun toward the sound. It was real, but the man wasn't Sebastian. In the doorway was a fair-haired man wearing a clerical collar.

"Reverend Kane." Panic rushed Hannah's voice. "I didn't think you'd be back until this evening. I didn't know what else to do. They—"

He held up a hand. "It's all right, Hannah. Why don't you head back to your house? I'm certain God has seen to this moment. I'll handle it."

She nodded, scurrying out the door as the *Reverend* came farther in.

"Reverend?" Alec said, moving closer. The cabin light was dim, but this was clearly not the man in his memory.

"I'm Reverend Kane," he said, his gaze darting between the two brothers. "Ezra Kane. And I knew you'd both be back someday. What is it I can do for you—Alec?"

CHAPTER THIRTY-ONE

1984

Good Hope, Pennsylvania

IF THIS WAS A DREAM, EVIE DIDN'T WANT TO WAKE UP. IF SHE WAS DEAD, she'd been given a greater reward than she deserved. She and Sebastian crumpled together onto the cabin floor. Her breathing was so erratic, speaking was impossible. She focused on tangible elements. Sebastian's arms were around her—one in a cast—the two of them rocked in a calming motion. *"How...?"* she managed.

"It's a long, incredible story." The grip of his un-casted arm grew tighter. She knew his touch, recognized his smell, and the beat of his heart.

"Sam, he said... he showed me photos."

"I know—and he was almost right."

The way they'd fallen, Evie's back pressed against his chest. She broke from his grip and spun on her knees. She grasped either side of his face, staring into it. It was gaunt and showed fading bruises. But his eyes—his eyes were alive and looking into hers. "I don't understand. How.... How is this possible? It's been months since Sam came to me, even longer since anyone heard from you. And the picture... Your eyes—they were... *dead.*"

"They were staring."

Evie swiped a finger through the tear on his cheek. She couldn't stop there, moving her hands over his face the way the blind might touch another person. But as she brushed a hand over his chest, he winced. Maybe this was it. Maybe this was where a cruel dream ended and Evie woke up. She grasped his T-shirt at the neck and tore it open. A patch of gauze was taped between his heart and shoulder. But she also saw the rise and fall of Sebastian's breath.

"Make a note," he said. "I am really not a fan of bullet wounds."

"Bullet wound." She stared, incredulous. "Sebastian," Evie said, heart and hands trembling. "If you're not a ghost... if you're not some wicked punishment for..." Her gaze rose from the wound to his face. "Tell me how you're alive."

"What did Sam tell you about my last assignment?"

"That it was *soft*. That you were guarding civilian workers from a company called AmeriTex. Their employees were taken hostage—not by rebels. Thugs, a street gang."

"That's right. A vicious street gang but better armed than some of the guerrilla factions I'd fought."

"Sam said there was a ransom, and that the company tried to negotiate it themselves. They thought they'd do better without government involvement. The first photo he showed me... you were chained to a pole—badly beaten but alive."

He nodded. "They never ID'd me as government, but they did think I was in charge. The AmeriTex employees—they were totally unprepared, scared shitless." He shook his head. "Hell, so was I—anybody would have been. At least with rebels there's some predictability, a point of negotiation. These guys were beyond ruthless.

"The beating ended up saving my life. I was separated from the rest of the hostages. After they got their payoff, I thought there was a chance they'd let them go. The ringleader said, 'Fuck 'em—dead men can't finger you. Kill them all.' It happened so fast. Twenty or more innocent men, they just smoked them. I've seen brutal shit, Evie, but I've never seen anything like that."

"But the photo—I saw it, Bash... You were in the pile, your eyes just staring."

"After they shot the others, they staged that gruesome photo op. They'd almost forgotten me—so jacked up on their crime, their payoff. One guy saw I was still chained to the pole. The asshole in charge said, 'Throw him on—but make sure he's dead first.' I got lucky—the shooter given the direction was a boy, maybe fifteen. His aim was that bad. The bullet hit—while it hurt like a son of a bitch, I knew it was a flesh wound. He stared. I stared back. I wasn't giving the little fucker the satisfaction of begging for my life." Evie inched back, cupping her hand to her mouth. "He was about ten, maybe fifteen feet away. I told him if he wanted to do it right, like a man, he should step up and hold the gun right to my head."

"Bash... no," Evie said, dropping her trembling hand onto his.

"In the moment, I preferred the alternative. I saw those guys, feet away—a human pile of suffering. Some weren't dead yet, but they were all badly wounded, in agony, bleeding. I saw the gas cans and I guessed what was coming. The boy stepped closer and raised the gun. I kept my eyes open and my mind on you. He could take my life, but he couldn't take my last thought. After a second or two, he..." Sebastian widened his eyes. "He couldn't do it. He just turned and walked away. I was quick enough to think to play dead. There was so much confusion, a river of blood. No one was paying attention to me. The kid and another guy threw me on the heap. It took everything I had to keep still, keep my wits. The one in charge said 'take the picture—something for their families' Christmas cards.' I wasn't sure how much longer I could hold out, but I literally managed not to blink. My arm," he said, lifting the casted limb toward Evie, "was busted pretty bad..."

Evie tipped her head, breathing deep at what had to have been excruciating pain. "Dear God... I can't begin to think..."

"Don't," he said. "I've been in some close scrapes, bad shit situations. I've never been in anything like that. I was surrounded by bodies—if they were lucky, they were already dead. If they weren't... The next thing I knew, I smelled gasoline. They tossed a match, but I guess they weren't prepared for the backlash of flames. They just grabbed their money and took off. From where I'd been chained, toward the rear of the building, I'd seen an exit. The fire was moving fast. I squeezed out from under the bodies and hauled myself to the back door a step ahead of the fire." Sebastian closed his eyes for a moment. "I turned back, but it was too late. There was an explosion, the building engulfed."

"But, how... then what? That was months ago."

"Sam might have said how remote the AmeriTex work location was. The warehouse where they held us was even farther—on the edge of the Amazon Basin."

"The rainforest." Evie knew of the vast, dense forest, human population was sparse—tribal mostly. But it was the terrain that would most likely kill a person, an impenetrable wild region.

"I started walking... dragging myself really. At that point, I figured it was a matter of time—my wounds or exposure. I dropped over on something that looked like a road. Days later, I woke in a village. It made La Carta look like a booming metropolis."

"But you were alive."

He nodded. "I was alive. I'm not even sure how. A family—native clan—had taken me in. The only medical means were something between a witch doctor and spiritual healer. He did splint the arm, which is probably the only reason it's still attached to me. My injuries were bad, but before long communicating became a bigger problem. The bullet was lodged in my shoulder. I knew it had to come out. So with the doc's help, I managed to get him to boil me a knife and..."

"And..." Evie said, dropping from her knees onto her bottom.

"And I cut the fucking thing out..."

From there Sebastian went on, telling Evie everything. How afterward infection set in and he'd spent time—he didn't know how much—drifting in and out of a feverish state. The Amazon tribe spoke in an odd dialect, a hybrid of Spanish, Portuguese, and native tongue. It made verbal communication nearly impossible. There was no electricity, no phone, no way to get a message to her or to Sam. Eventually, Sebastian did improve. The family, the tribe, seemed to look upon him as some sort of North American novelty. He said they were gracious but incredibly primitive, their contact with the outside world as unlikely as the region in which they'd survived for thousands of years. In time, Sebastian healed enough to move on. The tribe packed a tarp filled with food. Evie listened as he ticked off the native offerings—smoked armadillo, boiled plantains, indigenous plants, which Sebastian said he was most grateful for. "You really had to know which plants were edible and which ones would kill you. It seemed like a fifty-fifty split." Sebastian went on to tell Evie that the tribal elders took him by boat to the other side of a crocodile filled river. Then they pointed toward a mountain trail, indicating that the other side was the way out. "What were my choices?" he said, Evie's eyes locked in a wide stare. "I had to get back to you... the boys."

After sitting for some time on the cabin floor, they helped one another to their feet. She inspected Sebastian from top to bottom, the T-shirt hanging open. "It made more sense to get to Sam first," he said. "And when I did they sent a ride."

"A car?"

"Helicopter," he said, shaking his head. "We tried to get in touch right away. Sam sent some agents to the Rose Arch—you weren't there. I thought for sure you'd gone to Bim."

"Bim..." A breath sunk into Evie. "I... things were so different than when you wrote that letter years ago. I just... I didn't do it."

"When Bim said he hadn't heard from you, I didn't know what to make of it. He'd been waiting all these years for a chance to repay me. He was as distraught as me when you didn't contact him."

Evie glanced toward the feather bed and whispered, "I so wish I had... You've no idea how much." Her gaze cut to his.

Sebastian smiled, touching her face.

"For one wild second I thought I might never find you. I didn't... Well, I didn't think you'd come here. But then, it occurred to me, for better or worse, this," he said, glancing around, "probably seemed like the closest thing to home."

Evie wanted nothing more than to get out of the cabin and out of Good Hope. Hannah's reaction to Sebastian was stunning enough. Evie did not think she could bear to witness Ezra's. Hannah agreed to tell him she'd left, which he would be expecting. News of Sebastian's survival would be a shock, salt in Ezra's reopened wound. Evie's single, saving grace was that she'd been honest—whether Sebastian was dead or alive reuniting with her husband was not Evie's choice. Solace was also found in the fact that she'd never told the boys about their father's presumed demise. His return wasn't traumatic. Instead, Aaron and Alec were merely overjoyed to see Sebastian. Evie clung to those thoughts and feelings as they headed home to Nickel Springs. Riding in the passenger seat next to him, she closed her eyes, letting the sound of Sebastian's voice wash over her.

That night the caretaker's cottage eventually grew quiet. In the living room were the things that made them a family—a collection of history books Evie had given Sebastian, one every Christmas. The native souvenirs they'd collected in South America, a toy box so full the lid had no hope of closing. Evie breathed deep, thinking mostly of the people in the next room. Sebastian had fallen asleep in Alec's bed, his eldest son crooked between his body and cast, his uninjured arm cradling Aaron. Standing in the doorway, Evie saw perfection. It was why she chose to go to bed alone. She didn't want to disrupt that state of mind. Just as she drifted off, Evie felt the weight of the mattress shift—she'd nearly gotten used to the sense of being alone in the bed.

"Hey," he said, kissing her shoulder. "Did you want me to spend the night with the boys?"

She didn't answer.

"Evie?"

An onset of tears was hardly unexpected, Sebastian perceiving them as the aftermath of the whole horrid experience. When he reached for her, the way he had in Evie's dreams, in the way that had kept her alive, she could only respond in kind. She banished the previous night from their bed and her mind. She welcomed Sebastian home passionately and without hesitation, in the ways they both wanted.

Sebastian had been given several months' leave. It allowed them to be a family again while giving everyone time to readjust. Weeks into their old lives Evie saw differences, little fissures in Sebastian's personality that weren't there when he returned from other assignments. He was unable to sleep and grew snappish with her and the boys. He drank more than she ever recalled. Faced with his edgy, odd mood, it seemed like reason enough to keep her night with Ezra a secret. Then, two months later, Evie's secret took on a life of its own, landing at the forefront of everything. She received confirmation of what she already knew—the obvious signs of a third pregnancy. With a baby due in June, the basic math was alarming—she'd slept with both Sebastian and Ezra within a day of each other. Sebastian's reaction, thrilled by the news, was a contrast to Evie's. The prospect of a baby seemed to smooth his emotional scars in a way nothing else had. Evie tried to soothe herself with the odds—it was almost a certainty that Sebastian was the father. She'd lived as Ezra's wife for more than a year, and there'd been no child. Two nights in the cabin with Sebastian had resulted in Alec. And for a while longer, Evie let probability dominate.

But when Evie learned there'd be twins, she grew more anxious—or perhaps her guilt doubled. Hiding her concern became increasingly difficult. Sebastian began questioning her, wanting to know if she was unhappy about having another child. He prodded and coaxed, insisting there was something different in her demeanor. Evie's outlook wasn't dreamy like it had been with Alec and Aaron—acting as if these babies were somehow a burden. "I don't get it," Sebastian said. "After everything that's happened, I thought for sure you'd label this baby... *babies*, heaven sent."

Evie didn't know how much longer she could keep up the façade. She nearly choked on his words—on his hopeful, heartfelt sentiment—needing to rush from the room.

CHAPTER THIRTY-TWO

1985
Nickel Springs, New York

AT THE BEGINNING OF EVIE'S EIGHTH MONTH, SEBASTIAN WANTED TO know when she planned on preparing—not for one but two infants. There was no crib, no new clothing. She hadn't suggested a single name. She didn't wonder out loud, "Boys or girls?"

He wanted to know why.

The question pounding at Evie's brain wasn't *"Why"* but *"What if...?"*

She remained evasive and Sebastian grew agitated. On a sunny Sunday morning, he cornered Evie in the kitchen, demanding she explain herself. Sebastian fired question after question, almost an interrogation. She was stunned by his adeptness—clearly this was a skill he'd acquired while in the government's employ. Was there something wrong with the babies? Did the doctor tell her something she hadn't shared? Maybe it wasn't the babies. Maybe it was him. Was there a chance she simply didn't love him anymore?

And Evie's culpability hit tilt. Her deception had caused Sebastian to borrow trouble that didn't exist. Leaning against the kitchen counter, barefoot and largely pregnant, Evie couldn't lie any longer. Her legs grew wobbly and her whole body trembled as the confession about her night with Ezra spilled out—the precarious timing. Last time she'd been in such a state, Sebastian had rushed forward, catching Evie as she fell.

This time she'd no choice but stand on her own two feet. This time he backed away.

It was a twofold reaction. Evie understood that intellectually, Sebastian grasped the facts: Evie and Sam and the United States government thought he was dead. Viewed through that lens, it wasn't as if she'd cheated on him. No. Evie knew she'd done something far worse. She slept with her husband—the one man Sebastian could not be. It tore at him for days, like fall leaves through a shredder— reducing him to fragments of the man she knew. The unpleasant fact wasn't enough and he insisted on knowing more, like the setting for her and Ezra's long awaited reunion.

"The cabin," she said, her voice barely audible. "The night before you came back."

He nodded, growling something about adding insult to injury. She'd never seen such an unreadable look on Sebastian's face. Finally, he broached the rest of the conversation, the part Evie had been dreading most of all. "So what do we do?" he asked. "Just wait to see if they're mine... or his?" It broke Evie, so many truths gushing like blood from an open wound. Evie Neal had always been a wonderer, curious about places beyond Good Hope and what it might be like to live a life beyond its confines. In all her wondering, Evie had never imagined anything like this.

When she returned from the store the next day, an even fiercer argument ensued—mostly because Evie fought back. Sebastian was highly agitated, saying hateful things to Evie as his sons cowered in a nearby corner. "Maybe you should have never left Good Hope in the first place," he boomed. "Maybe your marriage really was a holy proclamation. As it is, you couldn't even divorce the son of a bitch— and I let you get away with it. Maybe we were just the devil's joke."

He was unnervingly angry—drunk, really, she surmised from the half-empty bottle on the kitchen table. Angry yes, but she couldn't believe he drank that much while minding his sons. Sebastian's surly state angered Evie and this time she didn't shrink from his accusations. When added to his on-going, ill-tempered mood, it left Evie with a man she didn't like very much. She yelled back, telling Sebastian he had to take some of the responsibility. If it weren't for his life-threatening choice of job, the circumstances with Ezra would have never existed in the first place.

"So it's my fault?" he yelled, his large frame looming. "My fault that you chose to fuck your husband at the first reasonable opportunity? That you decided to crawl back in his bed while I was doing everything I could to crawl back to you. No, Evie. You don't get to blame me for that."

It hurt more than any strike to the face Ezra or his father had delivered. It'd hurt because it'd come from Sebastian. He stormed from the cottage, leaving Evie in a puddle of confusion and despair. The next morning when he didn't return, Evie didn't know what to think—and maybe she didn't as she took the boys, got in the car, and drove away.

Hours later she arrived in Good Hope. It wasn't a conscious effort, more of an autopilot response. Her car idled just outside the gates and Evie held firm to the keys. At more than eight months pregnant, Good Hope was the last place Evie expected to find herself. She almost threw the car into reverse. But as she looked over the seat, the question was obvious. *Back up and go where?*

Once she was safely inside Hannah's house, her friend listened to the tale, her eyes barely moving from Evie's oversized belly. Evie hadn't told Hannah about the pregnancy because she *had* confessed to her friend about sleeping with Ezra. The omission of her subsequent pregnancy had been part of Evie's avoidance. Hannah would have insisted, months ago, that she deal with the many truths that now confronted her.

"And the babies?" Hannah said on a whispery breath.

"They're not due for a few weeks."

"Evie, that's not what I'm asking you."

She folded her arms, resting them on her oversized stomach. "They're Sebastian's, of course. You know Ezra can't... Well, we were together for more than a year and nothing..." Evie's crossed arms rose and fell on the breath she took. "No matter who the father is..." She stopped, blinking back tears. "Either way, I'm feeling rather alone." Overwhelmed, Evie sunk into the room's most comfortable chair. "I came here to think, Hannah. Can you let me do that—for a few hours, maybe a day? When we last talked, you said Ezra would be away this whole month—a retreat. I thought... Well, I don't know what I was thinking, other than maybe you'd understand."

Hannah was quiet, perhaps gauging the myriad of possible replies. "You're right. I did say Ezra was gone on a theological retreat. What I didn't mention was his father. Reverend Kane is on leave from his South American missions, filling in for Ezra. Evie, if he finds you here..."

She shifted, her back aching from her condition and the drive. "Then our visit will be briefer than I thought." Evie pulled herself out of the chair more quickly than she'd sat. "We'll go now."

"Don't be ridiculous. You're not leaving here—not unless it's to go back to..."

"Who, Hannah? My husband? It's a tricky question. Sebastian and I, we thought we were so clever—that what we felt for one another would be enough to keep a binding piece of paper from mattering. In the end, it's only made the truth we've avoided worse."

"Perhaps now," Hannah said, her gaze cutting to Evie's stomach, "Ezra will agree. He'll allow you a divorce."

She almost asked Hannah if she'd been drinking. "Do you think so?" Evie said, teary-eyed, shaking her head. "Do you really think Ezra's compassion runs that deep? That in the history of the Fathers of the Right, the grandson of its founding leader, the current clergy to oversee all sect members, should be the first one to divorce?" Evie laughed. "Better still, Ezra was always quite good with math. He'll see this," she said, her hand grazing her girth, "and wonder the same thing we all do—if God's finally seen to it that the Kane lineage continues." Evie brushed tears from her face. She was in no condition to drive—not with her sons in the car. "Fine. We'll stay the night, in the cabin—away from any of the others. No one will come down the path. We'll leave at daybreak."

By early evening, after settling in the cabin, Evie had calmed a bit—long enough to eat some supper and take a bath. She gratefully accepted when Hannah said she'd keep the boys for a few hours. Even so, Hannah was leery about leaving Evie alone. "I'm fine, really," Evie had insisted, rubbing her round belly. "They've been quiet considering all the fuss. I don't think there's much room left in there to move." Evie had raised a brow and glanced toward feet she could not see. Nevertheless, Hannah said she'd be back to check on her. In the meantime, she'd sent Tobias by with an upholstered chair. It offered Evie something besides the bed or the wooden kitchen chairs. In his quick entry and exit from the cabin, Tobias didn't say more than hello, barely making eye contact.

Evie was half-dozing, half reading a book when there was a knock on the door. On a cumbersome struggle out of the chair she began a conversation with Hannah. "Such formality. Really, Hannah, I hope it's because your hands are full of lemon meringue pie. I wasn't joking entirely when I said I had a wicked crav—"

Reverend Kane stood on the other side of the door. Evie hadn't seen him since the night she'd struck him on the head with the metal easel—the same night he'd tried to force himself on her in an effort to continue the Kane pedigree. A scar was evident on his temple, and she wondered how he'd explained it to his followers.

"Wicked. An excellent choice of words, and a fair place to begin this conversation," he said. Evie tried to push the door shut, but she was no match for the Reverend. She stumbled backward, catching herself on the stone edge of the fireplace. A forceful slam of the door followed, shaking the cabin's frame.

"I'll be gone by morning," she said, hoping it might end the exchange.

"It's exactly why I'm visiting tonight. I've waited a long time for this meeting, daughter."

"Don't call me—"

"Oh, do you prefer your true name? Slut… whore… harlot. Choose one."

He stood so close she could smell Adah's mint iced tea on his breath. But Evie was in no mood to be bullied. She glanced at the fire. "It's hot enough. Perhaps you'd like to brand me with a scarlet A. Call me whatever you like—I don't give a damn what you think."

"A foulmouthed slut at that. You've always been so quick to dismiss what I think."

"If you've come here to name call, I'll take a turn." Evie inched even closer, words ticking off her tongue. "Liar, drug dealer, gun runner… rapist, if you'd had your way."

He'd been staring at the hearth and his cool gaze met Evie's. "A common rapist?" he said, incredulous. "Think harder, Evie. You'd been married to my son for more than a year. It was… it still is crucial that the Kane bloodline continues. As the anointed leader of this community, it was my obligation to make certain—"

Evie inched back. "Obligation? Is that what you tell yourself? If Ezra only knew…"

"What Ezra knows. It's another fine topic." He glanced at her swollen stomach, smiling thinly. Evie spied the iron poker, slightly concerned that it sat to his right. "Here you stand, on the verge of spitting out—*two*, I understand—more bastards belonging to *the mission*."

Evie's arms folded.

"That's, of course, assuming they are *the mission's.*" And his thin smile grew wider. "Your friend, Hannah..."

"Hannah would never betray me."

"Perhaps not. But she would confide in her husband. Tobias has always been a loyal and obedient follower. He shared with me your visit nearly nine months ago, how much time you spent with Ezra. How grateful you were that my son saved your life. I'm here now to explore the possibility."

Evie kept a firm poker face. "Possibility of what?"

"Must I spell it out for you? Sleeping with your husband before your lover rose from the dead. Tobias tells me the paternity of the children is unknown. And if those children are Ezra's," he said, pointing to Evie's belly. "They belong to him. They belong to the Fathers of the Right. They belong to me. They're my legacy. You will not defy me nor deny my right to them."

"Are you insane?" Evie said, though she wrapped her hand protectively around her stomach. "You won't get anywhere near my children."

"Another quick assumption. I'm well versed in what separates church from state, Evie. I know every right and religious freedom this community possesses. No court will rule in your favor. Choose to award two innocent babies to their adulteress mother and a man unrelated to them, an infidel with mafia ties and a history of drug-running. Not when their cleric father, a man morally and legally entitled to them has so much to offer. The bloodline shall not be severed—not by you."

"That... that's absurd."

"Is it?" he said calmly. "I assure you, the state will be greatly reluctant to interfere in a religious matter of this magnitude."

Evie opened her mouth to object—to tell him that the state might be interested in the Reverend's own lurid activities. But as Evie tried to speak, outrage turned to pain. The Reverend cocked his head and for a moment concern filled his gray face. The pain subsided and Evie caught her breath.

"It never crossed your mind, did it?" he said. "You never considered how coming back to Good Hope is an opportunity from the Lord, your chance to make things right." Evie didn't respond, the pain gripping her again. It wasn't her intention to reach out, but there was nothing else near. The Reverend grasped her arm, his eyes lighting as if his anointed plan was falling into place.

"You understand? You agree? You'll remain inside this sanctuary until those children are born."

Evie shook her head, now struggling against his hold. "No..." she said, her teeth gritted. "I'd never do anything of the kind." But pain was quickly overtaking any ability to respond. Her actions were the opposite of her words, squeezing harder to the Reverend's arm.

The cabin door burst open and Alec came tearing through. Aaron followed, looking sleepy and dragging a Teddy bear. Reverend Kane jerked her closer and the boys froze in their steps. "These must be your heathen spawn," he said. "See. God is merciful. Afterward, you can take them and go. Have a dozen more. But I know from heaven to here in Good Hope, those two," he said, poking at Evie's stomach, "are Ezra's... *and they're mine.*"

Alec was immediately aware. Evie saw the look on his face change, focused and angry. He shouted for the Reverend to let go of his mother. Evie tried to quiet him, assuring Alec everything was fine. But the tension heightened as Aaron sensed trouble too, wrapping his small arms around his mother's leg. Both boys clamored for Evie—Aaron out of fright, Alec out of suspicion.

"Wild, little animals, aren't they?" he said as if fascinated. "Feral, like their father. Tell me, daughter, has he turned you out? Did *the mission* learn of what you've done? Is that it, the reason you're here—alone?"

Evie no longer struggled. She couldn't risk further alarming Alec. He was so much like Sebastian; his protective instincts couldn't be fooled. His small body was ready to pounce. Evie pictured it too clearly, the Reverend Kane backhanding her son right into the fire. "Alec, no," she said, seeing her son eye the fireplace poker. Evie turned her attention back to the Reverend. "Fine," she said negotiating pain, her sons, and the Reverend. "If you want to discuss it rationally, let's go to the meeting hall or to your office." Evie tried turning for the door. The Reverend pulled her back.

His grip was tight, her condition too cumbersome. "When I insisted Nolan Creek move out of this cabin, I almost asked that it be torn down. There was something unsavory about the way he lived here. I understand now why God counseled me otherwise. Man could never imagine this den of iniquity producing my legacy. Though I do suppose," he said, a wild-eyed gaze traveling the room, "it is a fitting place with you as the vessel."

With every bit of strength she had, Evie pulled away. But she jerked like a spring as the Reverend yanked her forward. She resisted and felt a terrific thud as her head collided with the mantel. Through a woozy gaze, looking up, the last thing she saw was the fireplace poker clenched in Alec's small fist. The last thing she heard was Sebastian's voice.

CHAPTER THIRTY-THREE

Present Day
Good Hope, Pennsylvania

As Ezra spoke, they'd listened like a sermon in church—Jess and four members of the *Tribe of Five* crammed around the cabin's kitchen table. Jake and Troy had joined them from the center of Good Hope not long after the younger reverend arrived. Ezra had elaborated on Hannah's story about Evie returning to Good Hope for a second time. She'd come back because of a fierce fight with Sebastian. He went on to say how his own father had violently confronted Evie that night. "Sebastian, he arrived just in time."

"I remember that part," Alec said. "Your father, he kept saying something like *'they're mine'* and I remember reaching for the fireplace poker. Then Pop came in—charged in maybe. I went from terrified to relieved, in all of two seconds."

"Your father had that gift, always showing up at just the right moment where Evie was concerned. As usual, I lagged behind. Once Hannah got word to me, I returned to Good Hope immediately. I couldn't believe how my father had come after Evie. Of course, that paled in comparison to my shock over your mother's... *condition*."

As he spoke, Alec's gaze remained on the fireplace poker, frustrated by a child's vague recollections. He looked at Ezra. "Why would my mother's condition come as a shock to you? Why would it matter?"

Ezra's thin chest rose and fell. "How, um... What did Hannah tell you about your mother and me—our relationship."

"That the two of you grew up together here, in Good Hope," Alec said. "That you were best friends. Between you and Hannah, I could see why she might have chosen to come back after she thought Pop was dead."

"Alec and I only remember bits and pieces, this cabin mostly," Aaron added.

Ezra stared thoughtfully at his folded hands.

"Praying, Reverend?" Alec asked.

To his surprise, Ezra nodded. "Praying for the wisdom to know how much of this story I have a right to tell."

"Sebastian and Evie would want you tell us all of it."

"How can you know that?" Ezra asked.

"Hannah didn't tell you about the plane."

The Reverend shook his head. "Only that Evie's sons were here and that I needed to come back to Good Hope."

Alec pulled his phone from his pocket. "While Jess was on a story assignment in a remote area of Colombia, she discovered a plane crash on an island off the coast. It was the plane my father was piloting the night it vanished."

"The plane—" Ezra touched his mouth, his hand trembling. "You'll forgive me. After all these years, to know how she... *how they*..."

"That was our reaction," Jake said, removing the ball cap he wore and placing it on the table. He dragged his hand through dark blond hair. "Jess and Alec went to the island. They saw the wreckage, Isla de la—"

"*Muerte*..." Ezra said.

"You know the island?" Alec asked.

"Duncan, my father, he... I've heard of it," Ezra replied. "It's about a hundred miles south of the area where I once did mission work."

"Okay," Alec said. "We'll circle back around to that. For now, take a look at this." He handed Ezra the phone, showing him the image of the crash site, the bloody initials on the side of the plane.

Ezra's startled look grew more distraught.

"I think we're now clear that E.K. is you. All the messages Evie and Sebastian could have left us, and it's your initials on our family tree that we find. So yes, sitting here, right now with 'E.K.'—I believe it's a direct request that you explain. I'd even go as far to say that it's Evie's last wish."

"Be careful what you wish for, Alec," Ezra said, his face grim.

Alec held steady but had the distinct impression the cryptic message wasn't going to be anything he wanted to hear.

"Fine. So be it," the Reverend said. "It's not as if I could ever deny your mother anything—including a last wish. So let me go back to the story of that night, here in the cabin. It's where it begins, the explanation you've come for," he said to Alec.

"Evie ended up going into labor—a result of the stress and circumstance—surely my father's actions. Hannah had been only a few paces behind Sebastian, following you boys to the cabin." Ezra pointed a finger at Alec and Aaron. "But it was long enough for Sebastian to assert himself into the situation. Hannah said she'd never seen anything like it. Your father was furious at mine, and not without cause. Sometimes... Well, I think if your mother hadn't been in such distress, Sebastian might have killed Duncan. As it was, he struck my father so hard he knocked out two teeth. My father's disdain for Evie ran deep. Only his contempt for your father surpassed it. It'd seemed that way from the moment he'd arrived in Good Hope."

"All because Evie Neal chose to leave this place with Sebastian Clair... Christos?" Alec said.

"Not quite." Reverend Kane looked to the empty hearth then he looked at the Clairmont faces in front of him. "Not hardly. When your mother left Good Hope with Sebastian she was married to me."

"She was..." Alec leaned in. "You're going to have to say that again."

"Married to me." Ezra's Adam's apple bobbed through his reedy throat. "It's true. Evie and I were married for over a year. What's more, we remained man and wife until the day she died."

"To our mother?" Jake said, going for pinpoint clarification.

"To your mother," Ezra replied.

Troy blinked hard, speaking to no one in particular. "Damn. If that doesn't answer Nickel Springs most burning question since... well, before I was born."

"It was a marriage sanctified by the Fathers of the Right leadership since we were children. It was always to be, Evie and I would marry."

"An arranged marriage," Jess said.

"For one of us, that turned out to be an apt description. As Hannah told you, Evie and I were the best of friends. We never questioned the proclamation of marriage. I loved her very much. I never saw it as an arrangement, but a gift. For a time, I believe Evie felt the same way."

"Until *the mission* showed up," Alec said.

Ezra nodded. "Your father was brought to Good Hope to provide a safe haven. He was in a great deal of trouble with his Greek mafia ties—the Godfathers of the Night."

"The what?" Jake said from the chair he straddled. "This is starting to sound like my next movie script."

"I suppose it's what they say, truth being stranger than fiction." They all paused for a moment, almost taking a collective breath. "I don't know the details of what brought Sebastian here, and I'll spare you the parts of the story that no longer matter. But know that when Evie chose to leave here, she did so married to me."

Alec eased back in his chair. "Why didn't she just divorce you?"

Ezra shook his head as the question left Alec's mouth. "Just divorce me, end a union considered a godly decree?" His tone had shifted to something that didn't fit with any modern-day, easy-fix on the matter. "It's not possible. Evie knew that. No matter how far from the Fathers of the Right she strayed, our marriage would always be."

"And that doesn't strike you as a little... *hard-assed*—especially after she and Sebastian had five kids?"

Jess reached out, giving Alec's thigh the squeeze that said *calm down*.

But the accusation didn't ruffle the cloistered man across from him. He took a deep breath and continued. "Your inability to comprehend our ways is a large part of the reason we live as we do. You perceive it as us shunning the outside world. We know it preserves our way of life—a life we have a right to if you check the Constitution. Good Hope isn't about accepting what's popular or common. And within our doctrine, there's no bond more sacred than marriage. Except," Ezra said, tugging at the edge of his clerical collar, "perhaps children.

"And so the subject brings us back to that night and the reason for my father's fury. Speaking strictly from the standpoint of doctrine, the elder Reverend Kane felt he was entitled to the children your mother was carrying—if they extended our family bloodline."

"And why the hell would he think that?" Alec said.

"Because there was a reasonable chance I was their father."

It seemed unlikely in such a small space, filled with so many people, that utter silence would prevail.

Hannah's words rolled through Alec's head and out of his mouth. "Two visits to Good Hope less than a year apart. That's what they'd fought about, why Pop was so angry, because..."

"In your mother's defense, she believed he was dead. She'd been told as much by the people he worked for. Still... a man like your father..."

Aaron leaned back in. "I'd guess pissed off wouldn't begin to describe his reaction."

"Not the language I would choose, but yes." Ezra cleared his throat. "I ask that you take my word as proof of the possibility. I prefer to keep the details of that night private."

Four sets of Clairmont hands shot up at once. Only Jess spoke. "I guess that's a hell of a story all on its own."

"And mine to keep," Ezra said.

Realization traveled from one brother to the next, all eyes eventually ending up on Jake, whose stare burned through Ezra. Confident was a word that readily described movie-icon Jake Clairmont. Not at the moment. At the moment, Alec saw raw nerves dangling off of him like the fate of a cliff, everything he'd ever known coming into question.

"After arriving back in Good Hope, I went on to the hospital. You were there with your sister," he said to Jake. "But I barely glanced in the nursery window. In that second, I only wanted to know if Evie was all right." He smiled at Troy. "She would be fine, or so I learned. Your father... He was, understandably, not overjoyed to see me. Before any of us had a chance to say much of anything, a nurse wheeled in two bassinettes. I was unaware that three people could hold their collective breath for so long. No one said a word until after she left. Even then..."

Jake's gaze moved anxiously from brother to brother. Alec knew what he was doing—assuring himself he was a Clairmont. Out of the four boys, he looked the least like Sebastian, which was to only say he wasn't the mirror image of Alec and Aaron, didn't bear quite the resemblance Troy did. But given the circumstance, Alec did wonder if they'd merely seen what made sense over the years. "And..." Alec finally prodded.

"I think we all knew at once. Evie was the first to say that Jake, in her mind, looked like his older brothers. Clearly, he was... *is* Sebastian's son. Then we all looked at the girl. She was like silk fallen from heaven, wispy but feisty. One thing was for certain, she was half Evie. Your father," Ezra said, his blue eyes damp, "he was the first to pick her up. She quieted for him right away—like she knew his voice. We, um... we traded a most civilized look, which I assure you was an odd thing for Sebastian and myself. The girl, she opened her eyes—wider than you'd think a newborn might. The color was so like mine and... well, it seemed a certainty."

From around the table the Clairmonts' looked at Ezra, looking into Honor's eyes—lagoon blue, Evie had always said.

Troy cleared his throat. "Wait. I don't get how..."

"Yeah... I'm a little shaky on that myself," Jake said.

"I, um... I'm not sure how to explain the science. But I assure you, it's possible. While you're most definitely Sebastian's son," he said to Jake, "the little girl was mine."

Troy looked between Ezra and Jake. "If he's... How would... Does that still make Honor your twin?" he said to his brother.

Jake's jaw hung and Alec could see his world shift a bit. "Yeah," Jake finally said, his confident tone emerging. "She is. Always... Same way she's your sister."

"I was amazed when your father handed the baby to me," Ezra said, his eyes glassy. "It showed tremendous courage, forgiveness, and a sizable heart—perhaps because he understood how much he'd taken from me. He said, 'I believe she belongs to you.'"

In that moment, I don't know what your parents thought would happen next. But I knew what my father had threatened. Of course, it would require my cooperation. It would require me to tell him she was my daughter." He looked away from the boys and out the cabin door where a full moon eavesdropped on Good Hope's secret. "I held her for a time. She was exquisite—the most perfect thing I'd ever seen. If I'm being honest, I thought of bringing her home— to here. Despite any judgments you've made, we're good people. It may not be a life you understand, but I trust in its purpose. Yet, I had to make the best choice for her. I thought it was what any good father would do. I chose to give my daughter three... and eventually four," he said, glancing at Troy, "brothers. I chose to give her one life, one family. To have brought her here... it would have made her a pawn in my father's war against Evie and Sebastian. It was more than I was prepared to take on—in this community and more importantly my own life."

"Just like that," Alec said. He'd tilted his chair back to keep his breath and mind steady—he let it fall forward. His brothers and Jess looked at him. "You walked away? I'm not sure I buy it. This place is all about rules and what you believe is right."

"You are indeed your father's son," Ezra said. "The abruptness is uncanny." A stoic glance, maybe a glare, wove between them. "Much time has passed. I tell the story now with more reflection than I would have years ago. That night, I asked your father if I could speak to Evie alone. He agreed, which I also don't believe was easy for him. We talked. Evie, she tried to suggest an alternative. She asked me to visit, implied that we could work things out in some modern, non-traditional way—that no one in Good Hope need know. While I was tempted, I couldn't fathom it. Perhaps I'm just a weak man because I could only think how hard such a thing would be."

Throats cleared and Alec guessed they were all thinking the same thing—*weakness* did not describe Ezra's actions.

"After a time, I handed her the baby. Evie had such huge tears in her eyes. And I think, that day, it was me who broke her heart. She could barely speak, saying how sorry she was that she couldn't properly honor our marriage."

I kissed your sister on the head and said, 'But you did, Evie. The fact that she exists is honor enough.'" Tension filled sighs rumbled from around the table. "I was quite pleased to learn Honor was her name, as it would be the only legacy from me she would have."

"And Duncan, he never found out?" Alec asked.

"No. While Hannah knows, she was amicable about keeping the fact a secret, even from her husband. She told him both children belonged to Sebastian, which I'm sure was reported back to Duncan. For many reasons, my decision was the right one."

"I'm sure that's been difficult," Jess said, offering audible sympathy.

"To a point. It's one of the many up sides of relying on faith. Without my cooperation, my father wouldn't have prevailed. But he also would not have let it go. Until your parents perished, he would have made their lives miserable. Only in the past year has that fact changed at all."

"And why's that?" Aaron asked.

"More recently, Duncan's mind has begun to fail—confusion, irrational thoughts. I admit, your timing is a bit eerie. After not speaking of Sebastian for... well, years, my father talked about him upon returning from his last mission trip."

"Talked about him?" Alec said. "In what way?"

"Nothing discernable. Thoughts that make no sense. He'd mutter over and over, *'the mission remains sequestered...'* I'm sure it's just yesteryear babble, having kept Sebastian sequestered in this very cabin. I've been praying for guidance about him. Father is lucid most of the time. Still..." Ezra said thoughtfully. "Not that it matters to you, but that's where I was today—in Lancaster meeting with those who carry out similar mission work, trying to decide how best to handle... *his condition.*"

As the conversation drew to a close, Ezra asked, "It's, um... it's purely a selfish thought, but I've always wondered... Is she a good person, your sister?"

It seemed the question belonged more to Jake than anyone else at the table. "Better than a Clairmont in some ways," he said, his eyes wet.

"I'll second that," Aaron said. "I, uh... I've had a rougher road than my brothers. It's a long story—almost as long as this one. If it wasn't for Honor.... Well, know that she saw me through all of it."

Ezra's glassy gaze reflected the table full of Clairmonts that he faced. "That's good to hear. Undoubtedly, you know your sister well. I'll continue to pray for her—and now guidance for the four of you in deciding what knowledge best serves her happiness."

CHAPTER THIRTY-FOUR

Before dawn, Ezra left the cabin saying it would be a brief sermon that Sunday morning. Jess had gone with him, asking for an escort to the edge of the Good Hope compound. They'd parked there, and she wanted to go in search of coffee. Alec guessed it was more about giving the four of them space. After talking it through once more, Troy and Aaron fell asleep on the bed. Alec felt that twisting in his gut—the one that lingered on months after a precarious military tour. He wouldn't be sleeping anytime soon.

"All I keep thinking..." Jake pointed to the seat where Ezra had sat. "Is how I'd feel right now if it was me. If that guy had said... If we'd sat around the table listening to bombshell after bombshell and it turned out that he was..."

"He's not. Ezra Kane is not your father." Alec's tone was so identical to Sebastian's it sent chills up his own spine. He wanted Jake to feel the same, the inbred confidence of being Sebastian Clairmont's son. "Don't doubt it. You know it's the truth."

Jake nodded.

"Of course that does leave us with a hell of a question."

Jake's eyes met firmly with Alec's. "Who the fuck is going to tell Honor?"

He squeezed his eyes shut. "I, uh... I don't know. I can't think about that right now."

"Alec, I made an A in basic biology, but I'm still not sure I understand how..."

"I think I can clarify." Alec scrubbed a hand over his face and sighed. It was a SEAL story wholly removed from the usual variety. "A frogman buddy—Ty. He's African-American, his girlfriend was Asian. He leaves for a nine-month tour. I guess it was a big good-bye because they end up pregnant. Eventually, she tells him they're expecting twins. Ty's ecstatic about the whole thing. But when he flies home to meet his kids... Well, it turned out the girlfriend had some explaining to do. Two boys. One looked just like Ty, the other as white as a sack of flour—redheaded and a mirror image of their Irish-American neighbor. Ty guessed he wasn't gone more than a day when she went across the street for a little comfort. Anyway, technically, that's how the, um... window of opportunity works." Alec pointed at the chair where Ezra had sat. "Given the right circumstance and timing, it can happen—twins by two different fathers."

"I guess I never thought about anything like that. It's, um... it's a lot to get your head around."

"And it explains a good chunk of why this place and Mom's past was such a secret." Alec glanced around the cabin, feeling like the walls were closing in. He looked toward the bathroom. "I need a shower or to take a run..."

"Go running in this place and somebody will probably take you out with a shotgun." Jake looked wide-eyed at Alec, as if he'd dodged his own bullet. "This Ezra... the Reverend... He seems like a decent person—but as for the rest of them, especially his old man..."

Yeah, he was bad news when I was six. I'd say old Ezra made the right choice—but I can also understand how Mom, maybe even Pop, wouldn't want to take that secret to their grave."

"I suppose," Jake said. "Do you think they always planned on telling us... or at least Honor, and then just..."

"Ran out of time?" Alec rose, needing to separate himself from the emotion beating at his brain. At the edge of the bathroom, he pounded a fist into the doorframe. "Great. A fucking tub. What good is a fucking tub?" He turned toward Jake. "Jess should be back any minute. I'll just get some air."

"Go. I'll be fine. I'll get the two sleeping beauties up in a few minutes." Jake motioned his square chin—Sebastian's chin—at his snoring brothers. "I still can't believe Aaron is here, after everything that went down."

Alec slapped his brother on the shoulders as he passed by. "Let it be part of today's reminder about timely events, bro. Good or bad, we never know what's around the corner."

⸻

In the pre-dawn light, Alec made his way to the parking area beyond Good Hope's gates. The barrier was only thigh-high, yet he still had to hurdle it—a homage to the reclusiveness of the community. Jess was pulling up, getting out of the SUV they'd rented. "Hey," she said on Alec's approach. "You look as if your world's been rocked a little."

He was often irked by her ability to zero in on what he was thinking. Worse, how he was feeling. At the moment, he couldn't be more grateful. "Sorry I was such a dick back in La Carta—that fight in my hotel room."

"Don't worry about it," she said. "The day I can't handle a few rounds with Alec Clairmont... well, I hope I never lose my edge." She tilted her head. "Is that how we're going to avoid what's happened here, by focusing on an argument from three-thousand miles ago?"

Alec shook his head. "No. I guess even you and I couldn't have a fight big enough to push this aside. It, um... It's just..." The wedge in his throat cut off his words.

"It's a lot, Alec. Don't gloss over it. It's okay to feel something—and, right now, that just may be a lot of confusion... frustration. Honor will always be a card-carrying member of the *Tribe of Five*. But the story Ezra Kane told, it can't *not* affect a person, even you."

Alec slung his neck back, looking heavenward. Stars dimmed one by one, the family past he knew flickering in their wake. He blinked—the stars were blurry. Jess's arms moved around him. Alec couldn't combat it. He didn't want to. He just held on. It'd been years since he'd gripped onto anything but self-sustaining mantras and a hard-ass attitude. A moment later, his mouth covered hers, kissing his roommate—the woman who lived across the hall. They edged backward until they were against the side of the SUV. No one spoke, Jess reaching for the buckle on his belt. Alec glanced down. *A skirt...* Naturally she'd be wearing a fucking skirt. "Jess..." he said.

"Don't think," she said, her hands moving over the stubble on his face. "Just for right now, go with whatever helps."

It wasn't like borrowing a clean towel because he was out—but Jess had done that before too, often giving Alec what he needed to get by. At times it was stuff, but mostly it was space, room to be himself—which didn't tend to make Alec the life of the party. And right now, space was the last thing he wanted.

Alec glanced at the SUV.

Too clumsy.

The cabin.

Too fucking full of Clairmonts.

Jess didn't appear deterred by logistics, shoving his pants down to get her hand around his rock-hard cock. Alec kissed her again. He skimmed her bare thigh, his fingers hooking around her underwear. *A thong?* Underneath the skirt, which had bothered him enough, she was wearing a thong. Sure, he'd seen them in the wash.

He didn't let it register—like maybe she'd been doing laundry for a friend. He spun her around, Jess's hands landing against the hood of the vehicle. Alec pressed his body into hers. "You need to say it if you don't want…"

"I know how to say no, Alec. It hasn't crossed my mind."

He glanced toward sleepy Good Hope, the blue-gray dawn, the distance giving them privacy. Alec considered the fast, hard fuck that normally described how he went about this. The urge was there, but so were other things. Things that made this different. With his dick throbbing against Jess's exposed backside, Alec did something unlikely and passive. He reached to her long hair and gently pushed a wave of kinky curls over one shoulder. He kissed her neck, pausing to breathe her in. Alec's fingers edged between the steel of the vehicle and Jess's taut stomach muscles. Dismissing the barely there front of the thong, Alec made subtle contact with a swollen nub. Jess's body had been rigid, almost disagreeing with her lack of objection. But the second Alec touched her, he felt Jess meld into the moment. She widened her stance, inviting more. Her breath quickened. "Jesus, Alec…" she whispered.

She turned her head to a deeper angle and Alec kissed her neck harder. His other hand slipped under her shirt, past a lacy bra. It made his breath shudder. Fuck. He'd noticed the bras too. His dual touch—half rough, half delicate—was all it took and Jess's entire body shuddered against his. He slid a finger inside her, nudging her legs farther apart with his. It summoned an achy gasp from her—a sound Alec was damn sure he'd never heard Jess make. Pleasure traveled from her to him as Alec repositioned his hands, gripping her firmly at the small of her back. His dick was all but begging, and he drove into her, letting urge take over.

Honest to God, it wasn't his best showing. He was too anxious to get to a feeling that would make recent days not matter—too anxious for Jess to be on the other end of that explosion. Her hands made dewy humid imprints on the SUV's hood, counterbalancing against Alec's wicked thrusts. As he came, Alec held onto her, which was not something he did in this moment. He let himself think only of her as deep, shaky breaths pulled in and out of Jess. Normally, he couldn't exit a bed or get to his pants fast enough. After a moment she disengaged with the steely hood, sliding around in his arms. Alec focused on the SUV—an inhuman object. He didn't want to be the colder, harder thing Jess encountered in that instance and he kissed her. He kept kissing her, standing in their half-naked places until the sun exposed them and Jess said something about coffee getting cold.

CHAPTER THIRTY-FIVE

With everything buttoned and zipped, skirt and thong adjusted, Jess retrieved the tray of coffee from the SUV. The everyday action neutralized the moment. The two of them didn't speak, walking side by side through the middle of Good Hope. Alec didn't offer to carry the coffee, and he got what he deserved for being a chivalrous-less shit. Her phone, balanced on top of the cups, vibrated. Julian's name lit up. It seemed extra bright. The phone shook, shimmying across the plastic lids. Alec snatched the coffee tray away, forcing Jess to grab her cell. He shrugged. "How the fuck else are you supposed to answer it?"

"I was thinking I wouldn't right now."

She didn't.

As they passed by the Blyth house, Alec was reminded of the rules and reasons for fucking women with whom he shared no personal attachment.

"So are you going to answer me?" Jess said. "I want to know what you think."

Alec stopped midstride. Great. Just fucking great. Jess, of all people, was going to demand a detailed emotional assessment of what had just happened. "I don't know," he snapped. "I'm going to need more than a minute to figure it out. I can't say fucking you against a rented SUV was part of my op strategy when coming to Good Hope."

She narrowed her eyes and took a step toward him, which made Alec take a step back—slightly concerned there was a tray of hot coffee between them. "Alec Clairmont, you fucking, ungrateful prick. Open your ears! That's not what I asked you. I wanted to know if you'd given any thought to the other things Ezra Kane said."

He blinked at her. Clearly, he'd been the one fixated on their parking lot rendezvous. "Sorry," he said. "It was just... Well, I didn't come out here..." He pointed toward the distance and SUV. "You didn't find that at all... *unexpected*?"

"I thought that was how you liked it—impersonal. I took a page from the Alec Clairmont handbook of instinct, need, and survival. Fucking you seemed like an optimal choice since I didn't bring a knife to bite on, weapon to unload, or whiskey flask to share." An angry growl rose from her throat. "Do you want to keep going?"

There wasn't much spit in his mouth, but Alec forced down a swallow. "What do you mean, the other things that Ezra said?"

"His father. When Ezra mentioned Isla de la Muerte you said you'd circle back around to it. You never did. I get why—the rest of what Ezra told us was enough to make anybody's brain overload. But given a little hindsight, I thought you might have—"

"Asked how the hell either of them knows about that island?"

"It'd be my next question... and it was. Do you really think I needed an escort to the parking lot in the middle of no-fucking-where?"

She seemed furious with him, but Alec smiled. Jess's cleverness and ability to compartmentalize was better than his. "And did the good Reverend have anything to add?"

"Not so much him. From the gist of it, Ezra didn't travel back to South America after the mid-eighties. It became his father's sole domain. But he said that over the years Duncan talked about the island from time to time. He called it his personal haven, his reward, from the mainland infidels. If nothing else, I thought it was odd because of the island's gruesome history."

"Unless gruesome stories about cannibalism were just that—or better still, a good way to keep unwanted people out. Seems like a lot of sudden coincidence, doesn't it, Jess? The remote island, my parents' plane, no bodies... and it all somehow links to Duncan Kane."

"Kind of where I was going with it."

"Do you still have those papers Hannah gave us—the letters and that contact doc?" Jess plopped her cell into her tote bag and retrieved the larger envelope. They traded the coffee tray and information. Alec took out the paper he'd identified as CIA. "Can I have your phone? Mine's in the cabin." She fished her cell back out. It was vibrating again. *Julian*. Without asking permission, he ignored the call. Then Alec started dialing.

"Seriously?" Jess said. "That contact number can't possibly still be valid."

"I guess we'll... Uh, yeah." Alec widened his eyes, responding to a voice then reading off the code of letters and numbers. In the moment his SEAL background was a godsend—Alec having a solid idea about what to say to the person who'd answered. After a brief exchange, he ended the call. "I guess we'll..." He looked up. Aaron was coming toward them.

"What the fuck happened to you two? Honor called. I put her off, but I didn't feel too good about it. Maybe that should be our priority, deciding how and if we tell her about— "

"Just wait," Jess said. "We might have a fresh lead about your parents."

"A fresh lead? From where?"

"Langley," Alec said. "I just spoke with the operative at the call-in desk."

"You did what?" Aaron said, reaching for a coffee cup.

"Langley—the phone number Pop left for Mom years ago, it still worked. But it could be days—maybe longer until we hear back, if ev—" The phone vibrated again. Alec was prepared to see Julian's name light up. His heart jumped a few beats as the screen read "Private Caller." The three of them exchanged a look as he answered. "Alec Clairmont."

—•◦••◦•—

By the time he ended the call, Jess's phone was almost dead. For the past half hour, Alec had listened as he and Jess and Aaron sat on the steps of Our Daily Bread. Alec didn't get a last name, but *Sam* provided a wealth of information neither Hannah Blyth nor Ezra Kane could have possibly known. "And that's where things ended up after Mom and Pop disappeared," Alec explained. "After a serious search and rescue, with nothing to show for it, Sam, regretfully closed out the case. But here's the part that will blow your minds: Seems Duncan Kane was more than a minister with an overly righteous attitude. According to Sam, he was once a drug-runner, which somehow tied into Pop's background." Jess gagged, nearly spitting out her coffee. "Your father was a drug dealer?"

"No—I don't think so... Sam said that part was complicated, too hard to explain in a phone conversation. But his father—Andor Christos—definitely was."

Aaron inched back. "A drug-runner... Pop's father?"

"Yeah. Greek mafia ties from what Sam said. Seems Andor passed away in the late eighties. Before that, the elder Reverend Kane was the US point of transfer for cocaine shipments out of South America. Apparently it was an undetected and lucrative operation for years. But when it finally went stale, the Reverend switched to gun running. Remember how I said the rebel forces ran that country for years?" Jess and Aaron nodded. "That's where Pop came in, but he worked with Sam, ultimately destroying Reverend Kane's newest endeavor."

"So why isn't his ass sitting in a cellblock similar to my old address?" Aaron asked.

"Sam didn't give me all the details, but he did indicate that Duncan Kane served a better purpose by carrying out real mission work. Between Sam and Pop, they had the Reverend working the straight and narrow for years."

"Then you were right about your assumption that your father worked for the government," Jess said.

"Seems so. Sam said he could be more specific with a face-to-face meeting back in Nickel Springs. He retired from active service about five years ago. But he warned me to be suspicious of Duncan Kane. According to Sam, it'd been part of Pop's job to monitor the Reverend's activities. In the years after they disappeared, Sam admitted that there wasn't enough manpower to keep a close watch on the Reverend. That the area had quieted in terms of rebel insurgence. Trouble started gravitating toward the Middle East and most operative forces withdrew from La Carta and the surrounding cities."

"Meaning Reverend Kane was probably left to his own devices," Aaron said.

"Meaning we're not leaving here without taking last night's discussion to the next level."

Alec and Aaron stood, heading down the dusty main street of Good Hope. "Hey! Where are you two going?" Jess said.

The brothers turned at the same time. "To see Duncan Kane."

CHAPTER THIRTY-SIX

ALEC AND AARON STOOD OUTSIDE THE FATHERS OF THE RIGHT MEETING hall. "Good a place as any to start," Alec said. They took the steps two at time with Jess following. He turned the knob. "It's not locked."

"I'm guessing crime isn't an issue in Good Hope," she said.

Inside a dark vestibule were another set of double doors. Alec didn't hesitate, flinging one open. The sunlit sanctuary was startling—a plain, simple setting with the exception of one magnificent piece of stained glass set in the side of the building. Alec headed up the aisle. Suddenly Aaron wasn't beside him. He turned back. His brother had stopped midway and was staring at the glass. Alec took two steps back to where Jess met up with Aaron. "It's very pretty," she said. "The colors, they're the most vibrant thing we've seen in Good Hope."

"Especially the green," Aaron said.

Jess glanced between Aaron and the robe of one of the men depicted in the scene. "Huh. You're right. It's also the exact same green as your eyes."

"And we're wasting time critiquing it because...?" Alec said.

"Nothing... no reason." Aaron shook his head. "I just saw it, and I had this weird sense of déjà vu, like maybe I'm not the first person to have noticed the green."

"Come on," Alec said, though with a bit more reverence.

As they neared the altar a man entered through an adjacent door. He must have thought them early worshipers, his greeting going from, "Good Sunday morning" to a startled gasp. The words, "Lord help us…" came rushing from his mouth.

The man ogled them as if they were ghosts. He backed up at a furious pace, knocking over a vase of wildflowers. Glass crashed to the floor, but it didn't disrupt his frantic retreat. "I… I must tell Reverend Kane immediately!" He never turned, stripping glasses from his face and wiping his eyes with a handkerchief as he stumbled backward through a swinging door.

"What the hell?" Aaron said.

"Wait!" Alec chased after him, and Aaron was right behind. They pounded over broken glass and wildflowers, pushing through the swinging door. The light dimmed again. Alec could hear the man rambling. He stopped and listened. He sounded terrified—as if the three of them had entered the sanctuary waving assault rifles. Alec held up his hand, indicating the need for stealth-like silence.

"I'm telling you, Reverend. He's come back—and not as one demon but two! I saw them. It's exactly as you prognosticated, we needed to be vigilant in our sequestering of *the mission*. You were right! He is cunning and dangerous. He… *they*, they've come to finish us all. I swear to you—"

"Brother Creek, it's early for hysterics." The voice was low and heavy, certainly unconcerned. "I'm sure it's nothing… your mind playing tricks again. Something like those perverse dreams you finally confided to me about you and *the mission—together*." The man cleared his throat. "These demons you think you've seen, it should serve to reinforce the need to keep secret *the mission's* true fate. I told you his presence here, years ago, was direct temptation from the devil. Now get ahold of yourself before someone hears you babbling."

Alec knew the voice. It belonged to Duncan Kane and his boyhood memory.

"I assure you, Brother—" the elder Reverend went on, "I've followed God's direction. I've seen to it that *the mission* spends his days on Earth serving penance. From there I shall be satisfied to let the devil deal with him."

Alec bolted forward. Aaron grabbed him in a choke hold. Preparation might have been an advantage, but it wasn't what the moment delivered. Alec went for a surprise attack. He broke from Aaron's grip, executing with the precision of any Navy SEAL raid.

On sight, Duncan Kane's composure crumbled. He was visibly shaken, his weight on his arms as they pressed hard into the desk. "How... how is this possible?" He looked to his panic-stricken manservant then looked back. As Aaron turned the corner, the Reverend fell back into his chair. Alec didn't give a fuck. He went right across the desktop, grabbing the elderly man by his vestments, yanking him to eye level.

"You son of a bitch. I swear to Christ and anybody else who is listening. You tell me what you know about my father, or I will end you right here, right now!"

Voices yelled from behind—Jess and Aaron shouting, as well as Ezra Kane who'd likely heard the commotion. "Stop! You'll stop this instance. Let him go! He's an old man—he doesn't know anything about your father or Evie."

Alec held the power of life and death in his hands. He could easily deliver the latter. But a small part of his brain comprehended that taking out Duncan Kane would not be to his benefit—not this second. Jess was grabbing him from one side, Aaron from the other. He released the Reverend, who sank back into the chair, his gray eyes wide and wary.

Alec, slightly calmer, turned toward Ezra. "I know what I heard... What we all heard. He just spoke in the present tense. Duncan Kane just indicated that he was overseeing *the mission's* penance while here on Earth. Unless you've got anybody else who you identify by that name, I suggest you start asking questions."

Clearly stunned, Ezra's gaze flicked from Alec to his father.

"You can do it, or I can," Alec said. "But be aware, Reverend. My methods won't be sanctioned by God. Just the United States government, and they made damn certain I know how to get results."

"Father?" Ezra said, his voice shaking. "If there's something you know... something I'm unaware of, I think now might be a good time to be forthcoming."

The elder Kane eased back in the chair, smoothing his vestments. "Surely, son, you don't believe a word of what these heathens have spewed. I was startled when they came in. Obviously, after so many years, their resemblance to *the mission* is apparent. I don't deny knowing him—saving his life, in fact. But I'm not sure what they think they heard."

"I know exactly what I heard." Alec looked toward the weaker prey, the man with glasses who seemed to be trying to blend into a bookcase. He cocked his head. "What about you... *Brother Creek*, was it? What do you know about—?"

"Nothing," he said, his voice pinched. "I know nothing."

"Brother Creek," the Reverend said, interrupting. "You're to leave here immediately. Remain in solitude until I come for you. Do you understand? You're not to speak to these men or that woman."

"Yes, Reverend." He started for the door.

Alec was having none of it. "Try again, *Brother.* You may bend over obediently and regularly for your Reverend. Not here. Not today."

"I've never done any such thing with the Reverend," he said, mortified.

Alec furrowed his brow at the curious reply. "Think it through, Brother Creek. It'll only take one Clairmont, but you'd have to get through four of us to keep whatever you know quiet." Alec came toward him. "Those are pretty shitty odds." Brother Creek backpedaled until he hit the wall of books again. Alec was on him, his arm cutting decisively across his throat.

"Alec!" Jess said. "Calm down."

"We won't stand for it—not that kind of violence," Ezra said. "Not in our sanctuary."

Alec didn't give a rat's ass, pushing harder into the man's throat, knowing the precise pressure that balanced life and death.

"Brother Creek, tell him what you know—if anything. *Please...*" Ezra turned toward his father. "Do something! I don't doubt him. He'll kill him. Will you have that on your head, Brother Creek's blood on your hands?"

Duncan Kane smiled, tipping his head at Brother Creek, whose color faded as he wheezed for air. Alec looked over his shoulder. "Smile if you want, old man—but know the second he's of no use, you're next."

"He's alive!" Nolan Creek hissed in a metered breath. Alec swiveled back around, keeping the pressure steady.

"Brother Creek!" Duncan Kane shouted, slamming a fist on the desk. "I'll not tolerate this insolence."

Glasses sat crookedly on Nolan Creek's face, and his eyes bulged as he looked into Alec's. "It's true. *The mission*, he's alive."

"How? Where?" Alec demanded, not letting up. Aaron drew closer.

"I... I don't know..."

Alec pressed harder.

"Somewhere in South America—I don't know the exact location. God told the Reverend he was to punish *the mission* for the sin he brought to Good Hope, spiriting Evie away—dishonoring his son as she did." Brother Creek's panicked gaze moved to his Reverend. "I'm sorry. But I'm not ready to die, Reverend. I can't yet face the hell and wrath to which I'll be banished for my sins."

"How do you know he's alive? Proof... I want proof—now!" The muscle in Alec's forearm tensed, a vein rising from the pressure he held against Brother Creek's neck.

"The safe... behind the painting."

"What safe?" Ezra said.

Everyone in the room followed Brother Creek's teary gaze. Aaron was on it, tossing a Last Supper painting aside. "Alec?" he said, faced with a combination lock.

Alec turned back to his captive source. "I don't know the combination," Nolan Creek said. "I swear it."

With his weight still on Brother Creek's windpipe, Alec looked back at the Reverend. "If I have zero qualms about taking out you and your brother here, imagine my indifference to blowing open a safe. Your choice," he said shrugging.

"Father, you'll tell them the combination immediately—or I'll aid his effort myself. If Sebastian... *If Evie...*" he said. Ezra gripped the leather of a high back chair, his hand as ghostly as his face. "With God as my witness, I'll kill you myself if you've done anything to harm her."

The Reverend's expression shifted, his smile settling to a humorless line. While he'd been caught, it was also as if he'd been waiting to twist the knife. "She's dead," he said. "She's been gone since the night their plane crashed into my island and God saw fit to deliver them to my hands. Evie survived a few hours—a slow bleeding, inside and out. That was how it was described to me."

"Described by who?" Jess said.

Duncan Kane blinked, looking as if her confusion were unwarranted. "Why, by *the mission*, of course."

"The combination... *now*," Alec said, his mind whirling, his body rigid. He released Nolan Creek and moved toward Duncan Kane, tossing a chair aside like it was made of paper.

Ezra stepped in his path, facing the elder Reverend. "I'll give you but one chance, Father. Then I'll turn him loose on you."

He was angry but compliant and a few moments later Jess was the only one steady enough to spin the safe's dial, the combination clicking into place. The safe creaked open and Aaron reached inside. He discarded miscellaneous items onto the floor. But as he withdrew a clear plastic bag, shudders were audible. Inside the bag was a familiar strip of leather with a rugged-looking emerald stone attached. Aaron took it out of the bag. The stone and leather strip lay in his palm. His glassy gaze rose to meet his brother's. Alec cocked his chin at the other item in the bag. A phone. Aaron held it out to Alec, his hand shaking. He turned it on.

"What?" Jess finally asked.

"Text messages." His voice was sharp and stricken. "They're reports. 'The mission's status remains as instructed' over and over... that's all it says." He scrolled back. "Jesus... they go on for forever..."

"Only a dozen years," Duncan Kane said. "He's not yet met with his eternal damnation."

Warily, Alec's thumb hovered over the photo icon. He traded a look with Aaron. Alec clicked on it. For all his bravado, it was all he could do to stay upright. "Holy..." Aaron raked his hands through his hair, his green eyes staring at the screen. It was like slow motion, Alec holding the phone out so Jess and Ezra could see the photos— some dated only weeks ago. They were photos of Sebastian Clairmont, caged like an animal, but very much alive.

"You miserable son of a—" Alec went after Duncan Kane like a rabid dog. It took the combined strength of his brother, Ezra, and Jess to pull him off.

"Alec, stop!" The shouting came from all three of them, though it was Aaron's voice that finally got through. Maybe that and the iron grip his brother had around him—not so different from the one he'd had around Nolan Creek. Alec struggled, snorting like a bull until he finally began to get ahold of himself. "If I let you go, are you going to stop, control yourself?" Aaron had a firm lock around him, his voice right in his ear. "I may not have your skills, Alec, but I've taken down my share of crazies behind bars—don't make me do that to you. Don't do anything to make Duncan Kane the victim here." Alec nodded, jerking free as his brother eased his hold.

The room, the whole fucking world was spinning. He focused on Aaron. It was too much, too personal. He couldn't deal, couldn't make a rational decision. "What... what do you want to do?"

It wasn't like Alec to relinquish control and for a moment Aaron looked flummoxed. Then, through the crazy haze of what they'd learned, he smiled at his brother. "Pop's alive. He's alive, Alec. So add that good news to this: I spent seven years planning a prison break—I always knew the odds were better if I had you with me. Looks like now's our chance."

About L.J. Wilson

L. J. Wilson is the pen name of award-winning author Laura Spinella. The Clairmont Series Novels are an extension of her mainstream work with *The Mission*, Book Two, following *Ruby Ink* in the series. *Ghost Gifts* is her new #1 Bestselling Laura Spinella novel; also look for *Beautiful Disaster* and *Perfect Timing*.

L. J. Wilson novels are sensual reads for discerning book lovers—stories that delve deep into her characters' suspense-filled lives and steamy romances.

For more information visit LJWilson.com and LauraSpinella.net

Printed in Great Britain
by Amazon